DEAD SPY, COLD GRAVE

DEAD SPY, COLD GRAVE

Michael J. Goodspeed

DOUBLE‡DAGGER

PRAISE FOR DEAD SPY, COLD GRAVE

Dead Spy, Cold Grave establishes Michael Goodspeed as Canada's pre-eminent author of espionage fiction. This classic spy story entertains with meticulous detail on post-war intelligence rivalries played out in a 1950's Ottawa winter. Street smart Mounties navigating the dark world of Soviet versus western spies and clever cameos will surely charm cold-war intelligence aficionados. With luck, this is the first of series.

- Alan R. Jones. Assistant Director, CSIS (ret'd)

Goodspeed's Dead Spy, Cold Grave is a page turner: historically and organizationally authentic; credible, engaging characters, well written, brimming with treachery, intrigue and sudden twists. The early Cold War complexities Goodspeed describes still resonate today.

- Major General (ret'd) Lewis Mackenzie - UN Commander in Sarajevo

Mounties, Soviets, spies, murder and sex. What more could we want in a Cold War mystery set in 1951 Ottawa? Goodspeed knows his stuff, sets the scene well, and tells a gripping tale.

- J.L. Granatstein, historian and co-author of *Spy Wars*

Whether your life was shaped by the drama of the Cold War or you're someone keen to discover what those early years were like, Dead Spy, Cold Grave is a feast of a book. Readers who loved Goodspeed's character Rory Farrell in his World Wars I and II military intelligence operations in Three to a Loaf and Our Only Shield are once again rewarded in Dead Spy, Cold Grave's realistic story of clandestine guile, and deception.

- J. Patrick Boyer, former Parliamentary Secretary, External Affairs.

Dead Spy, Cold Grave is an outstanding addition to the fascinating roller coaster story of Canada's counter-intelligence capability development. The attention to detail, intricate plot, suspense, and character development is of a very high standard. As a professional Intelligence Officer, I have read many intelligence-related books, both fiction and non-fiction. This is, without a doubt, one of the best.

- Colonel (ret'd) D H Neil Thompson, Canadian Forces Intelligence Officer

A must-read for anyone interested in the dangerous game of international espionage or the Cold War in Canada. A gripping fictional account grounded in reality. Intrigue, sex, murder and deceit ... what more could one want?

- Dr. Craig Leslie Mantle, Assistant Professor, Canadian Forces College.

Dead Spy, Cold Grave is a cracking good spy tale that captures, with precision, all the tension and uncertainty of early Cold War Canada.
- Douglas E. Delaney, Canada Research Chair in War Studies, RMC

Michael J Goodspeed has created a gripping and distinctly Canadian tale of Cold War intrigue. Cleverly paced, shrewd plot twists, appealing characters, a discerning eye for historical detail, and an easy fluid style, Dead Spy, Cold Grave is a massively entertaining read.
- Brian Hodgson, Retired Canadian Security and Intelligence Officer and former British and Canadian soldier.

Dead Spy, Cold Grave by Michael Goodspeed is a genuine rarity: a Canadian spy thriller set in 1950s Ottawa: the coldest capital of the Cold War. The characters, dialogue and scenes ring true with the flavour of the times. The chilling scenario - a dead diplomat in the dead of an Ottawa winter - sets the reader on a path of intrigue, deception, and betrayal toward an unexpected climax. This is one to keep you up reading through the darkest hours before the dawn.
- David A. Charters, author of *Canadian Military Intelligence*

Apart from being the most readable and absorbing espionage novel that I've read in years, Dead Spy, Cold Grave provides a compelling historical analogy of some of the major security problems that continue to plague the West. Absolutely first rate!
- Colonel (ret'd) JP de B Taillon, CSIS (ret'd)

Michael J Goodspeed has written a believable, compelling counter intelligence story. It is exceptionally well told. He has a practitioner's understanding of the nascent RCMP Security Service in the very early days of the Cold War, which unfolds six years following the defection of Soviet Military Intelligence (GRU), cypher clerk, Igor Gouzenko. The RCMP is fighting to keep the CIA and Britain's MI6 from encroaching on their investigation and claiming ownership of it. Mr. Godspeed has done his research well. The politics and the economics of the day meld seamlessly into the story. If I didn't know differently, I would believe that Mr. Goodspeed was a member of the RCMP Security Service himself in the early 1950's. Be prepared to be taken on a ride back in time, murder, betrayal and for unexpected twists and turns.
- Donald G. Mahar, former CSIS and RCMP, author of *Shattered Illusions KGB Cold War Espionage in Canada*

Goodspeed immediately carries you to a time when Stalin is still around, the Korean War is still fluid, most men had been to war - and an RCMP officer in a new intelligence function has to investigate a naked dead man in a snowdrift with a bullet hole behind one ear. I was entranced from the first page.
- John C Thompson, military historian, author of *Spirit over Steel*

To my grandchildren,
Mina Lazic and Owen and Rory Goodspeed.

Library and Archives Canada Cataloguing in Publication
Goodspeed, Michael. author
Dead Spy, Cold Grave / Michael Goodspeed

Issued in print and electronic formats.
ISBN: 978-1-990644-31-3 (soft cover)
ISBN: 978-1-990644-32-0 (e-book)

Editor: Jennifer McIntyre
Cover design: Battlefield Design/Paul Hewitt
Interior Design: Winston A. Prescott

Double Dagger Books Ltd
Toronto, Ontario, Canada
www.doubledagger.ca

There are three kinds of enemy: the enemy himself, the friends of your enemies, and the enemies of your friends.

– Russian proverb

Chapter 1

IT WAS STILL DARK OUTSIDE. A January wind coming off the Ottawa River blew granulated snow into the bushes on the American ambassador's lawn and over a frozen corpse. The body had been dragged over a snowbank and dumped beside an evergreen shrub. Three miles away, the wind was moaning around the windows of Inspector Declan Connelly's Ottawa apartment.

Connelly slipped on the jacket to one of his two civilian suits while he hurried into the kitchen to turn up the volume on the radio's morning news summary. Despite the discouraging nature of the content, the CBC announcer's voice was deadpan.

The Communist Chinese Army has now occupied the South Korean capital city of Seoul, and military analysts are speculating as to whether General MacArthur will order a complete withdrawal of United Nations forces from the Korean peninsula. In Poland today, Joseph Stalin is convening a meeting of East European defence ministers in Warsaw to examine the creation of a new military alliance. And in the United States, the House Un-American Activities Committee has announced that it will reopen investigations this spring into reported communist subversion in Hollywood.

For months now the news had been an unrelenting stream of international calamity. Connelly grimaced as he sipped at a scalding hot cup of instant coffee. He was convinced the world was once again scrambling toward another global war. But there was another reason he was paying close attention to the broadcast.

In the last two days, all of this turmoil had come crashing into his life. Two days ago, he had been notified of his transfer from criminal intelligence to the RCMP's recently formed 'B Section' of Special Branch. He'd had only the shortest of briefings on the new posting and still hadn't been told exactly what his new duties would entail. All he knew was that he was going to spend the next several years of his life working to thwart the efforts of Soviet intelligence agents on Canadian soil. Today was to be his first day on the new job; and although he wasn't the sort to admit it, he was apprehensive.

The uncertainty didn't last long. The telephone rang as the newscast ended. Connelly snatched up the receiver.

"Connelly."

"Inspector Connelly, this is Sergeant Collins speaking." The man's voice was expressionless. "I'm the duty sergeant at National Headquarters. I've got a message for you from Assistant Commissioner Murray's office. A body's been found on the grounds of the U.S. ambassador's residence. There are two cars there now from the Rockcliffe Village detachment. You've been detailed to investigate it as a probable murder. Because of the body's location, the assistant commissioner wants the case managed exclusively by Special Branch."

"Okay," said Connelly. "What else do we know?"

"Well, sir, we don't have much to go on, but the AC is concerned it may become an issue for the government, and since you're Special Branch with a background in major crimes, he's asked for you by name."

"Have you got any other details?" Connelly asked.

"No, sir, not yet."

"Right. Thanks. I'm leaving now." He put the phone down. Breakfast would have to wait.

* * *

Connelly parked his car up against a snowbank and walked two hundred yards along the road running past the lightly wooded parkland that encircled the American ambassador's official residence. The cold snap was showing no signs of ending. It was twenty-one below zero with a fierce wind out of the north. Connelly pulled down the brim of his hat and put his hands over his ears to keep them from freezing. It was utterly insane, he thought, that for the sake of fashion professional men like himself should be wearing fedoras on a day like today.

Whistling off the Ottawa River, the wind carried with it the sour odour pumped into the sky by the massive pulp and paper plant downstream at Thurso, Quebec. Shards of snow and ice crunched under Connelly's feet. The cold was so severe that deep within the pine trees sap was freezing, sporadically exploding veins of solid amber, cracking and splitting branches, and cascading showers of pine cones onto the road below.

Connelly checked his watch. It was 7:22. Off to the east, dawn was beginning to crawl feebly above the horizon. Its promise was illusory. On days like today, the anemic January sunshine was little more than a cruel joke. Connelly walked up to a large, hump-backed, black and white 1948 Ford Tudor sedan with the Mounted Police's Buffalo crest on its doors. The engine was running. The red roof light was flashing, and the car was parked horizontally across the road, blocking both lanes. He tapped on the window.

"Where's the body now?" he said to the constable in the driver's seat. The younger policeman, engrossed in pouring coffee from a steaming thermos, almost spilled his drink.

The window opened immediately. "Sorry, sir, I didn't see you. We didn't think you'd get here so fast." The constable put the cap on his thermos, opened the door, and clambered out of the car. "Corporal Wilson, my boss—he's up by the body. His car's in position further up the road. There's been no traffic this early in the morning and nobody's come near here. Probably won't get any traffic for another twenty minutes or so, until people start heading to work." He gestured behind him, down to where the road curved past the snowbank, toward a landscaped, wooded rise of ornamental bushes and massive white pines. "Body's up there. We're going to spell each other off every ten minutes. You know, because of the cold."

"That's fine." Connelly nodded. "How long have you been here?"

"Just twenty-five, maybe thirty minutes, sir. The body was found by a retired colonel. He called us around six twenty-five this morning, and we got here shortly after. Colonel Crawford lives half a mile or so away. He'd been walking his dog, and the dog found the body. Aside from the dog and the colonel, nobody else has been here since. I think the colonel initially walked over the same path that the killer used to get in and out. He seemed to have his wits about him, as he went back out on a separate path. Doing his best, I think, but the dog's made a complete mess of the crime scene, and I don't think there'll be much now in the way of useful footprints in the snow. Detachment's ordered a photographer and a forensic team. I think the photographer is coming from the Ottawa police department, but the team will be one of ours from the national lab. They should be along soon."

"Right. Finish your coffee, but make sure you don't let anyone past. I'll find my way up. Thanks."

Connelly walked around the bend and found Corporal Wilson standing beside his car beating his hands together and stomping his feet. He wore a navy-blue regimental parka and a muskrat hat, with the flaps pulled down over his ears. Connelly noted that Wilson had chunks of frost rimming his bushy eyebrows and black moustache. It was evidence that Wilson wasn't doing his turn on watch from inside his car.

"Morning, sir!" Wilson saluted, forcing a tight smile. "I hope the others get here as quickly as you did. It's no weather to be hanging around outside." He spoke with a Nova Scotia accent. "Body's up there, just at the top of that small rise. Do you mind if I take you in? I've been in and out on my own separate trail so I wouldn't disturb anything. Thought we'd use the same route. Whoever it is up there, he's totally naked, frozen solid as a side of beef. By the looks of him, he's had some rough treatment."

Corporal Wilson led Connelly over the snowbank and onto his track around and past the body. They ducked under low-hanging pine branches so that they could come at the corpse from behind, looking down at the head. The body was that of a fit, lean, mature white male. There was a light dusting of frost over the clean-shaven face, and the skin on the rest of his body had turned a greyish blue in the cold. Connelly guessed that, whoever it was, he might have been somewhere between thirty-five and forty. Now he lay naked on his back in a foot of snow, face upwards; his mouth was open wide, showing a broken front tooth, and one bloodshot, half-closed eye stared blankly at the sky. One arm was folded across his chest; the right leg was bent at an unnatural angle. Connelly took a step closer, then squatted down and leaned in carefully, taking care not to lose his balance and tumble onto the body. He saw what looked like a bullet wound behind and above the man's right ear, a neat black hole surrounded by thick white frost. An ugly, frozen black rivulet ran from the wound into a neatly tapered hairline. There was no blood pool in the snow.

"He wasn't killed here," Connelly said, and pointed to the beaten path through the snow. "Someone's dragged him here. Must have taken an effort on a night like last night — if that's when he was dumped here." He looked around at the beaten snow surrounding the body and then nodded half to himself. "It probably was last night; otherwise, the trail they made dragging him in here would have more snow drifted into it." Connelly shifted his weight and looked out at the roadway. "Whoever he is, I don't think it's a coincidence the killer, or killers, brought the body here. I'd guess that somebody's making a statement." He stood up. "It would have been a lot easier to dump him across the road, over the rock face near where I parked. If they did that, the body would have rolled down into the scrub by the river bank. Unless you were looking for it there, nobody'd likely find it until spring. They wanted the body to be found here."

Wilson nodded, unsure whether Connelly was talking to him or just thinking aloud. "That's what I thought, too, sir."

"Yeah." Connelly pursed his lips, deep in thought. Dumping a badly beaten body on the American ambassador's property seemed more like someone trying to make some kind of a crude statement. He couldn't be sure, but this didn't feel like a sex crime. It would be interesting to see what the forensic team and the pathologist would have to say. From a cursory study of the crime scene there wasn't much else to go on. He turned to Wilson. "Do you have a radio in your car?"

"Both cars in the Rockcliffe detachment have radios, sir." Wilson grinned. "You get new equipment when your detachment's responsible for the embassy district."

From the passenger seat of Wilson's car Connelly spoke deliberately into the hand mike.

"Tell Staff Sergeant Cormier that I'll meet him back at the office, probably about nine or nine-thirty. Before that, I'll need to speak to whoever's in at the American ambassador's house. I'm also going to talk to this Colonel Crawford and anyone else around here he might recommend. In the meantime, please have Staff Sergeant Cormier telephone the Ottawa City Police, the Ontario and Quebec Provincial Police forces, as well as the Hull Police, and see if any men in their late twenties to early forties have been reported missing in the last few days. One other thing. Advise the city coroner that I'll need a priority for this one. See if you can get me an early slot with him once the body thaws out. Thanks."

He re-cradled the microphone. Outside, the younger policeman was shouting. He sounded frustrated.

"No ma'am, you can't be up here. Ma'am, ma'am — stop, please!"

Connelly stepped out of the car. A woman in her mid-thirties was striding up the road with the young constable in close pursuit. The first things Connelly noticed about her was that she was pretty and exuded confidence and style. She wore a long burgundy wool coat with a large fur collar, and a navy-blue wool cloche hat pulled down over dark red hair. In her gloved hands she clutched a steno pad and a pencil. An older man in a long gabardine coat stumbled along behind them, struggling with the bellows of a large press camera. When he caught sight of Connelly, he stopped and began snapping shots of him. The inspector ignored him and strode toward the woman.

"Stop right there." He stepped in front of her and gave her a withering look. "Who are you, and what do you think you're doing unlawfully barging into a police restricted area?"

She stopped and folded her arms. "I'm Oriana Soroka. I work for the *Ottawa Tribune* and I'm looking for Inspector Connelly." She eyed Connelly, deliberately assessing him from the ground up, before she continued. "You are Inspector Connelly, I take it? I've got some questions for you."

For a fraction of a moment Connelly was taken aback. He'd never seen this woman in his life.

Sensing an opening, Soroka continued. "Do you know the victim's name? Also, why's Special Branch doing this investigation and not the murder squad?"

Connelly turned and glared at the younger constable, who shrank backwards and raised his hands in protest. "Not me, sir! I didn't say a word!"

"Oh, no," Soroka said, smiling. "This officer, he's been wonderful — believe me. He's told me nothing. Our newsroom has a receiver tuned to the Ottawa police dispatcher, and forty minutes ago they sent out an unencoded update describing this crime scene and who was handling it. I got a phone call telling me to get right over here. Now, Inspector, I know there's a body here and you've been sent to run things. So, how about answering my questions?"

Connelly regarded her coolly. If this woman wanted a confrontation, he wasn't going to give it to her. She had a determined look about her. There was a better way to handle this. Connelly took a breath and spoke quietly. "I give you top marks for your initiative, ma'am. I'll do what I can. Let's talk down at the other car, shall we, Miss... Soroka, you said?" She nodded. "I'll tell you everything I can right now, and I promise you, when I know more, because you've been so resourceful, you're absolutely going to be the first to hear about any press releases. But we can't talk here. This is now officially a crime scene, and it's restricted to all members of the public."

He took her by the arm and gestured with an affable wave for the cameraman to come with them. "Come on. You, too." He turned back to the woman. "My name's Declan Connelly, and I'm an inspector with the RCMP. As you've heard, there's been an incident here on the edge of the American ambassador's property. I've only been here for a few minutes myself, so that's about all I know and all that I can possibly tell you right now. You can't photograph the body, but I'd be happy to help in any other way I can. Like I said, I'll make sure you get a scoop before the press release. What do you say — if I can get you some information by noon, will that meet your deadline?"

Oriana Soroka smiled.

"Wonderful," said Connelly. "I'll do my best; that's a promise. Give me your phone number and I'll be in touch."

Soroka handed him her business card. Connelly tucked it into his pocket and led her and the cameraman away from the crime scene.

While the two journalists walked back to their car, Connelly turned to Wilson. "I'm going to leave you here to keep a lid on things when the photographer and the forensic team arrive. You know the drill. I want to get up and make some inquiries at the ambassador's house before people leave for the day. I'm sure things here are in good hands." He paused. "Good job. Thanks."

Corporal Wilson and the younger constable walked back to the police car parked up at the crime scene.

"You know," the constable said, "it was killing me trying to figure out who this Inspector Connelly was. I remember now where I heard of him. It was a couple of years ago, summer of 1949, out west. Wasn't he the one involved in that big internal investigation where one of our guys got shot? A lot of people thought he shouldn't have got off."

Wilson cut him short. "Yeah, well, you didn't actually hear any of the evidence, did you? If this guy was such a dick, do you think they'd send him here today? Your job's to listen and keep your eyes open." He locked eyes with the constable for a moment. "Now, it's your turn to stand watch. I'll relieve you in ten minutes."

"Well, you know, he seemed like an all right sort of guy to me," the constable said, backtracking quickly. "He's not like what I've heard people say about him."

Wilson rolled his eyes. "Right. I'll be back here at ten to eight."

✳ ✳ ✳

The iron gate at the entrance to the U.S. ambassador's residence was closed. Connelly pushed a buzzer on the gate post and an elderly commissionaire emerged from the small stone guard hut tucked discreetly among the shrubbery. Connelly noticed that there were no tread marks in the thin layer of snow that covered the driveway. There were two sets of footprints leading from the guard building to the road. The commissionaire bobbed his head when he saw Connelly's ID.

"Gotta phone the Marine sergeant up at the house first, though, sir."

Two minutes later, Connelly was standing in the foyer of 'Lonardo,' the massive grey stone mansion that was home to the American ambassador. The chief steward and a uniformed duty Marine sergeant were on hand to meet him. Both men said that no one had been in or out of the house since nine the night before, and the Marine confirmed nothing untoward had been reported by either the outgoing or incoming commissionaire at the guard house at six-thirty. The daytime cleaning and kitchen staff weren't due to report until after ten this morning, and nobody else had heard anything. Just as Connelly was leaving, the ambassador came downstairs. He was much younger than Connelly expected, apparently in his early forties; fit, with an athletic spring in his step, he looked more like an intense hockey coach or a brash salesman than a senior diplomat. He extended his hand to Connelly and the two men shook.

"Alan Wright," said the ambassador, introducing himself. "I heard what the chief steward just told you. I was upstairs in my study working till past midnight last night and I can tell you, there were only the three of us here last night. My wife's gone to the Florida Keys to visit her family. I didn't hear a thing." He looked Connelly in the eye. "I want you to personally keep me in the loop on this one, Inspector. I wanna know what goes on here." He reached out to shake Connelly's hand again. "I really appreciate having the Mounted Police on top of this one. Anything you need from me, you just call."

* * *

The Ottawa and Carleton County coroner was a large, jovial man in his early sixties. He wore a green rubber apron and rubber gloves, and looked out at the world with mischievous eyes through thick horn-rimmed glasses. His voice boomed as Connelly and Staff Sergeant Cormier entered his pathology laboratory.

"Ah, Inspector Connelly. They told me you were coming. I haven't had the pleasure of meeting you. My assistant tells me that you're a Special Branch officer. So, they decided not to send a workaday city homicide detective to do the sleuthing for this unfortunate man." The coroner smiled broadly, gesturing to the thawing corpse lying on the metal table before them.

Connelly smiled back at him. "Thanks, Doctor. Yes, I'm Inspector Declan Connelly, and this is Staff Sergeant Cormier. I'm sorry — I didn't catch your name?"

"I'm Dr. Peter Thompson. Now, tell me, Inspector, have you discovered a name yet for this poor man?"

"I'm afraid not. Nobody's been reported missing by any of the local police forces, and there's been no match so far to the fingerprint samples you sent us. That will probably take some time. There was nothing else of value from the crime scene that would indicate who he was or the exact circumstances of his death. I'm hoping you'll be able to give me some information."

"I'm certain I can be of some assistance, Inspector. My secretary is typing my report as we speak, but I can give you something now that you can go on before you get the report."

Dr. Thompson was obviously enjoying himself. He folded his arms and pushed his glasses back up his nose. "I estimate he was between the ages of thirty-eight and forty-one. At the time of death, he was in reasonably good health, well-nourished, and, judging by his hair and nails, he was well groomed. Despite the body being found naked, there's no evidence of any kind of sexual assault. I can't give you a precise time of death because of the freezing. But I can say that this man was dead for at least an hour and he lay undisturbed somewhere warm before being frozen. Rigor mortis had not started to set in."

The coroner pointed as if he were giving a class. "You see the eyelids, the jaw, the neck, across his face, and down through his chest, abdomen, upper arms, and legs — they hadn't begun to stiffen. The fingers and toes were equally supple. Also, if you look on his back, here," he rolled the body and pointed to the corpse's lower back, "you'll note the very beginnings of a reddish-purple colour here. Being frozen has altered the coloration somewhat, but that doesn't change things substantially. His body must have lain somewhere warm, probably for at least an hour, as I said, in the same supine position before being moved. We call that a 'post-mortem stain.' If you leave a body unmoved for a few hours, the parts of the body nearest the ground develop this very characteristic discoloration. It's just the blood seeping downward, gravity leaving its imprint. In this case this discoloration was just beginning, so I would assume that the body had not been moved for an hour, maybe an hour and half. I can't be more precise than that.

"Now," Dr. Thompson went on, warming to his task, "let's see what else I can tell you about this man and who he was. As you've also no doubt figured out, there's no question as to the cause of death. A single cranial gunshot wound. Notice the large stellate effect surrounding the entrance wound. This indicates a contact gunshot wound. He was shot once from very close, from above and to the rear of his right ear. The round exited the lower left jaw. Death was instantaneous. My guess is that likely the victim was on his knees or in a chair. I'll get to more of that in a minute. This was almost certainly not a wound inflicted by a rifle. Someone shot our boy with a pistol. Medium-calibre bullet. Without the actual bullet, I'd only be guessing at the exact calibre. The wound measurements are imprecise because the wound itself is a bit more jagged around the edges as a result of the body having been frozen. You didn't by chance happen to find a bullet at the crime scene?"

Connelly shook his head. "No. The only thing they found was a half-empty package of Lucky Strikes. No bullet."

"No?" Thompson nodded his head. "That's unfortunate. Well, it appears to be a fairly high-velocity round, leaving clean tunnelling. There's no projectile breakup whatsoever and not much neighbouring tissue damage. The round moved through his head quickly. The exit wound is fairly round, only slightly more irregular than the entry wound. Death was instantaneous. There's no evidence of significant bleeding.

"Now, the rest of the body is very interesting. Right off the bat I'd bring your attention to his teeth." Thompson reached over and gently opened the corpse's mouth. "The dental work jumped out at me. It's definitely not Canadian. And he has a broken front tooth, which has no associated stain and so likely was broken within hours of his death. That's consistent with the bruising around the face. Other than that, his front teeth aren't in bad shape. His back teeth, however, aren't nearly in such good shape: numerous cavities and cheap fillings. And in place of the maxillary second bicuspid," he pointed, "you'll notice a stainless-steel tooth. I'd almost certainly guess our man is from Eastern Europe."

Staff Sergeant Cormier peered over the corpse's face, examining his features and making small, appreciative noises. "I think you're right, Doctor," he said after a moment. "When I was in Manitoba, they used to call that a 'North End of Winnipeg' face."

"Um, yes," Dr. Thompson said guardedly. "These could well be Slavic features, but judging from his teeth, I'd say he didn't come from Winnipeg. Now, gentlemen, if you look at his wrists and his ankles, they're badly chafed. This poor man was tied up before he died, and none too gently. From the markings on him, I would bet he was tied to a chair and was executed while he was in that position. The other gruesome detail you need to know is that there are numerous burns between his toes. Probably cigarette burns. That would be an excruciating experience. Whoever burned him almost certainly knows something about torture and how to inflict pain. This would also explain why he was stripped naked: it increases the victim's sense of vulnerability. I think you have a very experienced and ruthless killer on your hands."

Connelly and Cormier said nothing; both merely raised their eyebrows and nodded. After a silent moment Connelly spoke again.

"Those scars on his legs — are they shrapnel wounds?"

"Very good. Yes, they are, Inspector. We did a body X-ray and found there are small fragments of metal still in his legs. My guess, from their size, is that they're grenade fragments. I take it you're familiar with shrapnel wounds, Inspector?"

"Yeah," Connelly replied. "I've got a couple of those marks myself."

Dr. Thompson raised an eyebrow. "You were in the last war?"

"Yeah. Sicily and Italy. My war ended at the Gothic Line."

The doctor's cheery manner evaporated. "I was in the Great War. I worked in a hospital in Canada for most of the war. I didn't go over until right near the end, in 1918. I didn't see much action, but I saw far too much of this sort of wound." The doctor rubbed his sleeve against his nose and exhaled noisily, then cleared his throat. "Anyway, I think it's safe to say that this man was probably a veteran. I'll leave it to you to determine for which side." He turned to the corpse again, all business once more.

"Internally, this man hadn't eaten much in the last several hours before death. He was a heavy smoker, and the state of his liver indicates he drank a fair amount, and over many years. He may not have been what we'd call an alcoholic, and although he was still reasonably healthy, he drank an unhealthy amount. He had a considerable amount of alcohol in his blood when he died, enough to declare him legally intoxicated. As I said earlier, he was well groomed, and from this I'd hazard that it's likely he was, outwardly at least, a stable personality.

"So, Inspector Connelly, in summary I'd say that this man was in early middle age, probably an East European national or an immigrant, a war veteran, and someone who either possessed some kind of information or had crossed someone such that some very nasty people were willing to torture and murder him."

Chapter 2

AT JUST PAST FIVE O'CLOCK, the street lights had come on and the mercury on the thermometer still hovered just above the minus-25-degree mark. Staff Sergeant Cormier drove Connelly back from the meeting with the coroner in one of the Special Branch's unmarked 1950 Ford sedans.

"That was an interesting session," Cormier said. He flipped open his Zippo lighter and, with a practised hand, lit an unfiltered Player's. "Want one, sir?"

"No, thanks. Haven't had a smoke for months now, but thanks anyway."

Cormier flipped the cigarette pack onto the steel dashboard and exhaled a blue cloud. "Yeah, I had my over-fifty medical last week. Doctor said I'm in great shape but told me to keep my smoking to under a pack a day. I'm getting there, but it's hard." He took another drag off his cigarette. "You know, there can't be too many missing guys who match that description in Ottawa. Do you want to go home, sir, or back to the office?"

"No. Take me back to the office, thanks, Marcel. I want to see whatever's come in on the daily summaries, if anything, and I really should get around and speak to Superintendent Ferrall. First day on the job. I'm sure he's got something to say to me." He glanced out the window. "Can you pull up beside the corner store just up here on Bank Street? I want to see what our journalist friend wrote for this afternoon's paper."

"Don't burn yourself out too early, boss. You single officers have a habit of going flat out from day one. The superintendent's still gonna be here tomorrow. Besides, there's nothing obvious for us to go on now. I don't expect anything's going to break overnight. The forensic team haven't found anything to go on, and I've just got a feeling this one's only going to be cracked by slogging through weeks of interviews and some good luck."

Connelly grunted. "You may be right. Stop up at the corner here. I'll just be a second."

Connelly got out and clambered over a three-foot bank of rock-hard frozen slush. Tinny bells on top of the door jingled as he entered the dingy confectionery. He came back with a couple of Oh Henry! chocolate bars and the evening's *Tribune*. He handed one of the bars to Cormier.

"Here. This'll keep your energy level up." He shook the paper open. "Look at the front page. Our new friend, Madame Oriana Soroka, has my picture right next to breaking news about the war in Korea! Look at this." He held up the paper, which showed a picture of him, snow swirling in the background, a large gloved hand raised in the stop position. "They haven't got much of a story either." Connelly read aloud. "'Police are being guarded in releasing information concerning the discovery of a frozen body on the grounds of the U.S. ambassador's residence in Rockcliffe Village in the early hours this morning. Inspector Declan Connelly of the RCMP Special Branch, pictured above, is leading the investigation. Sources at the American embassy say they have no knowledge of the incident and are cooperating fully with the police.'"

Connelly read silently for a moment and then shook his head in disbelief. "Wait a minute — listen to this! 'So far it would appear police investigations are at a complete impasse.' I never said that! And there's more: 'The body was found this morning by retired Colonel Jeffery Crawford.'" He read on. "Yeah, yeah... It goes on describing the colonel's dog." He turned to Cormier. "I never said anything like 'a complete impasse.' I said, 'That's all the information we can reveal at this stage of our inquiries.' What kind of paper is this? Chinese troops are attacking Seoul, we're about to start the Third World War, and these people are giving this single murder case equal prominence on their front page! Do you believe this?"

Cormier smiled tolerantly. "Boss, we both know a local murder sells more papers than ten thousand deaths on the other side of the world. Besides, we haven't heard the last of that reporter. Before we went to the coroner's, she was downstairs rooting around at the front desk for information. She's a determined lady."

At the RCMP office on the second floor of the Queen Street building, Shirley Agnew, the superintendent's secretary, was organizing her desk before heading home. She was an efficient, relentlessly cheerful fire-hydrant of a woman.

"Glad I caught you, Inspector Connelly," she said. "Superintendent Farrell wants to talk to you. He's still at his desk."

Rory Ferrall was in civilian clothes, reading from a red-labelled file. He looked up as Connelly tapped on the frame of his office door. Ferrall had only one eye, which some found disconcerting. The empty socket, the result of an old war wound, was covered by a stiff black patch. Connelly liked the man, but always felt Ferrall used the eye patch for dramatic effect. Ferrall's good eye never seemed to be looking at you as much as it studied you. In the Mounted Police, Ferrall was a larger-than-life but understated legend. In uniform, he wore two and half rows of war ribbons. His medals included campaign service in both World Wars as well as the Military Cross, the DSO, a Croix de Guerre, and the Dutch Bronze Cross. It was an open secret that, in addition to service in the trenches, he had served as a spy at the end of the First World War and in Special Operations Executive in the Second. Like everybody else, Connelly was drawn to the man, but found him slightly intimidating.

The two men had first met just after Connelly got home from the war, but they had never worked together. On the few occasions when they had met, Ferrall had always been cordial and cheerful. He had a reputation for being fair and friendly, but, according to informed gossip, he was ruthless with lazy, inept, or amateurish subordinates.

On his desk, a copy of the *Ottawa Tribune* lay beneath a black telephone.

Ferrall stood up to greet Connelly and extended his hand. "Welcome to Special Branch, Declan. Helluva a first day you've had in your new job. You're being thrown into the deep end on this one. Sorry about that." He motioned for Connelly to sit. "I'd have preferred your introduction to be a little more gradual." He waved his hand. "Ideally, you should have a series of proper briefings and some specialized training in Britain and the States. But I'm afraid we're going to have to leave that for later. One thing I'll point out to you right as you start your new job here, though: our mandate in Special Branch is to safeguard the country's security, not apprehend criminals. Some people have trouble getting their head around that one. In that respect, we're different from every other unit in the RCMP." He chuckled.

"But now that I've told you that, the first task you're getting in Special Branch is to investigate a murder," Ferrall continued. "Hopefully, this investigation won't take you too long. But up front, you should know my priorities. Part of my job is to organize and plan for the expansion of Special Branch. There may not be bombs dropping on Ottawa, but we're in a new kind of war, and the counter-intelligence business is going to grow — quickly, if I have anything to do with it. So, I'm going to be busy with other matters, which means I'm giving you a high degree of latitude in your job. I know you won't let me down."

Ferrall paused and scrutinized Connelly with his good eye. "You seem to have landed somewhere in an institutional twilight zone. You'll have to keep your wits about you on this one, Connelly, because the differences between being a policeman and being a counter-intelligence officer aren't always apparent. I have no doubt you'll manage. I guarantee you'll find that the job brings enormous frustrations, but you'll see that you're in the same boat that we all found ourselves in a few months ago when they established this section. Now, tell me what you know about this new case."

Connelly outlined Dr. Thompson's findings, while Ferrall swivelled slightly in his chair, lips pursed, fingers steepled.

"Interesting. Anything else?" Ferrall said when Connelly had concluded his summary.

"Yes, sir. I went to the American embassy, and I actually got to speak to the ambassador. He hadn't left for work this morning. He was very concerned about this and asked to be kept abreast of any developments. He promised to provide any help he could, but nobody at the ambassador's residence knew anything about it. I also checked with the guard who manned the security booth at the entrance to the grounds. There was no report of anything untoward all night."

"What have you done by way of getting a positive identification of this victim?"

"Well, sir, I've asked that one of our photographers get a facial shot of the victim. We'll circulate it to the local police forces in the morning. I checked on the way in, and there are no missing persons on record locally or across Canada that match our description of this guy."

"Right. Thanks, Declan. It sounds to me like you're on the right track. Keep doing what you're doing." Ferrall smiled. "I want to give you a bit of background for your first day here. Because you've had to hit the deck running, consider this my welcoming chat with you. I'm sure it's not news to you, but the organization you've just joined is still in its infancy. Compared to the rest of the world, Canada has been," he paused, rummaging for the right word, "reluctant to recognize the need for a counter-intelligence service. To be brutally honest, we're still dog-paddling around in the shallow end of the pool. That'll change, and I need you to help be a catalyst for that change.

"Right now, we're understaffed, under-resourced, and inexperienced. Here in Ottawa, in B Section, including you, I have exactly seven uniforms, nine civilian analysts, and a dozen men in what is our surveillance team. In this business, it takes twenty men to provide adequate covert surveillance on a single individual. Like I said, we have twelve men in our entire watcher service. It's ridiculously small. So, a major part of my task is to convince those above me of the need for a much larger and more capable security service." He looked at Connelly, who nodded. "Your job will be more focused on working at the coal face, as it were, chasing spies. We're all still feeling our way around.

"Up until now, Special Branch was supposed to handle all politically sensitive files, all sedition and espionage files, all counter-intelligence matters. Before this section was created, Special Branch had been involved almost exclusively in hunting for Soviet agents in the trade unions and hounding homosexuals out of the civil service. Not for repetition outside this office, it's been a stupid policy. It's wasted our time and, as a result, we've been almost completely ineffective as a counter-intelligence service. On the few legitimate files we actually pursued, we operated like a normal police force. We tended to drive toward resolution in court. That's the right thing to do with criminal work. But you'll find counter-intelligence is different. Most of your files will never see the insides of a courtroom — and our files here tend to stay open indefinitely. As a police officer investigating a crime, you'd keep the file open until you had either a conviction or an acquittal in court. We can't do that. In fairness, a conventional police approach was more or less workable when we had to deal with the Nazis. Fascist agents usually stuck out like sore thumbs, and, luckily for us, they weren't particularly concerned with Canada before the war. When the war came, we could just lock them all up."

Ferrall sat back in his chair. "After the war, it all changed: the Soviets began to take a serious interest in us. In the world of subterfuge and intrigue, the Russians are the world's ugly, battle-scarred veterans. They've been the most ruthless and vicious players in the cloak-and-dagger business for a hundred years, long before the Communists came along. They see clandestine operations as a normal way of doing business. They've been at it so long, it's in their blood. I don't know if this new case of yours involves the Russians, Declan. You say the coroner thinks this victim is East European, yes?" Connelly nodded. "We'll wait and see, but it wouldn't surprise me if that were, indeed, the case.

"Personally, I think the assistant commissioner was hedging his bets when he gave this to Special Branch. You'll find ninety-eight percent of the work you're going to do here involves the Soviets. They don't regard themselves as being at peace with the West. Although most people here don't like to think of it like that, we're in a period of simmering conflict, and, unlike the wars you and I know, this one has no discrete beginning or end. For the Soviets this is an initial preparatory phase in the global revolutionary struggle."

Ferrall shifted in his chair. "I've told you what I think about our counter-intelligence efforts up to now. This section won't be doing that.

Now that the government has raised B Section, we're responsible for serious counter-intelligence operations. We prevent foreign intelligence agencies from gathering and collecting intelligence. That almost exclusively involves political, scientific, and military secrets." Ferrall paused and picked up a pipe. "Perhaps most importantly, the Russians see Canada as a springboard for intelligence operations in the United States. We shouldn't kid ourselves: America's their big prize. But, as you'll discover, whether or not it's on this case or on whatever follows for you, they're working hard here."

Ferrall struck a match and began sucking furiously on his pipe. Clouds of smoke billowed up around him. Satisfied, he lowered the pipe and regarded Connelly with his one good eye. "When you work here, Declan, I want you to remember that the concept of 'mass' is the Russians' most important principle of war. They apply the same principle to their secret intelligence operations: they conduct espionage and subversion operations here in the West on a massive scale, but we shouldn't think that because the scale of their effort is huge, it means they're clumsy. Quite the opposite. They're the most experienced nation in the world in clandestine warfare. They're good at it and they're ruthless. I suspect that they have far more people operating in Canada than we have operating against them. Let that one sink in."

Ferrall pointed his pipe at Connelly as if he were about to pronounce judgment. "Having said that, it's important we approach this kind of problem in a discriminating manner. If we go overboard and start running around screeching the 'Red under every bed' refrain, we'll end up overplaying our hand and going after innocent people — and that'll only make us look foolish and incompetent. If that happens nobody will have any faith in us. We can't fall into that trap. In this game the public will only ever hear about our failures. Any successes we have will almost always go unreported. And that's how I want it."

He waved his pipe in a circular motion. "That brings me to you. One of the reasons I asked you to be posted here is that I want discreet, imaginative officers who will bring balance and common sense to the organization. Uncurbed enthusiasm is fine — if you're a boy scout. But it's disastrous in a counter-intelligence agency. As we grow, I want you to be a steadying influence here, Declan. But at the same time, I need creative solutions. It's easy to get tunnel vision in this job." Ferrall puffed on his pipe. "Anyway, we're going to talk in detail later. That's it for now." He stood up. "The long and short of it, Declan, is that none of us in happy little Canada has had much experience in counter-intelligence or politically sensitive operations. And we still don't. We're absurdly small for the job we have to do. We're learning this game as we go along, but at the same time we have to keep our heads above water. So, if you're unsure of something, don't hesitate to ask for advice or help. We'll get there, one way or the other."

Connelly stood up. "Thanks, sir." He turned for the door.

"Oh, one further point, Declan," Ferrall said. "I see the *Tribune* has described your efforts as being 'at a complete impasse.' Is that how you described it?"

"No, sir. I said our investigation had just begun. I told them we hadn't heard from the coroner yet, that we were working on things, and that that was all the information we could reveal at this stage of our inquiries. That was it."

"I thought as much. The reason I raise the issue," Ferrall said, "is that after reading this article, the U.S. ambassador called the minister to express his concern. I then got a phone call. I told the minister's Chief of Staff that I had complete confidence in you, but be advised: you're in the limelight now. As far as the federal government and the cabinet are concerned, this case is now politically sensitive."

* * *

Connelly was tired and hungry when he got back to his apartment. The place was in darkness. He had lived in this small space for two years now, but it still didn't feel much like home. He switched on the overhead light in the living room and hung up his coat. The few rooms he inhabited were about as bare and depressingly functional as could be. Apart from his work, he'd been living like a hermit. The ironing board was still set up in the living room from two days ago when he'd ironed a week's worth of shirts. Aside from that, everything was neat, orderly, and drearily purposeful. There were no pictures on the walls. The only concessions to pleasure were his table-top tube radio with its built-in clock and a large bookcase neatly lined with modern histories, novels, and oversize reference volumes.

He frowned. There wasn't much in the kitchen to stimulate him. Although he was hungry, the only food in the fridge was his usual cache of eggs, milk, and bread. He'd have to make do with yet another late-night meal of fried eggs, fried Spam, toast, and tea. He assembled his ingredients on the tiny countertop, plugged in the kettle, and began to make his dinner. Someday he was going to get a proper cookbook and put some variety into his life. He smiled wryly. If a cookbook was going to make any change in his dining habits, he'd have to take enough time off work to do proper grocery shopping. He poked the eggs around the cast-iron frying pan. Cookbooks might be fine, but who was he kidding? A woman in his life would add a hell of a lot more variety and charm for him than another book.

As he prepared yet another unappetizing dinner, Connelly wondered how things had got to this state of affairs. Not that he was unhappy. He had been raised to believe that it was a sign of weakness for a man to admit to being lonely, or any other sign of melancholy. The posting to Special Branch was a welcome, if unforeseen, turn in his life — two years ago he'd probably have turned his nose up at it. Now Special Branch offered him fresh opportunities, a chance to prove himself again, the chance to rebuild a career and a life that had been sidetracked by circumstance and bad luck.

When he finished eating, he sat with his tea at the small kitchen table thinking about where life had taken him. He was phlegmatic enough about it. Things could be worse. He was in good health. The new job looked interesting and he liked his boss. Now, there were new avenues open to him. He was determined to give it everything he had.

He thought about the chain of events that had brought him to this point, wondering if he would have done anything different given the chance. He had been a dirt-poor farm kid who'd graduated at the top of his high school class and got a place in the Mounties during the Depression. He'd been posted to New Brunswick, and that had been followed in rapid succession by a promotion and posting to Nova Scotia, getting married, volunteering for the army during the war, getting a commission, and then almost as promptly being wounded in Italy and shipped back to Britain, where there was a Dear John letter waiting for him at the convalescent hospital. When he was repatriated, he went back into the Mounties and became a serious crimes detective. Soon after that, he was accepted for a commission and given his own detachment in Saskatchewan. That upturn was followed by Jim Walker's death and the ugly consequences of that tragedy.

Now, Special Branch offered fresh challenges and the chance to get himself back on track. His life had followed an arc that looked a lot like the stock market in the last ten years: a few big slumps, but for the most part slowly moving upwards. He put his teacup down and looked around him at his modest little apartment. When he had some spare time, in addition to that cookbook, he'd do something to make things look a little more cheerful. For now, there was an East European corpse with a bullet hole behind its left ear to keep him occupied.

✳ ✳ ✳

Superintendent Wallace Graham stared at the reflection in his office window. He was a burly man: five foot six with thinning red hair, freckles, and a paunch that in the last four years had ballooned inexorably past his belt. He didn't like the look of the man glowering back at him: pasty-faced, flabby, cantankerous, and discouragingly unremarkable, a man in the throes of late middle age who was becoming vinegary and more brittle with age.

It bothered him to think that the image staring back at him was what his wife saw these days. This morning she'd slammed the door in his face. The words she'd spat at him still stung. "You haven't been any fun for the last ten years, but since we've come to Ottawa, living with you has been sheer, fucking agony. I'm sick of it." Over the years, they'd fought often enough, but she'd never spoken to him like that. He knew her well enough to know that it meant she was a hair's breadth away from separation and divorce. By itself, the idea of their marriage ending didn't bother him, but a divorce — that was another thing. Divorce would torpedo him. It was frowned upon in the most senior ranks of the RCMP. This morning's quarrel had flared up over his refusal to go out to the movies the night before. But they both knew that wasn't the only reason.

Before coming to Ottawa, Graham had been a zealous and highly regarded policeman. Over the span of three decades, he'd developed a reputation for staid, single-minded competence. It didn't bother him that he'd been tagged with the nickname 'Chuckles' by a bitter subordinate. The sobriquet had dogged him for the last twenty-three years. What rankled him was that he was distrusted by his subordinates and peers, that he had no real friends among his contemporaries. But much more importantly, he knew he was admired by several influential superior officers for being reliable, cautious, and austere. He was happy with that. He liked to think of himself as 'a crusty old senior officer.'

Coming to Ottawa and getting a job with the Privy Council had been a big step up. He'd earned it the hard way. It was a clear signal that his superiors trusted him and had better things in mind for him — and why not? He'd sweated buckets for it, leaving dozens of lesser men in the dust behind him.

Graham massaged his temples. In Ottawa's bureaucracies, some of the most coveted and influential government positions were in the Privy Council Office. He was now one of three key advisers in the office of the Assistant Secretary to the Cabinet for Defence, Security, and Intelligence. Everything to do with the Mounted Police that went to the minister was filtered through him. If he used his influence properly, it was one of the most powerful jobs in the RCMP. By definition, among many other things, Graham had access to all communications going to cabinet that dealt with Special Branch and counter-intelligence operations within Canada. It was an advantage he intended to capitalize on.

He prided himself that he had gotten this far by being a capable cop but also by being discreetly cagey. He had long since figured out that carefully insinuating yourself with the right people was not only an acceptable career skill, it was an essential aptitude. He walked around his desk, gently closed the door to his office, and exhaled heavily.

Until this morning he had never really thought about it in such blunt terms. He'd reached a point where career success was the most important thing in his life. If his wife couldn't appreciate that, that was her problem. Her rant this morning had crystalized things: now was the time to make a move. He'd already made the decision to cozy up to his opposite number in the Prime Minister's Office — even though he knew that entailed a certain degree of risk.

When he'd first taken the job, he had been explicitly warned to keep his distance. Assistant Commissioner Murray, Graham's immediate superior in the force and a man Graham regarded as a moralistic stuffed shirt, had explained the rules.

"The Prime Minister's Office makes government policy. That's fine. Your job in the Privy Council Office is very different. You work entirely on implementing the government's policy decisions. Politicians and their staffs in the PMO don't operate under the same rules as public servants. They both serve, but in different ways. Your first duty, Wallace, is to the system, not a political party. When you meet with anyone from the Prime Minister's Office, you've always got to have another member of the Privy Council with you. That's standard procedure. You start showing the slightest bit of political favouritism to political staffers, you've become partisan. You cross that line, it eventually becomes public knowledge, and the RCMP will lose credibility when it comes to investigating anything with any kind of political consequence. We can't afford to look like we're playing political favourites, or like we're working for any particular political party.

"Other than that, your only permissible communication chains are with your assistant secretary in the Privy Council and back to the RCMP through me. The Prime Minister's Office is an entirely partisan political institution whose members provide the prime minister and his cabinet with political advice. There's nothing wrong with that, but that's not what we do, Wallace. Part of your job is to safeguard the integrity of the force, and to do that, you have to remain an impartial government servant. In a healthy government, at your level the Privy Council and the Prime Minister's Office operate in different spheres."

That was fine for some, but Graham understood career success was the product of ability reinforced by connections. He'd already made a valuable contact in the PMO. It was time to build on that. No one would be the wiser.

He wouldn't act impulsively. He still needed information from B Section of Special Branch — and if word got out that he'd stepped over the line, he'd just say it was routine passage of information.

He slowly picked up the phone and spun the rotary dial.

"It's Superintendent Graham. Please put me through to Superintendent Ferrall." He drummed his fingers until Ferrall came on the line. "Rory, there's a problem. I understand that you spoke to the deputy minister about this case involving the American embassy. I don't know anything about it. I only heard about this from the minister's office just before lunch. That's unacceptable."

Ferrall paused before replying. "I don't think that constitutes a problem, Wallace. The deputy minister phoned me directly, and you heard about the conversation in due course. Sounds like things are working normally."

"No, no. I can't do my job, Rory, if I have to hear about issues second-hand. You know that."

"You aren't in my chain of command, Wallace, but believe me, whenever there's anything that I think you need to know, I'll keep you in the loop."

"You do that, Rory. I've also heard that you've put Connelly in charge of the case. Is that right?"

"It is. I happen to think he's the right man for the job, but for the record, he was handpicked for it by the assistant commissioner."

Graham was silent for a moment. "You know my feelings about that man. He should never have been sent to Special Branch, let alone been allowed to stay in the force."

"Thanks for your opinion, Wallace," Ferrall said icily. "If there's anything else you ever want to get off your chest, call me."

Graham hung up the phone. He licked his lips. Special Branch didn't know who they were dealing with. He walked to the window. His tiny office on the Quebec side of the Ottawa River was on the third floor of one of the temporary government buildings that had sprung up during the war. His window overlooked the massive industrial scar that was the Eddy Match and Paper Company: a mountain of softwood logs, grimy factory buildings, and smoke stacks. It was an ugly sight. He inhaled deeply. If Connelly wanted to screw up a case that was potentially of national importance, he could legitimately turn it to his advantage.

He picked up the phone and slowly dialled. "Hi, Francine, it's Superintendent Graham." He forced a smile into the phone. "Yeah, I'm fine. How are you today? Great. Is your boss in? No, that's wonderful. I'll wait."

Two minutes later Paul Norman, the prime minister's thirty-one-year-old deputy political advisor for justice and public safety, came on the line.

"Hi, Paul. Hope I'm not disturbing you, but I want to keep you up to date on things. It's a bit unusual, and I wouldn't be calling if it wasn't important. I see it as part of my job to keep you guys out of the soup. You've heard about this new case that's come up with the dead body on the lawn of the U.S. ambassador's residence? Yeah, I read the piece in the paper too. I'm concerned it could come back to bite you politically. I don't know how it's happened, but the officer managing this case has a pretty checkered record." He let out a theatrical sigh. "If he screws it up, there could be some unpleasant diplomatic and political ramifications. Personally, I'm certain they have the wrong guy on the job, but there's not much I can do about it from where I sit."

"What do you want me to do, Wallace?" Norman said.

"Nothing just now. I'm keeping you posted, but just between the two of us, I know the reporter for the *Tribune* who wrote that piece. I could quietly advise her on this matter. An article in one of the local papers might stimulate some action. I just didn't want you to be blindsided when this thing comes up in the press, and I figured I'd let you know where it's going. You don't want to be seen to be meddling, and you can honestly advise the minister to say that he's aware of the issue and it's being handled by the appropriate authorities."

"Thanks, Wallace. I appreciate the call. Keep me advised if you think this thing's likely to blow up."

Chapter 3

STAFF SERGEANT CORMIER KNOCKED on the side of the doorway. "Sir, the American embassy case? I think we have some movement on it."

Connelly looked up from his desk. "Okay?"

"This afternoon the prints from the facial photos came back from being developed. I sent a car around to all the local police forces with copies of the prints, and I put a copy on our bulletin board."

"Yeah, I saw that. Thanks."

"Well, Corporal Russell saw the photo and came back just a moment ago with a match. This case is going to be front-page news everywhere. It's not a run-of-the-mill homicide." Cormier raised his eyebrows. "The guy was an accredited diplomat with the Soviet embassy."

Corporal Russell was the gangly, youthful second-in-command of the Ottawa Photographic Surveillance Section. At six foot five, he looked much too big for his desk. A glass thermos and sandwiches in an open waxed-paper wrapper lay beside a solidly built Remington typewriter. He smiled as Connelly and Cormier entered.

"I know what you're here for, sir. I'm pretty certain this is the same guy — Anatoly Shemyakin. I normally see pictures of him about every two days. Haven't seen him around for the last week or so, but that's him, all right. I'd bet the farm on it."

Russell went over to a steel filing cabinet and pulled out a fat manila accordion file. "As you know, sir, to keep a handle on things we've got a camera that gets a picture of everyone who goes in and out of the Soviet embassy." He handed Connelly an eight-and-a-half-by-eleven photograph. "This picture was taken in November. I don't think we've missed anyone in the last year or so. I've got good photos of all of them. We took this photo from the third-floor bachelor apartment across Charlotte Street, right across from the embassy. We have an automatic camera set up in the attic. I get an update with contact prints every day, and I can get a blow-up like this within an hour if we need it."

Connelly studied the picture.

"This is your guy, sir," Russell said.

"Mmm." Connelly grunted noncommittally. After a moment studying the two photos he said, "I think you're right. What do you have on him?"

"I don't have a lot on him in this office, sir. Mostly his comings and goings." Russell pulled out a clipboard from his in-basket. "Shemyakin went into the embassy on foot on Monday at 1432 hours. So far there's no record of him leaving, but that doesn't mean he didn't leave. There's been a parade of cars in and out at all hours for the last two weeks. He could have been in any one of them. That's not unusual. They have their busy periods fairly frequently, and they often get a lot of traffic coming and going throughout the night. Most likely people going in to send messages or talk on the phone to Russia. It's a seven-hour time difference, so they don't really have any down times. They're busy most days. They usually have two officers on duty inside the embassy around the clock."

Connelly nodded, and Russell continued. "Sir, I assumed you were going to ask, so I've advised Sergeant Simard down in Soviet and East European Records to bring you up to speed on this guy. He told me he's putting things together from various files, said he'll bring it up to you."

Sergeant André Simard, a uniformed officer with a Roman nose and thin pencil moustache, was waiting in the hallway by the time Connelly and Cormier got back upstairs. Connelly smiled, reaching out his hand in greeting.

"André, I'd no idea before this morning you were working here."

"Welcome, sir. I just heard that you were transferred into Special Branch. We do move around, don't we?" Simard spoke English with a slight French accent. "We're glad to have you aboard. I haven't seen you since... geez, before the war, I guess. It's been a long time. You're an officer now. Always knew you'd do well."

Connelly smiled broadly. "Thanks. Hard to believe the last time I saw you we were both in New Brunswick." He was anxious not to embarrass his old friend. Back then, Connelly had been a constable and was working for Simard, who had been a corporal. "How do you like working here in Special Branch?"

Simard pursed his lips and fluttered his left hand. "Oh,

comme ci, comme ça, sir. It's a new organization. The work and the people, they're good, and I get to go home to Montreal more often. But you'll see, we don't have enough people to do the job, not nearly enough. Let me put it this way, sir. Our job is like putting together a jigsaw puzzle. The problem we have is that we have to search for all the pieces, and we don't know what the overall picture is supposed to look like. So, we get little fragments here and there, and if we can make some of them match up, that's a big victory. That's the frustrating part. Maybe it'll be a little different for you because this is a murder, and that's different from what we normally deal with in Special Branch. Anyway, I have Shemyakin's file here for you. At least that's the name we know him by."

Connelly motioned for them to go in and sit in his office. "What do you know about this guy, André?" he asked when they were seated.

"Well, sir, on paper he was a third secretary for Science, Technology, and Industrial Trade. He got his accreditation two years ago. We're not entirely certain what his real job is or what his real name is, but we've been keeping tabs on him on and off since he got here."

"Okay. What does 'keeping tabs on him' mean in practical terms?"

"In practical terms, it's about as loose a form of surveillance as you can imagine. Let me explain." Simard took a deep breath. "For one thing, none of these guys are probably who they say they are. We think Shemyakin worked in London for a time after the war. Then, he was called Evgeny Zhirkov, and when he was there, he was listed as a low-level clerk. We asked a couple of times, but the Brits didn't give us anything more on him. The only one we are certain is actually doing the job that his accreditation says he does is the ambassador. We've been watching all of them as best we can, but you have to understand there are thirty accredited diplomats in the Soviet embassy, more than in any other embassy, and there are more than seventy other diplomats accredited in all the other East European embassies. As far as we're concerned, when it comes to espionage and subversion, we have to assume they're all working for the Russians. We don't have enough people to follow even a few of them, never mind finding the illegals." He shrugged.

"So, tell me about Shemyakin."

"He got here two years ago. Lived with his wife, Irina Shemyakin, in an apartment in Sandy Hill, six blocks from the embassy. Spent a lot of his time travelling to trade shows, visiting industrial plants, going to public lectures at universities. We've followed him on and off, enough to let him know we're watching him, but I don't think he's been fooled by that. He was turned away once trying to get into an Air Force base, and we complained about that, but since we don't have enough people to tail these guys all the time, he's been pretty much free to come and go as he pleases."

"What did he claim his official interest was?"

"Air safety. He makes a big effort to show he's studying air safety issues. He showed up at all the cocktail parties the Russians put on. That's all he talks about. We had people chat to him a few times."

"Okay. What did you learn?'

"We thought it was a ruse to plant information. He claimed one of the jobs he was tasked with was doing research to upgrade Soviet civilian airfields with improved radar and civilian air traffic control technology. Said he wanted to improve their safety records. There's probably a grain of truth in that."

"That would give him some thin cover for nosing about military technology."

"Yes, sir, but he was interested in other things too. He did some work around the auto and aeronautical industries. He was interested in how we set up manufacturing plants in Ontario and Quebec. Actually, that part was all fairly innocent. But it turned out that Mr. Shemyakin had another side to him."

"What was that?'

"Well, we discovered that Anatoly Nikolayevich Shemyakin was a bit of a womanizer. Either that or he was just lonely. He used to visit a hotel here in Ottawa on a monthly basis. We assumed he was meeting with a hooker. Not much to go on there, but we nevertheless kept some photos of him going in and out of a hotel off the Byward Market in case we ever needed some dirt on him. We also know that he was interested in the Air Force's new radar identification system for the new Pinetree Line radar chain. Made a bit of a nuisance of himself once at an air station in Montreal, but after that he hasn't drawn a lot of attention to himself. We've spent most of our time watching other, higher-value diplomats."

"So, if we knew he was trying to get information about a classified project, why wasn't he expelled as a spy?"

Simard gave a small, tolerant smile. "Well, sir, that's a question you can ask Superintendent Ferrall, but I'll tell you this. In Special Branch we put in regular reports, but if we expelled every Soviet diplomat who looked like he was sticking his nose where he shouldn't, there'd be no Soviet embassy in Ottawa. Usually, we have to let them run. We do our best to keep an eye on them, but running even a small watcher service uses up a lot of manpower, people we don't have. And you know," he shrugged, "all the Soviets and East Europeans are after information one way or another. And God only knows how many illegals they've brought in or how many Canadian recruits they have working in the country."

"This doesn't sound too good. You guys have your work cut out for you," Connelly said.

"No, sir, it's not good. But to answer your original question, to expel a diplomat, Superintendent Farrell advises the assistant commissioner, who in turn advises the deputy commissioner and the commissioner. Then the decision to expel a diplomat goes to cabinet. It's usually the prime minister himself who decides to kick one of these guys out of the country. It doesn't happen that often."

✳ ✳ ✳

Alexei Glinin, the Soviet ambassador, clutched his desk and looked distastefully at his first secretary. Like they always did in the cold weather, the ambassador's legs hurt from his war wounds, and the pain left him even more short-tempered than usual. "Why do they want to talk about Shemyakin?"

"They would not say, Comrade Ambassador. The Canadian police said it was urgent and they needed to come and speak to you in person."

"When do they want to talk?"

"I think they want to come over now."

"This is quite irregular. Has Shemyakin done something? Has he been arrested? Where is he now?"

"No one has seen him since yesterday at around three o'clock when he left the embassy, Comrade Ambassador."

The ambassador sniffed, wrenched himself around in his chair, pulled off his glasses, and wiped his eyes with the back of his hand. He glared at his first secretary. He had taken two days off at home with leg pain and a migraine, and now he had to come back to this shitstorm.

"Where did he go?"

"I don't know, Comrade Ambassador; I can ask around. He probably... Well..." He licked his lips. "I suppose he went back to his apartment. That's most likely."

"Did he sign out? Did he phone? What entry did he put into the duty sign-out book? Did he tell one of the duty officers where he was going?"

"I don't know, Comrade Ambassador. I can check."

"Why do you come to me without having some basic answers? What do you think I'm supposed to say to the police?"

"Yes, Comrade Ambassador, I understand, but—"

"You don't understand anything, or I'd have some answers already to some simple questions. Find out what they want. Tell them to supply their questions in writing to you, and tell them they will under no circumstances violate diplomatic immunity and trespass on sovereign Soviet embassy

28

property."

* * *

Connelly hung up the phone on his desk. He had been kept on hold for over forty minutes. "Stupid bastards want me to send my queries to them in writing. They say under no circumstances are we to go to the embassy and try to speak to anyone."

"That kinda puts a crimp in our investigation, doesn't it?" Staff Sergeant Cormier said.

Connelly frowned and rubbed his lower lip with two fingers. "Okay, we'll play their game. I'll draft a statement and a list of questions for the ambassador. We'll get one of the guys to run it over once it's been typed. We won't wait around for them. André Simard can scribble an illegible signature over my signature block. We're not entirely at an impasse yet. Where did you say he and his wife lived?"

"They have an apartment in Sandy Hill. I've got the address in my notes."

"Give me five minutes and I'll draft a memo with the questions. In the meantime, can you get a car ready and ask André to come up here, please? After that, we'll go and see Mrs. Shemyakin."

* * *

The Shemyakin apartment was a plain, one-bedroom walk-up on the third floor of a four-story brick building that had been hastily built immediately after the war to house returning servicemen and their families.

Connelly tapped respectfully at the door. It was opened by a fair-haired woman wearing a green house dress and a cardigan. She had a medium build and looked to be in her late thirties, with a clear complexion, flat cheeks, and dark blue eyes. She looked at the two plainclothes policemen suspiciously.

"Mrs. Shemyakin?"

"Yes. Who are you?"

"Mrs. Shemyakin, I'm Inspector Connelly of the Royal Canadian Mounted Police. This is Staff Sergeant Cormier." He showed her his badge.

"I have done nothing wrong." Her English was clear, with a faint hint of a British accent.

"No. ma'am, it's not about you. May we please come in?"

"No. What do you want?"

Connelly and Cormier exchanged glances.

29

"Ma'am, I'm afraid we have some very bad news about your husband."

Mrs. Shemyakin looked at them blankly.

"I'm very sorry to have to tell you, but your husband has died, ma'am."

Mrs. Shemyakin turned and looked away for a long moment. Connelly thought she shuddered, but he couldn't be sure.

"Have you told embassy?" she said.

"Yes, ma'am. We have, and we thought you should know as soon as possible."

She stared at the two officers. Connelly couldn't read her reaction. Her eyes darted back and forth between the two of them. She seemed to be thinking things through. Connelly thought she showed no visible signs of grief, anxiety, disbelief, or even concern. It was as if he was telling her that the electricity was going to be turned off tomorrow. After ten or fifteen seconds she dropped her head and whispered, "What happened?"

Cormier replied, "Perhaps you should sit down, ma'am."

"No. I am fine. What happened?"

"It appears he was shot."

She said nothing.

"At this stage we don't know much more than that. Ma'am, we will need to have someone come to the hospital to make a positive identification."

"In such case, you must deal with embassy. I cannot help you." She stepped back and began to close the door.

Connelly spoke in a quiet voice. "I'm very sorry for your loss, ma'am, but can you tell us where he might have been in the last few days? Anything? It would be of great assistance in helping us find out what happened to him."

"Last week, I saw him on Thursday. He said he would be gone several days. He said he was going to Montreal to Commercial Consul Office. Now, I cannot help you. If you desire assistance you must talk to embassy." She closed the door quietly.

* * *

Outside at their car, Cormier raised his eyebrows.

Connelly said, "What do you think, Marcel? Did you get the impression this was a surprise to her, but not a shock?"

"Not exactly a stunned, grieving widow, sir."

"I can't say I know how to read her. At the end of that little exchange, her Russian accent seemed to get a little more pronounced."

"Probably distress and the shock of the whole thing sinking in."

"Maybe, but something odd is going on."

"I'm sure you're right." Cormier turned the key in the ignition and grimaced as the engine squealed. "Belts are probably slipping in the cold." He turned the key again. "But you know, sir, she may not even have been married to Shemyakin. It's not unusual for the Russians to do this. Maybe Anatoly Shemyakin's real wife, if he had one, is back in the Soviet Union, and Mrs. Shemyakin is a Russian operative. We've seen this before. Ever since Gouzenko flew the coop with his wife, the Soviets have been pretty wary about having couples posted together when they're abroad. If you keep an operative's family back home as permanent hostages, it's an arrangement that reduces the chances of a defection."

Chapter 4

BACK AT THE OFFICE, SHIRLEY AGNEW handed Connelly two sheets of paper. "Inspector Connelly, you have two phone calls, sir. One is from the Soviet and East European Section of the Department of External Affairs. The other is from your favourite reporter, a Miss Oriana Soroka of the *Ottawa Tribune*. Both say they need a call back urgently." She grinned, eyes sparkling behind her glasses. "I'm dying to find out which one you're going to call first. Oh, yes. Superintendent Ferrall wants to talk to you when you've got a minute."

* * *

Connelly strode into his office, picked up the phone, and dialled. "Yes, this is Inspector Declan Connelly of the RCMP," he said when the call connected. "I'm returning a call from a Mr. Charles Fischer of the External Affairs department."

While he waited for Fischer to come on the line, Connelly toyed with a brass letter opener. Mrs. Shemyakin's behaviour didn't suggest a quick resolution to things. She posed three questions: was she hiding something, was she frightened of the Soviet authorities, or was she perhaps both? He pulled out a pad of foolscap paper to take notes on and began to write. He wondered if the Brits or the Americans had anything on Irina Shemyakin. He put it on his "to do" list. In the meantime, he had to see what else, if anything, André Simard had on her in his files.

Finally, Fischer came on the line. "Hello, Inspector Connelly. Chuck Fischer here. Sorry to keep you waiting. I've been in a meeting. Inspector, I've had a call from the first secretary of the Soviet embassy. He says that they believe there's been an incident with one of their diplomats and that you have phoned them trying to arrange an interview with them. Is that correct?”

“Yes.”

“Right.” Fischer cleared his throat. “I, uh, I understand what you’re trying to do, but, um, normally government communications with the Soviet embassy go through our office. We have a certain protocol, and...”

“Thanks, but I have a dead body in the morgue, and I can’t find anyone who’s willing to identify it. So, yeah, I do have a small problem.” As soon as the words were out of his mouth, Connelly reproached himself. Putting this guy’s back up wasn’t going to help. “Tell you what, Chuck. Can you help me? Can you bring some influence to bear on these guys? I need someone to identify the body.”

“Well, we haven’t had to face this kind of issue before, and the director general here in my department wants me to draft some guidelines for dealing with these—”

“Anything you can do now, Chuck,” Connelly broke in, cutting him off. “Anything at all to get this thing moving. I need help now.”

Fischer’s voice dropped, and his next words sounded furtive. “Okay. I hear you, Inspector. I don’t want this to turn into a bureaucratic merry-go-round either. There is something. You see, the first secretary just phoned me and told me he only wants to talk to me or a journalist. He thinks that if one of his diplomats has been murdered, he doesn’t trust the Canadian police to deal with it. He wants everything done in the open.”

“Well, that would be a first for the Soviets, wouldn’t it?”

“Yes, it would. Now, the journalist he wants as an intermediary is from the *Ottawa Tribune*, Oriana Soroka.”

“Really?” Connelly blinked in surprise.

“You know her?”

“Not well. Why Miss Soroka?”

“I have no idea. She used to be the chief parliamentary reporter for the *Tribune*. I used to read her stuff regularly. She wasn’t bad: fair, shrewd, pretty decent reporter generally. Now she’s doing some kind of local beat. Bit of a comedown.”

“Okay, that’s interesting. She’s left me a message to call her.” Connelly rubbed his fingers across his lower lip. He needed some time to think about this. “Let me work on this one, Chuck. In the meantime, can you try to get someone from the embassy to identify the body?”

Fischer was silent for a beat. “Well, actually, they’re very angry that you contacted his wife.”

Connelly grunted. “They’ll have to get over that. Tell them we do things differently here than in Russia. We have laws they have to respect. I also need answers to the questions I sent them.”

"I'll see what I can do, Inspector. Can you have someone run a copy of your questions over to me?"

Connelly nodded. "Sure."

"Okay. I can't make any promises, but I'll do what I can. Just some background information, though: I spent eighteen months in Moscow shortly after the war. You're dealing with people in a vicious system. They make a mistake, they literally get a bullet in the back of the head. This isn't going to be like your normal murder case."

"Yeah. I'm starting to get that sense. Thanks."

❋ ❋ ❋

Connelly considered whether or not to go in and see Superintendent Ferrall first, or call Oriana Soroka. The superintendent probably only wanted an update, but if that wasn't what he wanted, Connelly didn't want him imposing further restrictions on his range of action. Not yet. The case was wonky enough on its own merits. He'd talk to the superintendent later and get whatever information he could from the reporter now.

She answered on the first ring.

"Miss Soroka, this is Inspector Connelly. You called?"

"Inspector Connelly, thank you for calling. Listen, before I say anything else, I really want to apologize for that 'complete impasse' phrase. I'm very sorry, but I did not write it."

"No? Who did? Fairies?"

There was a pause at the other end. "My editor, actually. I was furious. He did it without my knowledge. I told him that you had been very helpful and that inserting that comment didn't reflect the true nature of things or anything you said. He told me not to worry, that his job was to sell newspapers. Like I said, I do apologize."

"Okay. It's in the past, I suppose. Now, what is it specifically that you want?"

"Well, I... um, I had a call just an hour ago from the Soviet embassy. They asked me to be the intermediary for them in dealing with you. It's a bit perplexing. I've had nothing to do with the Soviets. I don't know any of them, and I don't know how they got my name."

Connelly shifted in his chair. "My guess, Miss Soroka, and it's only a guess, is that they assume from your front-page article that you're hostile to the police, and that your views will suit their purposes. Unless, of course, there's something you're not telling me."

"No, I'm telling you everything I know. I thought I'd follow this, see where it leads, but I wanted to hear your opinion first."

"I can't, or won't, tell you what to do, but I'd suggest that you might not want to do anything that could be construed as obstructing the course of justice. I will also add that it's possible that much of what we are going to find may end up being covered by the Official Secrets Act. That may put a crimp on your reporting down the line. With a dead Soviet diplomat found on the American ambassador's property, it's shaping up to be a very sensitive case. This may put you in a delicate situation if they try to use you for broadcasting their views."

"I realize that. The first secretary has asked me to come around to his embassy for a briefing tomorrow morning."

"That's not against the law. If I was you, I'd go. I'll be interested in what they have to say."

"Well, thank you, Inspector, and again, I apologize for what happened. I threatened to resign if it happened again."

"Well, let's hope it doesn't come to that. Thanks for calling." Connelly hung up, tapping his lower lip thoughtfully. If the Soviets were going to be deliberately awkward, Oriana Soroka might be the only means of finding out what they were trying to hide.

✳ ✳ ✳

Superintendent Farrell motioned Connelly to sit. He looked impatient. "What have you learned?"

Connelly outlined the results of his day's activities while his boss steepled his fingers and studied him with his good eye. When Connelly finished Ferrall glanced up at the ceiling.

"Okay. What you're doing sounds reasonable. Just to keep you advised, I'm getting calls every few hours from very senior and influential people. They want to know about this one. It sounds to me like you have things in hand. Do you need any more people?"

"Not just yet, sir, I'm sure I will. When I do, I'll shout."

As Connelly walked out the door, the superintendent's secretary waved a piece of paper at him. "Mr. Fischer from External Affairs called. He said you should be at the morgue tomorrow at nine. The Russians have agreed to identify the body."

✳ ✳ ✳

The porter at the morgue was a short, swarthy man. He had a fussy and pretentious air about him, but in an odd sort of way Connelly liked him — probably because he was genuinely trying to be helpful.

35

As he rolled Shemyakin's trolley out to the centre of the floor, the porter said, "If you'd like, sir, I'll show the family in and then I'll just wait outside. Usually, it's better if there are fewer people around when they see their loved ones for the first time after death. It can be quite horrific."

"Thanks. These people probably won't be family, but it'll still be best if there are fewer of us in the room." Connelly resisted the temptation of telling the porter he'd done this kind of thing scores of times before. It was always unpleasant, but it was often the only time to hear things that people might not otherwise reveal when their grief was less intense.

The porter left, and Connelly rocked back on his heels, looking at the steel trolley with a white sheet covering the body. It was cold in here. The bright fluorescent lighting only added to the clinical atmosphere. He looked at his watch, walked over to the stretcher, and lifted the sheet. Shemyakin's eyes were closed now, but the facial bruising was more prominent. He looked at the small hole behind the left ear and the ragged exit wound under the jaw line. It was hard not to sympathize with someone who had endured such a terrible death. What kind of man had he been? What had he done to end up this way?

Connelly thought that the two of them almost certainly had several things in common. This guy was just about the same age as him, and both had found themselves in the intelligence business. Shemyakin had probably been a veteran, most likely fighting in the same war against the same enemy Connelly had fought. Both of them had suffered in that war.

Connelly put the sheet back in place. Was anybody grieving this man's death? Was there a family back in Russia? Would a small child somewhere be stunned to hear their father was dead? His widow certainly didn't seem too distraught. He looked at the door. There was no sound in the hallway. He looked back at the inert form on the table. For all their similarities, there was one big difference. Shemyakin was working for Joseph Stalin, a grotesque dictator who had killed far more people than Hitler. Connelly looked down at his salt-stained shoes, wondering if he was actually going to make any difference in this new cloak-and-dagger world he found himself in. Would he just be thrashing about ineffectively, or would he actually accomplish something tangible to protect the rule of law on behalf of a democratically elected government? He took a deep breath, tasting the cold antiseptic air of the morgue. There wasn't much to be gained from getting too sentimental or self-absorbed. He exhaled slowly. It was unfortunate, but for all their similarities, the differences between the two of them made Shemyakin a kind of enemy.

Connelly checked his watch again. Maybe the Russians had decided not to come after all? They were already fifteen minutes late. Connelly suspected the timing might be a crude means of establishing dominance, but then changed his mind. They weren't expecting him to be here.

At nine sixteen the swinging doors opened and three men entered the room. Two were grim faced, clad in identical, military-cut brown trench coats. The third man, in an expensive grey mouton-collared coat, was tall and confident looking. He extended his hand.

"You must be Inspector Connelly. We talked on the phone. I'm Chuck Fischer, and this gentleman," he indicated one of the grim-faced men, "is First Secretary Pavel Bodrov." Bodrov glared at Connelly but did not extend his hand. Fischer grimaced. "Yes. And this gentleman is the second secretary, Commercial and Cultural Affairs, Vitaly Privalov." Privalov nodded guardedly and, like his compatriot, pointedly refused to shake hands.

Connelly spoke first. "Gentlemen, I wish we were meeting under different circumstances. I know that this can be a difficult time. Was Mr. Shemyakin a close friend?"

Bodrov pushed his hands deep into his trench coat pockets. "He was a colleague, Inspector. Why do you ask?"

"I'm afraid it's a matter of routine, sir. You see, I have to confirm that you knew the deceased well enough to give a positive identification. You probably have the same procedure in your country."

"He was a friend, Inspector. He was a comrade and a colleague. We don't wish to make small talk."

"I appreciate that, sir. This is not small talk. Can you tell me how long you knew Mr. Shemyakin?"

The two Russians exchanged glances. Their faces remained impassive.

"Two years," Bodrov said at last.

"Have you any idea who would want to do this to Mr. Shemyakin?"

"We do not come to answer questions of the police. Diplomatic immunity means we keep out of police investigations. We are diplomats and speak only to Mr. Fischer on this matter."

"I understand your position, sir. However, according to our laws you have to cooperate with the police in criminal matters or you can be declared persona non grata and deported."

Fischer's eyes widened. Connelly wasn't sure if this was true or not, but he continued. "I'm sure you're not trying to hide anything, but before you identify the body you have to prove you were in fact familiar with the deceased and his circumstances."

Bodrov was defiant. "You seriously ask such question? Who else would want to kill Soviet diplomat? The Americans. You know that like we do, but you do not investigate them. You are working with them; they are your friends. We can expect no fair investigation. Now, let us see Anatoly Shemyakin."

Connelly indicated with a nod that they should all step forward to the trolley. He lifted the sheet back, revealing the head.

Bodrov studied the dead man for a few seconds. "This is him. You know murder like this is disgrace and mockery of international rules of behaviour. Why are Soviet diplomats treated like this in your country? You do nothing to protect. This would never happen in Moscow." He turned, strode back to the swinging door, and pushed it open.

Once the doors swung closed again behind Bodrov, Privalov turned to Connelly. "They were friends. I'm not supposed to talk, but the first secretary is very upset. The last time any of us saw Anatoly was when he left the embassy at about three o'clock on Monday afternoon. One of the chauffeurs drove him to do shopping on Rideau Street. He was going to walk home." He nodded politely. "Now, I must go."

*   *   *

Cradling a mug of coffee in his hands, Connelly stepped into Ferrall's office. Cormier was with him, talking rapidly in French, and Ferrall threw his head back and laughed.

"Join us. Take a seat, Declan," Ferrall said. "Marcel was just telling me about his ice fishing trip last winter. Tell me how your morning went with the Russians."

Connelly took a sip of his coffee. He was embarrassed that he couldn't speak French; that was something for his to-do list. He recounted his morning meeting in the morgue. "So that's pretty much what happened this morning, sir," he concluded. "I don't know if we're any farther ahead or not. If Privalov's telling the truth, Shemyakin was last seen alive on Rideau Street at three o'clock on Monday afternoon."

"Except that his wife indicated he was out of town and expected to be in Montreal for several days," Cormier said. "You can't believe any of them."

Connelly put his mug down. "The one certainty is that Corporal Russell has a photograph of him going on foot into the Soviet embassy at two o'clock, but he could well have left around three, as they claim. If he was in one of their cars, we wouldn't likely catch him on film. We also know that Mrs. Shemyakin's statement is at odds with the first secretary's."

"It's possible both are telling the truth." Ferrall blew out a cloud of pipe smoke. "He could have gone to Montreal and come back. He almost certainly didn't tell his wife about all his activities. Even if she's not who they claim she may be, she could be telling the truth as she knows it. She's likely been told information on a need-to-know basis — and it's probably not always the truth. But nonetheless," Ferrall studied his two subordinates, "I think she's still a big question mark. If she really was Shemyakin's wife, she's the only one we know so far who has a motive to kill him — if he was a womanizer. But torturing him like that and then moving the body would require more than one person, and that would be inconsistent with a woman acting in a crime of passion."

"Well, sir, that's about all we have to go on at this stage." Connelly stood up. "We can't legally compel testimony from any of the diplomatic staff or their families, so I'm going to begin interviewing anyone who knew Shemyakin. André Simard has given me a list of known contacts, and I've provided a list of basic questions for the embassy to answer. I'll be interested to see what sort of answers we get. From the Russians' behaviour in the morgue, it sounds like they only intend to talk to us through Chuck Fischer, their contact in the External Affairs department. Fortunately, he seems like a reasonable sort. The other wrinkle is that they plan on making formal statements to the press through Miss Soroka of the *Ottawa Tribune*."

Back at his desk, Connelly found a handwritten note beside his telephone asking him to call back a Flight Lieutenant Jerry Parsons from the Directorate of Technical Intelligence at National Defence Headquarters. The name meant nothing to him. He dialled the number.

"Thanks for calling, Inspector Connelly," said Parsons when he picked up. "I'm working on the radar project for the new Pinetree Line system. Your Sergeant Simard called me and suggested I talk to you." Parsons spoke in a slow, deliberate manner. "Don't know if this is any help, as I can't say much about this over the phone, but Mr. Anatoly Shemyakin was very interested in a project we've been working on. I think Simard gave you the gist of things, but you'll want to talk to a Professor Jason Adams and his wife. Professor Adams does applied research in theoretical physics at the University of Ottawa, and we know that Shemyakin was very interested in his work. We don't have much on Shemyakin, but what I can tell you was that he came to our attention a couple of times. We monitored him nosing about at trade shows, which was fine, but when we caught him in an amateurish attempt to bluff his way onto the airfield at the RCAF Station at Saint Hubert, we threatened to expel him. That was last summer, in early August. He was trying to get in to see the preliminary test setup for the project we're currently working on. He's kept a low profile since then."

* * *

Connelly wondered how it was possible that anyone who grappled with such complicated problems all day could manage in such a chaotic-looking office. Every surface in the tiny room was stacked two feet deep with piles of papers, files, books, and journals. There were no decorations on the walls. The room smelled of fermenting garbage.

Jason Adams shook Connelly's hand limply and dropped into the chair behind his desk. He was tall and unnaturally thin. His tie hung limply around his neck like a noose. There was irregular grey stubble on his cheeks and chin, and his skin had a greyish pallor.

"What can I do for you, Inspector?"

Connelly showed him his badge. "I'm from the Special Branch of the RCMP. We're investigating the death of a Soviet diplomat, Anatoly Shemyakin. Did you know him, Dr. Adams?"

Adams smiled and swallowed painfully. "Yeah, I've met the man. You say that he's dead. I can't say I'm in any way sorry to hear that."

"Why do you say that, sir?"

Adams looked down at his desk and then back up at Connelly and crossed his arms. "I'm happy to see that he's dead because I hated him."

"Why do you say that?"

Adams forced a thin smile. "I hated him for two reasons. But let me start from the beginning. Shemyakin started off as a nuisance. He started showing up here two years ago, trying to find out exactly what we were up to. He'd show up uninvited at lectures and seminars. The only problem was that he had no real understanding, no scientific appreciation of what we were doing. He's not a scientist. He just wanted to hoover up information. He claimed his diplomatic status allowed him access to unclassified scientific briefings, that we all had a common interest and a moral obligation to share information on commercial flight safety. I reported him to the RCMP, and, as far as I know, he stopped showing up at the university. That was about a year ago. Since then, we've had instructions to keep him and his like away."

"Why was he after unclassified information? Couldn't he get that from the library?"

"Yes, he could have bought or borrowed the journals we published. He was using the university as cover. He was really trying to establish contacts in the scientific community. To be more precise, he wanted to establish some sort of a relationship with me."

"What exactly do you think he was after?"

"No question about that." Adams pursed his lips and looked down at his desk again. "I suppose if anybody has a need to know, it's you. Shemyakin wanted to discover everything he could about radar coverage in the new Pinetree Line. I'm sure you've heard; the Pinetree Line will be a radar chain that faces north and provides radar coverage over northern Canada and Alaska. It will identify future fleets of Soviet nuclear armed bombers heading south to strike at North American cities. I've been working on the program in conjunction with a few others here in Canada and the United States. My work is essentially helping to develop a system that allows our radar to differentiate with absolute certainty between the different readings on an operator's screen — to help the operator identify at very long distances such things as flocks of geese, environmental clutter, and commercial passenger traffic — to distinguish them from the radar signatures of Soviet manned bombers."

Connelly nodded, and Adams continued. "It's complicated. In addition to the actual transmitters, which I don't have anything to do with, my work involves some of the theoretical calculations involved in antenna design." He made a weak wave. "I've been factoring in matters such as pulse strength, pulse width, echo patterns, and frequency repetition. That's the part I've been working on, the physics of the thing. I'm sorry to say, I haven't got it right yet. You see, if the Soviets get an insight into how we build and manage our radar systems, they can decoy us or send deceptive signals. In the worst case, they could conceivably have an undetected approach for their bombers to inflict nuclear strikes on the North American heartland. A nuclear attack like that would, at a conservative estimate, kill somewhere between fifty and a hundred million people." Adams tilted his head back. "So you see, Inspector Connelly, the stakes are high. That's the main reason I'm glad to hear he's dead."

"What's the other reason?"

"He'd been screwing my wife."

There was a difficult silence. "How did that come about?"

"I'm not certain when it started, or how long their affair went on, but my wife had too much to drink one night and confessed to me. I didn't want to hear any of the details. You see, I have lymphoma. It's in an advanced stage. I've had the new radiation treatments, but they haven't worked. My wife said she didn't want me to die without forgiving her. In her own self-indulgent way, she thought she was being noble." He pretended to laugh. "More likely, in addition to being disloyal, she was her normal thoughtless and melodramatic self." Adams looked down at the papers strewn in front of him. "I wish she hadn't told me. I'd rather die an unwitting cuckold, Inspector Adams."

"I'm very sorry to hear this, sir." After a suitable pause, Connelly quietly ventured, "Did you report this development to anyone?"

"No. No, I didn't. To my shame, I've kept this to myself. As far as I know, Shemyakin didn't get any useful information from my wife. Neither of them understood what I've been doing anyway. So, I thought, to hell with it, I'd leave it there. In the last months of my life, I didn't have the strength or the courage to manage this kind of intrusion. I didn't want to deal with that kind of worry. I got the diagnosis a few months ago. I'd hoped to finish my work here and see my garden in bloom one more time, but my doctor tells me that I won't live to see the end of this wretched winter."

Chapter 5

CORMIER SWIVELLED IN HIS OFFICE CHAIR, dangling a sheet of paper in front of him. "The Russians have answered us, sir. This just came, hand-delivered from Chuck Fischer's office. How did it go with Professor Adams?"

"Not much different than what André Simard briefed us: Shemyakin was trying to get information from him. It appears that Shemyakin also had an affair with Adams' wife. We're going to go see her right after I read what the Soviets have to say."

Connelly scanned the sheet. Instead of answering his list of questions, in reply the Russians had sent a formal statement. The paper was typed, laid out in a dense, single-spaced format with numbered paragraphs. He ran his eyes over each of the paragraphs. The gist of it was that Shemyakin was an accredited diplomat, an honest man, and a valued colleague. He had left the embassy with one of the drivers at three PM on Monday the eighth of January, 1951. He was last seen alive by his driver, who let him out of his car on Rideau Street to go shopping. The Soviets were demanding immediate release of the body so the embassy could have the remains cremated and sent home. They were also demanding that all autopsy and police reports be handed over to the embassy forthwith.

The second half of the page went on to say that diplomats, no matter where they were from, must under all circumstances be accorded the highest degree of security possible, and that the RCMP had been criminally negligent in carrying out their duties. The RCMP was not cooperating with the Soviet embassy and furthermore could not be trusted to conduct an impartial investigation, as they were widely recognized as one of the repressive forces of Western capitalism and had close and official relationships with forces hostile to the USSR. The last paragraph demanded that the Soviet Union be allowed to bring in one of their own expert investigative teams to work alongside the RCMP in finding the culprits. The document was signed by the ambassador.

Connelly looked up and sighed. "Has Superintendent Ferrall read this?"

"Yes, sir, he's already phoned the commissioner's office and External Affairs. Basically, he told them the demand for a joint investigation is nonsense. They've agreed."

"Well, if there was ever any doubt that we weren't going to get any cooperation from the Soviets, this officially confirms it." He tossed the paper onto Cormier's desk and got to his feet. "Come with me. We are going to talk to Mrs. Adams."

* * *

Connelly rang the bell of an elegant brick house in the Glebe district. A dark-haired woman in her early forties answered. She was heavyset, had a pinched face, and wore a green cashmere sweater, a pleated plaid skirt, and pearls.

"Mrs. Betty Adams?"

"Yes. What can I do for you?" Her voice was an equal mixture of suspicion and hauteur.

"Ma'am, I'm Inspector Connelly from the RCMP, and this is Staff Sergeant Cormier." He flashed his badge. "Could we come in and talk, please?"

"No. Whatever it is, you can talk here."

"This will take some time, ma'am, so in that case I'm going to ask you to come down to the station, where we can interview you at length."

Mrs. Adams stiffened. "Oh. Well... I didn't realize... No, please come in. I — I'm reluctant to bring strangers into the house."

Inside, Mrs. Adams ushered the two detectives into a stylish living room. She motioned for them to sit and took a seat on the edge of a floral upholstered wing chair.

"Can I get you gentlemen coffee or tea?"

"No, that's fine thanks, ma'am." Connelly pulled out a pen and a small notebook. "Is there anyone else at home just now?"

Mrs. Adams shook her head. "No, my husband's at work. We live alone. We have no children."

Connelly resumed. "We're here as part of an investigation into the death of a Soviet diplomat. Did you ever know a Mr. Anatoly Shemyakin?"

Mrs. Adams looked alarmed. She put her hand to her mouth. "Well, yes. I knew Mr. Shemyakin, but I haven't seen him for, oh my goodness..."

She began to straighten the pleats of her skirt. "Well, oh, for quite a long time. Has anything happened to him?"

"Yes, ma'am. I'm afraid he was found dead on Tuesday morning." Connelly paused and put the tip of his pen on the paper as if to record something. "Could you please tell us what your relationship was to Mr. Shemyakin?"

She inhaled and sat up as straight as possible. "Well, I'm very sorry to hear that. He seemed like a nice gentleman. You say that he's dead?"

Connelly pursed his lips and nodded.

Mrs. Adams collected herself and tilted her hear head. "Well, I met Mr. Shemyakin socially at the Faculty Club, at one of the events sponsored by the university. It was a meet and greet, and he was there. He told me he was a scientific attaché and was working on a project for commercial airport safety."

"And what was your relationship to Mr. Shemyakin, Mrs. Adams?"

"I, um, I saw him occasionally, on social occasions. He had a habit of turning up at events. My husband says he was a nuisance. They didn't want to give him any information about their work. You see, Mr. Shemyakin worked for the Soviet embassy and they didn't trust him." She raised her eyebrows at Connelly as if to imply she had told them all there was to say and she was ready for his next question.

Cormier shifted in his chair. "Mrs. Adams, we've spoken to your husband. We know that Shemyakin had been trying to get classified scientific information. We're doing a thorough investigation, and if it turns out he has obtained classified information, and if any of it can be linked back to you, you could find yourself on the receiving end of a very long prison sentence."

"Mrs. Adams," Connelly said softly, in his most reassuring voice, "we need your help. We are going to get all the information related to this case, one way or another. We know of your relationship to Anatoly Shemyakin, so please don't play any more games with us. If I have to, I'll arrest you now, and to start with I'll charge you with obstruction of justice. There are very serious matters at play here, so please, tell us everything you know. Let's start from the beginning."

Mrs. Adams' eyes turned teary. She sniffled. "Well, I did meet him like I said, at a university function. It was last year, just before Christmas. He was very charming, so different from all the other boring science professors. He called me later the next week," Mrs. Adams tilted her head, thinking about how to frame her words, "and I agreed to meet him. We had a drink at the Queen Street Grill." She looked around her as if bewildered. "It went from there." Her voice rose. "Anatoly was funny and exciting, and I was unhappy.

After that, we'd meet at various hotels or his apartment. Things hadn't been going well with Jason. He was so involved in his work. I was lonely."

Connelly nodded sympathetically. "When did Shemyakin first ask you to get him scientific information?"

"I never gave him anything important, I swear. In early June he asked if Jason ever brought work home. I laughed; I remember thinking, 'What a ridiculous question!' Jason brought work home every night and every weekend. It's the only thing he lived for. Anatoly told me that he wasn't providing his boss with any useful information and he needed something new and useful or they were going to send him back to Moscow. I didn't want him to leave."

"What did you give him?"

"I knew it was wrong, so at first, I tried to tell him that I couldn't do it. But I believed him when he said they were going to send him home in a couple of weeks if he didn't produce anything of value." She paused and started to weep.

Connelly handed her a handkerchief but said nothing.

"I was frightened, so I brought him some pages from an article Jason had been working on. I knew it wasn't anything secret because Jason told me he was going to have it published. Anatoly seemed to be happy when I gave him the notes, but when I saw him the next week, he said he needed more, that if I didn't get it, not only were they going to send him home, but then he said the Russians were going to expose my affair with him. They were threatening to ruin me. I knew I was in way over my head, but I was desperate. I felt I had nothing to lose."

"So, what happened next?" Connelly said.

"I got some more papers, but I never gave them to him. I wanted to surprise him. I waited in my car outside his apartment one night last summer, late June or early July. It was very hot. He pulled up in his car and before I got out, I could see he was with another woman. They were laughing, and they went inside. He phoned me later that week. He'd always phone when he knew Jason wasn't home. He wanted to meet me, but I broke it off then. I told him he was a sneaky, lying, miserable bastard, and if he ever called me again, I'd go to the police."

"Did you ever hear from him after that?" Connelly asked.

"No."

"Do you know who the other woman was that you saw that night?"

"Yes. It was Lucy Kendall. She was married to Howard Kendall. We had them to dinner once last winter. They're from Montreal. Her husband is vice president of a company that manufactures radar systems for the government. Jason and he became friends last year when they started working together on the project. I haven't seen her since."

"You're quite sure of this?" Cormier said.

"Oh, yes, I'm very sure."

＊ ＊ ＊

Once they were in the car again, Cormier lit a cigarette. "She's a piece of work. Didn't say a word about her husband dying. Didn't seem too upset that her lover was just found tits-up in a snowbank, either. Do you believe her?"

"Yeah, most of what she says." Connelly rolled his window down halfway. "Not that I trust her. My gut feel is that she's left out some of the more disreputable bits. I may not have been in Special Branch for long, but I can recognize a classic honey-trap operation when I see it. She may be the victim here, but I still don't like her. She's not terribly clever. She's selfish, a bit of an overbearing snob — and we know she's completely disloyal. She was probably an easy mark for Shemyakin. But I believe her husband. He says he never had anything at home that was classified. I don't think she did it, or that she had a hand in the murder. This kind of killing wouldn't be her style," Connelly took a breath, "but we may not be finished with her yet. If we find we need more information, we can always dangle a charge of seditious conspiracy to help us. Lucy Kendall, on the other hand, is a woman we'll want to talk to tomorrow."

At the office, an open copy of the afternoon's *Tribune* was sitting on Connelly's desk. On page three a picture of the Soviet ambassador ran above the headline: 'Soviets Demand Role in Investigation of Diplomat's Death.' Connelly did his best to look nonchalant as he picked up the newspaper.

The article, written by Oriana Soroka, was brief. Connelly read it carefully.

> *In an exclusive interview with the Tribune, Soviet ambassador Alexei Glinin expressed serious reservations as to the reliability of Canadian police in investigating the recent death of Anatoly Shemyakin. Glinin stated that he has sent the government a formal complaint demanding to have Soviet police participate in the investigation. Glinin said that at a dangerous time of rising world tension, the criminal mistreatment of diplomats is totally unacceptable.*

Glinin went on to say that Shemyakin was a quiet, peaceful man, dedicated to bettering peace and understanding between Canada and the Soviet Union. He leaves behind a wife, Irina Shemyakin, who he says has today returned to the Soviet Union to be with her family. Glinin claims Mrs. Shemyakin was subject to an insensitive and callous interrogation by police.

Charles Fischer, an External Affairs department spokesman, said Canada deeply regrets Mr. Shemyakin's death. Fischer further stated that bringing Soviet police into this investigation would be a violation of sovereignty, and that the RCMP are tactfully and energetically investigating the case and will comment on its development in due course.

The RCMP have requested that anyone with information that may have a bearing on this case should contact them at Central-37345.

Connelly handed the paper to Cormier. "This doesn't surprise me. Looks like Mrs. Shemyakin won't be around to give us any more information."

Cormier scanned the article "Whose side is this Oriana Soroka on anyway? She's given the Russians more space than us. What's with her?"

"Actually," Connelly said, "I don't think the Russians sound too crisp on this one, Marcel, and Soroka's giving them exactly what they want to hear. I'm not certain that I wouldn't have done the same thing if I was in her shoes." Connelly tilted his head thoughtfully. "Sounds like she's keeping the lines open to the Soviets, and since we're obviously not getting any cooperation from them, we're probably going to need her."

The office coffee percolator bubbled away on top of a battered hotplate. Connelly looked at it with distrust. The appliance was probably a fire hazard. No one, he thought, had bothered to replace it because it was still functional and gave off such a wonderful aroma. While he was pouring himself a cup, André Simard bounded into the office clutching a sheet of flimsy teletype paper.

"Sir, I've got something interesting here for you. Last night I sent out a request to see if anybody had anything on Betty Adams. Nothing came back from Canada, but the FBI just responded. Very interesting. Betty Adams' maiden name was Betty Wendell. She was originally from Harrisburg, Pennsylvania. Apparently, back in 1934 she had an affair with a married architect. It only becomes significant because when the affair came to an end, Miss Wendell tried to blackmail the architect by threatening to expose their relationship. The architect went to the police and Miss Wendell was charged with felony blackmail, but it never went to trial. The prosecution eventually dropped the charges for lack of evidence. Miss Wendell then left town and moved to Toronto, where she met Professor Adams, who was doing his PhD at the University of Toronto. They married that same year. I don't know how things went with Mrs. Adams, sir, but I think you may have a very hard-nosed little lady on your hands."

＊　＊　＊

It had been a frantic week. The weekend didn't look like it was going to be much better. Connelly sat at his desk scratching out his to-do list in his pocket notebook. He numbered each task in priority. At the bottom of the list, he had 'Pay electric bill' and 'Groceries.' At the top he had 'Read files,' 'Travel to Montreal,' 'Interview Lucy Kendall,' 'Interview husband,' and 'Interview Soviet Commercial Consul.' He noted wryly that there was nothing on the list between the most basic, life-supporting maintenance tasks of his daily life and his responsibilities at work. He screwed the cap back on his fountain pen. It wasn't the first time he'd noticed that his life had become one-dimensional. He wondered if he'd become obsessive about his work. Perhaps that was why Ferrall had asked for him to be posted to Special Branch.

He closed the notebook and put it in his suitcoat pocket. Depending on how things went with the interviews, the trip could take the better part of two days. He got up and walked to the outer office. "Shirley, could you please phone and book two rooms for tomorrow night for Marcel and me in Montreal? Somewhere central. We'll drive there, first thing."

Just as he was about to ask André Simard to run background checks, his phone rang.

A woman's voice said, "Inspector Connelly?"

"Yes. Who's speaking, please?"

"It's Oriana Soroka. I think I need to talk to you."

"Okay. What can I do for you, ma'am?"

"I don't think it's a good idea telling you what I have to say over the phone. Can I meet you for coffee somewhere?"

Connelly looked at his watch. "Okay, how about I meet you in an hour and a half? Do you know Levi's Delicatessen? It's a tiny place just down from the Nelson Theatre on Rideau. Good. I'll meet you there at six."

Connelly parked just off Rideau Street and walked to the diner. It was

49

warmer now. The heavily salted roads had turned to slush and the wisps of falling snow had an amber tinge under the streetlights. As he entered the diner, he stomped his feet, shaking off the snow.

"Declan, you're early tonight," Mrs. Katz called out from behind the counter.

"I'm hungry, Mrs. Katz. What's good on the menu tonight?"

"You say that every night," she said and laughed, wiping her hands on her apron. "I keep telling you, it's always the same and it's always good. But you — you need to eat more. You're way too skinny. Levi agrees with me: you need someone nice to take care of you."

"It'll never work, Mrs. Katz. Nice women are always too smart for me. Can I have the back booth? I've got a business meeting tonight."

"Oh yeah, of course. You're catching criminals, protecting society again! That's what you do, eh? You want coffee now?"

"Yes, please," said Connelly, and made his way to the back booth, where he sat facing the door. Oriana Soroka appeared at two minutes past the hour. He stood up to greet her.

"Inspector Connelly, thanks so much for meeting me tonight. I'm sure you're busy."

"No, that's fine." Connelly looked at his watch. "Listen, I'm a bit pressed for time and I've got some things I've got to do later tonight. Have you eaten?"

She smiled. "This isn't a date, Inspector."

"Absolutely not. I have a rule about not dating women who've tried to ruin my career. "

"I'm really sorry..." She looked thrown off her guard.

"That was a joke," Connelly assured her. "I'm hungry. I missed lunch and I do have to work late tonight. I hope you don't think I'm being rude. Can we eat while we talk? Club sandwiches here are the best in Ottawa. Is that all right?" Oriana nodded. "Great." Connelly raised his arm. "Mrs. Katz, two club sandwich specials and another coffee. Thanks."

Connelly pulled out his pad and pen. "So what do you have to tell me, Miss Soroka?"

Oriana exhaled heavily, took off her hat and gloves, and unbuttoned her coat. Connelly noticed she didn't wear any rings.

"I'll start from the beginning. As you know, the Russian ambassador said he only wanted to talk to me and Chuck Fischer. You've probably read my article?"

"Yes."

"Well, I got a phone call this morning at home asking me to meet the Soviet ambassador at eleven at the embassy. My editor's very keen on this story and he agreed I should go. Anyway, I went, and it wasn't the Soviet ambassador who met me but another man, a Mr. Vitaly Privalov. He's a commercial and cultural attaché. He apologized for the ambassador, said he was tied up. Mr. Privalov thanked me for the article and promised me that there would be more information to come. He rambled on about the injustice of Shemyakin's murder and then told me he had reason to believe that the RCMP killed Shemyakin because he knew something about illegal activities being carried out by the RCMP here in Ottawa. I asked what those activities might be, and he said he couldn't tell me just now, but if I waited a week or two, he'd have more information for me. He also asked me what I knew about you. I told him nothing. He strongly suggested I should investigate that angle."

Connelly nodded. "Okay, anything else?"

"Yes,"

Oriana stopped talking while Mrs. Katz brought the coffee. Connelly smiled in thanks. Mrs. Katz stepped back behind Oriana, arched her eyebrows, and nodded approvingly.

Once Mrs. Katz was safely back behind the counter Oriana continued. "After I left the embassy, on my way back to the office, I went to my bank on Sparks Street. Just a routine withdrawal; I had to get some cash. Anyway, when the teller made up my bank book, I noticed that there was an extra fifteen hundred dollars deposited in it. Inspector Connelly, that's more money than I make in four months. I said there had to be a mistake, but she said no. At eleven this morning a man deposited that amount in cash into my account. I asked to see the deposit slip, but the name on it was an illegible scrawl. She couldn't give a very good description of the man — forty years old, tall, and he had a slight accent of some kind. I think it's got to be the Russians. What do you think?"

"I wouldn't be surprised. They're probably trying to set you up."

"That's what I thought. What do you suppose they're doing?"

"They pay you now, then they ask that you do something for them later on. Usually their requests start off small, something innocuous like getting a phone book for them, but then they soon demand things of a more serious nature. If you go along with them and later don't cooperate, they blackmail you by threatening to expose you. Which in your case means, at a minimum, you're disgraced and lose your job. Worst case, if there's any truth to it, you face espionage or subversion charges. My guess is that because you're a journalist, they'll be looking either to get information from you, or use you to plant stories for them later on. They call it 'influence operations.' They wait until there's a crisis or problem and then they get an agent or a compromised journalist to write up their point of view. It sounds like a crude technique, but you'd be surprised how effective it can be. Journalists are high priority for their recruitment. As you know, they can be very effective in moving public opinion."

"What do you think I should do?"

Connelly was quiet for a moment. "Nothing. You've already done the right thing. I'll make an official note of it for Special Branch. We'll record it, and we'll watch and see what their next step is. If they ever try to blackmail you, you're in the clear."

"So, what do you suggest I do? You want me to get information from them for you?"

"Only if you agree. There's an outside chance this could get rough. These people are deadly serious."

"What if I choose not to work with you?"

"That's fine too. You can stop meeting with the Russians and act like nothing happened. You've been a responsible citizen and reported this to the police. They'll be out fifteen hundred dollars, and you'll find something else to report on."

"Won't they try something to get their investment back?"

"Probably not at this stage. If you stop having anything to do with them, they'll likely regard the loss on their investment as a cost of doing business, and they'll move on to someone else more cooperative. My guess is right now they think you're sympathetic to their cause, that you have good potential to be recruited as an agent of influence. But if you walk away at this stage, there's nothing in it for them to go after you. That might not be the case later on if they come to trust you for whatever they want." He sipped his coffee and met her eyes across the table. "You don't have to make up your mind tonight."

Oriana was quiet for a while. Mrs. Katz brought their dinners and they ate in silence for a few moments.

"There is one other thing I need to discuss with you," Oriana said, setting down her fork. "Do you know a Superintendent Graham?"

Chapter 6

THE SOVIET COMMERCIAL CONSUL in Montreal had his office on the top floor of a three-story soot-stained building on the corner of Rue St Hubert and Rue Villeray. The display board in the dimly lit vestibule showed the building was occupied by a small firm of lawyers, an import export business, insurance offices, and an ophthalmologist. The Soviet consul was marked as "G. Alexeev — Commercial Consul."

Cormier knocked on the door and walked in, Connelly behind him. A bald, middle-aged man sat reading a newspaper at a desk in an outer office. "Yes? Can I help you?"

"We'd like to speak to Mr. Gennady Alexeev, please," Cormier said.

"He's very busy now. I will take your name and he can call you when he is free."

"Is he in? We're from the Royal Canadian Mounted Police and we have to speak to him now," Cormier said.

"You don't have appointment. Mr. Alexeev cannot see you without appointment."

Cormier stepped forward and opened the door to Alexeev's office. He flashed his badge. "Mr. Alexeev, we're from the RCMP. We need to talk to you now."

The bald man got to his feet and spoke rapidly in Russian, and Alexeev answered him angrily. Turning to Cormier, he switched to English. "You cannot come in here and question me. I am a diplomat and you must follow protocols."

Connelly answered. "No. You're not an accredited diplomat, Mr. Alexeev. We checked before we came here. If you need reminding, you are a consular agent and you are in this country on a commercial visa, not a diplomatic one. If you don't cooperate with us, I'll make sure that the visas for you and your friend here are revoked this afternoon. Now, shall we talk?"

Alexeev said nothing for a moment, then waved the bald man away and slumped back into his chair. Connelly and Cormier stepped into the office. Cormier closed the door behind them, and the two men sat down on the wooden chairs opposite Alexeev's desk.

Connelly spoke now. "Mr. Alexeev, we're investigating the murder of a Mr. Anatoly Shemyakin. I have reason to believe he was here on the seventh of January. What was he doing here?"

Alexeev looked hunted. "Mr. Shemyakin came here often, several times a year. I don't remember anything."

"What was he doing in Montreal, Mr. Alexeev? Who did he come to see?"

Alexeev shrugged and said nothing.

"Okay, we're going to discuss this down at the Montreal police station. Get your coat and hat. We'll read you your charges down there." Connelly stood up.

"No, you must understand," said Alexeev, leaning forward and lowering his voice. "I have been advised I cannot talk to police. Please, sir, this can be very dangerous for me."

"It'll be a lot worse if you don't tell us what we need to know. A man has been murdered and you were one of the last people to see him alive. That makes you a person of interest to the police. I'm sure you understand that."

Alexeev sighed. "Anatoly was here last week. He came to see me on Friday. He told me he came here to talk with businessmen about safety equipment for Soviet airfields. We only talked about these things for a short time. He said he came to Montreal on Thursday and was going back to Ottawa on Monday. That's all I know."

"Who did he come to see in Montreal?"

"I don't know."

"Where did he stay?"

Alexeev swallowed. "I think he stayed at the Windsor Hotel."

"That's a pretty pricey hotel, Mr. Alexeev. Not exactly the choice of the proletarian working class. How often did he come here?" Cormier said.

"Three, four times a year, I think. I don't know. He did not always come here to my office, I believe."

"Who do you report to at the embassy, Mr. Alexeev?"

Alexeev inhaled sharply and sat back in his chair. "I send my reports to the ambassador."

"What exactly did Shemyakin do when he came to Montreal?" Cormier said.

"I don't know. He did not report to me. He was a second secretary, and his rank was higher than mine."

"What kind of man was he? Did you like him?" Connelly asked.

Alexeev shrugged. "He always let me know he was above me. I would only talk to him about business. He wanted names of people and companies he could talk to here in Montreal."

"What else can you tell me about him?"

"He was fine, a good Soviet citizen." As he got into the rhythm of answering Connelly's questions, his initial defensiveness and misgivings seemed to disappear. He became almost smug.

Connelly narrowed his eyes, scrutinizing him. "What are you not telling me?"

Alexeev smiled, showing the hint of a gold filling in one of his back teeth. "Nothing. That's all I know."

"Do you know why anyone would want to kill Mr. Shemyakin?" Connelly said.

"No, of course not. Unless it was because he wanted Soviets and the West to live in peace. Then maybe one of your people, or the Americans or the British — they would want to kill him."

Connelly looked unconvinced. He stood up and offered his hand to Alexeev. "Thank you, Mr. Alexeev. We'll be in touch."

Outside on the street, Cormier lit a cigarette. "You shut that down pretty abruptly, boss. What was that about?"

"We got whatever information we were going to get out of him. He thought he was playing us for fools at the end. Much as I'd like to, we don't have time to rake him over the coals. We've confirmed that Shemyakin was here last week, and we now know that he stayed at the Windsor Hotel. That's more than we knew going in there. Anything else Mr. Alexeev was going to tell us would have been bullshit. I'm sure he's on the phone to Ottawa now. Let's go see Mrs. Lucy Kendall."

The parking brake crunched as Cormier pulled their unmarked car up in front of the Kendalls' house. It was a large stone building in Westmount, the affluent English-speaking enclave in the centre of the island of Montreal.

Connelly looked impassively out the passenger window. "Add both our salaries together for twenty years, we still couldn't buy this place."

"You're right, sir. It appears that our friend Shemyakin wasn't too keen on stirring up the revolution among the workers and peasants. He stayed at the Windsor Hotel, and this is where his mistress lives. He liked to live in style," Cormier said as he butted his cigarette.

The doorbell had a pleasant five-tone ring, like someone playing a set of Chinese gongs. An attractive woman in her mid-forties answered the door.

"Mrs. Kendall?"

The woman smiled. "And who would you two handsome men be?" she said, clutching the side of the door with one hand and clutching a crystal tumbler with the other.

"We are with the RCMP, ma'am. We'd like to ask you some questions," Connelly said.

"I was wondering when I'd hear from you gentlemen," Lucy Kendall said. Her voice had a smoky rasp. "You know, I read about Anatoly in the *Gazette* yesterday. I suppose it was just a matter of time until you sent someone around to see me."

Connelly could smell alcohol on her breath. "Ma'am, could we please come in? We would like to hear what you can tell us about Mr. Shemyakin."

"Yes, come in," she said theatrically, standing aside and ushering them in. "Are you going to arrest me for being indiscreet with a Russian? I think that would be fun. We weren't in love, you know. We were just having a good laugh. Now poor old Anatoly's dead." Lucy Kendall led the two men through a wood-panelled foyer into a large sitting room and waved for them to sit. "Can I get you a drink? I'm going to freshen mine."

"Perhaps, Mrs. Kendall, if you don't mind, you can hold off having that drink until we've had a chance to talk," Connelly said.

She looked at him condescendingly. "I'll take that to mean you don't want a drink. Oh, you're no fun at all." She slumped into a chair and raised her tumbler as if to make a toast. "Okay, let's talk."

"Mrs. Kendall, you knew Anatoly Shemyakin. Tell us about him."

Suddenly she seemed to drop her role play; her eyes teared up. Connelly noticed her makeup had smudged into the crow's feet around her eyes. "Of course I knew him. That's why you're here. Now you want to get all the dirt you can on the poor man, now that he's dead."

"No, Mrs. Kendall," Connelly said, "we want to find out what we can about who killed him and why he died. Can you tell me how you met him?"

"What's there to tell?" Her tone had become angry. "I went to the opening of the Montreal Electronic and Mechanical Exhibition at the Forum. Howard had a display there — my husband, the vice president of marketing at Canada Radiotech International. They always had a private suite set aside to entertain clients. Anatoly showed up at one of these and told Howard that the Russians wanted to buy one of the new weather radar systems they were building. Howard was busy with another client." She smiled now and waved her glass. "Foolish man — he asked me to talk to Anatoly for a few moments. I did. After that, it was heaven."

"When was this, ma'am?" Cormier said.

"Oh, sometime last year, late October or November. Now I suppose you want to know all the lurid details, do you?"

"No, just the ones we're interested in," Connelly said. "I take it you saw him regularly after that?"

"Oh, yes. Anatoly always stayed at the Windsor Hotel. A couple of times I met him in Ottawa. Howard had to go there regularly for meetings. Anatoly and I would meet there. Dinner and then..." She smiled coquettishly. "Oh, you guys are big boys. You know what follows."

"Did he ever ask you for information, things relating to your husband's work?" Connelly said.

"Oh, yes. Well, not directly. He was always after me to get my husband to meet him. You see, it turned out that Howard wasn't allowed to sell anything to the Russians because they have some kind of law about not selling radar and radios and things like that to them. Howard wanted to sell them the weather radar. It would have been a contract worth," she giggled, "millions, I guess. He said they couldn't use it for their air force, so who cared? It's only weather instruments."

"Did you ever meet any of Mr. Shemyakin's colleagues?"

"Nope, only Anatoly."

"How often did you meet?"

Lucy Kendall waved her glass, frowning. "Once a month, maybe once every six weeks. Always at the Windsor, except for twice in Ottawa at his place when his wife wasn't around. He'd phone me when Howard was out. Listen, Officer, I was there for a good time. Anatoly was funny and it was always a good time with him That's all."

"When did you last see Mr. Shemyakin?"

"Last Friday, in his room at the Windsor."

"And did you notice anything unusual, anything at all?"

"No, nothing. He was relaxed, happy. Nothing out of the ordinary. We had lunch. He was like he always was, you know? He said he was going back to Ottawa the next morning."

"Mrs. Kendall, does your husband ever work at home?"

"Yeah, all the time. That's his office over there." She motioned to a wooden door across the hall. "He's locked in there most nights, most weekends, except he's at the office again today. How do you think he pays for this?" She waved her hand to indicate their surroundings. "Could one of you guys give a girl a cigarette?"

Cormier offered her one.

"Player's Navy Cut." She batted her eyes at him. "Oh, very manly, I must say…"

"Mrs. Kendall, did you ever lose your keys after one of your meetings with Mr. Shemyakin?" Connelly asked.

The question caught her off guard. "Yeah, once, but I think… I'm pretty sure I lost them in the taxi. I had a lot to drink and, no…I don't think Anatoly would've taken my keys."

"Mrs. Kendall, do you know anyone who would want to kill Mr. Shemyakin?"

"No. Like I said, we never met any other people. We never talked about his life or mine. I can't imagine why anyone would want to kill him." Her tone changed and she became playful again. "Unless, of course, he was some kind of spy."

Connelly stood up. "Thanks, Mrs. Kendall. We will almost certainly be in touch."

"A big handsome boy like you, and you're not going to arrest me?"

"Not today. Thank you."

Cormier waited until he was in the car. "You know, boss, Shemyakin knew how to pick them. I still can't figure out if she's as stupid as a bag of hammers, or she's having us on. Think she's telling us the truth?"

"Yeah, I do. She doesn't seem the type to leave anything out if there's a possibility of being dramatic, but you know, I don't think she's decorated her story too much. I think what you see is what you get with Mrs. Kendall. She'll probably be disappointed if she doesn't get her name in the papers." Connelly looked at his watch. "I'll be anxious to meet her husband. Tell you what — the Windsor Hotel is just four or five blocks from the head office of Canada Radiotech International on Peel Street. Drop me off there. You go and talk to whoever you can find at the hotel, and I'll pay Mr. Howard Kendall a visit. I'll take a cab back to our hotel and I'll meet you for dinner there."

* * *

For a Saturday, the Canada Radiotech International's head office was busy. At least half the offices were occupied by men in suits, all of them studiously absorbed at their desks.

"Mr. Kendall will see you now," the secretary said to Connelly as she opened the door into Kendall's inner office. Howard Kendall was mid-fifties, a tall, athletic-looking man with a thin, neatly trimmed moustache.

Connelly thought he looked like a senior army officer from the last war.

"Get the door on your way out, will you, please, Madeleine?" said Kendall, getting to his feet. "Inspector Connelly, what can I do to help you? I've just had an emotional call from my wife, so I was more or less expecting you." He shook Connelly's hand and then indicated a chair in front of his desk. "Please be seated."

"I'm here as part of the investigation into Anatoly Shemyakin. I assume you knew of him?"

"Yeah. I knew him," said Kendall, resuming his own seat. "I suppose you are also well aware of the relationship he had with my wife?"

Connelly nodded. "Tell me about that."

"You don't beat around the bush, do you?" said Kendall, cocking an eyebrow. "Okay. Shemyakin started nosing about here a year or so ago. Pestering us to give him details about our new airfield weather radar system. We're designing and building it in cooperation with an American consortium. We are also building radar components for the new Pinetree Line. We contacted the RCMP, told them that this guy was sniffing around here."

"Who did you talk to?" Connelly asked.

"A corporal something or other. I forget his name." Kendall waved his hand. "Came here in civilian clothes. Look, we can't lose our security clearance on this thing. A lot of jobs depend on us."

"I understand, but I don't have anything to do with security clearances, Mr. Kendall. Let's not worry about that now. What happened with Shemyakin?"

"Well, as you know, he and my wife, they... they had an affair. He came to one of our functions and they met, and I guess it turned into something a little steamier."

"You don't seem to be perturbed by any of this, Mr. Kendall."

Kendall took a deep breath. "Okay, I'm not asking for your approval, Inspector, but you have to understand, Lucy and I have had a different kind of marriage. It works for us. We don't do things the way other people do. She's seen other men, and I've seen a couple of other women on the side. It's been that way for several years. We try to be discreet. I don't think people here at my firm know about our relationship." He licked his lips and looked down. "We're the best of friends. It works for us. I don't want this to become public knowledge."

"I understand, Mr. Kendall. Tell me about Shemyakin. What do you know about him?"

"I didn't know Lucy was seeing him for some time. We don't make a habit of going into any detail about our other relationships. We just say we we're visiting a friend. Anyway, Lucy let it slip one night. She'd been drinking heavily. She's been doing that a lot the past few years. She said that Shemyakin wanted to do business with us." Kendall looked away from Connelly for a moment. "I hit the roof. I told her she could lose us our government contracts, I asked her what the hell she thought she was doing. She laughed, told me I was being ridiculous, that she and Shemyakin were just friends and there was nothing more to it."

"Did you tell any of this to the RCMP corporal you spoke to?"

"No, I spoke to him before I knew any of this."

"And you didn't think to advise him once you discovered what was going on?"

"No. Shemyakin was seeing my wife, not me or one of our employees. I knew there wasn't a problem. Besides, with all the Red Scare nonsense going on these days — McCarthy turning up lists of communist sympathizers in the States, the Parliamentary Commission here — do you think I'd risk losing our most important contracts? That would be suicide. It's my life's work. We do almost all our work for the Canadian and American governments. We're a patriotic firm, Inspector, and I've done my share for this country. This company built almost all the VHF radios used by the RCAF during the war. That was a helluva contribution to the war effort, believe me. We're not traitors, but if I reported this, we'd go under."

"What did you tell your wife when you found out she was seeing Shemyakin?"

"I told her to find someone else." He took a deep breath. "Look, I know this sounds pretty bizarre. Lucy and I aren't the only ones who live this way, believe me. In every other way we have a strong marriage. We're a team."

"Mr. Kendall, I'm not really interested in your marriage. Tell me what you know about Shemyakin."

"Not much. He was a good-looking, smooth-talking guy. He approached us, the company, a couple of times that I know of. I told him if he wanted to do business with us, he had to go through the government in Ottawa. As far as I knew, except for Lucy seeing him, that was the last of him."

"When was it that Lucy told you she was seeing him?"

Kendall pulled his head back as if he needed distance to think. "Three months ago? Yeah, it was in late October. I had just come back from my last golf game."

"Where were you from last Friday until Tuesday morning, Mr. Kendall?"

"You don't think I did this, do you? Lucy's had several ... friends. Jealousy isn't an issue," Kendall said.

Connelly spoke quietly. "No, just keeping things straight for our records. It eliminates all possible suspects."

"I worked late at the office Friday night. Saturday, I came in here for a few hours from eleven to two or so. Lucy and I had dinner with friends at the golf club on Saturday night. Sunday, I worked from home, and Monday and Tuesday I was here, at the office."

"Do you know anyone who would want to kill Shemyakin?"

"Like I said, I didn't know him other than a meeting at a trade show, and he came to the office once before that. Both times we spoke for maybe a couple of minutes."

"Has anyone else in your company had anything to do with Shemyakin?"

"I don't think so."

"Well, Mr. Kendall. That's all for now." Connelly stood up and handed him one of his cards. "I'm going to ask you later on this week to come down and provide us with a written statement. Consider what we've discussed as classified information, Mr. Kendall. I'll advise you now that you can't talk about this to anyone else. If you do, you could make things very difficult for yourself. That includes going to a lawyer at this stage. If you think of anything else I should know, give me a call."

"Can I be charged with anything?"

"Let's not get ahead of ourselves, Mr. Kendall. I'm sure you're an honest citizen. We're just asking for a witness statement. It doesn't mean you're a suspect. Your statement helps give us the big picture. We're just going to need all the facts for our records."

"I hope all this — you know, Lucy and me — stays private."

Connelly spoke soothingly. "I shouldn't worry yourself too much on that score, Mr. Kendall. Thanks for your help." The two men shook hands.

* * *

"Could I please speak to the manager of the front desk?" Cormier flashed his badge to a young woman in a blazer. "It's a routine investigation, nothing to do with the hotel."

Within seconds the front desk manager of the Windsor Hotel emerged from the back office. He was serious looking, in his early thirties, a balding man with glasses. "Yes, sir, I know of Mr. Shemyakin, the diplomat. He was here just last week. Terrible what happened to him. He stayed with us many times and was always very pleasant. Always paid his bill on time. Never a problem."

"Can you tell me which dates he stayed here?"

"Certainly." The manager snapped his fingers and a woman at the front desk turned toward him. "Marie-Thérèse, can you please prepare a record for this gentleman of the times Monsieur Shemyakin stayed with us?" The woman nodded and hurried away, and the manager turned his attention back to Connelly. "In the meantime, sir, is there anything else I can do to be of service?"

"No, thanks. I'm just going to talk to the bar manager. I'll be back in a while to get that list from Marie-Thérèse."

Cormier entered the bar, hat in hand, and looked about him. It was a large room. The dark mahogany panelling was discreetly lit by recessed pocket lights; the carpet underfoot was a plush green. There were twenty or so small tables with expensive leather barrel chairs, and a young man in a far corner played a Chopin piece softly on a grand piano. At five in the afternoon, except for three couples talking quietly in distant parts of the room, the place was nearly deserted. The barman eyed him quizzically.

"Yes, sir? Can I help you?"

Cormier smiled and took a seat at one of the leather stools. He answered in French. "Yeah, please, I'm sure you can." He took out his badge. "I'm Staff Sergeant Marcel Cormier. I'm with the RCMP, doing some work on a murder. Were you at all familiar with a Mr. Anatoly Shemyakin?"

The bartender's face brightened. "Oh yes. We saw Mr. Shemyakin a lot. I read about him in the paper yesterday. That was terrible."

"What can you tell me about him?"

"He was in here a lot. A very quiet man, pleasant, always tipped well. He could handle his booze. He was never a problem."

"Was he alone when he came here?"

"Well, yes, he used to always come here alone, but in the last few months he would meet a lady, pretty expensively dressed. She wasn't a hooker, I'm pretty sure. She spoke English, never French. She was not so pleasant. You know, often a bit drunk, rude to the staff, but Monsieur Shemyakin and her seemed to have a good time. There was never a problem." He shrugged. "That's about it. Can I get you a drink? On the house."

"No. Thanks anyway. I appreciate it. I'm on duty. Can you tell me if Mr. Shemyakin ever met anybody else here?"

"Yes, last week. There was a man he met; they spoke for about an hour. It was about this time early last week. He was an American."

"How do you know that?"

"The way he paid the bill."

"I don't follow."

"Well, he asked for the check. Only the Americans ask for the check.

English Canadians ask for the bill." He chuckled. "And sometimes they pay you with a cheque. You know, and this guy, he also used American expressions like 'y'all', and he asked for the restroom. We get good at telling things about people here."

"Maybe you should be a detective too." Cormier smiled. "What did this guy look like?"

"Tall, well dressed, a very good suit..." The barman thought for a moment. "You know, let me get Gino Barone. He's a waiter here. He was here that night as well."

Barone was a young man in his early twenties, short, with dark, intelligent eyes. "You want to know about the man here with Mr. Shemyakin last week, sir?"

Cormier nodded.

"What can I say? He was tall, had short, curly, fair hair, thirty years old, maybe thirty-five, going a little bit bald at the front." He smiled. "Sort of the same hairline as you have, sir. I noticed this guy because he was with a Russian. I know Mr. Shemyakin is Russian and this guy is an American. To me it just seemed a little bit funny. The whole time, they were always a little bit distant, you know? Not laughing, but talking very seriously and quietly. When I came up to their table they stopped talking. The American guy had good teeth, smiled a lot — and one other thing. I noticed he wore a ring, a big ring, on one hand, with a green stone. I've seen a lot of American guys with that kind of ring. You know, I think it's a college-type ring. I noticed that because my wife, she likes jewellery and she's always looking at what people are wearing."

"Anything else?"

"No."

"Did you ever see that man before?"

"No."

"If I got you a photo, would you recognize that man?"

"Yeah. Yeah, I think so."

Cormier slipped off the bar stool. "Thanks, gentlemen. This might help."

Chapter 7

IT HAD BEEN A PRODUCTIVE DAY. Connelly and Cormier cancelled the hotel rooms they had booked for that night and chose to drive back to Ottawa. Connelly tried to write in his notepad while Cormier, both hands clenching the wheel, steered over the bridge at St-Anne de Bellevue. He cursed under his breath as the car swerved unexpectedly.

"Sorry about that," said Cormier. "I didn't see that coming. There's black ice on these long bridges in this weather..." He slowed down. "If I go any faster, I'll put us over the side. They oughta to put more salt down. It's treacherous." He paused. "Talking about treachery, sir, what do you make about this description of an American meeting Shemyakin? Do you suppose Shemyakin was working for the Americans?"

"It's possible, but if he was, you'd think we'd know about it. I can't imagine us not knowing."

Cormier smiled. "Forgive me for saying, boss, but it doesn't surprise me. You'll get used to that here. This isn't like normal police work. There's a different attitude here. Most of the time it's frustrating as hell. I've seen it before, when information is kept back from a case officer, for a lot of reasons. If this were a normal criminal file, we'd expect to get flooded with all available information. We'd have a big meeting, everybody would show up and tell you what they knew, people from different departments — but here, it's different. Believe me." He struggled to drag a pack of cigarettes from his coat pocket. "People hang on to information partly because they're not allowed to reveal their sources, partly because the security environment is suffocating, and even though we're a tiny organization, we've become completely compartmentalized. The other thing is they're afraid of leaks. Then, once in a while, there's the asshole who won't give you anything unless you ask for it directly. You know, the information is power bullshit. Holding onto important information gives some people a bogus sense of authority, you know? They think it increases their status." He shook a cigarette out of the pack with one hand. "Some of the people we've had working in Special Branch Intelligence," Cormier shook his head, "remind me of the time that I was driving back to Moncton years back. My car broke down in the middle of nowhere, pissing down rain, and I had to repair it in the dark." Cormier flicked his lighter. "People kept driving by me in the night. All I needed was a light. That's all — a light. No big deal. All I had to do was reset the needle valve on the carburetor, but it took forever. Very frustrating."

"So, how'd you fix it?"

"Some good guy stopped, asked if he could help, and he lit up my car with his headlights. Only took a minute, once I could see what the hell I was doing and I could identify the problem. We need more of that kind of guy around here, you know?"

"I take my hat off to you, Staff Sergeant," Connelly said. "If it had been up to me, we'd still be at the side of the road. I have no idea what a needle valve is. Marcel, let's stop and eat soon. I know a good place up ahead, a restaurant in the village of Rigaud."

* * *

It hadn't been much of a weekend. On Sunday morning Connelly was back in the office reading files that might shed some light on his case. They didn't. On Monday morning he was back in the office shortly before seven. The commissionaire at the front desk handed him a note instructing him to call Howard Kendall ASAP.

He threw his coat and hat on the coat rack inside his office door, picked up the phone, and dialled. Kendall picked up on the first ring.

"Thanks for calling, Inspector. I just got in the door here. There was something that I remembered after you left on Saturday. Not about Shemyakin, exactly, but related to him. I should have told you then, but I didn't think of it. Anyway, I remember one of the engineers from the design test bed here in Montreal mentioned to me that an American had been around, asking if anybody had been talking to the Russians about our project. The engineer asked him for identification and the man showed some kind of government security card. Nobody said they had talked to or seen Shemyakin. I didn't think much of it after that. To be honest, the engineer wasn't much help with his description: average height, grey coat, smiled a lot. But apparently this guy reappeared the week before last and asked the same kind of questions to the manufacturing chief at the assembly line in Laval."

65

"Any kind of a description or a name then?"

"No name. Nobody thought of this as a big issue. We get U.S. Air Force and scientific teams up here all the time. They come and go, so everybody just assumed it was an internal security check. The manufacturing chief said the guy he saw he was average height, light complexion, curly hair, spoke with a slight southern accent, and he thought he went to an Ivy League school because he wore one of those big school rings that the Americans like. Other than that, not much. I was thinking the Americans might be able to help you if they discovered anything."

"Thanks, Mr. Kendall. Do you have a name and a number for your manufacturing chief? I'd like to talk to him myself."

"Yes, I do. Just hang on." Kendall put the phone down for two minutes, and then came back on the line. "My secretary's not in yet this morning, but I found it. It's Nick Meyers, and you can reach him during the day at his office. The number is Dominic 73988."

Nick Meyers didn't return Connelly's call until close to nine, but he remembered the incident well.

"Yeah," he said in a voice as gravelly as crushed shale, "the American gave me a number to call if any unusual people showed up at the plant. Wait a second, I think I still have it." Seconds later he came back on the line. "His name was Jay O'Neil, and it's an Ottawa number. He said to call collect. Sherwood 92960."

Connelly thanked him, hung up, and dialled the Ottawa number. He got a fast busy signal. He tried it twice more with the same result and then went downstairs to see André Simard.

Simard was back with the information in thirty minutes. "Sir, I talked to the Bell Telephone people. That number was put out of service last week. It was paid for with a check from a small American bank — First Washington Trust and Loan. I don't know if this helps."

A minute later Connelly dialled the American embassy switchboard. "This is Inspector Declan Connelly of the RCMP. I'd like to speak to Mr. Jay O'Neil, please."

The operator hesitated. "I'm not familiar with that name here, sir. Do you know the section that he works in? I can try there."

Connelly hesitated for a moment. "Could you try the FBI liaison office, please?"

The FBI liaison secretary was emphatic. No, sir, I've been here nine years and I've never heard of a Mr. Jay O'Neill here in the embassy. He certainly doesn't work for us. Are you sure you have the right name?"

Connelly thanked her and hung up.

✳ ✳ ✳

Rory Farrell's mind was turning over the possible reasons for this meeting. It was unusual. All he had heard was that the parliamentary secretary for the solicitor general had asked to see him this afternoon. He was still wearing his coat as he stepped into the conference room in the East Block on Parliament Hill. The booming theatrical voice that greeted him was full of confidence and energy.

"Superintendent Ferrall, thank you for meeting with me at such short notice." Kenneth MacBride, the parliamentary secretary to the solicitor general, forced a smile at Ferrall and invited him to sit in the single chair on one side of the walnut table. Ferrall thought the seating plan looked like it was set up for a job interview, or a sentencing.

"I appreciate your assistance," MacBride said. He was a stern-looking man with thick tortoiseshell glasses. Ferrall knew him only by reputation as a successful corporate lawyer from Toronto. He looked around the room. Seated across the table, dressed in civilian clothes, was Superintendent Wallace Graham; beside him were two other civilians in their early thirties. Ferrall didn't know either of them.

"I apologize, Superintendent Ferrall. You're actually a few minutes early," said MacBride. "But I'm a bit rushed, and Question Period is coming up in the House of Commons shortly. I need answers now. I won't beat around the bush. I know it's unusual, if not downright inappropriate, for a politician to be involved in an ongoing criminal investigation, but I think you will agree the Shemyakin affair is unusual. The solicitor general has asked me to keep abreast of developments in this case. We've been receiving communications from the Soviets on a daily basis, and it appears both the Americans and the British have taken an active interest in this case. What developments are there?"

"It's very early days, sir. I can tell you we are following a number of lines of inquiry. We have no suspects at this stage, but, to be blunt, we're getting no cooperation whatsoever from the Soviets. As I'm sure you are aware, they have demanded to assist the RCMP in a joint investigation, and the government has wisely refused. This is a Canadian investigation, and we intend to treat it as such."

Superintendent Graham lit a cigarette and blew smoke noisily at the ceiling.

"Perhaps, Superintendent Farrell, you might tell the parliamentary secretary exactly just how many people you have on the case today." The two civilians beside Graham exchanged knowing glances.

"Certainly," said Farrell. "Leading the case I have Inspector Declan Connelly, and he is ably assisted by Staff Sergeant Marcel Cormier. They can be backed up by any of the rest of my crew, which, less me, is precisely twelve men, all of whom are doing other jobs just now."

"Why do you only have two people actively pursuing such an important case?" MacBride asked.

"We don't need any more just now, sir. At this stage there are insufficient leads to justify assigning more men. If the case develops such that it needs more manpower, I intend to reassign some of my officers, and if for any reason we need more than that, I will go to the commander of "A" Division here in Ottawa and ask him for help. But right now, the work on this case won't be improved by adding more men. In fact, given the sensitive nature of the case, I'd argue that you might want to keep fewer of your best men on it. Think of it as a doctor performing an operation, sir. It may well be a delicate and risky procedure that your surgeon has on his hands, but the chances of having a successful outcome won't be improved by having more doctors with scalpels around the operating table. We should let the investigation run its course. That's my best professional advice to you, sir." Ferrall turned to Graham. "If anyone else here has a different opinion, I'd like to hear it now."

The two men beside Graham whispered to one another.

"I would add," Ferrall continued, "that this is not to say that I have anything like sufficient resources to monitor the Soviet embassy or to conduct routine operations to counter Soviet intelligence-gathering in this country." He looked again at Graham while he spoke. "I've made that point quite openly in the past in every one of my reports, so I'm sure that's not news to you, sir, but to be clear, that ongoing task should not be confused with this murder investigation."

"Well, Superintendent, now that you raise the issue of it being a Canadian investigation, the matter has come up of British participation in this case. The British have quite adamantly requested that MI5 officers be seconded to you to assist in this. How do you feel about that?"

"I'm certainly open to discuss British assistance in the form of advice — as long as that kind of input remains at my level, and of course we would welcome any timely supporting intelligence that they may have that bears on this case. I would expect them to provide that as a matter of course."

Graham sat back in his chair. "Now, come on, Superintendent Farrell. You and I both know that the Brits have many more years' experience in this kind of thing than we do. We used them to our advantage when Gouzenko defected. We've always looked to them for technical assistance on things, and bringing them in now couldn't hurt anything. In fact, it'll likely speed things along."

Ferrall ignored Graham and turned to MacBride. "Sir, we've come some distance since Gouzenko defected. Not as far as I'd like, but enough to allow us to handle issues in our own country. When Gouzenko defected back in 1945, we had no idea what to do with a defector. Special Branch was exclusively devoted to issues concerning Soviet influence in the labour movement. We may be understaffed for our day-to-day operations, but having British officers assume control over this murder investigation will do nothing to fix that problem or hasten the resolution of this case. This investigation is being conducted by my best man, who I might add was handpicked by Assistant Commissioner Murray. There's no reason to believe that bringing in British officers who don't know the ropes here, and who are unfamiliar with things in Ottawa, will move this case along any faster or more efficiently.

"There's also the matter of how this would play out in the press. Bringing in any outside officers would be tantamount to the government making a public admission of neglect and inadequacy in matters of domestic security. I probably don't need to point out to anyone in this room that we established a very capable reputation for ourselves in the last war, and given the fact that Canada has recently decided to send a brigade to Korea and a brigade to Germany, as well as an air division to Europe, I don't think any of us want to send the message that in matters of routine domestic security we can't manage on our own. If the press got a hold of that information, as they almost certainly would, it would look like the government still sees itself as a colonial dependency in need of the mother country to organize things for us."

MacBride grimaced for a moment, chewed his lower lip, and then looked at his watch. He turned to the two men beside Graham, then back to Ferrall. "Okay, you make a convincing case, Superintendent Ferrall. I've been told by a reliable source that this question's likely to surface in the House today. What I intend to say is largely what you have outlined." Turning to the civilians beside Graham, he said, "In the meantime, I want you gentlemen to find out where this information is coming from. If there's a leak, if someone on the inside is feeding information to the opposition, I want to put a stop to it." He looked at his watch again. "I've got to go now, but," he paused and smiled, "I can't resist. I know this is a classified meeting, but one last question. Completely off the record, who do you think killed this guy?"

"We honestly don't know yet, sir. And as I said, we are following up on a number of avenues of inquiry and we have to get it right. That may take some time."

MacBride nodded, then, addressing the two Mounties, he said, "Thank you gentlemen. I know this may take some time, but I can't guarantee you that you'll have as much time as you need. The Brits and the Americans both want in on this investigation," MacBride paused, choosing his words carefully, "and I'm not sure that the prime minister can hold out on them much longer, if you know what I mean. I'm not trying to put undue pressure on you, but if you don't wrap this up in a week or so, ten days at the outside, this will probably be taken away from you. It's not good news." He picked up his papers and stood up. The two civilians got to their feet as well. "Good luck," said MacBride.

Graham and Ferrall stayed behind as the civilians left the room. When the door had closed behind them, Graham turned to Ferrall. "You nailed that one down, Rory."

Ferrall didn't answer, leaving Graham in an uncomfortable silence.

"Look, Rory," said Graham at length. "I'm just doing my job. I call them the way I see them. Difficult questions have to be raised, and the government needs answers. We're here to provide them. No hard feelings."

"I don't have hard feelings, Wallace, but you and I both know you deliberately overstepped your authority on this one. We both know you put the flea in MacBride's ear that we should hand over control of this case. You're not up to date on the investigation, and you don't know what you're talking about in counter-intelligence matters. You have no experience in that field, and when you're briefing the government on policy and operational matters involving my responsibilities, have the common sense and decency to consult with me first."

"Come on, Rory. Things are different here," Graham said, adopting a more affable tone. "Things happen here quickly, more quickly than you guys in the field sometimes appreciate — or are used to. We can work these issues at our level. Remember, this one had a short fuse. I didn't really have time for anything else. We worked this one out. It's not a problem, and you know if I have time, I'll always call you."

"It wasn't the short notice, Wallace," Ferrall shot back. "You tried to interfere with the leadership and control of the investigation."

"Like I said, next time, I'll call you in advance." Graham raised his hands in a pacifying gesture. "I will."

"Right. Do that," Ferrall said. He picked up his coat and left the room.

* * *

The only sound in the office was that of Shirley Agnew down the hall typing furiously. Connelly lifted the phone and put it back in its cradle as Cormier appeared at his door.

"Marcel, I was just going to call you. Can you please go back to Montreal and interview the people at the hotel and at Canada Radiotech International? I want to see if we can find out anything more on the American who was in contact with Shemyakin and the people at the radar plant. I don't think I have to tell you, that's going to require some digging."

"Sure. No problem, sir. I'll see what I come up with. Do you think this guy, if it's the same person, had anything to do with Shemyakin's death?"

"There's no evidence for that, but it's possible there may be a link. Besides, I want to know what he was up to. It might tell us something more about Shemyakin."

Cormier looked at his watch and stood up. "I'm on to it, boss." He picked up his hat and stubbed out a cigarette in the metal stand-up ashtray. "Oh, one thing, sir. Tomorrow, my daughter, Madeleine, is in the debating semifinals at the Ottawa Regional High School Senior Championships. I promised her and my wife I'd go see them. We were in Montreal and I missed the first round of debates on Saturday. Any problem in me taking tomorrow afternoon to see her? Probably take me most of the afternoon."

"No, no, that's great, Marcel. Your daughter sounds pretty sharp. I guess the brains run on the female side of your family too, eh?"

Both men laughed. The phone rang. Cormier raised a finger and whispered, "I'm gone, boss."

Connelly lifted the handset, his face impassive. After a few seconds he said, "I'll be right up, sir."

* * *

"Declan, I've tried to keep this thing from getting out of control on us. I won't go into the details. Evidently, I haven't been successful. At ten thirty this morning, the second secretary to the British embassy in Washington, a man by the name of Guy Burgess, is coming to see me. The Brits have sent him up to convince us to let them take an active role in your investigation. I've been delegated to hear him out."

"If he's a second secretary, he could be with MI5 or SIS."

"No, not this one." Ferrall shook his head and made a sour face. "He's some kind of diplomat. Once a month they send up one of their intelligence officers and we chat. Seems this time they've sent up one of their more senior people, but he's not from one of the security services. A friend at the high commissioner's has advised me that this guy has a notorious reputation in the Foreign Office. He apologized in advance, called him an embarrassment

71

and an out-of-control problem drinker. Nobody understands how he got into the Foreign Office or why he wasn't fired years ago."

"What do you want me to do with him, sir?"

"I'm going to talk to him in my office, a courtesy call, and then I'm going to hand him off to you. Promise him you'll keep him advised as to what's going on, but don't tip your hand on anything. Then ditch him. I'm handing him off to you because this afternoon I've also got the Americans dropping by — Hal Mauro from the FBI. I'm sure it's about Shemyakin."

Connelly said, "Okay, sir."

Ferrall gave him a sharp look. "Don't look so reticent. I realize you've got enough on your plate as it is, Declan, but there's no one else to handle this and everyone from the minister on down has ducked out."

Connelly looked unconvinced.

"Understand this, Declan. It's not just about this particular investigation. If we screw this up, we might as well wave goodbye to Special Branch and any independent Canadian counter-intelligence capabilities. Our two major allies will happily eat our lunch. In the short term that's not a problem, but over time, if we can't manage our own security, for all intents and purposes we'll end up reverting to being a colony again. I'm not asking you to like this task, just to stick-handle this guy."

Guy Burgess arrived at 11:30. Mrs. Agnew phoned for Connelly to go up to the superintendent's office at 11:35. "I think you're going to find this one a handful, sir," she said, sotto voce. "He's in with Superintendent Ferrall now."

Upstairs, Connelly stood at Ferrall's office door taking in the scene in front of him. Burgess, a dark-haired, slender man in his early forties, sat sprawled in the visitor's chair front of Ferrall, his eyes bloodshot and his face a pugnacious snarl. He waved a nicotine-stained finger in the air.

"That's the problem with you fucking Canadians. As a country you're as rich as Croesus, but once the war was over, you went and shrank your armed forces to a shadow of what they were, and because of Korea you think doubling them in size again makes things hunky-dory. Jesus, man! Look at you. You have absolutely no intelligence services to speak of. For God's sakes, you have the fucking Mounties doing your counter-intelligence! We aren't chasing mad fur trappers in the Yukon, Superintendent! No offence to you, but you are only a superintendent and you are running your counter-espionage out of Special Branch." Burgess lit a cigarette with a Zippo lighter and exhaled noisily. "How primitive can you be? Our Special Branch is twenty-five times the size of yours, and it's run by an assistant commissioner, and you know what? We have MI5 to do the heavy lifting. Special Branch is a supporting act. You people aren't prepared for this kind of work, so of course we want to help you with this file." Burgess ran his hand through an unwashed-looking tangle of hair. "We have the experience, Superintendent. And let me put it as succinctly as I can…" He wagged his finger at Ferrall. "Canada has its head up its arse if you think you can handle this by yourselves."

"Declan, good of you to drop by." Ferrall smiled grimly and waved him into his office. "Mr. Burgess here was just explaining to me his views on Canadian security. He makes some interesting points. I've promised him that you're going to do everything you possibly can to assist him with this file that you're working on. Unfortunately," he looked pointedly at his watch, "I'm really busy here, but you're more familiar with this issue than anybody, so why don't the two of you go to lunch and you can fill him in on things?" Ferrall smiled again and rose from his chair.

Outside the building, Connelly shoehorned Burgess into a cab and took him to the Lord Elgin Hotel. Earlier that morning, Connelly had made inquiries to the RCMP liaison office at the embassy in Washington. They were well acquainted with Guy Burgess. It didn't take him long to figure out a plan. He had made reservations for a corner booth and left detailed instructions for the waiter.

Throughout the meal, Connelly agreed with everything Burgess said and nodded his head at all the appropriate points in his rant. Two double scotches, a small steak, a bottle of Côte de Rhone, and a ridiculously large cognac later, Burgess was now close to being paralytically incoherent. Connelly stood up and motioned for the bill, then struggled to help Burgess to his feet.

"Come on old sport, let's get our coats." Connelly himself was more than a little woozy, but still pleased that he'd managed to remain relatively clear-headed. Whenever Burgess wasn't looking, he had been dumping his glass onto the carpeted floor behind him.

The maître d' whistled him up a cab and Connelly stuffed Burgess into the back seat. After closing the back door he scuttled around to the driver and handed him a ten-dollar bill. "Fast as you can. British High Commissioner's residence on Sussex Drive. Keep the change." He waved down the next taxi to take him home for a couple of hours' sleep. There was work to be done tonight.

Chapter 8

"I KNOW YOU TALKED to Inspector Connelly recently. That's why he asked me to come and see you," Cormier said quietly. "I just have to clarify a couple of things."

Howard Kendall frowned and crossed his arms. Cormier thought he was being pompous and melodramatic.

"What seems to be the problem?" Cormier asked him impatiently.

"Listen, I've just been trying to do my job as best I can. I've told Inspector Connelly everything I know." Kendall raised his voice. "What more do you people want? I've co-operated with your investigation. Now, can't you see I'm busy? I've got things to do. I don't have time for this."

Cormier sat back in the guest chair in Kendall's office. He looked away and said nothing for a few seconds, then leaned forward, nodded his head, and dangled his hat carelessly by his knee. "You know, Mr. Kendall, I came here just looking to verify a couple of things, and now, maybe it's my gut instinct, but I'm thinking that you aren't telling us everything. I smell horse shit. Why is that?"

"I don't know." Kendall looked sullen.

"Okay, let's start from where this American guy comes to you and asks you about Shemyakin. Tell me about that."

"Like I told Connelly, he came here, wanted to know about Shemyakin. I didn't give him any information and he left. That was it." Kendall shrugged his shoulders.

"Let me get this straight. An American, or a man you believe is an American, a foreign security officer..." Cormier paused. "You did see his ID, right?"

Kendall shook his head.

"Okay, why didn't you confirm that he was legitimate, or at least touch base with the RCMP officer who had been here earlier?"

Kendall licked his lips. "Like I told Connelly, I didn't think of it at the time. We have American suppliers and government people here all the time. For God's sakes, do you want me to call our lawyer?" Kendall shifted his gaze down to the desk.

Cormier stroked his chin and raised his eyebrows. "It's very important that you tell me everything you know. We're not out to hammer you, Mr. Kendall. We've got much bigger fish to fry," he said reassuringly. "But this is a national security issue, and I just have this feeling that there's something missing in your story. I'd like to give you the chance to straighten things out. Now, if you've left something out, if you aren't telling me something, that omission could change your life in unpleasant ways that you have never anticipated." Cormier sat back and put both hands out, motioning to the office around him. "Now, you've worked hard all your life to get this. So, let's get back to this American gentleman. I'm in the process of confirming some things from some other sources, and your picture doesn't seem to add up. What is it you're not telling me?"

"The guy told me he was with the American government. That he was working in conjunction with the Canadian authorities."

"Okay, keep going." Cormier frowned. "What happened then?"

Kendall looked out the window and then down at his desk. He exhaled heavily and looked up at Cormier. "He knew Shemyakin was having an affair with my wife. He knew all about our marriage. He asked me to bring some documents home with me. Leave them out so my wife could see them."

"He gave you these documents?"

"Yes."

"This was done on the assumption that your wife would pass these documents to Shemyakin?"

"I think so, yes."

"What were they? What was in these documents?"

"They were test results and prototype manufacturing design instructions for a radar receiver group, but they weren't the specifications we'd been working on. I didn't understand everything in them. I'm not a scientist, but I knew enough to know the information was bogus. They were modified, old summaries of our testing by stages. From what I could see, if Shemyakin sent these back to Russia, they'd spend a long, long time and a lot of effort testing and building a system that wouldn't work."

"What specifically did he want you to tell them?"

"It was technical stuff. The documents he provided had the calculations and diagrams that dealt with relative antenna size and long-wavelength radars, how they work in conjunction with narrower beam-widths. It was our old stuff, but the Americans changed some key parameters. There were some other sections he gave me that dealt with different types of dual and triple feed antennas, the ones we tried using in conjunction with monopole radars and rapid scanning dipole apertures." Kendall kept his eyes focused on his desk. He spoke rapidly, his breathing was shallow.

"The other major thing," he went on, "was that the documents the Americans substituted completely changed the nature of the signal fidelity. This would give false information regarding observation data. It really was credible stuff. It was written by someone who knew what he was doing. I'd been on the project for a couple of years and I knew what worked and what didn't. I knew enough to know it was fake, but only because I'd been down that road. It was cleverly altered from the experiments that we'd conducted a couple of years ago. We stopped all work on that line of development because the system would never work. You see, I wasn't giving useful information to the Russians, not anything they could ever use against us. I was working on our side. I didn't do anything wrong." He looked back up at Cormier.

"Did you receive any money for this?"

Kendall's eyes darted back and forth. He swallowed hard.

"I can have our people look through your bank accounts Mr. Kendall. It'll all come out and that could be grounds for obstruction of justice," Cormier said.

"Yes. He gave me money."

"How much?"

"Five thousand dollars."

"That's a lot. How did you receive that money?"

"It was deposited into a special account."

"I'll need all your account information."

Kendall started rifling through his top drawer.

"We can get to that later." Cormier waved his hand. "You said you couldn't remember this guy's name. Do you want to change that statement?"

"Yeah. He said he was Jay O'Neil. He had U.S. State Department ID and some kind of badge. I didn't look closely at the badge. Honestly, that's all I know about him. He was very convincing."

"Describe him for me."

"He was about your height, thirty-five or forty years old, fit looking, well groomed, slightly receding hairline, wore a nicely cut suit, curly brown hair." Kendall thought for a moment. "Brown eyes, I think. A light complexion. He spoke with a southern accent, not too strong but a bit of a drawl. He sounded well educated, very confident, very sure of himself. He told me that I wasn't allowed to talk to anybody about this. That both our governments were in on this and that he was exclusively handling security."

"Anything else about him?"

Kendall suddenly looked concerned. "Yeah, yeah — he had a big flashy green ring. I thought it looked out of place on him because everything else about him was understated, in good taste."

"Anything else you want to tell me?"

"No, I can't think of anything else." The pitch of Kendall's voice rose. "Listen, I didn't do anything wrong."

"Okay, tell me again, just so I've got it right. Why didn't you contact the RCMP?"

"Listen, sir, I don't understand all this secret stuff. I assumed the Americans are on our side. It seemed to me like I was doing something positive, something helpful."

"Thank you, Mr. Kendall." Cormier got to his feet. "This new information is going to be useful. I have no intention of charging you with anything, so you don't need a lawyer. However," Cormier casually twirled his hat, "if you do talk to anyone about this, anybody at all, as Inspector Connelly has already told you, you'll be in violation of the Official Secrets Act. And in that case, we will prosecute you and we will definitely take a second look at your decision to withhold important information, and at your finances."

✳ ✳ ✳

Mr. Hal Mauro had a downturned mouth embedded at the bottom of a face that looked like it hadn't smiled since childhood. The FBI liaison officer from the American embassy was a short, swarthy man in his late fifties. He wore a brown a suit, a starched white shirt, a brown tie, and black plastic glasses. He carried his overcoat and hat in one hand; on his feet he wore brown rubber galoshes with black buckles. He spoke in low, earnest tones, with a slow Queens accent. Anyone who didn't notice the quickness and intensity in the eyes might be lulled into thinking he was an easy mark.

"Thanks for seeing me, Superintendent Ferrall. I know the kind of pressures you guys are operating under these days. The ambassador's asked me to keep abreast of your investigation into Mr. Shemyakin's murder. He also wants to assure you that if you need any assistance in this, we're here to help in any way we can."

"Thanks, Hal," Ferrall said. "We haven't exhausted all our resources yet, but I'll certainly give you a shout if we need help. But in the meantime, I was hoping that you'd be able to provide us with whatever information you might have on Shemyakin. Our file on him is pretty thin, and to tell you the truth, we're hoping your people, or the CIA, might be able to provide some background on the man. As you know, the Soviet embassy has refused to waive diplomatic immunity and won't cooperate in any meaningful way, so that pretty seriously limits our investigation."

Mauro sniffled and took a handkerchief from his pocket. "I've got one helluva winter cold," he explained apologetically. "You guys have incredibly devastating germs up here in Canada, you know that?" He blew his nose and then took his time putting the handkerchief back. "We don't have much on him, Superintendent. Nothing more than you guys have, I'm sure. You know, I checked with the CIA and he's an unknown quantity to them too. But let me tell you, sir, we'd be happy to give you the use of some of our best FBI agents. Maybe we could also rustle up a couple of analysts from the counter-intelligence group to help beef up your team." He shrugged. "I know the limitations you guys are working with: a tiny force, no access to modern equipment, not much money. You're very professional, we know that, and you do a great job with what you have. But no offence Superintendent: let's build on your strengths. We can throw in some of our technical equipment. That would help you listen in on things in the Soviet embassy. A proper-sized surveillance team might also come in handy. What do you say?"

"Again, Hal, that's kind of you, but you know, that kind of decision would have to be made at a level much higher than mine."

Mauro shifted forward in his chair. "That may be, Superintendent, but I happen to know that your opinion holds some authority with those guys who make the decisions, and, I don't wanna be rude, but we are getting very anxious to find out just what the hell happened up here. We need some answers. The Russian's body, after all, was deposited on our ambassador's property, so we want a quick resolution to this problem. After Gouzenko defected, we were unhappy with the fact that your government refused to send him down to the U.S. to be questioned by our people. Now," he raised his hands, anticipating Ferrall's protest, "I know you didn't do that, but this time we want to play a more active role in things. My orders were to come and talk to you and get a fire going, and as far as I can see, things here are as frozen as an Alaskan reindeer turd in January. I need your help."

Ferrall smiled. "I hear what you're saying, Hal, but you have to understand where we're coming from on this."

Mauro stood up. "Okay. I don't imagine I'm gonna change your mind on this one, for now anyway." He rubbed the back of his hand across his nose and sniffled again. "Superintendent, I know through the jungle drums that you've personally worked closely with the Brits and that you have close relations with them, but on this one, let me warn you." He paused. "You didn't hear it from me, but you should know, there's a big leak somewhere in the British embassy in Washington. We're not certain who it is, but we know that everything that goes to them these days ends up with the Russians. In the last couple of years, the CIA tell me that we've lost almost every one of our sources behind the Iron Curtain. The CIA doesn't believe the leak's with the Brits in Washington, but that's because by law they're forbidden from doing any surveillance inside the U.S." Mauro paused and chuckled. "We have a different opinion and let me just say we in the FBI have very good reason to believe that the leak's in Washington, within the British embassy." Mauro paused. "I can't go into any details. You can understand that, but if you decide you want some assistance, come to us, the FBI, not the Brits or the CIA. We can make it worth your effort."

"I appreciate you telling me that, Hal. I've heard that about the leak. Believe me, if we feel we need help, I know who to call."

* * *

"Kenneth, we have a problem on our hands." The solicitor general, Gerard Warmington, stood at the office door of his parliamentary secretary, Kenneth MacBride. Warmington was a tall man in his late sixties with thinning white hair, wire-frame glasses, a slight stoop, and a faint whiff of talcum powder. He stepped inside the mahogany-panelled room, turned about, and carefully closed the door. His voice was a hoarse whisper. "You know Ken, I asked you to look into that matter of the murdered Soviet?"

"Sure." MacBride sounded defensive. "I've already had the meeting with the RCMP officer from Special Branch. Has something come up?"

"Yes. Yes, it has. I just talked to the minister of external affairs a couple of minutes ago. He wants to know what's going on with the investigation."

"As far as I can see the investigation's moving along. Actually, I was impressed with the officer from Special Branch, a Superintendent Ferrall. Very convincing guy, seemed to have a solid understanding and a grip on things. Why does Reg want to know? I've already briefed him."

"Well, apparently both the British and the Americans have just made some kind of direct informal representation to him. They're both insisting that we should let them in exclusively on the investigation. You know, I'm not comfortable with any of this. I've always thought that all this secret police, espionage, and surveillance business... Well, frankly, it's not Canadian. It's not who we are, or who we want to be." The solicitor general eased himself into one of the green leather barrel chairs. "What do you think?"

MacBride leaned with his back against the window sill and frowned.

"I've heard several versions of that argument, Gerard." He folded his arms and said nothing for a moment. "I've never believed in a vision of this country that's so pious and righteous that we don't have to take the same measures to defend ourselves as the rest of the world." MacBride paused and checked as to whether his minister had taken offence at his candour. He softened his tone. "Gerard, in regards to this particular case, nothing's changed as far as I can see. It's the same issue we had yesterday. The question didn't arise in the House of Commons, but I don't see any reason for us to get involved at our level. In fact, I see several good reasons why we should keep our distance from things. Unless we have solid evidence that the investigation is off the rails, we have to resist the temptation to breathe down our people's necks."

The solicitor general looked troubled. He was quiet for a moment. "Yes, Ken, I hear what you're saying, but at the same time, if the prime minister thinks we've let him down in front of our two biggest allies, our heads are going to be for the chopping block. Besides, I've heard through the grapevine that the Mounties have a weak link in the chain. The officer doing the investigation might not be up to scratch. Whatever the British and the Americans want in this, we won't be well served if we have anyone less than our best leadership in place, and I've heard that's one of their concerns.

"I don't know the case officer and I only met Ferrall briefly, but like I said, from what I can see, he seems to be fairly competent and understands what side is up. If we don't see a problem from where we are, I have to ask you what it is that the British and the Americans want in taking over this case. I should also emphasize the point the head of Special Branch makes about how this will look if it ever gets out that we threw in the towel on this one and let a foreign intelligence service take over our most important domestic file. We'll look like hapless clowns, and our allies will see this as an opportunity to walk all over us the next time. The opposition will make mincemeat out of you on this in the House and in the press. What they'll say is we can't manage routine security matters, and they'd be right. I don't believe in government management by innuendo. Where's this information about the case officer's abilities coming from?"

"It's not just from the Brits or the Americans," MacBride said. "It's coming from the RCMP. I'd rather not say who's giving us the information because I want to keep a back channel open. One of my men in the PMO has a trustworthy source. I think there's value in that, but I am concerned. The other thing that's been left unsaid in all this is that leaks to the press don't have to come from us. If the Americans or the Brits start surreptitiously feeding information to the press that this investigation is going sideways, then, as you say, we'll look like clowns."

"Look at it this way, Gerard." MacBride sat back and rubbed his chin. "If we cave on this, if we hand over our responsibilities to another country, I guarantee you we'll regret it. The thing's only a few days old. It's going to take time. The sky's not falling. Let me call Superintendent Ferrall and discuss it with him. Meanwhile, why don't you talk to the commissioner of the RCMP? We don't have to make a decision on this now."

"I hear what you're saying," the solicitor general said, "but I don't think you understand where I'm coming from on this one. If we don't have movement on this soon, the prime minister has already agreed to hand the entire case over to either the British or the Americans. He desperately wants us to be seen as an active and loyal ally. He says we're not going to jeopardize our international standing with the Americans for the sake of the RCMP's pride. I tried to talk him out of it, but he won't budge. Give them ten days, and not a minute more."

Chapter 9

"DECLAN, GLAD YOU CAME UP." Superintendent Ferrall waved his pipe in greeting as Connelly entered his office. "First thing, thanks for taking care of Mr. Burgess for me yesterday. How'd things go with him anyway?"

Connelly smiled. "No problem at all, sir. We went for a nice lunch at the Lord Elgin Hotel, had a few drinks, and then I saw him off in a cab to the British High Commissioner's residence." He smirked mischievously. "It was all very quiet. I gave the receipts to Shirley Agnew this morning."

Ferrall wrinkled his brow. "I think I've got the picture. I won't ask for details. Anyway, despite our efforts, we're not having much luck with this one. Both the Americans and the British remain a problem. Both countries have gone over our heads; they're applying pressure directly at the highest levels. I think we have some breathing space for now, but the minister of external affairs and the solicitor general are anxious to see this thing wrapped up quickly. I have it from a pretty good source that unless we can prove that we're making significant progress on this, the prime minister is giving us ten days. I understand 'significant progress' to mean that unless we wrap this case up before the end of the month, he's going to ask the Brits or the Americans to step in. What that will mean in practice is that Special Branch will become nothing more than a watcher service for the FBI or MI5, and you and I will both be out of this business and back on routine police work as soon as the handover's complete." Ferrall swivelled his chair away from Connelly and adjusted his eye patch. "I don't have to tell you that there are some influential people within the RCMP who would be very happy to see that happen." Ferrall laid his pipe down on his desk. "So, aside from that bit of happy news, what new developments have you got for me?"

"That's insane, sir. I've never had to work on a case before with a timeline like this tied to it. Ten days is absurd. How did they come up with that number?"

"This is a political decision, Declan. It has nothing to do with you or me, or the case. We've got ten days."

Connelly said nothing. In an instant, the implications of this development flashed through his mind. On a personal level this could be disastrous for him. One of the 'influential people' Ferrall was referring to was undoubtedly Superintendent Graham. Following a nasty run-in in a previous posting, Graham had become his implacable enemy. The man was already actively trying to sink him. Graham would use this as further proof that he was a hopeless incompetent. Connelly raised his head and frowned. Worrying about that now wasn't going to help with his immediate problem. He pushed that line of thinking aside.

"Right, sir. We'll get at it. Marcel Cormier did some great work yesterday in Montreal, but things are a little more complicated than we thought."

"How so?" Ferrall steepled his hands in front of his chin.

"It seems the Americans are already involved." Connelly got up and closed the door. He sat down again. "To make a long story short, I sent Marcel to Montreal yesterday to do a second interview with Howard Kendall. I thought that our friend Kendall was a tad reticent, there was something septic about him — push him a little harder and something nasty would ooze out. Turns out that when Marcel talked to Kendall, he had the same impression, that Kendall knew more than he was telling. He probed a little further and it turns out Kendall had been paid to provide Shemyakin with phony and misleading documents on the Pinetree Line radar system by an American going by the name of Jay O'Neil. I've checked out Jay O'Neil, and the U.S. embassy doesn't admit to anyone by that name working for them."

"Anything else?"

"Yes. I've had the payments to Kendall checked out. They come from a Washington, DC, account, a bank called First Washington Trust and Loan. It was the same account that paid for the Ottawa telephone number."

"Where was the phone installed?"

"At a small furnished apartment in the east end of the city, rented to a Jay O'Neil and paid for with a cheque from First Washington Trust and Loan. The bank has provided Sergeant Simard with some information. The account was opened by the same Mr. Jay O'Neil in early May of last year with a cash deposit of twenty thousand dollars, and there were two cheques deposited in the amount of five thousand dollars each to Howard Kendall's account in the last three months. This means that Kendall was lying to

Cormier as to the amount he received in total from O'Neil and probably about the number of contacts he had with O'Neil. It'll be interesting to see what else he's lying about. The account was closed two weeks ago when O'Neil withdrew the remaining deposit."

"Have you had anyone check out the apartment?"

"Yeah, the place is empty now. Nothing of value in it, but I've had a fingerprint team go over it and we're awaiting results on that one. Hopefully we'll get a set of prints that leads us to Mr. O'Neil."

"Sounds like the apartment's someone's safe house for the duration of an operation. Have you spoken to anyone in the FBI about this?"

"No, not apart from asking if Jay O'Neil worked at the American embassy. Oh, and a request to provide information on the Washington bank accounts."

"Okay, let's keep the queries restricted to those two issues for now. I don't think we want to go any further down that road for a while yet." Ferrall took a deep breath and pursed his lips. After a moment he spoke again. "Okay, a statement of the obvious: the Americans would appear to be running an operation out of Ottawa, and until now we've known nothing about it. The questions for us now are: What American organization is it? What do they already know about Soviet espionage in Canada that we don't? And what, if any, bearing does this have on Anatoly Shemyakin's murder?"

Ferrall picked up his pipe. "My guess is that it's the CIA, but it could realistically just as easily be the FBI, or even one of the defence intelligence organizations. But talking to Mauro the other day, I'd put my money on the CIA.

"No surprise to either of us, the Americans have been frustrated with the scale and impact of our activities, and they aren't happy with Mr. Shemyakin's efforts to discover technical secrets pertaining to the Pinetree Line radar system. They've decided to move things along on their own. Now, if they're running their own operation, why are they so keen to get us out of the way? Why wouldn't they simply make up some kind of story as to how they became aware of Shemyakin and advise us of his activities? We could easily have expelled him with what we now know."

"Maybe there's something about this operation, apart from the fact that they're running it, that they don't want us to know?" Connelly said.

"Oh, I'm sure you're right. My guess is that there are a lot of things they don't want us to know, and one of the first things is that they're running counter-espionage operations here in Canada without telling us. I suspect that this is probably not an isolated operation. They know something that threatens them about Soviet operations in Canada and they don't want us to know what it is." Ferrall paused. "If we confront them with our discovery, they'll almost certainly deny it. So, what we also need to know is how large an operation are they running and what have they found out?"

"Are there any advantages to showing them we have proof of their operations here?"

"Not at this stage. It's not like they're spying against the Canadian government, but they clearly don't want us in on the investigation. If they got caught red-handed running operations on our turf, it would cause an ugly international incident, and, on a more practical level it would be a career-ending embarrassment for the head of whatever agency is conducting their operation. This probably explains why Hal Mauro was in here yesterday. He was pretty adamant that the FBI wanted to take the reins of this thing and keep the Brits and the CIA out.

"Another thing. You phoned the embassy and asked for Jay O'Neil and then got the FBI to do a check on his bank. That's information that won't go unnoticed. I think we have to assume that whoever is running this knows that *we* know they're up to something."

"Do you think they killed Shemyakin?" Connelly asked.

"It's possible, but I think it's improbable. Maybe Shemyakin was onto something and they decided to shut him down. Alternatively, this could be the work of rogue agents."

"Shemyakin was tortured," Connelly said. "Torturing and murdering a diplomat in an allied capital — that's not really an American intelligence agency's modus operandi. Someone was sending a message by leaving the scarred body on the ambassador's property. If it was the Americans, who would they be sending a message to? The Soviets? And if it was the Soviets, what message would they have been sending, and to whom?"

"You're right," Ferrall said. "It could be the Soviets themselves who killed him. Maybe the Americans turned him? But if Shemyakin was working for the Americans and the Russians found out, their normal procedure has always been to sedate their man so he can't defect and then ship him home where they can deal with him at their leisure. We've seen it once before here in Ottawa. The Soviets are notorious for taking care of their discipline problems with a bullet to the back of the neck in the basement of the Lubyanka in Moscow. But you know, at this stage, this is all conjecture. There's no way of proving any of it if we can't even speak to members of the Soviet embassy. And we have no evidence whatsoever that the Americans had turned Shemyakin. So, we're really in a bit of a dead end here."

"If I may, sir," Connelly said, "I think there's something we can still do here to flesh out this picture."

"What's that?"

"Well, we don't have much to go on from the Russians, right?"

"That's an understatement."

"We can do something about that. Not only do we not have any information about the Soviets that's useful to us in this case…" Connelly paused and licked his lips. "Now, please don't take what I'm going to say as criticism of Special Branch, but from what I can see, even if we ignore this particular murder case, I can see that at the best of times we just don't get much information on Soviet activities here in Canada. It looks to me like we're always just nibbling around the edges of the problem. The Russians seem to be operating pretty much at will, and with our manpower restrictions we can't do much about it. We need a major break, something that will give us sufficient information to show that we're managing things capably on our own."

"I'm listening." Ferrall rubbed at the edges of his eye patch and stuck his pipe in his mouth.

"As you said, we're under the gun because the government's likely to ask either the Americans or the Brits to take this over if we don't have some kind of heart-stopping development in the next few days. If we let the case continue on the same trajectory that we're on now, we're dead."

Ferrall nodded noncommittally.

"Something has to give in the next few days. For that to happen, we've got to go out on a limb. We have to try something we've never done before." Connelly paused. "We need to find ourselves a defector, someone who has more of the information we're seeking. A defector will give us the leg up that we need."

"Are you suggesting that you have a plan to get us a defector?"

"Yes, sir. I am."

✳ ✳ ✳

"So, sir." Sergeant Simard laid a typed list on Inspector Connelly's desk. "We have fifty-one people at the Soviet embassy who've been granted diplomatic immunity. Which particular ones are you interested in?

"To start with, I want the top five who travel out of the embassy the most frequently. Oh, and André, could you also please annotate whatever information we have beside each of their names. Indicate their rank, their range of contacts, and any other information that we think has been worth noting."

Simard left the room, papers in hand, and was back in a few minutes with Corporal Russell.

"I brought Corporal Russell, sir. I think this will be faster, and you need to understand his system for categorizing our surveillance targets. He can give you any additional information about the people you want to look at." He handed Ferrall a new list. "The top four are the ones who move around the most."

Corporal Russell jumped in. "Sir, the patterns of life for Soviet embassy employees fall into three major categories. I've called them Groundhogs, Canines, and Jaguars. Category Threes are the Groundhogs. They're the people who work almost exclusively at the embassy. Frankly, that's the overwhelming majority of the fifty-one registered diplomats. The patterns of life and movement for Groundhogs are pretty limited. They go to and from work, perhaps once in a while they do some shopping, but those occasions are rare, and they're usually forced to go in pairs so they can keep an eye on one another. Apart from that, Groundhogs rarely move too far from their apartments or the embassy." Corporal Russell was obviously enjoying the presentation. He gestured with his long arms while speaking rapidly in an exaggerated, conversational monologue. "Groundhogs aren't usually very high-priority targets. We believe that they're completely restricted by their superiors, and if they're caught outside their authorized areas of movement, they're punished severely. Groundhogs, needless to say, are very obedient. We think of them as the least dangerous of the Soviet embassy staff. Some of them may be mid-level technical officers who are, for the most part, restricted to duties within the embassy. Groundhogs can be found at all levels of seniority. We think mid-level Groundhogs are analysts and duty officers. A very small number of them are operating under diplomatic cover, and these are the ones who we suspect direct the operations of their subordinates from within the embassy. The junior ones, about forty-five of the registered diplomatic staff, we believe are radio operators, technicians, switchboard operators, secretaries, clerks, and cipher clerks."

"Can Groundhogs be used for any other activities?" Connelly said.

"Yes, sir. I was going to get to that. Groundhogs have been used on a couple of occasions that I know of: to act as cut-outs, to pass information without compromising more active agents, or, occasionally, to manage the agent signals for use in a dead drop. Somewhat more frequently we've seen them here in Ottawa used from time to time as decoys to draw our attention away from the behaviour of an active agent. We've found out from the Americans that their equivalents to Groundhogs are sometimes used to service dead drops and act as cut-outs, but because of our manpower restrictions here, we can't say we've actually caught one in the act yet. I'm sure that'll come soon enough, though. On the other hand, we know Shemyakin managed to shake one of our tails using a Groundhog as a decoy against us a couple of months ago." Russell gave a self-conscious smile. "We learn from our mistakes in this game, sir. Now, if we see a Groundhog heading out with a high-value agent, we're usually sure something's about to happen."

"Great. What about the rest?

"I've got six here, sir, who I like to categorize as my Twos and Ones — my Canines and Jaguars. I know you asked for five, but there are six of them and these guys take up virtually all my watchers' time." He paused. "I'm not exactly sure what you want these names for, sir. Perhaps if I knew what exactly you're looking for or what you're planning to do, I could be a bit more useful to you."

"No, sorry. I appreciate that you're interested, Corporal Russell, but for now this one has to be on a strictly need-to-know basis, even here," Connelly said. "No slight to you, but I'm sure you understand. Now, if I can just have your Canines and Jaguars, please."

"No problem, sir. I've only three Category Twos. These are the 'Canines.' Canines are the only people in the embassy who I think are allowed to move around at will. They seem to be the most trusted members of the embassy. Given the nature of their jobs, Canines aren't dangerous, as a rule. They're pretty tame. My three Canines are the ambassador, his first secretary, and the Defence attaché. The Defence attaché was rotated back to Russia last month in what we think was a normal posting cycle, and he's yet to be replaced. We try to keep tabs on the remaining two Canines, but we don't have anything like sufficient resources to keep them under surveillance on a regular basis. Given their positions, they're unlikely to risk conducting overtly illegal activities outside the confines of the embassy. That has to be left to other embassy staff. So that leaves me with my four Category Ones, my Jaguars.

"Jaguars are dangerous, predatory, nocturnal animals. We don't like to ever turn our backs on a Jaguar. Jaguars are the most active members of the embassy. They seem to be tasked with making most of the contacts within the country. Much of it's perfectly legal: seeking out trade union leaders, scientists, journalists, cranky professors, that sort of thing. Other activities, however, are illegal and prohibited. They try to find and corrupt disaffected members of the civil service, the police, the armed forces, and so forth."

Russell raised a finger in the air. "I should correct myself. I said I have four Jaguars. I don't anymore. Now that Mr. Shemyakin is no longer with us, we have just three." Russell grinned and raised his eyes to the ceiling. "God rest his communist soul."

He looked back down at Connelly, still grinning. "Now that Shemyakin is dead, I have a little more flexibility to schedule my guys' shifts so that they can actually get some regularly scheduled time off. When they send a replacement for Shemyakin, that will change. Needless to say, Jaguars are cunning and resourceful, and when they want to, with our small watcher teams, they can easily give a one- or two-man tail the slip."

"Okay," said Connelly, impressed, "I can see that with the number of watchers you have in your surveillance section, you're seriously limited in what you can do. Can we use your watchers as decoys to distract the Soviets in an operation?"

"Oh, yeah, we could do that, sir, and I'd be happy to, but I'd need some advance notice as to where and when they'd be used. I'd want to disguise them beforehand. I don't have very many of them, and I need to keep their identities secret."

"Excellent. Now, who are your three remaining Jaguars?" Connelly said. "I like your categories, by the way. Very imaginative."

"Shemyakin was my most active Jaguar. Next is Vitaly Privalov, followed by Fedor Nikolaev and Valery Burdin. Burdin's fairly young, middle twenties. I think he's in training. His pattern of movement gets to be predictable. They never try to shake a tail. They're happy just to walk around and waste my watchers' time. It almost seems like they're just getting to know the lay of the land, get familiar with the language. These guys, their English isn't strong, and I suspect that we'll probably see Burdin surface with a different name in another English-speaking country in a few years. I'd guess that he'll be much more dangerous in a year or so. I imagine he's been very carefully selected. He's bright, level headed, aggressive, and seems to know what he's doing, but for now he's seriously hampered by his English skills, although he's learning their game. That'll change soon.

"Nikolaev is a driver and we've rarely seen him out alone. We don't have a lot of detail on him. That brings me to Vitaly Privalov. If anyone is a Jaguar, it's Privalov. The category was invented for him." Russell leafed through the file he was holding and pulled out a grainy black and white photograph. "I personally took this one at the Ottawa Winter Fair last year in Lansdowne Park. Jaguars like to move around busy public places like bus stops, grocery stores, movie lobbies, hockey games, that sort of thing. Anywhere there's a good crowd. It gives them an opportunity to conduct a brush pass and secretly exchange a document or instructions with one of their contacts. To photograph Privalov, I used one of those tiny cameras concealed in my coat lapel. When you're indoors under artificial light, you have to be close or you quickly lose the detail."

Connelly took the photo and examined it. Privalov was standing in line at a hot dog stand, dressed in a suit and tie and looking out toward the crowd as if he was expecting someone. Connelly had seen Privalov before in the morgue, but now he studied the man closely: mid-thirties, dark hair, a high forehead, a broad, intelligent-looking face. He appeared to be relaxed and poised.

"What information do you have on this guy?" Connelly asked.

"What we have is pretty sketchy, sir. He's a second secretary, responsible for commercial and cultural affairs. He speaks reasonably good English with a slight British accent. From what we can see, he's responsible for disinformation operations and penetrating the media. We don't think he's been too successful here so far."

Russell paused and flipped through several pages of his file. "Apart from providing interviews to the *People's Voice* and the Canadian Socialist League and a couple of other crank organizations, we don't think he's managed to gain much of a footing so far that way. We've seen a number of attempts with the Soviets trying to implement active disinformation measures with regard to the Korean crisis, but so far these have all been pretty clumsy. We suspect that these actions have in some way been instigated or supported by Privalov, but that's only conjecture at this stage. We would have thought he'd have been more active in trying to drum up support against Canada's participation in the war in Korea, but so far, he's kept a low profile. It's probable, sir, that there are other clandestine contacts he's made that we don't know about, but so far those haven't shown up in any of the major newspapers or radio chains." Russell looked down at his file. "Of recent note, he's been nominated as the press contact for issues regarding Shemyakin's death. He's been dealing exclusively with Oriana Soroka of the *Tribune*, but I imagine you know more about that than I do, sir." He looked back up at Connelly again. "That's about it for what I have, sir."

"That's great, Corporal Russell. That's certainly a help. I imagine that we'll be able to flesh that file out somewhat in the future. Thanks."

* * *

The Cathay House was a cavernous restaurant decorated in jungle greens and peppered with rice-paper prints of rural Chinese landscapes. At noon, except for one other Asian couple with a toddler, the place was empty. Off in the kitchen a radio was faintly playing the honky-tonk pain of Hank Williams' 'Cold, Cold Heart.' Connelly and Oriana Soroka were in the far corner in a velvet booth, a pot of green tea and two cups before them on a black laminate table.

"Do you always choose such exotic locales to have your meetings?" Oriana said. "I don't know if you saw the motto underneath the sign outside — 'Where East Meets West.' I feel like I've just wakened up in some kind of movie set."

"No, nothing staged or dramatic. I enjoy their food. Like Katz's deli, it's one of my favourite places to eat. Nothing too mysterious in that." Connelly looked around him before continuing. "Oriana, I do have a reason to talk to you today. Something's come up and I need to know now if you've made up your mind about whether or not you agree to working with me on this case." He shifted his gaze from the table to her eyes.

Oriana laughed. "Well, because of your rule about not going out with anyone who's tried to sabotage your career, I assumed that this wasn't a date." She sat back and stopped smiling. "I was expecting you to get to that, just not so quickly. You're pretty straightforward."

"Fair enough. I'm not a great one for small talk. If I wasn't straight up with you, you'd think I was concealing something and that there was something shady in all this. But you still haven't answered my question. Are you in?"

Oriana leaned forward. "I'm certainly tempted, but when we last spoke you promised to tell me why Superintendent Graham is out to get you. If I agree to work with you, I want to know exactly what I'm getting mixed up with." She swirled the tea in her cup. "You know, Graham's told me that he has some information that would make for excellent copy. He still hasn't told me exactly what he has. He phoned and left me another message at the paper last night. I haven't called him back. I wanted to hear your side of things first."

Connelly looked uneasy. "Yeah. I did promise that. I don't have anything to hide, but I'm sure as an efficient reporter, you've probably done some kind of a search on me. Did you find anything in the newspaper's archives?"

Oriana blinked and looked blankly at him, saying nothing.

"Okay. I'm certain that you'll find that, four years ago near Prince Albert, Saskatchewan, my name surfaced in the news."

Oriana remained inscrutable. Connelly continued, "I was a detachment commander at the time, and we had an incident where one of our young constables was killed responding to a domestic call. We had an internal investigation. That's normal in these cases. The investigators found that the call came from a rural house that had a history of incidents associated with it. Because of the history of this particular place, the officer who took the call should have responded to the tasking with at least one other officer. He didn't. He was young and keen and didn't want to wait around for another officer to accompany him. The long and short of it is that he got to the farmhouse and was shot and killed as he got out of his patrol car. When the backup officer arrived, the assailant was found dead. The autopsy ruled it a self-inflicted wound."

Oriana spoke softly. "So why would any of this have any bearing on you now?"

"Well, Superintendent Graham was one of the officers on the board of inquiry looking into the incident. He should never have been on the board, but he was. He kept the information to himself. The young officer who was killed, Constable Jim Walker, was his nephew. He was Graham's older sister's only son. Graham was understandably grief-stricken, and he was of the opinion that his nephew wouldn't have died if proper procedures had been followed. Graham didn't want his nephew's death attributed to his failure to follow standard procedures. He maintained that I was unfit to command the detachment, and that if the detachment had been run properly, if there had been adequate leadership, junior police officers would have followed the procedures and the incident would've had a very different outcome."

"What were the final findings of the board?"

"The board found that Constable Walker had acted rashly, and although he showed considerable gallantry in carrying out his duties, he failed to act in accordance with the detachment's policy and the training he had received in the force. I was exonerated, but Graham continued trying to smear me. I was posted to Ottawa after only a year in the detachment. Graham has since then gone around telling anyone who would listen that I was an incompetent and that I blamed Walker's death on the only man who couldn't defend himself. He says I should have been dismissed from the RCMP."

"Who else was on the board?"

"The board consisted of three officers, all superintendents. Two of them found no fault with my leadership, and their findings were reflected in the report. But Graham was adamant that under different leadership, Jim Walker would still be alive."

"Did Graham have any reason to believe that you had acted improperly in any way?"

"He heard in the course of the testimony that my wife, Betty, had left me and moved to the United States. She was in the process of obtaining a State of Nevada divorce in Reno. Apart from him being one of those who believe that divorced people are immoral and dissolute, he was convinced that I was too distraught to manage things properly and that, as a result, the detachment was in a state of chaos."

"Was it?"

"No. Not at all. My wife had left a few months before. It was our second breakup. The first was when I was overseas. I was in hospital. I was in the army and was wounded in Italy and evacuated to England. I got a Dear John when I arrived at the convalescent hospital. She'd moved in with a dentist." Connelly pushed his fork around the tablecloth. "They made me an inspector and I got sent to Prince Albert. Meanwhile, things didn't work out with my wife — we hadn't gotten a divorce — and shortly after I arrived in Prince Albert, my wife showed up. I agreed to give it a second try. That was a huge mistake. Let's just say it wasn't a very happy relationship. She left again within a few months. That second time she left, it was for a wealthy American businessman. It was two months before Constable Walker was killed. We didn't have any children, and frankly, it was a relief to have her gone. The two of them went to Reno and she filed for divorce."

Connelly stopped. Oriana was transfixed, following every word. He went on, "I'd never met Graham before then. He seemed to be obsessive, maintaining that I was too upset by my domestic life to run the detachment. The other two investigating officers on the board of inquiry disagreed, as did the members of my detachment who testified on my behalf. I was officially exonerated, but Graham's tried to make my life a misery ever since. I'm pretty sure he was the one who pulled strings with one of his buddies to have me posted out of commanding my detachment and into a desk job in Ottawa. Normally, that would be a career-ender. Superintendent Ferrall eventually gave me a second chance. So, here I am. Whatever Graham tells you, it's probably going to be something along those lines."

"That's quite a story." Oriana looked poker-faced. "Do you suppose Graham has somehow managed to put a flea in the ear of the Russians, saying that you're not up to the job?"

Connelly thought for a second. "No. He's a jerk, but I couldn't imagine him doing that. I've no reason to think he's passing information to the enemy."

"Just a thought. For the record, I did try to find out information about you. I wasn't very successful. Our archives aren't that responsive, so I called your Staff Sergeant Cormier this morning. He hasn't returned my call."

"I hadn't heard that. Marcel's a good man."

Oriana sighed. "That's a remarkable story you have. You've had a lot on your plate in the last few years."

Connelly looked sheepish. "I certainly hadn't expected to tell you my life story. In my job, normally I'm the one listening to tales of woe." He took a deep breath. "I figured that with Graham on the scene and me asking you to buy into a fairly sketchy operation, I owed you a proper explanation." Connelly picked up the menu. "Whatever you choose to do, I'd ask that you please respect my privacy. Should we order lunch?"

"Okay. Maybe over lunch I can tell you my story. After that, we'll see if you're still interested in having me on your team."

Chapter 10

AS HE READ THE DECODED 'Of Special Importance — Ambassador's Eyes Only' message from the Ministry of Foreign Affairs, Alexei Glinin, the Soviet ambassador, put his hand down on the desk to stop it from trembling. The message was brief and to the point.

Ministry of the Interior Police sending Colonel Investigator Yevgeny Tarabin and Major Investigator Georgy Shubenkov from the Ministry of State Security to conduct an enquiry into the death of Anatoly N. Shemyakin. Full Stop. — Investigation Party accredited with United Nations New York and will arrive Ottawa via New York on Trans-Canada Air Lines Flight 107 at 1950 hours on 23 January. Full Stop — Team is travelling as routine audit of embassy finances. Full Stop — Soviet embassy in Ottawa to provide every possible assistance to these officers in conduct of investigation. Full Stop. Message Ends

Glinin took off his reading glasses and said nothing. He had expected this.

The cipher clerk standing beside him asked, "Will you be needing me for anything else, Comrade Ambassador?"

"Who else has seen this message?"

"No one, Comrade Ambassador. The duty signals officer brought the encrypted message to me and I decoded it and brought it to you. No one else has seen this. You have the only decoded copy. The original encoded text is in my safe, and I have in my pocket the only copy of today's code."

"Good. Speak to no one about this." Glinin waved him away.

When the cipher clerk left the office, Glinin put his hand to his mouth. His heart raced. This was an alarming development. He had hoped someone would come from the Ministry of the Interior Police, not the MGB. In Russia everyone feared the MGB. It was Stalin's domestic counter-intelligence bureau and his principal foreign spy agency. Their methods were barbaric, and since the early thirties they had become a law unto themselves. In the last two decades they had "liquidated" millions of Soviet citizens and sent millions more to slave labour camps.

Glinin struggled to his feet and grabbed his cane for support. He stood at the window watching the grey clouds scudding across the rooftops beyond Strathcona Park. This didn't look good. If the MGB officers found evidence of anything slovenly or negligent at the embassy, whether or not it was in relation to Shemyakin's death, the ambassador had a sinking feeling that he would be the one accompanying Colonel Tarabin back to Moscow. That was a contingency he had to think his way through. These things routinely ended in calamity.

* * *

Oriana put her teacup down. "I should let you know where I stand in all this. I think I'd like to help, but you might not want my assistance after you hear what I have to say."

"Why do you say that?" asked Connelly.

"I'm a journalist by profession. My job is to report stories of importance and interest in an independent and impartial manner. I take that responsibility seriously. My concern is that if I work with you, I'll be restricting myself in what I can write. I'm not keen on that."

"That's true, but the articles you write get censored anyway. The only difference is that journalists call it editing. When someone else does it, it's called censorship. Besides, I'm not asking you not to write about us. If you did work with us, I'd want you to provide me with information, not necessarily suppress what you've learned."

"Not true. You wouldn't want me to write about you, for example. You wouldn't want names and photos of your people, your activities, your problems and issues written up in the newspaper, would you? You couldn't have that. You couldn't operate."

"Oriana, I don't pretend to have all the answers." Connelly raised his hands. "I just started this line of work ten days ago. I'm dealing with a man who was brutally murdered in very unusual circumstances. I have to get to the bottom of this; that's my job. But no, I think what we have to realize is that right now we're at war. It's not a shooting war, and it's more than just international political tension. It's a different kind of struggle. I'm not very good at putting this into an argument, but each side's trying to gain an advantage, an advantage that might possibly mean the difference between deterring a nuclear attack and having millions of people killed and our cities turned into smouldering radioactive ruins. If that means we occasionally have to limit the publication of certain aspects of our operations, I'm fine with that."

Oriana took a sip of tea and then pushed her plate away. "For what it's worth, I happen to believe in what you're doing. It's not that I think our people are any better, but we have more institutional restraints imposed on our leaders than the Soviets. I think it's possible for any society, given the right circumstances, to end up being led by sociopaths who turn into mass murderers."

She took a deep breath, focusing on what she was saying. "My problem is this: within those institutional restraints, where do you draw the line between restricting freedom of the press and security? I'm not being melodramatic, Declan. I'm not suggesting that for me to work with you will mean the end of Western freedoms, but there's a principle at stake here, and I have to be clear that whatever I do is principled. Like you, I take my job seriously. And right now, I'm not clear what the hell the right thing to do is."

"Let me put it this way. If this was a run-of-the-mill murder," Connelly shrugged, "say a gangland killing, would you have the same reservations?"

"I see your point. Probably not."

"So, what's the difference? If you could help out by bringing run-of-the-mill thugs to justice, it wouldn't cause you much grief. Stalin's regime is much worse than a small-time crime syndicate. He's killed millions in purges and who knows how many millions more with his gulags and famines."

"You don't have to tell me that. My father's from the Ukraine. He lost most of his family in the Holodomor. Millions were intentionally starved."

"I know your father's Ukrainian."

"Oh, do you?" Oriana glanced at him sharply. "How do you know that?"

"Okay, your last name, Soroka, was a bit of a giveaway, but I haven't just pulled this idea out of thin air. I had a quick background check done on you when I heard that the Soviets would only talk to you. It's just a sensible precaution."

"So, what did you learn about me from your sensible precaution?"

"That your father was a Ukrainian immigrant, and your mother was Italian. You are highly intelligent and well educated, you are financially responsible, you were married several years ago, and now you're divorced and devoting all your energies to your job. You grew up and lived in Winnipeg, and you have no known affiliations with hostile countries or domestic anti-democratic movements. That's about it. You're in the clear."

Oriana laughed. "You sound smug." She shook her head, smiling. "You did a background check on me?"

"Why shouldn't I?" Connelly raised his eyebrows. "You can't tell me you're outraged. Remember, you've already admitted to trying to get information on *me*. The only difference is that my research has been faster and more effective than yours."

"You know," Oriana grinned, "I almost have a blockbuster, career-making story right there. 'Canadian secret policeman with contentious background vets journalist and tries to recruit her for undercover operations.'"

Connelly didn't return her smile. "You could write that, but it would hurt us. Hell, it would hurt Canada and it wouldn't be a fair representation of things." He sighed and ran his fingers through his hair. "Yeah, I'm taking a chance, but I think you're honest enough to value the difference."

"That's a huge risk, and you may be missing the point. It's not a matter of honesty, Declan. It's a matter of perception."

"Maybe, but my gut instinct, reinforced by some background checks, reduces that risk a bit."

"I'm flattered."

"You should be. I've considered this carefully. I wouldn't have asked for your help if I didn't think you were up to it."

"Now you're being condescending."

"No, I'm not. It's the truth. Why would you think I'm being condescending?"

"Because I live in a world where men are condescending to women as a matter of routine. Why in God's name would you be any different?"

"Okay, you've lost me. I don't follow you now."

"Really? You tell me if you think I'm 'up to it.' I've heard that phrase my whole life. Right now, I'm the only woman reporter on our paper. I used to be the Parliamentary Affairs reporter. I worked bloody hard to get that job, but three months ago I was replaced by an inexperienced man fresh out of school. And guess what? I was relegated without warning to a junior position on a local beat. Not that I did anything wrong. My work was as good as or better than that of any man in the press gallery. But we got a new editor, and within a week I was off the job with a vague promise that if I was a good little girl, I could possibly work my way up again. Because I'm a woman in a man's profession, the odds are stacked against me and they always will be. Now I cover City Hall, petty crime, and teas at Government House. There's nothing wrong with that work, but I've already done that, for years. I didn't work myself to the bone for the last decade and a half to be given a cub reporter's job. That's why when you use a phrase like 'didn't think you were up to it,' I think you're patronizing me."

"I'm sorry. That wasn't my intention." Connelly dropped his upturned hands on the table in a gesture of mock frustration. "But I'm asking you for help, only because you're capable and in a position to assist me. And because, I think you'll agree, it's the right thing to do."

"Look," Oriana sighed, "this puts me in a huge bind. The other thing you should know is my editor wants me to produce a series of sensational articles on this case. He thinks that it can eventually become a book. He's told me to get whatever information I can on all the key players. Who was the victim? Who are the cops? What are their backgrounds? The juicier the information the better. He's dangled this one in front of me, saying that if I can produce something really sensational, he'll see what he can do to get me my job back as the parliamentary correspondent or even a position as a foreign bureau chief."

Connelly nodded. "I didn't know that, but I'm asking you to do whatever you think is right."

There was a very long silence, punctuated by the clatter of dishes in the kitchen and Patti Page on the radio singing 'The Tennessee Waltz.'

Oriana shook her head and exhaled heavily. "I'll do it." She said nothing for a moment. "You should know that Vitaly Privalov has asked me to come to the embassy and talk to him tomorrow."

✳ ✳ ✳

Connelly and Cormier sat in Ferrall's office with the door closed. "Gentlemen, we've never tried something like this before," Ferrall said. "I agree with Declan's assessment. I think making Privalov our target's the right move."

Much as Connelly liked his boss, it always amused him when he watched Ferrall render his decisions, like a judge pronouncing a verdict at the end of a complicated trial.

"Now that Shemyakin's dead," Ferrall continued, "Privalov moves into the number one spot as the most active member of the embassy. He's almost certainly an operative in the MGB or military intelligence. We don't know who he actually works for, and at this stage, I don't really care much one way or the other if he's MGB or GRU, but I agree, he's the man we want. But things aren't that straightforward. I've given this situation some thought. I have a serious concern with the legality of this operation, so I want to make my thoughts clear to both of you before we go any further." Ferrall paused. Connelly sat up and shifted in his chair.

"We're running a tiny security agency that's staffed at levels that might have been acceptable in Victorian times," Ferrall went on. "But the government doesn't care what problems we face, unless of course something goes wrong. Most days they're not remotely interested in what we do. The only advantage that gives us is that I've been given considerable autonomy in determining the conduct of our operations. But in conducting operations we're still required to respect the law. As I've told both of you before, our job as counter-intelligence officers is to deal with threats to our security. As a regular police officer, Declan, you were concerned with prosecuting criminals. However, you've heard me say it before: the two tasks aren't the same thing. We are not always concerned with gaining sufficient evidence to be successful in a court of law, yet we have to be seen to be acting within the law. So, our problem is that we have to detain Privalov. But, and here's the catch, we have to respect his diplomatic immunity and maintain secrecy, and we can't keep him against his will. I'm not splitting hairs here, gentlemen. This thing could go seriously off the rails, even long after it's over, if someone complains and we can't prove we've operated within the law. I don't pretend to have the answers to that now. But if I ever have to go before a parliamentary committee, we're going to have to prove that we've not only operated within the law, but also acted in a way that shields the government from any political or diplomatic embarrassment."

Ferrall waved his pipe. "The second aspect I'm concerned about is security. The only people right now who are aware that we are even contemplating this move are the three of us in this room. There will be one other key person involved in this caper, but for security reasons that individual must have only partial information. Nothing about this operation should be written down or discussed on the phone or outside of this room." Ferrall glanced at the two men in turn. "Fine. So, before we go much farther down this road, I want your opinions. Do you think we can get Privalov to defect?" Ferrall looked at Cormier. "Marcel? Your thoughts?"

"Sir, I'm not certain it's such a long shot as I first thought, but there are a couple of things that bother me. If we offer him enough money and a comfortable life here, I think we could get him, but I guess my big concern's his family. What happens to them if he goes over to us? The second thing is, can we be able to offer him enough money to make him bolt? We're really asking him to switch sides. But you know, lots of Soviets have jumped ship for all kinds of reasons. What do we know about this guy? Are the money and a life in Canada going to be enough to make him stay with us?"

"Good points. Thanks. Let's look at the first issue," Ferrall said. "I don't know if he has a family. I guess we're going to find out, but if he does defect, and reprisals are taken against his family, then, unfortunately, Marcel, we can't wear the blame for that. We can't let Stalin hold us to ransom by using his own people as hostages." He leaned forward. "We should all remember this. Comrade Privalov would have been in his mid-thirties at the height of the purges. You can bet the farm that as a state security or GRU officer, he has innocent blood on his hands, and buckets of it. If he's a foreign intelligence officer now, it would be a statistical impossibility that he didn't have an active part in the worst excesses of the Soviet police state. We know beyond any reasonable doubt that his organization killed millions in the purges before the war. They starved millions of their own people when they collectivized Soviet agriculture, and after the war they eliminated and uprooted millions more.

"I'd be equally certain that this guy is not troubled by conventional notions of morality. I don't think his conscience troubles him too much. I appreciate your concern, Marcel, but this guy, just like Comrade Shemyakin, has been involved in a bloody and ruthless business for a long time. Regrettably, his family, if he has any, aren't a part of our considerations. Your second point, don't worry about the money — I'll sort that issue out when the time comes."

Ferrall tilted the patch on his missing eye and rubbed the edges of his eye socket. "Damn thing's acting up on me today," he muttered. Replacing the patch, he turned to Connelly. "Declan, what are your concerns?"

"You know where I stand, sir. My mind's been made up for a few days now. One bit of good news: as of today, I have assurances from a judge from the Ontario Court of Justice that by mid-morning he'll issue me a writ allowing us to question Privalov in relation to this case."

"What did you tell the judge?" Ferrall asked.

Connelly grinned. "I told him the truth about the case. I didn't tell him where we planned to question Privalov, though. He agreed, said we could proceed as long as our actions were reasonable and proportionate."

Ferrall looked skeptical.

"I know what you're thinking, sir. Regarding your concerns about diplomatic or political embarrassment, the risks in this case are minimal; but I'd agree, there's an off-chance that this could get some unfavourable publicity. That's not a reason for us to do nothing. If we don't act, if we don't change the trajectory of this case, our risk approaches one hundred percent. We'll lose whatever counter-intelligence capability we now have." Connelly smiled and raised his hands — "And when it goes successfully, we'll have survived to fight another day."

"Good work getting the writ," Ferrall said, chewing his lower lip. "You must've been convincing. It does give us some cover if this ever goes public.

But understand that if this goes wrong, we'll be thrown to the wolves, and if it succeeds, we'll be unsung heroes. There's no glory or reward in this for us. That's the nature of our job. Marcel, you still look worried. What's on your mind?"

"Well, one other point, sir. I'm not sure if this is relevant to this particular aspect of our operations, but Sergeant Simard told me just before I came in here this morning that he'd been working late last night, and he dropped into the Sunset Café a couple of blocks away to buy a pack of cigarettes. He said he saw Constable Murphy in one of the booths having a coffee with Superintendent Graham. Both were in civvies and the two were pretty deep in conversation. Now, Murphy works in Simard's research section, and Murphy told him this morning it was no big deal, they just ran into each other, but it seems pretty fucking odd to me that a senior superintendent should be sitting down after hours to have coffee and a chat with a Special Branch constable twenty-five years his junior." Cormier turned to Connelly. "Forgive me, sir, but I know that Graham's been a pain in the ass — those rumours are all over the force — but I see this as suspicious behaviour. I'm not certain we haven't got a leak in our own organization."

* * *

Oriana Soroka stood at the gate of the Soviet embassy on Charlotte Street. She was apprehensive as she pressed the buzzer. The rambling old Victorian mansion was surrounded by a seven-foot-high black steel fence topped by sharp spikes disguised as decorative fleurs-de-lis. The windows of the building looked as if they had never been washed, and long, heavy icicles hung hazardously where the eavestroughs met the walls.

A heavyset man with a thin moustache in a black suit came out to meet her. After Oriana provided identification, the moustached man unlocked the gate and ushered her inside to what had once been a fashionable sitting room. The room was sparsely furnished with three wooden office chairs and a small maple table. The wooden floorboards were stained and warped. On the walls were two black and white photographs. In one, Lenin was lecturing a crowd, his arm raised in a defiant, angry gesture. Beside him in a much larger picture was a bust of Joseph Stalin, narrow eyed, with a wolfish smile and wearing a simple military uniform decorated with a single star-shaped medal. From somewhere upstairs she could hear a phone ringing and indistinct voices.

After a minute Vitaly Privalov made his entrance. He was a lean, good-looking man, with dark hair and a strained smile. He was well groomed, dressed in a well-cut suit, and sported a red star pin on his lapel.

"I am so glad that you could come, Miss Soroka. I know you must be busy, so, please, give me your coat and have a seat." He motioned to one of the chairs. "Please sit and we can discuss our concerns." He took her coat and set it on the maple table.

Oriana took a seat and Privalov clasped his hands together. "Please forgive me. Can I offer you a coffee or a cup of tea?"

"No thanks. I'm fine — really." She pulled a pen and pad from her purse. "Now tell me, Mr. Privalov, what exactly do you do here at the embassy?"

"I am a commercial and cultural attaché, madam. But tell me, with such a beautiful Ukrainian name like Soroka, how do you come to be in Canada?"

"My father came from the Ukraine when he was very young."

"Do you have family still in the Ukrainian Soviet Republic?"

Oriana smiled. "Well, not that I know of. My father told me that his family lost touch with them after they emigrated. Maybe someday we can find out where they are."

"Oh, yes. You should travel to the Soviet Union. We would love to have a Canadian journalist come and see us."

"That would be nice. Now, Mr. Privalov, what exactly does a commercial and cultural attaché do?"

Privalov smiled. "It is my job to try to ensure that the Soviet Union maintains close cultural ties to our host nation. Currently, I am working to have a cultural exchange between Canada and my country. I am hoping we can work out exchanges with the Winnipeg Ballet and the Red Army Chorus. We believe that such cultural activities can do so much to increase understanding and promote peaceful relations between our two countries. We don't do this now, and we need such activities in dangerous times. But you know, Miss Soroka, right now we have, as you know, a problem. The death of my good friend and comrade Anatoly Shemyakin." Privalov hesitated and looked earnestly at Oriana. His voice dropped. "You know, Anatoly's death makes me sad. He was my friend. But also, in our embassy we believe that the Canadian police are not doing what they should to catch the murderers. We have offered to help, but our offer has been rejected. This is why I hope you can do something in your paper."

"I understand your concern, Mr. Privalov, but I'm afraid we've already covered that. You see, I have to show my editor something new, some fresh information with each article. I need your help on that. When we spoke on the phone, you did say you had something new for me, and that's what I'm hoping you can tell me, so that I can put it into an article."

Privalov put his hand to his chin. "I see. Can I tell you about Anatoly's life, maybe something to help your readers understand the kind of man he was?"

"That would be wonderful. Do you have any pictures of him with his family? His wife, for instance — how is she coping? What about his work? Is anything unfinished?"

Privalov nodded vigorously in response. "Yes, yes, of course. His wife was crushed at the terrible news. Now she is at home with her mother and friends, trying to get over this loss. Anatoly was a good man. He was a dedicated patriot. He was from Novosibirsk, where he trained as an electrical engineer. He did engineering studies at Novosibirsk Technical University. During the Great Patriotic War, Anatoly fought as a tank officer in battles at Moscow, at the Dnieper River, where he was wounded, and later at Budapest. He was always grateful to work with Soviet allies, and after the war he joined the Soviet Ministry of External Relations and worked in Moscow and was then transferred to Ottawa. Anatoly was very keen to improve air safety in the Soviet Union and hoped that his work in Canada would allow for the development of peaceful mutual understanding of technical issues. You see, Anatoly had no enemies. He was a happy man, always ready for a good time. No reasonable person would want to hurt him. We feel that his murder is an attempt to drive a wedge between the Canadian and Soviet peoples. The Canadian government is not looking hard enough to find who killed him."

"Who do you think killed him, Mr. Privalov?"

Privalov sat back and raised his hands as if he was about to lead his congregation in prayer. His voice rose. "Let me ask you, who do you think hates the Soviet people? Who has declared themselves the enemy of the progressive socialist states? Who are the imperialists who would like to destroy Soviet efforts at friendship? Who would like to see Canada and the Soviet Union as bitter enemies? If you answer these questions, you will know where to look. These are the questions you should ask in your newspaper, Miss Soroka. These are the questions the Canadian police are not asking."

"That's very interesting, Mr. Privalov. I'm certainly going to try to follow up on that." She made a few notes on the pad in her lap and then looked up at him again. "Do you have any pictures of Mr. Shemyakin, perhaps with his family or while he was not working? That would be a great help."

Privalov nodded. "Wait here. I will go and see what we have."

Once Privalov was out of the room. Oriana noticed that the man who had let her in at the gate was now lurking in the hallway — a precaution to keep her from exploring inside the embassy, she supposed. She smiled at him and he nodded grimly.

Five minutes later, Privalov returned with a small black and white head-

and-shoulders photograph of Shemyakin looking as if he'd been surprised by the flashbulb. The photograph had glue marks on the back and looked like it had been recently peeled off a file or a passport.

Oriana smiled. "Thank you, Mr. Privalov. It's not exactly what I had in mind, but it'll do in a pinch." She stood up. "Can I telephone you if I need to clarify any points for my article?"

"Of course. I will get a pen and write down the number."

"That's fine, thanks. I'm sure the embassy switchboard will connect us." Oriana smiled, offered her hand to Privalov, and then put on her coat.

Privalov beamed. "Thank you for coming. Mr. Aliyev will show you to the gate."

* * *

"Of all places, why are we meeting here?" Oriana asked of no one in particular as she closed the door behind her. Ferrall, Connelly, and Cormier sat around a wooden table in one of the small, dimly lit breakout rooms at the back of the reference floor in the main branch of the Ottawa Public Library. Ferrall, rising to his feet, was the first to speak.

"Well, I'm delighted to see you're not shy. Have a seat, please, Miss Soroka. I'll answer your question, but first I'd like to introduce myself. I'm Superintendent Rory Ferrall. You already know Inspector Declan Connelly, and this is Staff Sergeant Marcel Cormier. I want to say how grateful we are for your assistance. As for the location," he dipped his head and smiled, "it was my idea to meet here. In this kind of work, we're discreet to the point of being obsessive. So, in the event that you were followed by the Russians, it wouldn't be a great idea to have you dropping round to a known RCMP building. A journalist coming and going to the library won't arouse any suspicion. Also, we know for certain this place isn't bugged. Having said that, we won't keep you long. This should only take a few minutes."

"Thanks for coming, Oriana," Connelly said. "You may think we're being overly cautious, but I didn't want to talk on the phone. It's also important that the other two members involved in this operation get a chance to meet you. We'd just like to tie up a few details for our next activity. Did you get to speak with Privalov yesterday?"

"I did. Afterwards, I phoned him back and told him I wanted to meet again to go over my notes for my next article. He invited me back to the embassy. I said that I didn't think it was a good idea. If it ever got out that I was regularly going to the embassy, it would look like I wasn't independent, that I was being told what I should and shouldn't write. I told him that kind of thing, even if it wasn't true, would sabotage my journalism career

104

and my credibility forever. He saw the sense in that and agreed completely. I suggested that we meet the next time someplace open where we could easily come and go."

"What did you agree to?" Ferrall said.

"I suggested the malted milk stand in the basement of Freiman's department store. He was delighted; he said that he goes there all the time. Turns out he loves the stuff. They don't have anything like it in Russia, and it's cheap."

"That's perfect! What time are you gonna meet him?" Cormier asked.

"Just after noon. It should be crowded then. That's what Declan told me would be best."

"Do you have anything to give him? He may want to see a draft or an outline," Connelly said.

"I can type up some notes. I was thinking of using the internment of Ukrainians in the First World War and the internment of Italians in the Second World War as a background piece. For what it's worth, my dad was briefly interned and then registered as an enemy alien. I thought that it would make a good talking point, and it might interest him, show him that there's some kind of cultural sympathy as well as an ideological connection."

"I like that. Can you keep him engaged in conversation for three or four minutes? That's all we need," Connelly said.

"Shouldn't be a problem. I'll ask him a few questions. I can ham it up a bit."

"Okay. Needless to say, when you see any of us there, whatever you do, please don't let on that you recognize us," Cormier said.

"I've figured that much out. Thanks."

"Please don't be offended, Miss Soroka," Ferrall said, getting to his feet. "You'd be surprised what we have to tell some people when we have to set something like this up. Marcel didn't mean to imply anything by it. Believe me, he's the voice of experience in these things." He looked at his watch. "Okay, this sounds like things are lining up nicely. We shouldn't delay you any longer. Again, we want you to know how grateful we are, Miss Soroka. It's been great to meet you. I think you're going to be splendid. We won't keep you any longer."

"We really appreciate your work, Oriana. Thanks," Connelly said.

Oriana stood up. "I'll knock 'em dead." She winked at the group as she closed the door.

Connelly was the first to speak. "She seems to have it figured out and she certainly doesn't appear to be intimidated by any of this. I think she'll be fine."

Cormier nodded. "I hope so, sir. We're about to find out."

"I know we all agreed to leave here independently," Connelly said, "so if you gentlemen don't mind, I'll slip out first by the back door. I promised to meet the lab people this morning to see if they have any kind of match for Jay O'Neil's fingerprints."

Once Connelly left, Ferrall spoke. "I think she'll be fine too. She seems bright enough, confident and alert. Maybe just a touch overconfident. What do you think, Marcel?"

"She's certainly sure of herself, no question about that, sir," Cormier said. "That's great, but..." He reddened slightly. "I'm not being disloyal, sir. I've got a lot of respect for Inspector Connelly. He's a good officer, a good man, but is it my imagination, boss? Did you see the way those two looked at each other? Am I the only one who noticed? There's some kind of electricity going on between those two."

* * *

Freiman's had fashionable, quality clothing at the best prices in the city. In late January the store held its door-busting winter clothing sale. Budget-conscious shoppers in heavy coats, scarves, and hats sorted and pulled their way through the store's remaining stock of men's and women's winter coats, flannel shirts, overshoes, sweaters, and children's snow suits — all of which, two days earlier, had been sitting on racks upstairs at full price. Freiman's was also known for one of the best lunch counters in the city. On any given day of the week, middle-aged women in white uniforms and red aprons served a ceaseless stream of fresh sandwiches, hamburgers, milk shakes, French fries, coffee, slices of fresh-baked pies, and one of the department store's top attractions, freshly made mini-donuts. Beside the lunch counter, behind a glass window, was a machine that deep-fried mini-donuts on a conveyer belt.

Today the basement was crammed with housewives and civil servants on their noon-hour break, all hunting for bargains. At the lunch counter, all the stools were filled. Customers stood two deep behind the counter, patiently waiting to order. Tucked away in a corner beside the escalator at the malted milk booth, thirty people crowded around the small concession as two attendants feverishly dished out thick, ice-cold, six-ounce malted milks for ten cents a glass. At the foot of the escalator was Corporal Eddy Russell.

Russell, wearing a dark overcoat and a fedora, was carefully studying the contents of a mid-winter sale flyer. Three of his surveillance team members hung back behind the lunch counter crowd, intermingled among the shoppers. The epitome of good manners, they discreetly allowed legitimate customers to move ahead of them. Standing in one of the aisles for children's snow suits, holding a cardboard Freiman's china box with a 50mm automatic Leica telephoto camera rigged inside, was one of Russell's photographic team. Further off, Connelly and Cormier nosed through the racks of flannel shirts and duffel coats.

Oriana came down the escalator at 11:58 and headed for the back of the crowd at the malted milk stand. At precisely 12, looking for all the world like he'd just stepped off a construction site, Privalov strolled over from the shoe and winter boot section across the room. He was unshaven and dressed in a concrete-stained working man's canvas parka. On his head he wore a large red, white, and blue Montreal Canadiens toque. He approached Oriana from behind and squeezed her elbow.

"Here you are, right on time."

Oriana turned and laughed with genuine surprise. "My goodness, Mr. Privalov. I never would have recognized you! Why on earth are you dressed like that?"

Privalov leaned forward and whispered, "You know, you told me you did not want to be seen talking to me in the embassy. I think that was true also for being seen in public. This is better. Do you have the article?"

"I do. Let me get it." She rummaged through her purse and handed Privalov an unsealed envelope. Privalov pulled out the paper and began reading. Seconds later, a tired, glassy-eyed Cormier, reeking of alcohol, carrying a shopping bag, his tie loosened at his neck and his hat pushed back to expose his forehead, sidled up behind him.

"Hey pal, are you gonna buy a malted or are you just standin' here readin'? I gotta get back to work, you know. C'mon, c'mon! The line's movin'!"

Oriana stepped back, bumping the man beside her. "Listen, mister," she said. "We are here waiting patiently, minding our own business. Why don't you just beat it?" Turning to Privalov, she said, "I'm really sorry. We're not all as rude as this guy — really."

Cormier looked at his watch. "Lady, I don't have all day, okay? Some of us work for a living."

Privalov turned about and snarled, "We are doing nothing. Don't talk like that to this woman. What is the matter with you?"

"Oh, yeah. Right. Mister tough guy, huh?"

Privalov stepped closer to Cormier, jaw thrust out, feet balanced in a combative stance.

Cormier raised his hands and his tone switched to a more placating mutter. "Hey, fuck. I don't need this, eh? Look, I'm sorry, okay? I'm just pissed off these days. I got lots goin' on these days. I'm late for my job and my kid's sick." He reached out and touched Privalov on the elbow. "Look, I'm sorry. I didn't mean no fuckin' harm, honestly." He tipped his hat and looked at Oriana. "Sorry, lady. I'm outa here. Have a nice fuckin' day, eh?" He turned, and, in a moment, was swallowed by the crush of shoppers surging past the lunch counter.

A few moments later, Constable Voigt from Special Branch walked up, brushing people aside. He was dressed in a suit and tie. "Excuse me. I'm the store security manager. I saw that incident. That man has been here before causing trouble. Are you two all right?" Voigt looked inquiringly at Privalov.

"No, I'm fine, really. Just some guy. It's nothing." Oriana stepped back. "He's got something on his mind, I guess."

"How about you, sir? I can have that man escorted out of the store."

"No, no. Everything is fine — please, please." Privalov motioned with his hands.

"Are you sure, sir? We can't have people behaving like that at Freiman's," Voigt said, staring at Privalov. "Okay. It doesn't matter. I'm going to go check him out." He strode away in the direction Cormier had gone.

Oriana turned to Privalov. "Let's get out of here. Why don't we go somewhere where it's not so crowded? We can have malted milks another day. This place is a zoo." She pulled Privalov by the arm and smiled. "Come with me. I want to hear what you have to say about my notes. There's a little café a couple of blocks from here where we can talk privately."

Chapter 11

IT WAS DARK AND SNOW WAS FALLING in the streetlight. Connelly and Oriana pretended to look over the vegetables in the produce aisle of Boushey's Grocery on Elgin Street.

"So, any indication whether or not he suspected anything was up at the department store this morning?" Connelly said.

She answered him with an impish smile. "You know, this is kind of fun, isn't it? Secret meetings, surreptitious photographing, lunch with spies. I'm going to hate going back to my real job and covering City Hall zoning meetings, snow storm damage, and the Kiwanis Music Festival. You guys should kill Russian spies more often."

Connelly smiled wistfully. "We didn't kill Shemyakin, but you did a really good job today. I almost believed you. So, did Privalov suspect anything?"

"No, I don't think so. I think he seemed much more interested in what I'd written than in the incident at the department store. Your friend's a pretty believable drunk, by the way. Privalov certainly didn't seem to be put off by it. When we went for lunch, he told me that confrontations with angry drunks on the street happen all the time in Moscow. He told me we got off lucky. Over there most of these things end in some kind of violence. In Moscow, a lot of the drunks carry knives."

"What did he say about your notes?" Connelly picked up a grapefruit and pretended to study it.

"He said he liked them, but he asked me to rewrite the part dealing with the internment of Ukrainians and Italians. He said it wasn't harsh enough. Canadians had to know the extent of the treachery inflicted on their own people by the government. I thought that was a bit rich coming from this guy. He wanted to meet again later this week, asked me to call him tomorrow and we could sort it out. I think he's lonely. He tried to be charming in an awkward sort of way. He's not my type — no sense of humour, very abrupt. Something I don't like about him." They moved slowly down the aisle into the canned goods.

"I'm sure you've got that right," Connelly said. "He's probably an officer in the Soviet secret police. He'd put a bullet in the back of your head as soon as look at you. He's as contemptible as a Gestapo officer, and just as dangerous."

"If that's what it is, it didn't show. He just seemed awkward and unpleasant. Tell me something, though. Why are we meeting here?"

"Well, like I told you before, I'm not really all that experienced in secret espionage stuff. When I was an ordinary cop, I just went out in the mornings and arrested the bad guys wherever I saw them. This job's different, I guess. You don't like grocery stores?"

A stock boy pushing a trolley of boxes stopped at the end of their aisle. "Anything I can help you folks with?"

Oriana flashed him a smile. "No, we're good, thanks." The stock boy moved on. She turned to Connelly. "Seriously, do you think we have to do this?"

"Okay, you probably have a point. I don't think they have the resources to follow you too closely. If they were going to keep an eye on you, it'd probably have been just before your meeting and just after lunch, and I don't think they did that. But then again, it's possible they could have had a Groundhog drop by to see what you're up to."

She looked at him askance. "What the hell are you talking about?"

"Sorry. I'm using the office slang. I've just picked up the term myself. Groundhogs are Russians who normally don't stray too far from the embassy. Sometimes they use them for simple low-level tasks — like checking up on an individual."

"Do you think we're being watched by a Groundhog?"

"I doubt it."

"Okay, in that case, I don't really feel like carrying on a conversation over the carrots and onions, and I don't want to walk around in the snow all night. Why don't we just go to my place and talk there?"

Connelly hesitated for a moment. "Okay, sounds good."

They walked slowly through the darkened streets. After a block, Oriana put her arm through Connelly's and rested her head on his shoulder. It seemed entirely natural.

"Where's this going to end, Declan?" she said after a while. "Are they going to drop atomic bombs on all of us?"

"I wish I knew. I think for now we're pretty safe here in Canada."

"I hope you're right."

Oriana's apartment was on the second story of a four-story, yellow brick building on Argyle Street, a downtown residential street of apartments and walk-ups that looked as if it had been cross-bred between London's Camden Town and Montreal's Rosemont. Her apartment was a small, one-bedroom flat. The living room had a view across the street of a tiny park and swing set covered in snow. The apartment was modest. In the living room she had a small couch, two comfortable chairs, and a coffee table. The room was freshly painted in a faint shade of grey and tastefully decorated with three colourful paintings of what looked like a Canadian city in winter. There were several bookshelves filled with modern novels, travelogues, cookbooks, and expensive-looking art books. A stack of newspapers lay neatly piled on the floor beside one of the armchairs.

"I don't have much to drink. Brandy or red wine? Take your pick." She hung her coat in the hallway and reached out for Declan's. "Actually," she put the back of her hand to her forehead, "the red wine's probably gone vinegary. I've had it since last spring. Do you like brandy?"

"Brandy's fine." Declan sat on the couch.

She poured drinks into juice glasses, handed him one, and sat sideways on the couch, her back leaning on one of the arm rests. She burrowed her toes under Declan's leg, straightened her skirt, and said, "Okay, tell me. What happens now?"

"We wait until you talk to Privalov next and we take it from there."

"You won't say any more?"

"I don't know any more just yet. Honestly, there's no point in getting too far ahead of ourselves. I'm taking this thing one step at a time, but when I figure out the next step, you'll be one of the first to know."

"You kept your word using that line once before. So, I guess I can believe you. Now, tell me about yourself. Who am I trusting myself to in all this," she flourished her glass, "whatever you call what we're doing? You owe it to me to tell me that."

Connelly paused and sipped his drink. "I'm Declan Connelly, the only child of Mr. and Mrs. Connelly. I was born and raised on a small farm near Cremona — that's in the Alberta Foothills. I suppose we were poor, but so was everybody else then. Both my parents died while I was away during the war. You know about my ex-wife." Connelly swirled his brandy. "Your turn now."

"Well, you already know I'm from Winnipeg. My Dad was a Ukrainian farmer who moved to the city and worked for the wheat pool as a driver. He lost the farm in the Depression. My Mum was an Italian immigrant. She moved here as a child fifty years ago. She met my dad at a dance, and here I am. So, what do you do when you're not catching spies and criminals?"

The conversation rocked along comfortably with Oriana's game, both of them enjoying the rhythm and the exhilaration of their disclosures, both tacitly recognizing this was a quick test to see if a romantic relationship was worth the effort. Connelly spent a lot of his off hours reading history and liked the outdoors. He'd joined the Mounted Police after high school. Even though he had the marks, he couldn't afford to go to university. He'd been posted to New Brunswick and Nova Scotia. He couldn't cook to save his life. He avoided talking about the war, but conceded he'd been in the Provost Corps and was wounded in both legs in a mortar barrage when he was escorting German prisoners from the front line.

Oriana had worked two jobs waitressing and put herself through the University of Manitoba, where she'd studied English and art history. The father of a university friend of hers was the city editor of the *Winnipeg Free Press*. There was an opening, and she'd got her first job reporting court news within a week of graduating. She'd met her ex-husband, a law student, at a party. The marriage had been a disaster. She'd left when she discovered that, from the beginning of their married life, he had had a stream of girlfriends on the side. After she'd moved to Ottawa and got a job with the *Tribune*, she had taken up skiing, cooking, and studying French. She wanted to try painting someday.

Neither of them had close friends in Ottawa. Both their sets of good friends lived in cities back on the Prairies. They both liked movies, especially anything with Humphrey Bogart and Lauren Bacall. Both of them dated on and off. Neither had developed much interest in the people they dated. Connelly wanted to stay in the RCMP. Oriana was sick of her job and didn't know what she wanted.

At 12:15 and three inches down the brandy bottle, Connelly looked at his watch. "It's late. I should go."

Oriana leaned forward and put her arms around him. Her hair brushed across his face, the spicy warm fragrance of her perfume stirring him. "I know, but I want you to stay," she whispered.

He pulled her in to him and kissed her, at first an unhurried, gentle, tentative brandied kiss that slowly intensified, building its own fused energy between the two of them. Neither spoke. Oriana stood up and led him by the hand to her darkened bedroom. He unbuttoned her blouse and reached around her, deftly uncoupling her bra catch. She laughed.

"You've done this before."

"Not for a long time."

She slipped out of her clothes and unzipped his fly. Pushing him back onto her bed she undressed him in seconds. Her body was both lithe and silky. He pulled her close and rolled onto her, kissing and stroking, aware of her every breath, enjoying the rocking motion of her hips and savouring her pleasured gasps, and later, a long, intense moan as her body stiffened and released. He climbed up and she arched her back as he entered her, rocking and pounding and thrusting. When he came, he rolled onto his side and they lay next to one another, breathing heavily, a sweet collapse. She nuzzled him and whispered, "Stay." Connelly said nothing, but in reply he pulled the covers over the two of them and pulled her close.

✳ ✳ ✳

In the morning, Oriana was up before Connelly. She brought coffee into the bedroom to find him awake, dressed, and sitting on the edge of the bed tying his shoes.

"I'm sorry, but I can't stay long," she said, handing him a cup. "I've got to go and cover the meeting of the Ottawa Transportation Commission, new bus routes. Not exactly thrilling stuff." She kissed him. "You and your spies are much more interesting. How do you want me to contact you after I hear from Privalov?"

"Probably the best thing will be to just phone the office and leave a message. After that, I can phone you here."

"Well, better still, why don't you come over for dinner?"

Shirley Agnew waved a sheet of message paper at Connelly as he entered the office. "I'm so glad I caught you, sir. I just had a call from Superintendent Ferrall. He wants you at a meeting with Assistant Commissioner Murray." She looked at her watch and raised her eyebrows. "The bad news is that the meeting's at ten and its over at National Headquarters in the Nicholson Building. Do you want me to order you a car?"

Connelly was ushered into the assistant commissioner's office to find his boss in the midst of an animated debate as to whether or not Northern Manitoba's trout lakes had better fishing than New Brunswick's Miramichi salmon rivers.

"Declan, thanks for coming. Assistant Commissioner Murray has asked us for an update on your case. I thought you should give it in person."

Smiling, Murray got to his feet and extended his hand to Connelly. "Our paths have never crossed, but I've heard only good things about you. Criminal Intelligence fought me tooth and nail to keep you, and Rory here was insistent that you move to Special Branch. Of course, you know who won. Now, I have to brief a parliamentary committee late this afternoon

113

and I need up-to-date information." He sat down, clasped his hands in front of his chest. "Declan, please, tell me how things are progressing."

"Right, sir," Connelly said. "The short answer is we haven't got a suspect yet, but how about if I start from the beginning?"

"Shoot."

"Shortly after six AM on the ninth of January, a retired Colonel Crawford was walking a large dog in Rockcliffe Park beside the American ambassador's residence. The dog was not on a leash. The dog found a body, frozen and stripped naked, in the bushes at the edge of the property. Crawford saw it, went home, and phoned the RCMP Rockcliffe detachment. Corporal Wilson and Constable Layton went immediately to the scene. They secured the area and radioed in. I arrived around seven. It was evident that the body had been dumped there, and that the murder had taken place somewhere else. I have Corporal Wilson's crime scene sketch with me if you wish to see it, sir."

"No, not just now. Carry on."

"An on-site analysis team came by at close to eight. I have the photographs and their reports. Not much to go on. No reliable footprints in the snow, as the body was dragged over the snow, and the dog and the colonel destroyed any that would have been left by the party that dumped the body. We had our people canvass the area around the ambassador's residence and we brought Colonel Crawford in for a statement, but there are no leads there.

"The autopsy confirmed that the cause of death was a gunshot wound to the head, fired at close quarters. The nature of the wound suggests the murder weapon was probably a medium-calibre pistol. Freezing and thawing left the entrance and exit wounds too ragged to make a precise determination. The body showed evidence of recent torture: burns between the toes. Based on a photo of the corpse, Special Branch subsequently identified the victim as Anatoly Shemyakin, an accredited diplomat at the Soviet embassy. Our identification was corroborated by two Soviet diplomats who viewed the body on the morning of the tenth.

"All efforts to question Soviet embassy personnel have been rebuffed. The Soviets claim diplomatic immunity and at the same time have demanded that a Soviet investigative team be allowed to participate in the investigation. Naturally, we have declined. We did manage to briefly interview Shemyakin's wife, or at least the woman who officially claimed to be married to him. She said that he had travelled to Montreal three days earlier. She flew back to the Soviet Union the day after our interview with her. While she is not at this stage a suspect, she's definitely a person of interest. We have since requested she return for a further interview.

The Soviets have been almost completely uncooperative. They'll take only written questions submitted through their Foreign Affairs contact, and they insist on dealing with the press through Miss Oriana Soroka of the *Tribune*."

"Okay. I've heard of her. Go on."

"At the autopsy I spoke briefly with the first secretary and one of the cultural attachés. They claim that Shemyakin had returned to the embassy on Saturday but left again, and that he was driven to Rideau Street and dropped off to do some shopping. I've had a team from our watchers canvass all the businesses in the area with one of our photographs, and no one has any recollection of Shemyakin going into any stores or restaurants near the area. The man who drove him is a low-level employee who has diplomatic accreditation, but the embassy refuses to let us talk to him. They have, however, provided a written statement confirming what I've just described.

"We've followed up on two leads concerning Shemyakin's recent behaviour. We believe that Shemyakin was probably an agent of Soviet military intelligence. He was primarily tasked with getting technical information about the new Pinetree Line radar system. To that end, he had seduced the wives of two Canadians: one was the wife of a physics professor, and the second was the wife of a senior executive in Canada Radiotech International. We don't believe he's managed to get what he was looking for, but we have, in the course of the investigation, discovered that an American agent using the pseudonym Jay O'Neil was monitoring Shemyakin's efforts and was using the Radiotech International contacts as a means of supplying the Russians with false information. We've had no luck trying to find Mr. Jay O'Neil, although we have been reasonably discreet and not very vigorous in our inquiries, as we want to determine in a later inquiry the full extent of American intelligence and counter-intelligence operations on Canadian soil."

"Sounds like you've been busy, Declan," said Murray. "This is fascinating. For reasons of security, I won't brief this to the parliamentary committee, at least not until you've completed your investigation."

"Thanks, sir," Connelly said, then continued. "As to either of the two husbands whose wives were sleeping with Shemyakin, they're possible suspects, but I think unlikely ones. The professor is on death's door from cancer, and the businessman and his wife have some kind of open marriage. We didn't rule out that it's possible that one of them hired someone else to kill Shemyakin, however. And to tie off that loose end, I've taken the liberty of getting a judicial warrant and had their bank accounts examined. Neither man has had a large or suspicious amount of money withdrawn in the last two years, so I think they remain unlikely suspects. We are at a bit of a standstill in this, although we have had one guy from out in Calgary confess to the murder, but he's confessed to several other high-profile cases in the last couple of years. So, we don't have a prime suspect at this point. Perhaps I should say *suspects* because, given the signs of torture, we can assume that more than one person was involved in this murder."

Connelly looked over at Superintendent Ferrall, who nodded almost imperceptibly. "So, going forward," Connelly continued, "we've enlisted the support of Miss Oriana Soroka. It seems the Soviets liked her first article and have announced that any dealings they have with the press will be first delivered through Miss Soroka."

"So, excuse me here," Murray waved a hand, "you trust this woman? Why do the Soviets like her so much?"

Ferrall jumped in. "Yeah, I think she's legitimate, sir. We've had a quick background check done on her, and there's no reason to believe she had any prior contacts or sympathies with the Soviets. We think they were influenced in their decision by a line in her first article deriding our investigation. She says, and we believe her, that her editor threw it in without her knowledge to spice the piece up. I just wanted to clarify that. Go ahead Declan."

"Right now," Connelly continued, "we're not quite at a dead end in this investigation, but we will be unless we do something to stimulate leads. With the Soviets refusing to be interviewed, we're at a serious disadvantage. So, going forward, we intend to encourage one of the members of their staff to defect, and with any luck we can get a better picture of what the situation was in the embassy before Shemyakin was murdered. Failing that, a defection will at the least provide us with a better understanding of how the Russians operate.

"Now, Miss Soroka has so far helped us in the initial stages of this operation, and I expect to be talking to her later today once she's spoken to the Soviets about her next article."

Murray said nothing for a moment then weighed his next words carefully. "Gentlemen, I'm not going to ask you just how you intend to find a defector. I won't lie or dissemble to the parliamentary committee. I'd rather just say that you are actively pursuing several lines of investigation." He wiped his finger across his lips. "However, I do want assurances from both of you that what you are about to do is legal, and that if whatever you're planning becomes public knowledge at any point, we won't become an international embarrassment."

"Let me speak to that," Ferrall said. "In a nutshell, I can tell you we won't kidnap anybody. We'll keep it legal. We're getting judicial permission to question our target. That will all be above board. Now, I certainly can't vouch for what the Soviets are going to say once we're done, but I guarantee you that they won't like it. They'll scream, have a tantrum, and make all kinds of accusations, but we can't be deterred by that. We intend to play hardball for a change."

Murray nodded and said nothing for a moment. "I suppose at some stage we have to take a bit of a risk if we intend to be a player in this game. I'll leave that one to your good judgment. Just before you go, could I speak privately with your superintendent for a moment, Declan?"

Connelly got to his feet and said, "I'll meet you back at the office, sir."

When the door closed, Murray spoke. "Connelly seems to me to have his act together. That's as succinct a briefing as I've heard in a while. What do you think of him?"

"Connelly's a good officer. I've got a fair degree of trust in his intellect, his energy, his integrity, and his judgment. I think he's got the potential to go much higher. That's why I asked for him to come to Special Branch. He's an unusual officer. He's got a wide range of interests outside of work; he reads a lot, he's self-educated, and he keeps up to date on things. When I interviewed him for the job, it was obvious he'd done a lot of preparation and research. Of all the candidates I interviewed, he was unique that way. Besides, he's probably one of the best interrogation officers I've seen. I think he's got good judgment, especially when it comes to reading people; that's important in this job. He's tactful, and his subordinates trust him. I haven't seen anything so far to make me question his abilities. Why do you ask, sir?"

"I raised the issue because Superintendent Graham seems to be doing his best to get this investigation moved out of Special Branch. I hear he may have the ear of the commissioner and the solicitor general. What's going on there?"

"Same thing as usual. He believes Connelly should have been held responsible for his nephew's death. You're familiar with that story?" Murray nodded. "It's gone a step further; he has a mole in my research section who's reporting to him."

"How do you know that?"

"Sergeant Simard saw one of our constables talking to Graham. Later, we asked him what that was about, and he admitted that Graham had approached him two weeks ago and asked for his cooperation. He said he wanted an informal means of knowing what was going on in some of the key sections in Ottawa. We've since transferred the constable."

"What do you suppose Graham's up to? Do you think he's the one who's fed the Russians the line that the investigation's being handled incompetently?"

"I can't imagine Graham's working for the Soviets, but you never know," Ferrall said. "Maybe there's some kind of connection. It could be a leaker out of the Privy Council Office, but I'd guess that Graham is playing some kind of bureaucratic power game."

Murray tilted his head back and pursed his lips. "Yeah, Graham certainly has his faults, but he's always struck me as being basically loyal, a dutiful officer, hardworking, honest about most things, I think. He's a terrible kiss-ass, though, and that's helped his career because he's not that smart. Whatever he's doing, he's got the ear of some powerful people. Leave this one with me, Rory. I want to get to the bottom of it. Thanks."

✳ ✳ ✳

It was long past lunch when Connelly got back to the office. Apart from a cup of coffee, he hadn't eaten in the last eighteen hours and his head ached. There was a handwritten note written in Shirley Agnew's distinctive green ink on Connelly's desk. 'Call Oriana Soroka — Central-23476.'

Connelly closed the door before calling. Oriana answered on the second ring.

"I'm in the office," she whispered. "I just talked to Privalov. He wants to meet me today. I thought that would be too soon, so I put him off. I said I'm getting a cold and I haven't finished the rewrite. I told him I'll meet him tomorrow at seven PM at the Normandie Soda Bar at 250 Elgin Street. How's that work for you?"

"That's perfect. Go ahead — meet him there. Act as if everything's normal. I'll phone you at home when it's over. It may take a few days until you hear from me, though."

"So I guess you aren't coming tonight?"

"Unfortunately, with this development I can't now. Things are moving fast, and I've got a reconnaissance and a rehearsal to sort out tonight." He lowered his voice. "Oriana, after tomorrow night, if anyone calls you asking after Privalov, tell them that after you talked, you left the restaurant and that's the last you saw of him. It'll be the truth."

"I can do that. Anything else?"

"No. Just be completely natural. We'll take care of the rest. After tomorrow night I'll be busy for a while, but I'll call you in a few days."

Oriana walked to the Normandie Soda Bar from her apartment. The weather forecast called for blizzard conditions overnight. As she walked, the snow began to fall, large lazy flakes drifting downward, blanketing Ottawa's downtown in a muffled serenity. The few cars on the road crawled

118

forward, their headlights penetrating just a few yards into a curtain of driving snow. As Oriana neared the restaurant, she did her best to look nonchalant, deliberately avoiding looking to her right or left. Except for an old man with a cane and an obvious limp, the sidewalks were deserted. Nothing was out of the ordinary. At 6:50 she pulled open the Normandie's glass front door and took a seat in one of the red leatherette booths. The only other customer was a tired-looking man in work clothes sitting on a stool at the counter. She slid out of her coat, took off her hat, and ordered coffee and a hamburger. Privalov came through the door precisely on the hour.

Oriana smiled at him. "I hope you don't mind. I'm starving and I've already ordered."

Privalov pulled off his hat and beat the snow off his coat. "No, no, that is fine. Your Canadian weather reminds me of my home." He grinned. "What is the best thing they have to eat here?"

"Milk shakes and hamburgers, no question about it."

A middle-aged waitress appeared from the back. Privalov looked at her sheepishly and smiled. "I will order the same as my lovely companion. You know, I love this food."

The waitress shoved her pencil into a mass of curly brown hair above her ear, the faintest trace of a cheeky smile showing. "Okay, you've got it."

Privalov was in a breezy mood. With the waitress gone he said, "I have looked forward to meeting with you again. You know, this could be the beginning of a very profitable relationship for both of us."

"I think that's great," Oriana said as she pulled a sheet of paper from her purse. "I've got the revised article you requested." She handed it to him. "Let's not go over this tonight. You can read it when you get home and we can discuss the final draft the next time we meet."

Privalov grinned. "I think that is a wonderful idea."

"I'm sorry, Vitaly, but I can't stay long tonight. I have to finish an article I'm writing on new bus routes. The city's growing faster than the public transportation can handle, and I have to have it in to my editor first thing tomorrow. Can we meet tomorrow, and we can go over the final draft then?"

"Yes. I think that is a wonderful idea, but you know, even more than this, I was thinking that you could write some articles for our newspapers. You know, we are happy to have Western writers in Soviet papers. *Pravda* has a much bigger circulation than any Canadian paper."

"Well, let me think about that one, Vitaly. It sounds like a very good idea, but I have to check my contract with the *Tribune*. I'm not certain if I can moonlight with other newspapers while I work for the *Tribune*."

Privalov looked crestfallen.

"Oh, cheer up, Vitaly. We can probably work something out." Oriana laughed. "I might have to use a nom de plume. Let me think about that tonight, and we'll discuss it tomorrow."

They both made room on the table as the waitress brought their orders. Oriana took a bite of her hamburger and then looked up at Vitaly. "Now, tell me about your home. If we're going to work together, I want to know more about you."

While Privalov shovelled down his hamburger, Oriana kept the conversation light and sparkly, alternately listening intently and complimenting him with the occasional question thrown in. It was obvious he enjoyed the attention. At 7:45 Oriana looked at her watch.

"Oh my God. It's getting late and I still have to get my article written tonight." She sidled out of the booth and grabbed her coat and purse. "Meet me here tomorrow night, same time. Seven PM. We'll talk about *Pravda* then. I've gotta run."

Privalov sputtered, "But Oriana, wait..." What the hell, he thought as he sat back. She was certainly a dynamo. Well, not to worry; he could claim her part of the bill against his expenses. He finished his coffee. At 7:57 he went to the cash register and paid the bill. Standing outside the front door, he noticed that the wind had picked up and the snow was now blowing at an angle. He stopped and pulled up his collar. As he did so, Cormier strolled up to him. The policeman smiled and gestured with an unlit cigarette.

"Excuse me, sir, have you got a light?"

As Privalov lifted his coat and reached into his trouser pocket for his matches, a black Packard sedan pulled up. The rear door opened. Cormier dropped his cigarette and slid in close, hugging Privalov, using his body to lock the Russian's hand below his waist. At the same time, Cormier seized Privalov by the elbow with one hand and gripped him by the neck with the other, squeezing his fingers sharply into the brachial plexus nerves between Privalov's shoulder joint and neck. Privalov was taken completely by surprise; the only noise he made was a shrill inhalation. For a moment, the pain was agonizing; at the same time, the pressure point squeeze caused him to feel temporarily stunned.

Cormier shoved the Russian violently toward the car. Within seconds, Privalov found himself in the back seat, firmly wedged between Cormier and Corporal Russell. The door slammed, the car lurched forward, and Connelly turned about in the front seat and smiled.

"I'm very glad to see you again, Vitaly."

Chapter 12

"THIS IS OUTRAGEOUS. Let me go. You can't do this! Do you know who I am?"

Connelly turned in the front seat. "I know exactly who you are, Vitaly. I also know that when you hear what I have to tell you, you won't be too upset. But I understand that for now you're a bit upset, so just relax and enjoy the ride. No one's going to hurt you. Not now, not tonight, not ever. You're perfectly safe. We are taking you to a cottage not far from here and we are going to have a little chat. If, at the end of our talk, you still want to go back to the embassy, we'll drive you there and drop you off, and you can make a full report to the ambassador as to where you've been and what you've done. For now, though, let's just enjoy the ride on this beautiful snowy night."

Privalov sat back without speaking. He looked closely at the men on either side of him. For a man who had just been abducted on the street, he seemed remarkably cool. Cormier took out a pack of his Player's Navy Cut and offered him a cigarette. Privalov nodded acceptance and took one from the package. He frowned and Cormier helped him light it, indicating a fold-out ashtray in the back of the front bench seat. Privalov took a deep drag and deliberately flicked the ash onto the car floor. Cormier shrugged and smiled agreeably. The two men smoked in silence.

Connelly turned about and saw that Privalov was carefully studying the route they were following. "Don't worry, Vitaly. We'll be heading up past Low Quebec to a beautiful chalet on Lac Beaulieu. I think you'll like it there. I can show you on the map exactly where it is once we get up there. I've rented a place for us to talk. It shouldn't be too cold. The owner tells me there's a magnificent fireplace as well as several cords of dried firewood, so we'll be comfortable even if it gets a lot colder than this."

They crossed into Quebec over the Chaudière Bridge and motored past the thundering cascade of the Chaudière Falls, past the looming pulp and paper mills of Hull Quebec, and north into the frozen woodlands of the Gatineau Hills and the Canadian Shield. The five men in the car sat in near complete silence — except for Connelly, who cheerfully pointed out spots of interest: the frozen log jams on the Gatineau River, a wonderful restaurant at Saint Pierre de Wakefield that was open in the summer, and the tiny hamlet of Brennan Hill, the location of Canada's only tax rebellion. He was an exuberant travelling companion, giving a chatty running commentary on their route, almost as if Privalov was a favourite relative visiting from out of town. Privalov butted his cigarette on the car floor and sat rigid, suspicious, and hostile, studying Connelly like a caged animal.

An hour and a half later they turned off the major highway onto the gravel road leading to Lac Beaulieu. The snowfall had stopped.

"We're in luck, Vitaly," Connelly told him. "The owner of the cottage told me the road was freshly plowed this morning. Almost there."

Privalov peered out at the woods and turned to Cormier. "This is where you will kill me, in this remote area?"

"No," Cormier said. "Inspector Connelly has told you the truth. No one's going to kill you. He'll tell you the rest of his offer once we get to the cottage. You're safe as houses, believe me."

Connelly turned around and nodded. "He's right, Vitaly. We don't do that kind of thing, but you know that. We'll talk in a while."

* * *

The 'cottage' was situated on a wooded bluff overlooking the lake. It was a magnificent building, a cottage in name only, designed more to replicate the extravagant tastes of the region's nineteenth-century lumber barons. The original owner had been a prosperous businessman who had spared no expense in its construction. It was built just a year before the Great Depression, a monument to the precarious banking practices and margin buying of the period. The foundation and chimneys were constructed from locally quarried granite; the rest of the house was made from logs hewn in a D shape and stained a dark green on the exterior. Behind the house was a smaller outbuilding, built from the same materials. It was large enough to house three cars, a generator, and a tool crib. The two buildings were surrounded by old-growth white pines and had the added advantage that they sat isolated on two hundred and seven acres of forest. The nearest building was a quarter of a mile away, on the far side of the lake, and was occupied only in the summer months.

Inside, the building was more luxurious than rustic, furnished with old leather and Oriental carpets. The naturally stained interior walls were decorated with antique wildlife prints. In the salon, the windows on the north wall looked over the frozen lake. Above the fireplace, a massive moose head protruded from a fieldstone wall. A couch, two easy chairs, and a glass-topped walnut coffee table were arranged to provide views of the lake.

Connelly led Privalov into the front entranceway, stamping the snow off his feet as he entered. "So, this will be your home for the next few days, Vitaly, if you choose to stay. I want you to be comfortable. We've managed to get it just for you. I think you'll like it here. Let me take your coat and hat." Privalov ignored him. Connelly took off his own coat and hat and hung them in a small closet by the door. Privalov stood tall, pulled his shoulders back, and looked around the room and at each of the RCMP officers in turn.

"Just put your coat and hat in the closet, then," Connelly said. "My men here will get us a fire going in the fireplace any moment now, and while they do that, I think you and I should have a chat."

Privalov rubbed his hands and looked about him for a second time before taking off his coat. Connelly thought he looked wary and apprehensive, but he was keeping his wits about him.

Connelly walked to the centre of the room and then turned back to Privalov. "You're not a prisoner here, Vitaly. You're free to come and go. In the morning, I'll take you to wherever you want. But in the meantime, we need to talk. Just know that if you choose to bolt from here, it's a long way down the road to the highway, and then you've got a few miles to get to the nearest village. Anyway, I don't think you're going to want to run away, so please, take a seat and I'll get you something to drink. I don't have a big selection, but what's your poison? Scotch or Cognac?"

Privalov sat in one of the armchairs and scratched his head. "This is a very strange kidnapping." For just a second, he permitted himself the faintest of smiles. "I have never heard of this kind of an abduction before. I'll have Scotch, but you must tell me, what is your name?"

Connelly smiled as Cormier went to get Privalov's drink. "Of course. My name is Declan Connelly, and I think you and I will get to know one another quite well over the next few days. We've prepared this splendid cottage for your stay, and I think you're going to be very comfortable with us here." Connelly sat down, utterly relaxed, with both arms outstretched on the back of the couch. "This is without doubt the nicest cottage I've ever been in. It's a bit of a hoax calling it a cottage, isn't it? More like a Tsarist hunting lodge. What do you think? Do you like it? I just love it."

Privalov smiled and raised his eyebrows. "It's certainly nicer than my apartment in Moscow," he said with a laugh, "and the one in Ottawa, too."

"Well, to tell you the truth, it's a lot nicer than my apartment as well, so I intend to enjoy it while we're here."

Cormier handed Privalov a crystal whisky glass with an inch and half of Scotch in it. Privalov took it without a nod. "Will you have anything, boss?" Cormier said.

"I'll have a brandy. Thanks, Marcel."

Cormier went back to the drinks table, picked up a crystal decanter, and poured a measure of cognac into a snifter, then returned and handed the glass to Connelly. Cormier noticed Connelly screw up his face as he sipped his drink.

Privalov sat back in his chair. "So it seems Miss Soroka is working for you?" he said, with just a touch of melancholy in his voice.

"No, unfortunately not," Connelly said. "I can't say she works for us, although I wish she was. We've been watching her closely and we have spoken to her. She knows nothing about what happened tonight after your meeting at the Normandie. She won't know you're missing until it becomes public knowledge, if it ever becomes public knowledge. It's you we've been following," Connelly added with a mysterious smile. "Does Miss Soroka work for you?"

"No, although I have to be honest, Mr. Connelly: like you, I wish she did. I think she sees some of the truth in what we stand for, but I don't think we have got her completely onside yet. Perhaps one day."

"I think she'd be quite a catch for you," Connelly said. "Anyway, Vitaly, before we get too far in this session, let me explain to you the ground rules." He paused to see if Privalov understood what he meant by the term 'ground rules.' The Russian nodded agreement. Connelly was impressed; the man's colloquial English was good.

Connelly put his glass down. "Now Vitaly —" He stopped. "You don't mind that I call you Vitaly? I'm not big on formality."

"No, no — please, go ahead. Vitaly. Yes, Vitaly."

"Wonderful. And you, please call me Declan. Now, Vitaly, as you've probably guessed, I'm going to make you an offer, but we can get to that in a minute. Upstairs, you will have your own room. We have pyjamas, a dressing gown, towels, and a shaving kit laid out for you. We honestly want to make your stay here as comfortable as we possibly can. One of our men will do the cooking for us. We've laid in some really good food, and you and I will just talk for the next few days. But as I said, tomorrow morning, you can decide if you want to stay with us or leave and go back to the embassy. However, in the meantime, I think you should see these." Connelly motioned to Cormier, who pulled out a sheaf of photographs from a briefcase he had beside his chair and handed them to Privalov.

Privalov thumbed through the pictures and handed them back to Cormier. "Okay."

These pictures," Connelly said, "were taken recently, and they show you talking to known officers of the RCMP. We also have photos of you making a brush pass with some of our officers from Corporal Russell's team. I'm sure you know about them, even if you don't know exactly who each one of them is. These photos are going to be handed over to some friends of ours who are in touch with your people."

"So, you think you can blackmail me into working for you?"

"No, not at all. Nothing like that."

"What do you propose?"

"We want you to come over voluntarily to our side. You tell us everything you know about your operation, what you know about Anatoly Shemyakin, and we will give you sanctuary here in Canada."

"You want me to defect, like the traitor Gouzenko?"

Connelly shook his head slowly, smiling tolerantly. "Gouzenko wasn't a traitor. He was a decent man, a rational patriot who didn't want to see the world destroyed in a nuclear war. There's a big difference. Love of one's country, love of Russia and its people are not the same thing as being loyal to Joseph Stalin and the Communist Party of the Soviet Union. In fact, if a Russian truly loves his country, he would be doing his utmost to change the system. Most Russians just aren't in a position to do that, Vitaly, but you are. And you know better than I do that if Joseph Stalin or almost anyone in his murderous hierarchy felt you were in the slightest way an inconvenience for them, or the Party, they'd put a bullet in your head or, if you were lucky, pack you off to a gulag without a second's hesitation."

"What do you think I have to tell you?"

"I guess we're going to find out. If you choose not to tell us anything, we'll just hand you back to the Soviet embassy and you can tell them what happened to you."

"This is not a very sophisticated way of operating. In fact, it's very crude, Mr. Declan. Is this your idea of decent conduct? Despite what you say, what you are doing is blackmail, sending an innocent man to his death." Privalov took a deep sip of his whisky.

"Vitaly, I'm sure you understand the way this game is played better than I do," Connelly said. "After all, you chose this life and these rules. Anyway, I don't want you to make up your mind right away. I want you to think about it. I want us to be civilized about this. In the long run, I think that it will only work if you come over voluntarily."

"It's not quite voluntary, is it? Either I join you, or you put my life in danger." Privalov sipped cautiously at his drink and said nothing for several moments. He looked at his glass. "For all I know, you have already put drugs in my drink."

"No. We don't do that. I don't even know how to do that sort of thing. We don't even have the people on staff to tell us how to do it. We're just not that sophisticated. You've been here long enough to know we don't operate like that. That's a Soviet trick; it's not in our rule book. Besides, we already have you here. Why would we drug you now?"

Privalov snorted. "So that is why you kidnapped me and brought me to a remote location to be interrogated?"

"We didn't kidnap you, Vitaly," Connelly said patiently. "As far as I'm concerned, you've been legally detained for questioning in connection with a murder. We're here to discuss our offer to you. You're not under arrest, and it hardly looks like you're being detained against your will."

"So, can I call a lawyer? Isn't that what your law allows me to do?"

"It does, and if you want, you can call a lawyer tomorrow. In fact, if you want, I'll personally drive you to a lawyer of your choice tomorrow. Whatever you want."

Privalov tilted his head sideways and swirled his whisky. "But I am an accredited diplomat. I have protections against this sort of thing."

"No. You have protections against arrest and prosecution. You have not been arrested and you aren't being prosecuted. Come on, Vitaly. Let's stop quibbling about legalities. Tell me what you know about Anatoly Shemyakin."

"I don't know anything about Shemyakin. I only know he was murdered, probably by your American allies."

"Well, I think you know more than that about him. You worked with him. You knew his wife; you knew a great deal about him. Just tell me what you know."

Privalov tilted his head back. "Anatoly was a good man. He had a wife. He worked hard for peace between our two countries, and someone murdered him. I think it was the Americans."

"The Americans? I thought you told Miss Soroka it was us, the RCMP, that killed Shemyakin. That's what you said, wasn't it?"

Privalov smiled innocently, as if he'd just been caught doing something mischievous but clever. "Yes. I was just looking to see what her reaction was. It was the Americans that killed Anatoly. We know it could not have been the Canadians. You people don't have the nerve to do that. Now, the Americans — they would kill him."

"Why would the Americans want to kill Shemyakin if he was so peaceful?"

"Because, as you know, the Americans — they are arrogant, the new imperialists. Look at them. They have sent an army into Korea, and now you are sending a little brigade to help them." Privalov chuckled. "And I don't have to tell you, the Americans are being badly beaten by the Chinese. In a few weeks, you won't have anywhere to put your brigade." He laughed again and took a sip of his drink. "And why are you being so... so..." He looked exasperated. "...*khanzheskiy*?"

"Smug?"

"Yes." Privalov's eyes narrowed. "So, you do speak Russian, don't you?"

"No. I just took a guess. It was the context." Connelly drained his glass. "You know, Vitaly, maybe the Americans did kill Shemyakin. I don't know. Although I do know it's not how they operate in this country, not here. If the Americans got caught killing someone here, they'd risk losing the support of an important ally. It would be a huge embarrassment. The problem becomes even worse for them if they get caught murdering a foreign diplomat in an allied country. But you and I know that the Soviets aren't above doing that kind of thing when it suits their purposes."

Privalov sniffed. "These are just stories. Disinformation to discredit the Soviet Union. We respect the law. Anatoly was a Soviet citizen. We would not kill him. Why would we kill him? If we were unhappy with him, we would recall him to Moscow. We respect the law."

Connelly rolled his eyes. "That's a good one, Vitaly. We know what being recalled to Moscow means for someone who hasn't performed well, never mind diplomats who fall out of favour. How many Soviet citizens has Stalin executed or worked to death in one of his camps?"

"That is just Western propaganda. Just as you do in the West, some diplomats are recalled for a normal posting, and only a few are brought home because they have not performed to the standard. As for the camps you talk so much about, you have never seen this kind of outrage that you accuse us of."

"No, I haven't, not in Russia. But you know, when I was in the army, at the very end of the last war, I was sent out from my convalescent hospital in Britain. My wounds were pretty much healed, and I could get around with a cane, so they flew me to Holland, to Herzogenbusch. It's a town in the Netherlands, the site of a concentration camp. After that, they sent several hundred of us to Ravensbrück in Germany. I had to be a witness to Nazi atrocities. Eisenhower ordered all the Allies to send large contingents of their officers to view these extermination camps. He was worried that no one would believe such a monstrous and massive operation could have taken place. He was concerned that the world would one day say, just as you do now, 'This was just propaganda.' Millions, *millions* of people systematically murdered. I saw the survivors. I talked to some of them. I saw the camps. I heard their stories. I saw the ovens. I saw the men and women who were so far gone our doctors couldn't save them. Women, children..."

Connelly paused. "You know Vitaly, those were the worst days of my life. I still dream of what I saw in those camps. For me, I think it was worse than anything I saw when I was actually involved in the fighting in Italy. I probably would have had trouble believing it if I hadn't seen those camps with my own eyes. These things are not only possible. They can and do happen when you have a closed and violently authoritarian system. When there is no accountability. They happen when evil men are in control. So, yes, I believe that Joseph Stalin has murdered millions of people. I know that Stalin is evil, and you know something, Vitaly? I know you do, too."

Cormier sat up. "Another drink, boss?"

"Yeah. Thanks, Marcel." He held out his glass, then turned back to Privalov. "So, Vitaly, let's not play games, okay?"

There was a long silence as Cormier took Connelly's glass and refilled it. Connelly took the snifter, sat back, and took a drink. Privalov stared at him, his defiance slipping.

"I'm sorry. I'm being rude," Connelly said. "I see your glass is empty. Will you have another drink?"

Privalov handed his glass to Cormier without speaking.

"So, let's get back to Shemyakin. Someone certainly killed him. And let me tell you, Vitaly, we now know what he was up to. We know about his contacts in Montreal. We just don't know who killed him, and you have to help us."

Cormier handed Privalov a glass with three fingers of Scotch. The Russian snatched it without thanking him and swirled the liquid around in his glass. After a few seconds he took a drink. "Anatoly worked in the field of aviation safety. Yes, he had contacts in Montreal. That was his job, but he did nothing illegal. He wanted peace. He was a good man."

"I'm sure he was a good man. Nobody is disputing that. Why would someone want to kill him, then?"

"I don't know," Privalov muttered.

"No. You know something. You think it was the Americans who killed him. Why do you think that?"

Privalov said nothing. He sipped slowly at his drink.

"Let's stop playing, Vitaly. You know as well as I do what's going to happen to you if we send you back to the embassy."

Privalov looked up. "You tell me that you think Stalin is evil, but you are prepared to send me back to him. Is this your idea of justice, of fairness? If I go back, I will be recalled to Moscow and, as you say, you know what will happen then. That makes you no better than Stalin."

"Those are the rules the Soviets play by, Vitaly. Your leaders made those rules. They're not my rules. Tomorrow morning you can choose to be with us, or you can choose Stalin and the thugs he uses to run his country. If they recall you to Moscow, I know the odds are pretty good that you'll be interrogated, tortured, and shot. But, if you're very lucky and for some reason they decide to believe you, you'll still have been interrogated and tortured, but they likely still won't entirely trust you. They will never use you working abroad again. My guess is that instead, just for good measure, you'll be sent to a gulag, and you'll be worked to death in some godforsaken camp in Siberia where you'll end your days eating nothing but rotten food, freezing all winter, and being sick and tormented by flies and mosquitoes all summer." He looked up at Privalov, who was watching him, stone-faced.

"Perhaps, if they do believe you, but your luck runs out and whoever is interrogating you doesn't like you," Connelly continued, "they'll send you to a mine in the sub-arctic. We both know how those operate. But we haven't put you in that situation, Vitaly. The Soviet government has. So, I'm giving you a reasonable alternative. You can take our generous offer, which guarantees you a comfortable, decent life, or you can turn your nose up at it and go back to the embassy tomorrow and have a very different kind of interrogation back in Moscow in a week or two."

"What will you give me if I defect?"

"We'll give you a new identity. We'll provide security and protect you. We'll give you a nice place to live in a new city, we'll help you train for a new career, and we'll help you find a decent job. Now, do you have a family?"

Privalov looked thoughtful. "Legally, I am married. I have no children." He exhaled heavily. "After the war I married, but after my training I was sent to England, to the British embassy, and after fifteen months in London I came to Ottawa. I have not seen my wife in three and a half years. She has since moved to Gorky. I have not heard a word from her in over two years. I am told she has moved in with a metallurgical engineer." He rested his glass on his knee. His voice dropped. "Everybody knows what she has done. We are no longer a couple, but if I apply for a divorce, I could lose my status in my job. No more overseas postings." He lifted his glass again and took a sip of his whisky. "She won't be in danger and," he raised his head, "I don't give a shit what happens to her."

"I'm sorry to hear that, Vitaly. I know the feeling. That kind of thing can be hard on a man — but it simplifies things for you and for us." Connelly shifted in his seat and collected his thoughts for a second. "Let's start from the beginning here. When did you first meet Shemyakin?"

"I met Shemyakin shortly after I arrived in Ottawa. He had been at the

Ottawa embassy a few more months than me."

"What job was he doing when you met him?"

"He was junior secretary for Science, Technology, and Industrial Trade."

Connelly spoke softly, trying to make his questions sound more conversational. "Who did he work for?"

"He worked directly for the first secretary. We are short-handed. There has been no second secretary for Industry for several years."

"What were his duties?"

Privalov shrugged. "He had many duties. The ambassador and the first secretary were responsible to outline his duties. They did not tell me, and I did not ask. All I know from overhearing a conversation once was that he had something to do with airports and radar. That's all I know. I didn't want to know more." Privalov took a sip of his drink. "You must understand, Mr. Declan, in the Soviet embassy, just as in the rest of Soviet government, you learn soon not to stick your nose into other people's business. Secrecy is important. Working hard on your own file, not showing too much interest in others and their work. These are survival skills. If you try to find out what others are doing in jobs that are sensitive, what their responsibilities are, how successful they are, you will find yourself in serious trouble quickly."

"But you knew he went to Montreal, that he had contacts there?"

"Yes. Sometimes you hear things. The canteen is a very good place to find out what is going on. Drivers who chauffer officers will talk about where they have been. You put two and two together. I can't remember exactly where and when I heard this, but I never talked directly to Anatoly about his job."

"Were you friends with Shemyakin? You're close to the same age."

Privalov chuckled "You think like it was Canada. Of course, I liked Anatoly. I think he liked me, but in the embassy, you have no real friends. You may laugh and share a joke sometimes, but you are never friends."

"Why is that?"

"Do I have to paint a picture for you?"

"No. I want to hear it from you. I want to get a complete sense of what it's like in the embassy. Why do you never have friends in the embassy?"

Privalov looked sideways and ran his free hand through his hair. "Trust. Friendship is based on trust. In the embassy there is no trust, so there are no friends. Instead, there is suspicion. Suspicion creates security. We have security because nobody dares do anything foolish. Everyone suspects everyone else and trusts no one. A friend can denounce you if it serves his purpose, so you have no real friends. We all know that. It can be dangerous for everyone involved if you find out too much about certain activities.

That's all I can say."

"No. It's not all you can say. You have to tell me more, Vitaly. That's the deal. What else do you know about Anatoly Shemyakin? You said you're certain it was the Americans that killed him. Why the Americans? Why not us, or one of the husbands of the wives he was screwing, or one of his contacts in the radar field, or someone in the embassy, for that matter? What aren't you telling me? This is important, Vitaly."

Privalov swallowed hard and drained his drink. "This is very new for me." He licked his lips.

"Of course it is. You're doing fine," Connelly said. "We're not here to see you fail, Vitaly. This is not a test. You are just providing us information. We're on the same side now. You have to believe that. So, let me ask you again, what more do you know about Shemyakin?"

"I know that the first secretary was worried for his safety. I came into a meeting once, in one of the meeting rooms on the second floor. I was to brief the ambassador and I heard the first secretary say he was worried for Anatoly's safety. That's all I heard, and they were angry with me for coming in unannounced. I left and waited a long distance away in the hallway until they were finished. That's all I know." He shrugged.

"So, what makes you think the Americans killed him?"

"Who else would kill him. Like you, I read the papers. That's part of my job. I know about the new radar system being set up across Canada and Alaska. Anatoly was working in the field of radars." He shrugged.

"So, you didn't believe that he was just a commercial and scientific attaché? There was more to his job than that?"

"Officially, we all believe what we are told, Mr. Declan. Believing what your superiors say is also a survival skill. No, I knew that Anatoly was being successful in his work. You could tell by the way the first secretary and ambassador talked to him. He became their pet in the last few weeks. They laughed and joked with him. They never do that with any others, and they never did that before. Suddenly he became someone they liked. It was very obvious. Now, if the ambassador and first secretary liked Shemyakin, why would they have him killed? You want my theory on this murder?"

Connelly nodded.

"I think Shemyakin was also working for the Americans, and they caught him. I think he was what you call a triple agent. He was working for us, and the Americans thought he was working for them, but all the time he was feeding them false information. That is my theory. Shemyakin was the ambassador's pet; he would never kill him. Shemyakin was his golden goose. But the Americans, they would kill him because I think he betrayed them. That is my theory."

"What evidence do you have to prove this?"

"None. I don't have a photograph or a letter or papers, but I know my people. I know how the embassy works. If Shemyakin was a traitor they would have sent him back to Moscow. They would make up an excuse, and he would go, and they would get the truth out of him in Moscow. They always do. You know that. That would be much easier — no risk. No, the ambassador and first secretary liked Shemyakin because he made them look good."

"Did Shemyakin speak to you at all about where he was going, who he was seeing, what he was doing?"

"No." Privalov smiled. "The only thing he told me was that in his job he had the opportunity to fuck some Western women. He could be very crude. That was not something I would have told anyone if I was Anatoly. The Communist Party of the Soviet Union can be very..." Privalov hesitated. "What is the word you use?" He took another long drink. "Puritan, that is it. Officially, the Party does not like people screwing around, you know. It's very bad, very... puritan, but it could also get him in trouble and be a big risk for his job here."

"When did he tell you this?"

"Oh, three months ago, I think. Yes, it was before the winter."

"Did he say who these women were?"

"No, he mentioned this once in the canteen. We had a party. He was drinking heavily. When he realized he was letting things slip, he became very quiet."

"Tell me, Vitaly, what did the members of the embassy do for relaxation? You can't work all the time. Very few of you are allowed to go out. What exactly do you do when you aren't doing your duties?"

"It is very boring most of the time. From time to time we have parties. They are drinking parties, like what you call a happy hour. They are also very dangerous, because most people get very drunk. Drinking is always heavy. It's like being in a job in the north. After work, people drink. People drink, they get drunk, and they go home to sleep."

"Why is it dangerous?"

"Because not everybody gets drunk. The counter-intelligence officer is always listening to hear if anyone slips up and says what they aren't supposed to talk about."

"Who is the counter-intelligence officer?"

"The embassy always has one man responsible for security. Six weeks ago, it was Vladimir Romankov. He was listed as a radio technician, but his real job was embassy counter-intelligence officer. He got a promotion and he has not been replaced."

"If you don't know what other people did in their day-to-day duties, how do you know who the counter-intelligence officer was?"

"Everybody knows the counter-intelligence officer. He is the third most important man in the embassy. The counter-intelligence officer is responsible for all aspects of security. He personally reviews all your contacts, looks at your paperwork, discusses your attitude. The counter-intelligence officer can go anywhere in the embassy and speak to anyone. The only other man to do that is the ambassador."

Privalov looked at his watch and smiled. "You know, I was supposed to check in with the duty officer an hour ago. When we return from going out, we have to check in with the duty officer, and later we write a short report: the purpose of our trip, who we met, where we went, who we talked to, what was said. Before, the counter-intelligence officer would read these reports and often would interview you after if there was something in it that interested him. You always felt guilty when you talked to the counter-intelligence officer. He was a man who frightened people, and he liked that. He liked people to be scared. It gave him power. Romankov never smiled, and he had a gold tooth that made him look like a rich *kulak*. I'm glad for the others that Romankov is gone, but they will replace him with another just like him. It's how our system works." He smiled thoughtfully. "By now, the duty officer will have phoned the first secretary and told him I have not returned."

"So, you would have had to go to the embassy and write a report tonight?"

"No. Romankov changed the process. He was a smart man. He made some things simpler, but he was still a tyrant. If I was out late, I could just phone and let them know I was back at my apartment." Privalov laughed. "It was one of the only sensible things he did. We know you are probably listening to our phone calls, so we would just ask for Alexander Siskin. Several years ago, Siskin was the first secretary's assistant. He is no longer with the embassy, so the duty operator would tell us, 'Alexander Siskin is not available. Phone back in the morning.' That was code for 'Everything is fine,' and my report would follow in the morning.

"Many times, the duty officer will send someone, usually one of the drivers, to your apartment to check on you. You never know whether they are coming or not. They go around to your flat, wake you up to ensure you have not just phoned in from somewhere else. If you are caught lying..." He snorted. "I don't know anyone foolish enough to lie about that kind of thing. Nobody is that stupid." Privalov smirked. "If I don't report in tonight, someone will be knocking on my door in the next hour or two."

"Well, even if you wanted to, you can't phone from here, so I guess the duty officer's going to raise the alarm tonight."

Privalov held out his glass for Cormier to fill. "You don't understand about Soviet Union and Russia, do you?"

Connelly nodded faintly at Cormier, approving Privalov's request. "What exactly are you getting at, Vitaly?"

"There are things wrong with my country, yes, of course, but it is my country. There are things wrong with every country, but I owe Russia and the Soviet Union my loyalty. I don't think you understand that. You don't understand loyalty. You don't understand why we love the Rodina," he said, using the familiar term for the Motherland. "You don't understand what we have been through. You don't understand the sacrifices we have made for the Motherland. For us, this loyalty is very real. It's something that is in our blood. We are building socialism. We have suffered more than you can imagine, Mr. Declan. You in the West, you don't appreciate that. You take things for granted; you think everyone wants to be like you. You think everyone thinks like you. You don't understand."

"What don't we understand, Vitaly? We fought as your ally in the war. We suffered too. I served for more than five years in the army. I was wounded. What don't I understand?"

"I don't want to tell you that your service does not count for anything, Mr. Declan, but your country has no idea what we have suffered. Not just Canada — America, England, even France. None of them suffered like the Soviet Union."

Connelly was tight lipped. He thought Privalov might be getting a little drunk, but he still had his wits about him.

"We lost over twenty million people, twenty million souls," Privalov looked anguished. "Your entire country is not even close to being that big. You don't have anywhere near that many people! We lost more people than all the Allies and the Germans combined. Our people won the war, not the West. You invaded France only when the Red Army had pushed the Germans completely out of Russia. By the time you came to France, we were pushing the Germans back through Poland. I was there! We were alone. We faced most of the German Army for almost the whole war! It was our soldiers who died in their millions defeating the Nazis." Privalov was close to shouting now. "We won the war, and you are asking me to turn my back on that sacrifice? Is that what you want?"

"No." Connelly spoke softly. "Nobody disputes the sacrifices made by the Russian people. But for the record, the Allies were able to invade the mainland only when they knew an invasion would be successful; and prior to that, without our aerial campaign, Hitler would have been much stronger and he would have overrun Russia. You seem to forget that, Vitaly. You also forget that you didn't join the war until two years after we did.

Stalin had a non-aggression pact with Hitler and refused to provide any assistance whatsoever to the Allies for the first two years of the war."

Connelly paused. "But I do agree that if those deaths, those millions of Soviet deaths, mean anything, Vitaly, your countrymen died fighting against one of the cruellest and most tyrannical regimes in history. You know that. You saw that, and so did I. Despotism and repression like that had to be destroyed. Hitler and the Nazis were the worst kind of barbarians — but Stalinism is only different in the details. Hitler killed millions of people because of their race or their religion. Stalin's killed millions of people because he's afraid they threatened his position as leader, they threatened his ideology. You know that." He paused again. "You know that Stalin has killed millions, *millions* of his own people. You've lived through that. You've seen these things for yourself. Stalin continues to rule through terror. People across the Soviet Union fear for their lives. You fear for your life. You've already described it for me in your own embassy. Normal people don't live like that, but it's how your system runs. It's different here. You've seen our elections. They're not perfect. God knows, many of our leaders are foolish or corrupt, or both, but we're free. We can get rid of them in an election. People here can choose their own government; they can write and speak freely without having the secret police knock on their doors at night. Someday, Russia and all the countries the Soviet Union occupies will be free. That's a long way off, but it will only happen when people like you act courageously against the system, when people like you love their country enough to do something to change it. If you work with us, you'll be one of those people, Vitaly. You will be a patriot."

Privalov said nothing, and Connelly wondered if he had overplayed his hand. The two sat in silence for a moment, then Privalov frowned and raised his eyebrows. He finished his glass.

"Maybe... I think you could be right." He stifled a yawn. "This has been a long day, Mr. Declan, and you have given me many things that I have to think about. I will have to give you my answer in the morning."

"Absolutely. Take your time, Vitaly. Think about it. If you choose to stay with us, we can talk about where you can go and what you'll do. If you choose to go back to the embassy, we'll have breakfast together in the morning and then I'll drive you back. I hope for your sake and for the good of Russia you choose to join us." Connelly smiled. "One thing. Don't be alarmed, but there will be one of my men outside your door all night. Just in case you need anything. Now, is there anything else you need before you go to bed?"

"Yes." Privalov turned to Cormier and shook his glass at him. "Give me what is left in that bottle of Scotch."

Chapter 13

CORMIER SHOWED PRIVALOV UPSTAIRS to his room and came back downstairs. He found Connelly standing in front of the shelves in the library alcove, peering at a book.

Cormier chuckled. "See anything you want to read, sir? You can take it right up with you to bed. This place is well furnished."

Connelly closed the book with a snap. "Whoever owned this house certainly bought a lot of books twenty years ago. Looks to me like he has every best-seller from about 1931 or so onwards." He put the book back on the shelf. "Funny thing, though — I don't see anything written after the beginning of the war. How'd you find this place on such short notice anyway?"

"I've been in Ottawa for a few years, sir. I got to know quite a few people on various cases. I ran into the owner during a smuggling case. Employees of one of his companies were involved in jewellery smuggling between Canada and the States. The owner was totally innocent. Anyway, I got to know him, as I'd been up here a couple of times a few years back. His son died in Bomber Command early in the war. That might explain why the books end where they do. Poor guy lost interest in just about everything after that. I'd heard he's living in town now and this place was empty. I contacted him, told him we needed it ASAP, and just like that he let me borrow it. When he gave me the keys, he told me he's gonna sell it."

Connelly nodded. "You did a superb job tonight, Marcel. How do you think things are going?"

"Overall, I think it went well. I'll have to talk to Corporal Russell. He's still in the basement fiddling with the tape recorder. I don't think there will be any problems there. The snatch from the restaurant went well." Cormier sat himself down in the chair by the library table. "Apart from that, though, I don't like Privalov. He's an officious, sneaky prick. I hope that didn't show, but did you see how he treated me? Like I was a serf. I guess the officer class treat the troops like dirt in the worker's paradise." He shook his head wryly. "Apart from my personal feelings about the guy, I'm not certain that I've got a strong take on him. I can't exactly figure out when he's telling the truth and when he's not, what his intentions are. I don't know. I'll be interested in what he has to say tomorrow. I thought he seemed pretty interested in what you were saying about a new life in Canada. He certainly perked up at that. I was doing my best to read his reactions as you talked to him, but to be honest, I couldn't get a sense of what he was thinking when you made an appeal to his higher loyalties. From what I can see from his personality, I don't think he's any kind of an idealist." Cormier tilted his head. "Yeah, he may be playing us for time. But that doesn't mean he's not genuinely interested in escaping and getting a new life. I wouldn't be surprised if we discover that he's a greedy, selfish little bugger. The one point that I'm certain of, and that came across loud and clear, was that he was telling the truth about his wife. No love lost there."

"What about Shemyakin?"

Cormier shrugged. "Yeah, unfortunately I'd hoped for more, but I think he told us what he knew. I don't know. Hard to read him on that one. He doesn't seem to know a helluva lot on that subject. It sounds like Shemyakin made some progress in getting information about the new radar line, and that accounted for his popularity with the ambassador. That makes sense, but Privalov is guessing it was the Americans who killed him." Cormier looked tired. "I suppose that was predictable. It's not much to go on, but it's more than anything we had before."

He yawned and rubbed his face. "Been a long day. I thought he seemed convincing enough when he was talking about the system in the embassy. We've assumed all along that life there is pretty strained. He's given us a better idea about that now, but things sound worse there than we suspected. No, if I was a betting man, I'd say that tomorrow he's going to come over to our side and try and dicker for the best deal he can get. My guess is that right now he's lying in his bed, three-quarters pissed, and can't believe his good fortune, but he's no idealist, sir. He'll go for the money, a new house in a new suburb, a car, and a new job. I don't think your pitch to honour and duty carried a hell of a lot of weight with that guy. That's just my guess."

Connelly chuckled. "Talking about getting pissed, that was really well done. I didn't expect the tea. It was a weird sensation. When you handed me my drink, I was expecting brandy. I took a sip and almost spit it out. I didn't see that one coming. I was worried I'd have to go into a drinking contest with a Russian."

"Yeah. Sorry about that, boss. I meant to tell you beforehand. I didn't know if this guy was one of those legendary Russian drinkers. But don't thank me, sir." Cormier chuckled. "I can't take credit for it. Again, that was Corporal Russell's idea when we came up here this afternoon. He showed me how to do it. He told me that, as a kid, he used to be an underage bartender at an expensive private golf club in Vancouver. He used to do that for businessmen trying to close deals. They'd give him the nod beforehand, and Russell would ply the guests with stiff drinks while the club member who was trying to close a deal swilled tea all night. He made great tips on those nights." Cormier grinned. "It's a good thing Russell works for us, sir. He'd be a fucking good criminal otherwise."

Connelly nodded his head. "I suppose you're right."

"Tell me one thing, sir?"

"What's that?"

"You said this operation was entirely legitimate. You told Privalov that for this questioning, he wasn't covered by his diplomatic status."

"I did."

"That's bullshit, right, sir? None of this is legal?"

"Not entirely. I've got judicial approval to question Privalov."

"So, what happens if this all goes on its head? What if tomorrow Privalov goes back to the embassy and they complain, or later on someone discovers you've run this operation without seeking higher approval?"

Connelly shrugged. "Yeah. I've thought about that. It's true, it's a gamble. It's true we picked up Privalov for questioning. I'd make the case that he came with us willingly and that he hasn't been forcibly restrained. He came here and remained here of his own free will. I know that's pretty thin, but we do have a court warrant to question him. If anyone pushed us on that, it may or may not hold up in court. I know — I'm gambling, but if he chooses to defect like I think he will, all that problem goes away." Connelly rubbed his fingers across his lips. "If he doesn't, we'll say that he was negotiating his defection and he returned to the embassy, which will also be true. The worst case is that nobody believes any of this, so if that happens, I guess the superintendent and I could be facing a formal disciplinary hearing." Connelly smiled. "On the other hand, if we're successful, we'll find out something about the Shemyakin murder, we'll find out what's going on in our own backyard, and we'll have given Special Branch the credibility it needs to do its job in Canada and with our allies."

"Yeah, that may be true, boss, but you're sticking your neck out." Cormier lit a cigarette. "You know that if this works out like you hope, neither you nor Superintendent Ferrall will get any fucking credit for it, but if it goes wrong, you'll be thrown to the wolves."

"I know." Connelly said nothing for a moment. "Neither Ferrall nor I took this risk to move our careers ahead. It was what had to be done. We were getting nowhere. If we did nothing, if we remained obedient little bureaucrats, we'd all end up looking like incompetents. If that happened, the country would hand over a key aspect of its security, probably to the Americans. I personally don't want J. Edgar Hoover running our counter-intelligence service, so we might have bent a few rules. We'll have to see what Privalov has to say in the morning."

* * *

By eleven that night, Colonel Yevgeny Tarabin and Major Georgy Shubenkov arrived at the Soviet embassy. The two men were MGB counter-intelligence officers from the First Main Directorate, working undercover at the new United Nations temporary headquarters on Long Island in New York. Both Tarabin and Shubenkov had served in the NKVD during the war. They rarely indulged in small talk and smiled even less.

Ambassador Glinin knew the two men by reputation and rose from his desk to greet them. The two MGB investigators terrified him. He took a deep breath and leaned into his cane. He lifted his chin and did his best to look composed. Neither of the MGB officers shook hands with Glinin.

Tarabin was here as the Soviet mission's chief accounting officer, and Shubenkov was listed as his senior bookkeeper. Tarabin, with a perpetually downturned mouth and sharp, intelligent black eyes, was fifty years old, round faced, and balding. It was rumoured in New York that Tarabin had been decorated for his role in eliminating the more prosperous kulak farmers in the late 1930s, and during the war he had been one of the officers involved in the identification and elimination of thousands of Polish officers in the Katyn Forest massacre.

Shubenkov was fifteen years Tarabin's junior: six foot four, powerfully built, with a brush cut. Shubenkov was an enigma in his profession. He was a man of numerous talents. Before the war he had trained as a classical violinist. In addition to being talented, he was also lucky, and had managed to secure one of the few positions available in the Leningrad Conservatory. In 1935, at the age of twenty, Shubenkov had made an abrupt career change. On a beautiful, sunny April morning, he walked into the local militia station and filed a statement that he had overheard Veniamin Buchstein, the music conservatory's director, criticizing the Soviet state. Shubenkov's signed testimony stated that his musical mentor was a counter-revolutionary and an anti-Soviet Trotskyite. Buchstein was arrested the next day and within a year died of diphtheria at one of the numbered labour camps on the Kolyma River. The elderly musician was just one of 18 million Soviet citizens to be sentenced to hard labour in one of the gulags. For Shubenkov, the denunciation was a good move; that week, he was accepted as an NKVD candidate.

Glinin did his best not to stare at Shubenkov. For some reason the younger officer frightened him more than the colonel.

Tarabin was the first to speak. "Mr. Ambassador, you know why we have come here. We will need a private office, twenty-four-hour access to your secure radio communications, and a car and driver. You will ensure that we have confidential access to all embassy staff for interviews as may be necessary — and let me be very clear: we expect the complete cooperation of everyone in your embassy. I will hold you, Comrade Ambassador, personally responsible for ensuring that our enquiry goes well. We will sleep and take our meals here in the embassy. Do you have any questions?"

Glinin gave him an unconvincing half-smile. Technically, as an ambassador he was superior in rank to Tarabin. In well-established practice, however, these senior MGB officers wielded the power of life or death over just about everyone. They were men to be avoided. Glinin took a deep breath and willed himself to speak slowly and deliberately.

"I have no questions at all, Colonel, but I want to say that I appreciate your assistance in this matter. We have had no success in finding out what happened to Comrade Shemyakin, so I am grateful for whatever experience and insight you can bring to bear on the problem." Glinin swallowed hard, desperate to project a positive image; his self-assurance was paper thin. "Colonel, in the event that you want to interview one of the embassy staff tonight, I have ordered all officers to be present and standing by their work areas." The ambassador forced a smile, hoping that the two counter-intelligence officers wanted to sleep instead. Everyone had shown up just as ordered, except Privalov. Where was that little shit?

✳ ✳ ✳

The first rays of the morning sun were turning the fresh fallen snow on the lake a pale pink. In the kitchen, Cormier looked out the window and turned to Connelly.

"Red sky at morning, sailors take warning. Do you believe in omens, boss?"

"Nope. I believe in fate, Marcel." Connelly put his coffee cup down. "I talked to Russell a few minutes ago. The tapes are good quality, so that's good news. After that, I went up to see Privalov. He's awake, shaved, and showered. The bastard's finished off that entire bottle of Scotch and looks none the worse for it. He must have a tremendous tolerance for the stuff.

I could never do it." He raised his finger in warning and cocked his head sideways. "Hear that? That's him on the stairs."

The watcher who had stood the last shift of the night outside Privalov's room followed him downstairs. The Russian looked refreshed and cheerful as he was led to breakfast in the dining room. Connelly joined them.

"Good morning, Vitaly. I trust you had a good night's rest. Nothing to disturb you?"

"No, no. I slept well, Mr. Declan. And this morning you will want me to give you my decision as to whether or not I stay or join you, yes?"

"There's no rush, Vitaly. We'll discuss business after we eat." Connelly motioned toward the table. Laid out before them on the sideboard were hot plates of bacon and eggs, fried tomatoes, hash browns, sausages, and toast. Urns of coffee and tea waited beside them.

Privalov smiled. "You know we don't have such breakfasts usually in the Soviet Union."

"No?" Connelly said. "When you were in Russia, what did you normally eat for breakfast?"

"I don't normally eat breakfast, maybe just a cup of tea with sugar, but most people eat porridge and jam, some bread and tea and maybe a couple of times a week a boiled egg. You see, unlike you, our most productive farms were all destroyed during the war. We have not recovered. It will take years. Times are still very hard. Food is still rationed. It is nothing like this."

"Well, if you make the right decision this morning," Connelly smiled, "you can eat better for the rest of your life." He pointed to the window. "I hear on the news that we're going to get some more snow blowing in from the Northwest later this morning."

The two men helped themselves to food and drink and carried their plates and cups to the table. Like strangers sharing their morning meal in a tourist home, they chatted about the weather and sports while they ate. Privalov was a well-informed fan of the Montreal Canadiens. He had been to the Forum in Montreal twice and considered Maurice Richard the best player in history. He listened to as many games as he could on the radio and was delighted every time the Canadiens beat one of the American teams.

"Hockey is a good game." He beamed. "You know, in Russia we are playing Canadian hockey now. We train harder than your athletes. In a few years, our Russian teams will beat you."

"Oh, I don't know about that," said Connelly affably. Despite the seemingly cheerful conversation there was a peculiar sense of anxiety in their exchange, as if both men were desperate to fill their time at breakfast with lively inanities.

When Privalov had finished eating, Connelly picked up his coffee cup and said, "Let's take our coffee and tea into the salon, shall we, Vitaly? We've got things to discuss."

In the salon, Cormier was already seated in his armchair. Privalov and Connelly took their places from last night. Privalov's jauntiness had vanished.

"So," said Connelly, "we have an important decision to make this morning. Shall we get on with it?"

* * *

Colonel Tarabin did not interview anyone the night he arrived. After he was shown his room, he said, "I'll start my interviews in the morning. I'm going to get some sleep now, Comrade Ambassador. I expect all members of the embassy to be present and available for questioning by zero-eight-hundred hours tomorrow. Have them standing by. Oh, and one other thing: the office you have provided for me. It is unsuitable. I want a bigger office, one that I know has been swept for listening devices in the last week. You can vacate yours and move in with the first secretary."

At twenty to eight the next morning, Tarabin and Shubenkov were deep in conversation in the ambassador's office. Glinin knocked delicately on the door frame.

"Is everything to your satisfaction, Comrade Colonel? You may have the use of my secretary as you wish, and I can have tea sent to you while you work." The pain in his legs forced Glinin to lean into his cane to stand straight.

Tarabin stared blankly at him for several seconds. "Comrade Ambassador, get me the nominal roll for the embassy staff and the duty officers' log book for the last three weeks. I also need the internal number to phone the duty officer. When I want something or someone, I'll call him. I want you to come back in fifteen minutes for the first interview." He turned abruptly toward Shubenkov and nodded. The major handed him a sheet of paper and whispered something inaudible. Tarabin scanned the document, deliberately ignoring the ambassador.

* * *

Five minutes before his appointment with Tarabin, Glinin leaned against the sink in the washroom on the embassy's second floor. He'd skipped breakfast. In fact, he hadn't slept much last night either, and at six this

142

morning he had thrown up. There was nothing left in his stomach. His mouth and throat were dry. He was shaky, his pulse was racing, and he had a hard time focusing his thoughts. He cupped his hands at the sink and took a drink of cold water. He looked in the mirror and straightened his tie. His legs ached, but he forced himself to stand straight. His face showed the strain. There were black circles under his eyes. He knew if he was to survive this coming ordeal, he shouldn't look so upset. He had done nothing wrong. If he played his hand properly, he should be exonerated. But getting control of himself was the problem.

Looking in the mirror, he saw a man he barely knew. Not so long ago, he had been a man of authority, somebody to be reckoned with and feared. He had been a good soldier. He had been awarded the Order of Suvorov and had survived the heavy fighting from the Demyansk Pocket outside Leningrad, and then fought all the way to Prague. He studied the black circles under his eyes and his pallid complexion. Where was the courageous Political Commissar from the Great Patriotic War?

Glinin had come to think of his years in the Great Patriotic War as the highwater mark of his life. He had joined the army as a Party member and soon found himself a senior lieutenant. He had fought his first battle in command of a company of half-trained infantry in the 139th Rifle Division. Back then, he had distinguished himself as a junior officer in the brutal fighting south of Moscow. The casualties in his unit had been horrific, and during the battles for Moscow he was promoted to command a battalion. Within a month, that appointment and his battalion came to a bloody and painful end. Leading a night attack in a wooded area south of Cholm, he was stitched by machine gun fire in both legs. But even back then, he hadn't experienced anxiety and fear like he did today.

Glinin took a deep breath. He wasn't a coward. He understood fear — he'd seen and overcome enough of it. While he was recuperating from his wounds, he was awarded the Medal of Courage for defending the Socialist Motherland. Once out of hospital, he was transferred to a senior staff job coordinating the distribution of equipment and the training and movement of newly raised Siberian divisions as they moved to the front. As a staff officer, Glinin's talents shone. In addition to his obvious analytical abilities and unquenchable enthusiasm, he was meticulous, determined, and utterly cold-blooded. He possessed one of the most important qualities of a Soviet commander: he never had misgivings about saying no to desperate men.

In early 1943, he was awarded the Medal for Battle Merit for his efforts in coordinating scarce resources in support of the 7th Army's winter campaign. Later that year, in part because of his Communist Party connections and in spite of his pronounced limp, he was transferred to duties as a regimental commissar.

He had ended the war as a divisional commissar in the 254th Motor Rifle Division. The 254th was a ministry of the Interior Division, one that was frequently tasked with eliminating the flow of deserters behind Soviet lines. Glinin's duties, among other things, had included two steady years of presiding over the division's standing courts martial.

Discipline in the Soviet Army was vicious and unforgiving. None of Glinin's trials ever lasted over five minutes. He had long since lost count of the number of men he had sentenced to death for being stragglers, or for not carrying out their orders with sufficient alacrity. Now, he was about to be standing on the other side of the prosecuting officer's desk, and he was in no doubt as to the mindset of the two MGB officers sent from New York.

* * *

While Glinin was preparing for his meeting with the MGB investigators, across the city in the RCMP headquarters building, Superintendent Wallace Graham was standing outside Assistant Commissioner Murray's office door.

"Wallace, come on in, please." Murray forced a thin smile. "Have a seat."

"Thanks, sir. What can I do for you?"

"Thanks for coming, Wallace. I just wanted to talk about a few things. As you know," Murray waved his hand nonchalantly, "I'm responsible for quite a mixed bag of organizations: your job in staffing the Privy Council, Special Branch, Criminal Intelligence, Interpol activity, all the exchange and liaison with friendly nations, that kind of thing." Murray sat back and folded his arms. "I just like to keep abreast of what's going on in each of these sections, find out what my folks are up to." He smiled. "How are you finding things these days?"

"Fine, sir. No complaints."

"Great. How's your wife doing? I know you're one of these guys who isn't afraid of putting in a few extra hours."

Graham shifted in his seat. "She's fine, sir. No problems."

"Perfect. Okay, then. I won't beat around the bush. I do have one question, then, that I've got to ask you, Wallace. What's your interest in Special Branch activities?"

Graham's jaw pushed out. "Nothing out of the ordinary, sir. Why do you ask?"

Murray gave a noncommittal nod. "Okay. Have you met with or discussed Special Branch activities with anyone?"

Graham sat up and took a deep breath. "No, nobody that I can think

144

of that's out of the ordinary."

Murray's face remained impassive. "Interesting. And who would the ordinary people be who you discussed Special Branch activities with?"

"I have to talk to a number of people about RCMP activities, sir. I don't understand. Is there some kind of problem?"

Murray smiled. "Come on now, Wallace. We're both trained in the art of questioning. Let's not shift the focus of the question. Who've you been talking to?"

"Well, Kenneth MacBride, the parliamentary secretary for the solicitor general. There was an aide there from Foreign Affairs as well." Graham shrugged. "I was called in to a meeting with them. Superintendent Ferrall was there too. There's been a lot of interest in the Shemyakin case."

"Okay. Anyone else?"

Graham shook his head. "No, not really."

"What about Constable Murphy? Until a few days ago he used to work in Special Branch."

Graham raised his eyebrows. "Yeah. I spoke to him a while back. Ran into him in a coffee shop. We didn't discuss his work. I think he used to be a friend of my nephew, the officer who died on Inspector Connelly's watch."

"Okay." Murray lowered his voice. "Actually, I've had someone speak to Constable Murphy. He said your meeting was planned. You phoned him, said it was part of an internal investigation, and you queried him on the files being run by Special Branch. By the way, Murphy never served with your nephew and they're from different parts of the country, so they probably never met, and it's unlikely that they were friends." He paused. "What's going on?"

Graham licked his lips. "Look, sir, I've just been doing my job to the best of my ability. I'm under a lot of pressure to provide timely information at the political level. I've never done anything to jeopardize or compromise an ongoing investigation." He shrugged. "I have to know what's going on across the country, and Ferrall's not providing me any information. He's playing the hush-hush secret agent game for all it's worth. I get a lot of requests for information, and Murphy's mistaken. I never asked him about the Shemyakin case."

Murray narrowed his eyes. "Why do you mention the Shemyakin case? I haven't said anything about that. We have several other files on the go in Special Branch. In fact, Murphy says that the Shemyakin case was precisely what you were interested in."

"That's just not true, sir. This sounds to me like Ferrall's gotten to him. Ferrall knows I didn't want Connelly sent to Special Branch, yet he disregarded my advice. Now look at the mess you've got." Graham rubbed his hand across his mouth and pursed his lips. "Sir, the file's a complete dog's breakfast, and I've been running top cover for him with the politicians."

"What do you mean, the file's a mess? What is it that has you so worried about this case?"

"This is a very high-profile case, sir. A murdered Soviet diplomat. I think that's pretty important."

"It is. That's why I have Special Branch handling it." Murray waved his hand. "But you know that. My concern is, why are you taking a special interest in it? That's well beyond the scope of your responsibilities. You know we've been under pressure from the government to hand the case over to one of the larger intelligence services of our allies. Both the Americans and the Brits are saying the same thing, that we should hand this over to a larger more experienced service. Somehow, they're getting inside information on our handling of this case. So, let me be blunt: who have you talked to about this case?"

"Like I said, sir, the parliamentary secretary. He could have talked to someone."

"He could have, but I don't think so." Murray tilted his head to one side. "The parliamentary secretary — I spoke to him, and he doesn't share your concern about Connelly. In fact, from what he's seen, he thinks Connelly's exactly the man for the job. I think the Brits and Americans are getting whatever information they have on this case from somewhere outside of official channels, because none of the routine reports we've passed on to them has breathed a word of concern about the quality of the investigation. So, where do you suppose they're getting their intelligence?"

"I don't know, sir."

"Let me get back to your meeting with Constable Murphy. Why did you decide you had to meet him?"

"Sir, I met Murphy because I thought Connelly and Ferrall weren't holding up their end of things. Murphy couldn't tell me much anyway, and I didn't pass on any information that I got from him to anybody." Graham's face was flushed now, and his hands were clenched.

Murray spoke barely above a whisper. "Superintendent Graham, you don't ever assess the performance of any of the officers in the other sections in my command. That's not your job. You have no responsibility or obligation to report on the performance of the RCMP. Your job is to deliver impartially the relevant news and information to the Privy Council Office. I'm going to end this interview — for now. But understand something: from what you've told me today, I've got serious doubts about your fitness for your job. So, if you want to keep your head on your shoulders, speak to no one about this meeting and keep your nose out of Special Branch activities. Now, close the door on your way out."

A few minutes after Graham left, Murray dialled Ferrall's number. "Any news on last night's activity?"

"From what I've heard, it went well, sir. I don't have anything specific beyond that just now, but as soon as I do, I'll come over and brief you."

"Good. Thanks." Murray hung up. He ran his fingers through his hair and lit a cigarette. He remembered sitting here at this desk two years ago when he'd taken over the job. At the time, he'd thought that the counter-intelligence business wouldn't be much different from police work. He smiled. He'd been so innocent back then.

* * *

Privalov swirled the remaining tea in his cup while staring out at the frozen lake. "You want me to just drop everything that I do with embassy? If I tell you everything I know about our system, our people, then you will give me asylum in Canada and set me up in new life. Is that correct?"

"Yes. That's pretty much correct." Connelly looked him in the eyes.

"How do you know I'm going to tell you the truth?"

"Okay, it's my turn. Do you really want me to spell it out for you?"

"What do you mean? I think that question is perfectly good."

"Vitaly, as you know, this is a rough game we're playing. If, for some reason, we find that we no longer trust you, or you've willingly deceived us, you know that we won't take your house away. You'll still have your new life. We intend to keep that part of our bargain. But what would happen if the Soviets found out your new identity and where you lived? What if that information suddenly became public knowledge?"

"You mean you would tell them? You would betray me?"

"Not if you tell us the truth, but if you deceive us, then it's not betrayal and all bets are off. Do you understand what I'm saying?"

"Oh, yes. You are very clear."

"Listen, Vitaly, I don't like working with people by threatening them. Like we said last night, we have to build a relationship on trust. I'm trying to make this as easy as I can for you. Coming to work with us is the right thing to do, but it takes courage. So, you have to tell me, what's your decision? Are you staying here this morning, or shall I drive you back to the embassy now?"

At that moment Corporal Russell came downstairs. He was holding a small Zeiss Ikon camera. He walked into the salon and, from ten feet, snapped off three quick shots of Connelly and Privalov sitting in their armchairs, tea and coffee cups in hand. "Excuse me, sir. I just had to get these for our files."

"That's fine, thanks, Corporal Russell. No need for any more of that." Connelly waved him off with a faint smile.

"Was that to add to your blackmail pictures?" Privalov said indignantly.

"It wasn't, but I suppose we could use them for that purpose. We want those pictures so that in the eventuality that you decided to tell people you were detained against your will, we'll have some photographic proof that you were treated with every possible courtesy. We also have one of those fancy new portable tape recorders. We recorded last night's conversation in its entirety, but I'm sure you expected that. Anyway, Vitaly, never mind all that. I really don't want to be threatening you. You are a free man. What's your decision?"

Privalov put his tea cup down and shifted in his chair. "You have made it so there is no choice. If I go back, my life is finished." He looked accusingly at Connelly.

"That may be, but like I said, those aren't my rules. We didn't create a tradition of suspicion or a culture of distrust. That's the Soviet way. You know that if the tables were turned and I was in your position in Moscow, and I went back to my embassy, I'm sure they'd believe me. They'd realize I have no reason to lie, and after a lengthy, non-violent interrogation, more than likely they'd let me go back to work. But I realize that it's entirely different for you." Connelly gestured with his open palms upward. "So, Vitaly, you can choose to work with us, live by our rules, or you can go back to the embassy and live by Stalin's rules."

Privalov exhaled a long, ragged sigh. It was a shade off being a sob. "I will work with you. Yes."

"Good. I guarantee you that you've made the right choice, Vitaly. I know it's early in the morning, but would you like a drink?"

"Yes. Yes, please." Whatever poise, outrage, and self-importance Privalov had displayed the night before seemed to have drained out of him. Connelly thought he suddenly looked shrunken and exhausted. Connelly walked over to the drinks table and poured several ounces of Scotch and a snifter of brandy. "I know it's early, but we both deserve this." He handed Privalov his drink and clinked his own glass against it. "You are a man of courage and principle. Cheers — to your new life."

Connelly sat down in his armchair. He spoke sympathetically. "Vitaly, I understand how hard this is, and I realize what you've done takes a strong backbone and a deep sense of integrity. You have my respect, sir." He raised his glass. "I salute you." He took a drink and sat back. "Let's keep moving on from where we left off last night, shall we? Tell me about you. Start with when you were born, and we'll end with this new chapter in your life. Tell me, who were your parents?"

Privalov let out a long breath. He looked relieved now that he had made his decision. "Thank you. You are very kind, Mr. Declan." He sat forward. "My parents both came from Chelyabinsk. It is a big city just east of the Urals. It was not so big then. During the war Stalin moved many heavy industries from Western Russia to there, and only then it became a much bigger industrial city. My parents were workers. You know, both sets of my grandparents were born as serfs. They couldn't read. They were owned by aristocratic farmers in the Eastern Steppe. After Emancipation they moved to Chelyabinsk. My father was the first in my family to learn how to read. He worked as a train driver and a mechanic, first in the rail yards and then on the Trans-Siberian Railway. He was away from home often. He did not serve in the army during the civil wars or in the First World War because he had a club foot. My mother was a housewife. They married before the First World War. I was born during the war, but just before the Bolshevik Revolution.

"My parents did not have strong political views. I don't know why, but I always suspected that my father liked the Tzar. He never spoke about it. My mother was secretly very religious. She kept a small leather prayer book hidden for years until my father found it and burned it. I remember that day. I had just turned seventeen. My mother cried, but my father said if we were caught with that book we would be denounced. I had told them that my teacher was asking students to report if their parents were counter-revolutionaries. Some of the children in the younger grades did that, and their parents were arrested and never seen again. It was a very bad time."

"What was your school like?" Connelly said.

"It was a very harsh school, but I had good grades when I was young. I worked hard and so when I was thirteen, I was put in the higher *teknikum* classes. I was being prepared to be an engineer, but in addition to mathematics, I was very good at languages, and so I was allowed to study English at high school for three years."

"Did you play any sports or games?"

"No. I was not good at sports, and there were not many sports to play in those days. My father was not happy, but I joined the Komsomol, the Party Youth organization, when I entered secondary school." Privalov ran his hand across his mouth. "It seems like such a long time ago now. I was also a member of the Vladimir Lenin All-Union Pioneer Organization. It was boring. Lots of political classes, marching and rifle drills, attending rallies and hikes. Our leaders were bullies, but even then, I knew that without belonging to these organizations my chances of university and a good career would not be good. I kept quiet and I worked hard."

"What happened after high school, Vitaly? You were, what, eighteen then? In 1934?"

"Yes. I saw what was happening in Russia during those years and I soon learned to keep my mouth closed. People disappeared. It was a frightening time. Because my father worked on the railroad, sometimes I would take his supper down to him at the railyard at night. My mother made his meal and she would put it in a small metal pail. Mostly just bread, pickles, and tea in a flask. At that time farmers in Russia and Ukraine were being forced onto collective farms. Tens of thousands were shot or deported if they resisted or complained. Stalin said he was liquidating the last of the kulaks and Sovietizing agriculture." Privalov took a drink and shook his head. "It was horrible. I saw that thousands of people were being shipped from the Ukraine to Siberia. They passed through the train yards in Chelyabinsk. My father sometimes told my mother of the things he saw. This was before the time of what you call 'the purges.' Those were the early days of the terror, but the period of forced collectivization, moving farmers onto large state-owned farms, it was much worse than the purges. Later on, people we knew were arrested in the night and we never heard from them again. I have heard that it was the worst in Ukraine. During the war I heard many stories. Maybe someday we will know. It was a terrible time to be alive. Some nights I heard my parents, both of them, crying. We were very frightened, but I knew if I was going to survive, I had to be good at school. I worked very hard."

Connelly nodded and spoke quietly. "I can't imagine having to live like that, Vitaly. I grew up on a poor farm, but I was never frightened for my life. We thought times were hard, but it was nothing like that."

"You don't know," Privalov muttered. "You think you know. You people believe only the things you want to believe. You don't understand what we have been through."

"What did you do after high school, Vitaly?"

"I worked for a year at the local Komsomol headquarters. It was a good thing to do. My bosses were all Party members. I worked hard, and they liked me and gave me a top recommendation to go to university. There were not many places at institutes of higher education. You could not get in unless you had Party connections as well as good grades."

"Where did you go from there?"

"Chelyabinsk State Pedagogical University. It was a new institute run by the Party. At first, I studied fundamental engineering and chemistry, but after the first term I changed my courses to study political theory, history, and languages." Privalov chuckled. "You see, I did not want to be a low-level engineer working in a factory. I had seen that in Chelyabinsk. An engineer had the same tiny apartment, the same shitty food. An engineer shared his bathroom with everyone else on his floor. He had the same life as a worker. I wanted better. I wanted to be in the Party, so my Komsomol work helped me." Privalov thumped himself on the chest. "I was the top student in political theory and languages at Chelyabinsk the year I graduated, so after I got my certificate, I was sent to Moscow to work in the Soviet Foreign Trade Secretariat of the Ministry for Economic Development. I said goodbye to my parents and left for Moscow in the summer. I thought things were going to get much better. I was wrong."

"What happened?"

"The job I had was nothing. I was a clerk in the Foreign Trade Secretariat Workers' Union. I was responsible for preparing the minutes of our meetings and writing endless reports on foreign trade statistics. Nobody ever read our reports. Most days we just pretended to work. My boss was a pig. He was harsh with his workers. No one who worked for him was ever promoted. We were afraid he would denounce us. I worked in the institute for three years, from 1937 to 1940. That was when I got away."

"How did you do that?"

Privalov laughed "I volunteered for the army." He waved his drink and arched his eyebrows. "I was bored and angry and it was the only way I could leave my job. They put me in the artillery. I was sent to an officers' school outside Donetsk and then posted to a Red Army divisional artillery group in the Ukraine. I finished my training just before the Great Patriotic War broke out with Germany."

Privalov looked morose. "I don't like talking about those days. It was a long, hard time. My unit was destroyed and re-established three times. Those years were the worst times of my life. But I was just one of twenty-nine million men who served my country in the Red Army. My story was not so different from most, except I was lucky. I survived. I started as a junior lieutenant and finished the war as a major. I fought in the Southwestern Front, from Kiev in 1941 right up to Vienna at the end of the war."

"Did you stay long in Vienna?"

"No. After the war I was repatriated. I went back to Moscow, and through an army friend I got put on an English language course. I did well on my training and was sent to the Ministry of External Relations. The rest you know about. I went to London and then to Ottawa." Privalov drained his glass. "And today I find myself working for you. What more can I tell you?"

Connelly looked sombre. "You've had quite a life, Vitaly."

"I've seen more things than a man should in his lifetime, Mr. Declan. Can I help myself to some more of your whisky?"

"Yes, yes, of course. We have lots and we can always get some more."

"I have done so much talking." Privalov scowled as he poured himself another drink. "Now it's your turn to answer my questions. Why did you choose me, Mr. Declan, and why did you choose to approach me on the night that you did?"

"I chose you because you were one of the few people in the Soviet embassy who could walk out freely. There was no one else we could monitor. We knew you were meeting with Miss Soroka, so we tapped her phone. We knew where you were going to be last night. We chose to act last night because that's when we were ready. Why do you ask?"

Privalov sat down heavily. He didn't speak for a moment. "No reason. I was only wondering."

Connelly looked out over the lake distractedly. "You know, I think we may get snow again today. That sunshine won't last." He turned back to Privalov. "But there are a few questions I still need you to answer, Vitaly. I'm a little troubled by some things that aren't in your account. You say you work for the Ministry of External Relations. I don't doubt that you may be seconded to them, but because you have been given a considerable amount of freedom to move around, unlike most people in the embassy you had the ability to move about outside relatively freely. That leads me to believe that you probably reported to the MGB or the GRU — you know, the Ministry of State Security or Military Intelligence. So, Vitaly, what exactly was your relationship to the intelligence agencies?"

Chapter 14

ORIANA HAD A HARD TIME SLEEPING THAT NIGHT. She was up and dressed an hour before her alarm clock sounded. As she walked to work through the frozen streets, the only things moving were huge dump trucks with massive plows, clearing the previous night's snowfall. At the newspaper, the only person in the building was the white-moustached commissionaire at the front desk. They smiled at one another.

"You're here early, ma'am."

Oriana raised a gloved hand. "Work, work, work. You know how it is, Leo."

Upstairs, Oriana took off her coat and hung it on the rack behind her desk. Her editor, Cedric Jacobsen, knew she was meeting Privalov last night and had insisted that she have six hundred words on the Shemyakin case by noon. Oriana usually got along well with her editors. Jacobsen, the publisher's nephew, was in his late forties, six foot four, fair haired, slender, and blessed with patrician good looks. He had the peculiar kind of brashness that sometimes comes from the advantages of a substantial trust fund. In his case, confidence in his own abilities was bundled with a deep-rooted sense of insecurity that stemmed from being raised by negligent parents who had sent him off to a badly run private school when he was nine. Oriana knew that, and there were days, when she was in a sympathetic mood, that she believed his overbearing disposition stemmed from social isolation in childhood. She was always quick to remind herself that she was only guessing; most of the time she thought he was just naturally an ass.

Last night, in his typically grating fashion, looking through reading glasses perched on his nose, he'd barked, "How the hell should I know what you should write? Use your feminine intuition, woman! Give me something new, something descriptive of the times. You're the one who's been to university. Think of something, but remember: I won't accept crap!" Jacobsen was the kind of leader who, in a few short phrases, habitually turned his employees' enthusiasm to dread. This morning she was at a loss as to where to start.

She took the kettle off the hotplate and poured boiling water into her cup. She had never really gotten used to the taste of Nescafé, but it was everywhere now. She still preferred brewed coffee. Instant coffee was like the new Wonder Bread: perfectly sliced and never stale — two of the time-saving products that had emerged during and just after the war. Instant coffee, powdered cheese toppings, sauces, canned soups, and atomic bombs. Within a year they were going to have television in Ottawa. Life was different now. Perhaps that was what she could use as an angle for her article? Tying together society's changes with the murder of a Russian diplomat might be difficult, but she could work it out somehow. The rising new prosperity existing alongside the new threats to global peace. No matter what she wrote, it would be better than another article on new bus routes.

She wondered how Declan was doing. She was comfortable with him in a way she hadn't been with other men. He'd been ready to trust her about her editor's change to that first article, and under his businesslike exterior, he seemed to have a warm heart and strength of character. Who knew? She wanted to think positively about him, but this morning she was uneasy. He'd said he was going to be busy. She knew that his job was demanding, but it still felt wrong that she hadn't heard from him. Did he think she was cheap? Oriana had never been in this situation before. She'd slept with him, and now she hadn't heard from him. It was the kind of con game she'd read about but had never thought of it happening to her. Anxiety, uncertainty, and self-doubt were themes that seemed to be playing a prominent role in her life lately. She sipped at her coffee. Perhaps those were ideas she could weave into her story, too. She went back to her desk and started to type.

* * *

"Come in, Comrade Ambassador." There was no warmth in Tarabin's voice. "Have you got everyone present and accounted for before I begin our investigation?"

Glinin winced. His leg was killing him, and his mouth was dry. "No, Colonel. There are two men missing this morning. They have all been told to be here. I have no idea where they are."

* * *

Privalov frowned and swirled the whisky in his glass. "You have to understand, Mr. Declan, we are all in one way or another tied into a kind of intelligence-gathering. That is what embassies do. We gather information *on* our host country, and we provide information *to* the host country. That is what intelligence is: the transfer of information. Nothing else. It is what your embassies do all around the world. So, if you ask me if I am in the intelligence business, my answer has to be yes. If you ask me if I am doing military intelligence, the answer is no.

"My job is to gather business and cultural information. Every day I read the newspapers. I listen to the radio. I speak to people. I write reports. I encourage trade between our two countries. It would be my greatest pleasure to have our two countries compete in an ice hockey tournament. That is how we should compete." He waved his glass. "I have worked hard to make a positive image of the Soviet Union. There is no big secret there. That is nothing different from what all diplomatic people do."

"Oh, come now, Vitaly. Don't play me for a fool. You mean to tell me that there were no military intelligence operations being run out of the embassy?" Connelly smiled. "You expect me to believe that Shemyakin was really interested in air traffic safety? What about all your Soviet theories of class warfare, the destruction of the international bourgeoisie, the inevitable overthrow of capitalist societies? That's not simply hot air."

"Maybe not, but do you really think we are all spies and saboteurs in the embassy? Who is being foolish now, Mr. Declan? I want to help you, but I won't be helping you by making up stories. I was not in the MGB or the GRU. Like I said, I do not know who was in the intelligence services. They deliberately conceal these kinds of things. Maybe Shemyakin was. I don't know. Like I said last night, you do not go asking or seeking to find out such information. It is not healthy. Most people in the embassy work to try to make things better for the Soviet Union. We work to buy your wheat and beef; we need those things. We work to set up cultural exchanges, to understand new technologies, to make our people better off. There is nothing hostile in this."

"Really? You expect me to believe that?" Connelly said. "Listen to the kind of life you've described for me. Despite every indication that the Soviet Union is a murderously aggressive country, you want me to believe that your embassy conducts normal diplomatic relations? If that's true, then why is everything in your embassy so secretive, so tightly controlled? Why is everybody watched all the time? No normal country would have exterminated its successful farming class. No normal country would have had purges. After defeating the Nazis, a normal country would have reduced the size of its armed forces. If you are a normal country, why do you publish so much about the inevitability of war with the capitalist states? Why is everything about the Soviet Union so closed and uncooperative? Why did you, Vitaly, have to check in after every single time you went out? What you're telling me doesn't add up."

Privalov sat up and banged his glass on the arm of the chair, spilling some of the scotch. "What do you want me to tell you? I can only tell you what I know. Yes, parts of my country are crazy. We were suspicious of the Germans. We are suspicious of you. We are suspicious of the Americans. You people want to destroy our society. We understand that. The West has always wanted to destroy the Soviet Union. There are twenty-five million dead Soviet citizens who are testimony to why we are suspicious."

Privalov took a deep breath, obviously attempting to control himself. "Mr. Declan, you are asking me things I know nothing about. I agree that we should not be ready to fight one another. But we are not all hostile to you. My job in the embassy was a normal job. I was working to set up cultural and sporting exchanges. Ask Miss Soroka. What did I talk to her about? It was innocent. I only want a fair representation of my country in the newspapers. I want people to see us as humans, not as bloodthirsty monsters. I don't want a nuclear war. After what we have just been through, you think we have no reason to be worried about security? Look at what is going on in America. Senator McCarthy, Red Scares. You have created NATO to threaten us, with every state in Western Europe and North America armed and ready to fight us. We watch the massive build-up of America's nuclear forces. Who do you think they intend to use those weapons on? In Europe there are fleets of the latest American airplanes ready to drop atomic bombs on Russian cities. Now, I ask you, why are you so suspicious of us?"

Privalov's hand trembled as he clutched his glass. He lowered his voice. "Mr. Declan, this is crazy. I do not want to be a part of it. Yes, I would like to see my country free. Yes, I said I will help you where I can, but I cannot help you with what I do not know." He licked his lips and took several deep breaths. "Mr. Declan, I have thought about what we discussed last night. Despite the fact that you have left me no choice, your actions have created a personal opportunity for me. I want to help you. I think you are correct about doing the right thing for my country. That I should do something to help change the government, to get rid of the Communist Party. You know, every one of us who lives here and works here in Canada, when we go to sleep at night, we think about how nice it would be to always live in a country like this: to always have enough to eat, to live in decent houses, to read whatever books we want, to live without fear, to be allowed to criticize the government.

"Now that you have pulled me away from my old life, you have changed things for me. I love my country, but you have left me no choice. I can never go back to the embassy, to the old ways. So, yes, I am on your side now, but I cannot give you information that I do not have. If you need something to trade for my asylum, I can help you assess things. I can translate and interpret for you. You can ask me for my opinion on what is possible and what is not. I can give you whatever information I have on the things that I know. But my fear now is that you will think that I am not enough value to you. And when the embassy realizes that I am here, they will demand that I be released to them, and because I have told you the truth and you think this is not the information you want to hear, you will send me back. That is what I fear."

Connelly said nothing for several seconds. "I can understand why you may feel that way; but no, I have no intention of sending you back, Vitaly." He turned and looked toward the kitchen. From behind the house there was the sound of a car door slamming and someone coming through the kitchen. One of Corporal Russell's uniformed constables came rushing into the room.

"Sir, sorry to interrupt, but can I have a second, please?" He jerked his head toward the kitchen. "In private? It's important." Connelly stood, and the two men moved into the kitchen. The constable whispered, "Something's come up in Ottawa, sir. I've no idea what it is, but Superintendent Ferrall wants you and the staff sergeant back there as soon as possible. He said I was to stay here with Constable Voigt. We'll keep a watch on Privalov, but you and Staff Sergeant Cormier have to get back to Ottawa immediately."

* * *

Cormier drove slowly along the twisting gravel road leading from the Lac Beaulieu cottage to the main highway. He sensed that Connelly was on edge. "I know we've got to get there quickly, boss, but with this snow on the road, I don't want to end up in the ditch or break an axle in a snow-filled pothole." He shifted in his seat and dug into his jacket pocket for his cigarettes. "So, what did you think of our friend Privalov's conversion?"

Connelly shook his head. "Like you said last night, he hasn't told us much that we don't already know. I still think he's hanging on to a lot more than he's telling us. It's probably going to take a while to get more information out of him. Like he said, I suspect he's still worried we'll turn him in because he hasn't given us much information that we can act on. What was your impression?"

"I haven't changed my opinion of the man. He's a shifty little weasel.

157

He'll latch onto whoever offers him the most, and he'll hedge his bets every chance he gets. He's a devious little prick, sir. Our prisons are filled with con men like that. I'm surprised he hasn't started yet to bargain for the things he wants us to provide him for his new life here in Canada. I just wish we had some means of comparing what he has to say with someone else from a similar position. As it is right now, we haven't got much to go on. I just don't trust this guy. But having said all that, I think there's a chance we may still get some useful information out of him. Like I said, I'd bet he's holding out to get a better deal. You know — a better job, better allowances, nicer car, that sort of thing." Cormier thumped the steering wheel in an expression of finality. "Anyway. Like you say, that'll take time. Why do you suppose Superintendent Ferrall wants us back in Ottawa in such a hurry?"

Connelly didn't answer the question right away. He looked out the window as they drove through the snow-covered woods. The trees in this section of the Canadian Shield were all deciduous: maples, red oak, and beech. He rubbed his fingers on his chin.

"It always surprises me how well you can see through these woods when the leaves are all gone. You take away their foliage and you can see a lot further. You see these, Marcel?" He gestured with an open palm at the view outside. "Seventy years ago, these were old-growth, hardwood forests. They stood here unchanged for centuries. A lot of the trees were seven or eight feet in circumference. Lumber barons cut them all down over a period of forty years and shipped the timber to Europe. With the leaves gone, you can see what's grown up instead. Nowadays we think these are big trees, that this is a massive forest, but actually they're relatively scrawny by comparison with what was here. But you know, when the leaves come out in the spring, when the foliage renews, the forest looks just as dense as it did in the old days.

"I think Privalov and his cronies are the same. Take the foliage away and they're not nearly as imposing as they once looked. I agree with you. I don't trust Privalov, so we've got to let him feel exposed for a while. Once we let him feel he's vulnerable, that's when I think we'll get what we're looking for. That's going to take a few days." Connelly turned from the window. "But to answer your question, I'm worried that Ferrall wants to see us because somehow this operation's been blown, and we may not have much time. My fear is that someone's talked, and the word's got out that we're holding a Soviet diplomat. Ferrall's probably doing damage control. I can't imagine any other reason he'd call us back."

Cormier exhaled a cloud of blue smoke. "Yeah." He nodded in agreement. "Unfortunately, that's the only reason I can come up with too, sir. What else could it be?" He rolled his window down an inch. "This smoke doesn't bother you, does it, boss?"

Connelly shook his head. "No, go ahead. It's character building. I've been dying for a smoke for the last few weeks."

Cormier rolled down the window a touch more and turned up the heater. "If you don't mind me asking, sir, do you know much about Superintendent Ferrall? He's kind of an unusual one, isn't he?"

"What do you mean?"

"Well, if this operation collapses, I'd like to know something more about the guy, whether or not we can trust him. Honestly, I don't have much of a take on the man. You're closer to him. What do you make of him?" Connelly looked askance at Cormier. "Well, you know, sir, I'm not asking you to be disloyal. Just that if I know something more about our commander, it might tell us what we're in for. If this thing's blown, I want to prepare myself for what's about to happen. I've been in Special Branch for six months now and I can't say I know him well yet. You've got a better take on him than I do."

He looked over at Connelly, who wasn't saying anything. "Like. I mean, sir," he went on doggedly, "Ferrall's a bit unusual for a senior RCMP officer. For one thing, sir, he's got one eye and he's missing a couple of fingers. How many senior officers would be allowed to stay in the force with that kind of condition?"

Connelly nodded. "Yeah. I hear what you're saying. I don't know the whole story, just what I've been told. He had a good war record from the First War, and the force let a number of returning veterans in if their wounds didn't interfere with their ability to do police work. I heard that in the war Ferrall won his Military Cross and then later lost his eye and a couple of fingers. He's half German, speaks the language fluently. After that, because of his language skills he worked in military intelligence and was decorated again with a Distinguished Service Order. As far as I can tell, nobody really knows why he got the second medal, and he doesn't talk about it. I do know that when he got home after the war, he joined the RCMP. When the Second World War broke out, he was pulled back into military intelligence and ended up in Special Operations Executive. He keeps all that information pretty close to his chest. He's never talked about it himself that I know of. I got all this from other officers who worked with him."

He tilted his head to the side. "So, no Marcel, I'm not too worried about Ferrall. He's got a good reputation. I've known some friends who worked for him back in Saskatchewan. They liked the guy, said that he's loyal to his subordinates, but he doesn't suffer fools gladly, and he's been known to rip into senior officers when they've done something remarkably stupid. I've never seen it, but he's got a reputation for being loyal to his troops to the point of occasional insubordination with his own superiors. So, I'd guess that explains why he's not gone higher in rank. I know what you're thinking, though. If this thing's gone sideways and we've been blown, we're lucky that we've got a senior officer like Ferrall in charge. We could have ended up with some cautiously obedient toady from headquarters. I suppose we're lucky in that respect."

"Well, that's fucking reassuring, sir. I've always thought that if I'm going to lose my head," Cormier grinned as he flicked his cigarette ash out the window, "I'd rather it drop into the basket alongside the heads of my superior officers. I take some comfort in that."

"Yeah. I think if we're going to get the chop, Ferrall's prepared to go with us. We'll see soon enough."

Chapter 15

SUPERINTENDENT FERRALL was lost in thought, holding a coffee cup and looking out the window, when Connelly and Cormier showed up at his door. Connelly knocked softly on the door frame.

"You asked us to come back and see you, sir?" Connelly said.

"Oh, yeah. Exactly the two men I want. Come in, please. Close the door and take a seat." Ferrall waited, leaning on the windowsill, until the two officers were sitting before he spoke again. "Okay, first things first. Before I give you my news, tell me how things are going with our friend Privalov."

"He seems to have come onside, sir." Connelly looked guarded. "We both agree, he seems reluctant; but he says he's grateful for the chance to start a new life here, and he wants asylum. Says he's a junior commercial and cultural officer and he'll work with us. But so far, he hasn't given us much information that we can act upon. He claims that the Americans were the ones who killed Shemyakin, but he can't provide any evidence other than the fact that Shemyakin was one of the ambassador's favourites. He thinks Shemyakin might have been a triple agent; but again, he says he has no proof of that." Connelly shrugged. "That's it so far. Not a lot." He paused. "But tell me, sir, have we been blown? Is that why you've called us back?"

"No." Ferrall took a deep breath and smiled. "I can see why you've asked that question, though." He sat down. "No, Declan, we haven't been blown, not as far as I know. In fact, the assistant commissioner's onside with us. I've briefed him. He understands the risks but still thinks your plan's worthwhile. . He's going to give us what the Air Force calls 'top cover,' but we do have another wrinkle in this case." Ferrall chuckled and picked up his pipe. He began filling it with tobacco from a jar covered in red leather on his desk.

"Believe it or not, we had an actual unsolicited walk-in defection this morning from the Soviet embassy. I've already talked to him." Ferrall struck a wooden match and talked in between inhalations on his pipe. "I'm not going to give you my impression of this guy. You've heard what Privalov has to say. Now, I'd like to hear what you have to say about our newest arrival." He put the pipe down. "He's waiting for you downstairs in one of the basement interview rooms. See what this guy has to say, and we'll sort out whatever differences we find in their stories later."

* * *

Connelly and Cormier were led downstairs by a uniformed constable and then followed him along a linoleum-floored corridor to the interview room.

"He's in the second room on the right, sir," the constable said to Connelly. "The man says he's Alexander Karazin. He was transferred to us by the Ottawa police early this morning. Apparently, sometime before six AM, he just walked into the central Ottawa police station and asked for asylum. He's been here for a few hours, and the only other people to have interviewed him are Superintendent Ferrall and the Ottawa duty sergeant."

"Okay," Connelly said. "Is the press aware that this guy's jumped ship?"

"Not as far as I know, sir."

"Great. Well, let's see him."

The constable opened the door and said, "Mr. Karazin, you have a couple of visitors."

Karazin looked up at them and forced a smile. He was sitting in a bare room on a metal folding chair at a metal table, nursing a cup of coffee. He was in his late twenties, a thin man with a swarthy complexion. He had a broad face, carefully combed thick dark hair, and a solemn and apprehensive look about him. He was dressed in an ill-fitting grey suit with a white shirt and a plain navy-blue tie. Connelly's first impression was that he resembled one of the earnest-looking Jehovah's Witnesses who regularly showed up at their farm house when he was in his teens. Those young men, warning of the imminent advent of God's Kingdom, had the same radiant, expectant look of vulnerability on their faces.

Connelly smiled and offered his hand. "Mister Karazin, I'm Inspector Connelly, and this is my colleague, Staff Sergeant Cormier. I hope I've pronounced your name properly?"

Karazin smiled again. "Yes, of course. It is fine."

"Is there anything we can get you? Are you well? Have you had breakfast? Cigarettes? Another coffee or tea?"

"Yes, please, sir. I am fine, but I am hungry, and I have not cigarettes."

162

"We can fix that right now, Mr. Karazin." Cormier offered him a cigarette and turned to Connelly. "I'll have someone send out for a hot breakfast, sir. Be right back."

"So, Mr. Karazin," Connelly said, taking a chair opposite him at the table, "this is a bit unusual. Could you please tell me who you are and what's brought you here?"

Karazin nodded. "Yes. My name is Alexander Vladimirovich Karazin. I work at Soviet embassy and I am asking asylum in your country." He stopped and smiled again at Connelly.

"Okay. What exactly did you do at the embassy, Mr. Karazin?"

"I am already telling superintendent, I am radio-technical officer second class, and when is no radios to repair, I work as duty officer. Most of time I am duty officer."

"Okay, and what made you decide to seek asylum, Mr. Karazin?"

"You hear of death of Anatoly Shemyakin, Inspector?"

"Yes, I am aware of it." Connelly nodded his head in an expression of heartfelt understanding.

"I was duty officer night Shemyakin died. At embassy they have started new investigation last night. I did not kill Shemyakin, but I know who did. I did not want to be part of such investigation."

Connelly rubbed his lower lip. "All right, tell me what exactly happened and why you don't want to be a part of the investigation."

Cormier slipped back into the room and took a seat off to one side of the table.

"Marcel, a quick update," Connelly said in a flat voice. "Mr. Karazin tells us that he's a radio technician in the embassy and he was serving as a duty officer on the night Shemyakin was killed."

Cormier raised his eyebrows. "Oh, we do need to talk, then, Mr. Karazin. But please, don't let me interrupt. A hot breakfast'll be here in a few minutes."

"Go on, Mr. Karazin," Connelly said.

"Yes. I was doing my duty on night Anatoly Shemyakin died. I took over shift at midnight in duty room in *referentura* in basement. It was quiet night. There was not so much traffic from Moscow on radio or teletype. Most of times, embassy is deserted during night time. When I took over from other duty officer, he told me that there was one duty driver as well as two officers still in embassy. He said officers were upstairs and drinking since dinner. He said I must be careful because Shemyakin and Privalov are both angry. They are shouting."

"Yes, go on," Connelly said.

"It was quiet for half hour. I thought maybe others were all gone home.

Sometimes when there is drinking parties, officers get too drunk and forget to sign out and they just go home." Karazin shrugged. "So, we cover for them. Then that is what I think was happening."

"What happened?" Cormier said.

"At about one in morning, I am hearing some screams and then music, very loud, from upstairs. I left radio station and go upstairs to see why there is screams. At MGB office room, Fedor Nikolaev meets me in hallway. He was duty driver. He is very big, strong man. He pushed me back, told me to wait downstairs. He said if I knew what was good not to come up again. I went downstairs back to desk. I stayed at desk. Music was very loud, and I heard more screams and then single shot. After that it is quiet. One hour later, Nikolaev comes to duty officer room and takes my cigarettes. Then, short time later, car leaving embassy and at around three-thirty Nikolaev coming back to embassy, tells me that to stay healthy and alive, I am hearing nothing all night, nobody had been here, and it was quiet all night. Then he took duty officer's log book and wrote some lines for two officers and himself."

"Who were the two officers?" Connelly asked.

"Anatoly Shemyakin and Vitaly Privalov."

"Are you sure? You say you didn't actually see these two men, so how can you be sure who they were?"

"I know these men, Inspector. Everybody in embassy knows these men. They drink together late at night, many times. Many times, we hearing fighting as they drink. Shemyakin was chief GRU officer in embassy, and Privalov was chief MGB officer. I am hearing arguments with these two men many, many times. Privalov is most powerful man in embassy next to ambassador, but Shemyakin also has special place in embassy. When I come to work, friends tell me, 'You don't want trouble, stay away from Privalov and Shemyakin.' Also, Nikolaev put writing in log book showing he was driving Shemyakin to Rideau Street in afternoon and Privalov was leaving embassy many hours before."

"You said Nikolaev took your cigarettes. What kind of cigarettes did you have?"

"They were American cigarettes. We get cigarettes and whisky sent every month from Washington in diplomatic bag."

"What kind of cigarettes did you have that night?"

Karazin shrugged and thought about the question for a second. "Lucky Strike, I think. Yes. Lucky Strike. We had many cartons this month coming from America in diplomatic bag. Normally, they are giving us Camels. I better like Canadian cigarettes."

Connelly nodded. "So let me get back to Shemyakin. You think

Privalov killed him?"

"Yes."

"Why would he kill Shemyakin?"

"I don't know." Karazin screwed up his face and shook his head. "Nikolaev has come back and telling me if I am reporting anything, *anything,* he will kill me. I believe him. Nikolaev is MGB. Nikolaev is working for Privalov. He is not man for having enemy."

"What happened in the embassy when they heard that Shemyakin was murdered?"

"Privalov and first secretary were conducting investigation. We all make statement. I am doing what I am told. I write I came to duty at midnight. I am hearing and I am seeing nothing all night. Maria Portunova in administrative office signed statement. She says she was signing out car to Nikolaev for afternoon before, so he could drive Shemyakin downtown. Daytime duty officer signed statement saying Shemyakin left in afternoon to go to Rideau Street on official duties. Maria, Nikolaev, and daytime duty officer write that last they were seeing Shemyakin alive was in afternoon going to Rideau Street."

"How do you know all that?" Cormier asked.

"I was doing duty when copies of all statements were being put in code and I am sending reports to New York and Moscow. I was putting in code final report and statements. That is my job."

"Where is Privalov now?"

Karazin shrugged. He looked tired and rubbed his hand over his forehead. "I don't know. I am not seeing Privalov for three days. He is often going away for many days. I think maybe he is back now with others at embassy this morning for new investigation. We were being told to be there last night and this morning for new investigation. When my shift is over, I am telling incoming duty officer I am going home for wash and eat, and I am coming back for investigation, but I went to police station and then they are bringing me here." He shrugged again. "What will be happening for me, Inspector?"

"You're safe here, Alexander. Don't worry about that. No one can get to you now. Do you mind if I call you Alexander? There are still a number of questions I need to ask you."

Karazin nodded.

"This may sound like an odd question to you, Alexander," Connelly leaned forward, "but why do you think that you couldn't tell the truth at the new investigation?"

"I am reading messages when coming in. New investigation was by MGB officers from New York. Because Privalov killing Shemyakin, MGB officers will be helping him. They believe their own man. Even when I am telling lies about night of murder, I am still being big danger to Privalov. I was only people to know, and I know in a few days something bad is happening to me."

"You think Privalov would kill you?"

"No, Nikolaev will kill me. Nikolaev does all dirty work for Privalov."

"What sort of dirty work?"

"Nikolaev's work is to threaten peoples. Many times, I see him threaten and push peoples — and..." Karazin waved his hand in a circular motion. "How do you say, how do you say? Bully — yes. He is bully for Privalov. Privalov is quiet man. Privalov, he is like many, many officers in MGB. He is quiet and talks nice always. It is to make you more scared. One of secretaries who was before working in Kremlin telling me, Privalov is acting like Beria. Beria is head of MGB. A little man, very quiet, never shouting, but he is dangerous killer."

"Aren't you afraid, Alexander, that by coming here and telling me this you are risking your life?"

"Yes, I am afraid, of course. And I have danger. But I am coming to you for help. I am taking chance. If I am staying at embassy, there is no chance for me. At embassy, if I am staying, soon I will be dead."

"What about your family? Do you have a family back in Russia?"

"Yes. I have parents and older sister. I worry about them. But situation is same for them. If I am being killed by Privalov, or he is making up some disgrace reason to send me back, my family would still have danger. Privalov will be denouncing me in report, and my family will be having danger same as if I am defecting. You see, for me there is no choice."

"Yes, I see what you're saying." Connelly spoke quietly. Karazin was straining to hear him. "Tell me, then, about Shemyakin and Privalov. What do you know about these two men?"

"Shemyakin was chief GRU officer and Privalov was chief MGB officer. Privalov was senior officer, but Shemyakin was same to him in ranks. He did not like Privalov as senior. He did not like to obey Privalov."

"How did you know that?"

"When I am being duty officer, I see, I hear many things. My job at night was I am encoding reports and sending reports to Moscow. I am encoding many reports. I am seeing what peoples do. Sometimes I am sending report for Shemyakin, and day or two later Privalov is coming to me and making questions about Shemyakin report. He is being angry. He is saying Shemyakin could not send reports unless Privalov is signing." Karazin exhaled a ragged sigh. "Sometimes I am hearing shouting, because Shemyakin reports going to Chief Intelligence Directorate of General Staff in Soviet Army. Privalov reports going to First Main Directorate of

Ministry of State Security. Two years ago, two departments were being together, but then they are change back to old way and split back with army and MGB. After that, there is bad competition. I am at Soviet embassy for three years and I am seeing many problems. Privalov wants all reports going to Ministry of State Security."

"You say that Privalov was the chief MGB officer, but his official title was that he was a commercial and cultural attaché."

"Yes, is normal." Karazin looked taken aback by the question. He shrugged and made a disdainful face. "MGB and GRU, they are always listing as different jobs."

"Who do you work for?"

"I am MGB. I am junior technical sergeant having special permission to see MGB and GRU messages and reports."

"Can you tell us any more about the activities of the MGB and the GRU in your embassy?"

"Yes. I am sending all their reports. Every night I am seeing reports and answers from Moscow."

There was a brisk knock at the door. Karazin stopped speaking and looked up, his eyes wide in alarm. The constable who had shown them in opened the door a crack. He was juggling a paper bag and a steaming china mug. "Sir, from the café down on the corner at Lisgar Street. I've got a couple of fried egg and bacon sandwiches, fried potatoes, and coffee for Mr. Karazin."

"Wonderful. Thanks. Bring it in." Connelly pushed his chair back and said, "Marcel, we're going to take a little break just now." Turning to Karazin, he said, "Excuse us, please, Alexander. Take some time now and enjoy your breakfast. If there is anything else you need or want to tell me, we'll talk again in a moment, but I have to speak to Staff Sergeant Cormier for just a few seconds."

Outside in the hallway, Connelly raised his eyebrows and whispered. "This guy's certainly got my attention. Marcel, I want you to go back to the cottage. Bring Mr. Privalov back here, in handcuffs, if you would, please? For now, we'll keep him away from Karazin. We'll keep him isolated in the cells at the Rockcliffe Park station. Don't let him talk to anyone there. It looks like we have a few issues to discuss with him. I'm going to stay here and finish up with our new comrade. Call me when you get Privalov to his new lodgings."

❋ ❋ ❋

Glinin pulled his shoulders back as he walked into his ambassadorial office. Shubenkov was sitting off to one side of his desk. He turned on the small

Philco tube radio on the credenza. The radio was set to a classical station with the volume turned up high, a standard procedure to mask sensitive conversations in Soviet embassies. Colonel Tarabin sat in the ambassador's chair, his face threatening and brash.

"Your people don't obey you," he said coldly. "What kind of an embassy are you running? How did you let it come to this?"

Glinin raised a finger in acknowledgement of the question, but also indicating that he would get to his answer. He stepped back and, leaning on his cane, eased himself into the wooden chair in the corner. His leg was throbbing, but now the way ahead for him was perfectly clear. The only chance to get through Tarabin's investigation without being found guilty of 'wrecking' or 'sabotage' was to act as if none of this was a personal threat to him. He took a deep breath and held his cane out in front of him like some tribal elder with a talking stick.

"Colonel Tarabin, for your records, I did not let this situation deteriorate. I was the one who requested the services of special investigators. I have done everything possible to control things. I was the one who asked for your assistance. Things here are very much in control."

Tarabin raised his eyebrows. "You have two people missing this morning."

"Yes. We don't know where they are, but I'm sure it is no coincidence that their disappearance has something to do with your arrival."

Tarabin looked like he had bitten into something sour. His eyes narrowed. "What do you mean by that, Comrade Ambassador? I don't like to speak in riddles. If you have something to say, speak directly."

"Both Privalov and Karazin are MGB." Glinin was doing his best to sound like he was speaking respectfully but with restraint. "Shemyakin was GRU. All three men worked for intelligence services and all three are missing. I think that perhaps whoever killed Shemyakin has probably done something to Privalov and Karazin. I can't prove that, but that's what I think."

"How would anyone outside the embassy know these men were with intelligence services? How would they know who to target?"

"Shemyakin was tortured. We know that. It's probable that, through his work, he was identified, and under duress he identified the others." Glinin waved his hand as if he was stating something blindingly obvious. "Now, I think it's possible the Americans have killed Shemyakin and they have something to do with the other two missing."

"Why not the Canadians?" Tarabin interrupted the ambassador. "This is their country. Why would they not have anything to do with this?"

"Comrade Colonel." Glinin leaned forward and locked eyes with

Tarabin. "Under my watch, this embassy has done very good work. Our people can operate almost freely. I am sure you have read my reports. I know that they are distributed to Washington and New York. The Canadians have very few people watching us, and it is very easy to shake them. The Canadians don't suspect much from us, and they don't feel threatened by us here in their city. That is not by accident, Comrade Colonel. I have worked hard to create these operational conditions. Despite this benign operational climate, however, it is possible that Canadians might have killed Shemyakin, but it is very unlikely. For the Canadians to kill Shemyakin would be very much out of character. Killing diplomats would cause them more problems than it would solve. If they thought there was a problem, they would get rid of him with a diplomatic expulsion.

"But the Americans — the Americans would do it in someone else's country, if they thought they could get away with it. Maybe the British would too. I don't know, but certainly not here. I think Americans killed Shemyakin, and so do Privalov and First Secretary Bodrov. So, Comrade Colonel, if I may be so forward, I would like to make the case that we need information about Americans operating in this country. We do not have such information. We do not have the people in position to tell us about that, but you, Comrade Colonel — you can talk to Moscow and head of mission in Washington to help get us the resources."

"You have no evidence for this theory about the Americans?"

"No, Comrade Colonel. This is not unlike playing chess. Sometimes you have to make a guess about the character of your opponent to understand what he is planning to do."

Tarabin sat back. He stuck out his jaw and thought about what Glinin had just told him. After a moment, he said, "So, are you criticizing the system? Are you saying that we have not given you sufficient information about threats to your operation by Americans working here? And are you suggesting, Comrade Ambassador, that I have not sufficiently assessed the nature of our business here in North America? Is that what you are telling me?"

Glinin swallowed hard. Before, he had been on thin ice. Now, whatever support he had was cracking wide open. "No. That's not at all what I'm saying, Comrade Colonel. I am not talking in riddles. I am speaking plainly, and I am merely suggesting that things are developing here, like in a battle or in a chess game. The situation is fluid and is always changing. There are factors at play beyond our control, and we must react to those changes. I am not criticizing our system or any of our people. I am merely giving you my loyal observations as to the lay of the ground and the enemy's disposition."

Tarabin looked from Glinin to Shubenkov without speaking.

Shubenkov nodded at his superior almost imperceptibly. Glinin was tempted to say something more in his defence, but he chose to hold his tongue. He had no idea what the two investigators were thinking. He didn't want to appear anxious or intimidated. Tarabin had to make the next move.

The music had stopped in the background, and the announcer on the radio was talking softly in French. Tarabin finally spoke.

"All right, Comrade Ambassador. We will consider what you have said in light of our other findings. You may go for now. Send in your first secretary when you leave."

* * *

Oriana pulled the last sheet from her typewriter, her eyes scanning every line judiciously. Her story was as good and as tight as anything she'd written in the last year. There was nothing in it Cedric Jacobsen could reasonably object to. Still, she frowned. With this guy, producing great copy was no guarantee she wouldn't get a blast of unfavourable criticism. She looked at her watch and debated whether she should take it in to him now or wait until the last minute so that he'd have less time to insist on any of his pedantic changes. She put the sheets of paper in her top drawer and went to get another cup of coffee.

On her way back from the coffee station, Jacobsen almost knocked the cup out of her hand as he rounded one of the filing cabinets.

"Oriana, nice to see that you're in early. Remember, I expect to see six hundred good words on that Russian case by noon."

Oriana flushed, more with anger than humiliation. Her eyes narrowed. "I've been here for two hours. The article's done." She instantly regretted telling him it was finished.

"Okay. That's a nice change. Drop around to my office in a minute. I'll give you my amendments to it then; besides, there's something else I want to tell you."

Oriana went back to her desk and sat seething for five minutes. She needed this job. She couldn't go in to see Jacobsen just now, knowing she was almost certain to say something that would get her fired. She yanked the drawer open and pulled out the article.

From the hallway she could hear that Jacobsen was talking on the phone. "Yeah, great, Scotty. Give me three hundred words on the South Ottawa Bantam hockey tournament. Yeah, sure. Okay. If you have to, then whittle it down to two hundred with a picture. Let's say tomorrow night. Does that work for you? Great."

Jacobsen looked up from his desk and brusquely waved Oriana inside. She noticed that he'd cut himself shaving this morning and still had a piece of Kleenex stuck to the wound. He motioned for her to sit. "Yeah, talk to you then, Scotty." He hung up.

"So, let's have a look at what you've got for me." Holding out his arm, he made a gimme motion, rubbing his thumb over his fingers. "So, Oriana, just so you know, I've decided to make some changes to the structure of our weekly staff meeting." He nodded his head in full agreement with himself. "I'm gonna make it a bit smaller. You don't need to come to those meetings anymore. I'll brief you on anything that's important, anything that affects you." He jutted out his lower lip. "This should save you a bit of time. Let you focus exclusively on your writing. You won't have to worry about any policy or editorial decisions." He forced a momentary grin. "Now, let's see your article. Sit right there while I scan this, and I'll tell you what changes I want to see."

Oriana stood up, flicked the papers onto his desk, and marched out without speaking. She grabbed her coat and headed for the stairs. As she neared the door and walked through the newsroom, she could hear the gravelly voice of Stan Jones, one of the junior copy editors, calling after her.

"Hey, Oriana, I picked up your phone while you were in with Cedric. Some Russian-sounding guy by the name of Fedor Nikolaev. Says he's from the embassy. He wants you to call him back. Says it's really urgent."

✳ ✳ ✳

Cormier thought it strange that no car was parked beside the cottage. There were fresh tread marks on the driveway. He ran a practised eye over the road but still couldn't tell exactly when the fresh tracks had been made. Earlier ruts had all partially filled with snow sometime after he and Connelly had left earlier in the morning.

He went inside and entered the kitchen, then stood still, listening. The building was quiet, unnaturally so.

Cormier reached inside his parka and drew his non-issue .38 snub-nosed police special from his shoulder holster. He shouted, "Staff Sergeant Cormier here. Anybody home?" There was no immediate answer. A few seconds later, he heard a muffled thumping from upstairs. Moving silently, he made a quick scan of the downstairs rooms and then went to the bottom of the stairs. Keeping his pistol trained in synch with his eyes, he moved upstairs in a crouch.

At the top of the stairs, he could see a set of legs, tied and lying immobile, on the master bedroom floor. He moved into the room. One of the constables, Voigt, was lying face down, bound and gagged, but motionless. Another officer was struggling alongside the bed. His hands

171

and feet were bound, and he had a hand towel stuffed in his mouth and secured by a shoelace. Cormier noticed the man's hands were turning blue. He motioned to the constable to wait for a second, then did a quick check of the other upstairs rooms. They were empty. He holstered his weapon, returned to the master bedroom, and untied the constable and removed his gag.

"What happened? Where's Privalov?" Cormier asked as he went over to the other man and gingerly examined him. From the back, there were no marks or obvious wounds. He began untying his hands, taking care not to move him.

The constable slowly got to his feet. "Privalov's gone. I think he must have smacked Voigt when he was coming out of the bathroom. Privalov called me upstairs, saying there was something wrong, and when I bent down to help, he clubbed me with something heavy. He knows what he's doing. He tied us up, took our sidearms, our wallets, and the car keys. I heard the car leave about an hour ago."

There was a large, swollen, purple and black mark on Voigt's left temple. His face was grey. Cormier gently removed the gag, and the man struggled to breathe.

"I think he's badly concussed," Cormier said. "He needs to see a doctor. How're you doing?"

"I've got a hell of a headache, but I think I'm okay, Staff."

"Good. Help me get him into the car. I don't have a radio. The nearest hospital's in Hull, an hour away on these roads. Let's go."

Chapter 16

PRIVALOV PULLED THE STOLEN UNMARKED CAR up to the gas pumps at the Sunoco station on Rue Isabelle in Hull as Cormier was untying the two guards. The odometer showed that he had travelled south for fifty-three miles from the cottage. He liked the car that he had taken from the Mounties. It was an unmarked midnight blue, four-door 1950 Ford sedan. It ran smoothly and still had that fresh new-car smell. Privalov squeezed the steering wheel contentedly. The capitalists made good vehicles. Privalov thought it more than likely that the police had bought this particular model to use as an unmarked car because it looked inconspicuous. Today, that served his purposes perfectly.

At this stage he wasn't exactly certain what his next move was going to be. However, if he planned on using the Mountie's unmarked car, he wanted a full fuel tank. A uniformed station attendant came out of the garage smiling, rubbing his hands on a rag. Privalov handed him a two-dollar bill and said, "Fill it, please." The attendant replied in French, something cheerful and unintelligible. Privalov shrugged. With the gas pump locked on 'fill,' the attendant laboriously cleaned the windscreen and then moved to the front of the vehicle. Privalov stared back at him blankly when he shouted something in French. The attendant grinned, motioning with his hand for him to pop the hood. It took Privalov a second to understand what the man wanted before pulling the release catch. A moment later the attendant came back to the driver window, saying something in French and handing Privalov thirty-two cents change. Privalov stared at the coins. It struck him that he not only had no idea what things cost, but that there were so many other commonplace things that he didn't know about in this society. He rubbed his chin and lower lip.

This incident was of no consequence, but now that he was a man on the run, he'd have to be careful that he didn't expose himself by obviously appearing foreign. He put the car in gear and headed for the bridges leading to Ottawa.

With that first rush of excitement from his escape wearing off, doubts began flooding his mind. Why hadn't he simply stayed on with the Canadian police? Now, he'd be a wanted man pursued by both the Soviets and the Canadians. He'd been foolish. He could have bluffed his way into a comfortable life somewhere here in Canada. He had been stupid and impulsive in escaping from the Canadians. The team from New York would never believe his story if he was to return now. There was no way he could know what had gone on there in the last twelve hours.

Because he wasn't there to steer the investigators onto a false trail, they would get to the bottom of things sooner rather than later. He'd missed the crucial beginnings of their investigation, and his absence would instantly raise their suspicions. It was likely that the MGB officers from New York would soon discover the truth of what had happened that night. Nikolaev knew what had happened, and Karazin and Portunova were likely to tell them about the changes to the log book. He checked his rear-view mirror. Nothing. Now that he had escaped from the Canadians he couldn't go back. They had tapes of him discussing the terms of his defection and photos of their meetings. He tightened his grip on the steering wheel; he could feel pressure in his temples and his breathing was shallow. He was trapped.

He stopped at a traffic light and took a deep breath. He had to think positively about this situation. He wasn't trapped. Trapped was when they caught you. For now, he had to believe that his range of action was only temporarily reduced. This was more like losing a couple of key pieces in a chess game. If he kept his wits about him, he could still pull it off. His choice last night to break free had been a deliberate one. The first thing he needed was confidence in his own judgment.

Privalov relaxed his grip and turned onto Eddy Street, heading for the Chaudière Bridge. He'd get out of this situation. He was going to avoid downtown Ottawa. He checked the rear-view mirror again. There was nothing out of the ordinary; the traffic was light. There were no police cars. No one was following him, not yet. Everything was normal. He knew what his next move was going to be. He'd survived tougher situations in the war. He intended to survive this one.

He was going home, back to the Soviet Union. After talking to Connelly last night, he knew that was the right thing to do. That was where his loyalty lay. Back home he could convince his own people that he had behaved loyally. Who did these Canadians think he was that he could be bought off with the promise of a more comfortable life, that he would turn his back on the country and the party that he had fought so hard for? It was a matter of pride. He was a stronger man than that.

Everything he had ever done in his life had been for the sake of the Soviet Motherland and the Party. He had been prepared to give his life for them, and that little prick Shemyakin had deserved what he'd gotten. When he got back to Moscow, he would convince them of that. His entire life had been a living and unassailable testimony to his loyalty. He would establish his innocence by revealing the truth about what was going on in the embassy, by demonstrating his loyalty to his country, how he had worked tirelessly to implement active measures to undermine his country's enemies. He would prove beyond a doubt that he was a loyal and competent MGB officer. By returning voluntarily and by rejecting the snare set by the capitalist police, he would prove his innocence.

His confidence was percolating to the surface now: perhaps he would be decorated for this. But for now, he had to think through the details of this problem. The first thing he had to do was get money. He could do nothing without money, and he knew exactly where to get it.

* * *

Cormier looked at his watch. He had been driving furiously for twenty-five minutes when he pulled into the gravel parking lot beside the stone-fronted church in the tiny village of Sainte-Thérèse-de-la-Gatineau. He hammered on the door of the rectory's small frame house. When no one answered immediately, he shoved the door open and shouted in French, "Police! I have to use your phone — now."

A small, elderly man in a cardigan and clerical collar scurried in from a back room. Cormier held up his leather wallet with his badge.

"Yes, yes, of course," said the man. "This way."

In the priest's cramped office, Cormier dialled the Special Branch number. Shirley Agnew picked up on the first ring.

"Shirley, give me one of the uniforms in the office now. It's urgent." Without saying a word, Agnew handed the phone to Corporal Russell.

"Corporal Russell, Privalov's escaped," Cormier told him. "He took the car an hour or so ago, and Voigt's been seriously injured. I think he's badly concussed. I'm in Sainte-Therese. I'm taking Voigt to Hôpital Sacré-Cœur de Hull. In the meantime, advise Superintendent Ferrall or Inspector Connelly. I'll touch base when I get to the hospital. Got it?"

"Understood, Staff," Russell said. "I'll phone the hospital and let them know you're coming in with a casualty."

* * *

Connelly had been listening intently to Karazin. "So, let me get this straight, Alexander. You're telling me that you encrypted Shemyakin's and Privalov's reports. Did you see all of them?"

"No. I am only seeing the reports that they are send at night, on shifts that I am working."

"What was in these reports?"

"Shemyakin was sending informations about new radar system. That was main job he was doing. Shemyakin told me he was doing most important job for embassy, and I heard Privalov was angry because Shemyakin had most important job."

"Privalov was jealous?"

"Yes, that is word — jealous. Yes, I think so. He was very jealous when he was drinking, very angry."

"Did Privalov drink much?"

"Yes. After ambassador left, every night he was at embassy he was drinking and being angry. Sometimes his reports did not make sense. I fixed reports for him."

Connelly nodded his head. "Okay. What was in Privalov's reports?"

"Privalov was sending reports about work he was doing, peoples he was meeting and projects he was working on."

"Did you know the names of the people Shemyakin and Privalov met?"

"No." Karazin shook his head. "For secret operations they are using codenames for peoples that are working in Canada. They are sending codenames first on different forms put in special code by Shemyakin and Privalov. Only people who could be seeing informations like this are Shemyakin and Privalov, and operator in Moscow who has first list of names in code. I was only seeing codenames."

"What kind of operations did you see?"

"Shemyakin was meeting peoples who built radar. Science people — technicians and engineers. He was sending technical and scientific informations. I am not understanding scientific informations. I just copied such things and put them in code."

"What about Privalov?"

"Privalov was sending informations about Canada and army going to Korea, about government. About many, many things. Privalov sent many reports, more than Shemyakin. Privalov was also sending many reports about peoples in Canada that are working for Soviet Union."

"How many people are working for the Soviet Union in Canada, other than people in the embassy?"

Karazin shrugged and made a face. "I am only seeing maybe twenty. I think yes, maybe twenty or thirty, but daytime duty operator was seeing maybe some more, but maybe some are same." He paused as he tried to remember. "Yes, I think maybe twenty, but maybe more. I don't know. I was not counting."

"We'll get back to these people later, Alexander. What kind of people were in these reports? What kinds of jobs did they do?"

"They are doing many different jobs. Some are in unions, some science people, students, engineers, one was soldier, professors, journalists. Many jobs." Karazin shrugged but suddenly perked up. "One name I am remembering was lady journalist last week here in Ottawa. Privalov was telling Moscow about meetings and money to give her. He was asking Moscow to be first checking if her family living in Soviet Union. I remember Ukrainian name: Soroka. There was no code."

Connelly sat back. "Okay. What did Privalov say about her?"

"He was thinking Soroka was not being good candidate yet, but to be checking for family so he could be putting some pressures on her. I did not see answer."

Just then Ferrall opened the door and smiled. "Sorry to interrupt, gentlemen. Declan, can we talk for a moment in the hallway?"

Outside and far enough down the hallway to be out of earshot, Ferrall whispered, "Privalov's gotten away on us. No idea where he is just now. Apparently, he clubbed the guards and he's got their car. Voigt's in serious condition. Marcel's taking him to hospital now. I'm putting him in charge of the search for Privalov. It's a routine police hunt for a criminal now, but I still want to keep all of this in Special Branch. I want you to stay here with Karazin. If he proves to be a serious counter-intelligence asset, he'll be important — and he just might be the card that keeps us in the game. I want you sticking with him. How's your interview going?"

"If he's a real defection and not a plant, I think he's going to be a gold mine, sir. So far, he's given us some details that could only come from a legitimate source." He exhaled heavily. "It's early days, so I'll reserve my judgment on this one. You know, I had some doubts about Privalov, but the bastard fooled me. I should have seen through him."

"Don't worry about that now. We're a lot further ahead than we were this time yesterday. Has Karazin said anything that would make you think he's a plant?"

"Nothing so far, but I suppose it's possible. If he is a fake, he's giving us valuable information that he couldn't possibly have coordinated with Privalov. There's a lot more substance to Karazin's version of things, so I'm thinking he's probably legitimate."

* * *

Privalov crossed the Portage Bridge over the Ottawa River and turned the car onto Wellington Street. Driving east to Rideau Street, he parked the car on a side street and went through the back entrance of Ogilvy's department store. On the main floor of the luggage department, he found the first item he needed: a brown leather briefcase. His next stop was to pick up a few articles at the Salvation Army's thrift shop in Lower Town. In just two stops, he now had all the accoutrements he needed to make good his escape. But there was one more item he still required.

Back in his car, Privalov drove west past the Parliament Buildings and the Supreme Court. He turned right onto Kent Street, searching for a parking spot. He thought it was funny that, as far as he could see, in this part of Ottawa all the major public buildings had the same massive, imposing character as the Victorian buildings in London. Except for the frozen snowbanks lining the streets, parts of this city could have been in Westminster. He wondered if the Canadians who'd built Ottawa had had a genuinely strong emotional bond to the British Empire, or had they just shared the same architects? It was a notion that was hard to understand. Who could take pleasure in being a part of an oppressive empire? It was an aspect of Canadians that puzzled him, especially when so many of them were fiercely proud of being French or Irish, or from somewhere else in Europe. He found a parking spot near Laurier Avenue and walked back three blocks to the Dominion Bank on Sparks Street.

It struck Privalov, as he entered the spacious main chamber of the bank, that here in the West, they built the main branches of their banks like little cathedrals: massive, solid structures with high ceilings; dimly lit, quiet, solemn places. Privalov looked about him disdainfully. They needed only a bank of flickering votive candles in the corner to complete the effect. Perhaps they worshipped money the same way they worshipped their God, he mused.

There were only a few customers lined up in front of the teller windows. Privalov went to the table and carefully filled out a withdrawal slip. He checked the account number on his bank book and went over to stand in line. The elderly lady in front of him was having a hard time understanding something about her account. Privalov looked impatiently at his watch. When his turn came, he stepped confidently in front of the teller, a pretty, young woman in her late teens. She wore a green sheath dress and had a beautiful smile and warm brown eyes.

"Yes, sir? How can I help you today?" Privalov forced a smile and handed her his withdrawal slip and bank book. She looked at the slip and said, "Is it six *hundred* dollars you want, sir? I see here you have six thousand written down on your slip."

"That is what I want to withdraw. Is there a problem?"

"Well, sir, it's just that I'm not allowed to authorize that much. I'll just speak to Mr. Cloutier, if you'll please just wait for a minute?"

Privalov nodded. What had he done? Was he not allowed to withdraw so much at once from his bank? This was another thing he did not know about. He had a hollow feeling in his stomach.

Mr. Cloutier appeared in seconds. A bespectacled little middle-aged man with a trim moustache, he was dressed in a baggy grey suit and had a worried look on his face.

"Sir, could you please come into my office?"

Privalov took a deep breath, resisting a rising sense of panic and the urge to turn and bolt for the door. He nodded and followed Mr. Cloutier into a tiny office.

"So, you want to draw out six thousand dollars in cash, Mister, um..." He looked at the bank book. "Mister... Mister Privalov. Is that correct?"

The dark-eyed teller appeared at the office door with a sheaf of yellow cards and handed them to Cloutier.

"Yes, that is correct. This is important embassy business," Privalov said abruptly. "I have my diplomatic passport and my identity card, if you want to see them."

"Yes, please. It's not that I don't trust you, sir. I just want to be extra careful when we're dealing with the funds of one of our embassies. We have to protect our clients." Cloutier studied the signature on the withdrawal slip against the signature on the account cards and then compared them with the signature and photo on the passport and the diplomatic status card. "Yes, this seems in order." He smiled. "Would you prefer a certified cheque, sir? That might be easier."

"No, thank you. I need cash. Put a hundred dollars of it in five-dollar bills, please."

"Very well, sir." Cloutier left the office and returned a few minutes later.

"I'm very sorry, sir, but would you mind if I gave you the last thousand dollars in twenty-dollar bills? We don't have sufficient hundreds or fifties, I'm afraid."

Privalov bobbed his head. "That will be fine."

Five minutes later, Privalov was standing on the frozen sidewalk, quietly exuberant, having just drained the bulk of the Soviet embassy's quarterly operating account. He had a spring in his step as he walked down the street, satisfied that he now had an excellent chance of getting home safely. It was everything he could do not to shout with joy. So why did he feel this wasn't going to work?

* * *

Nikolaev met Oriana in the lobby of the newspaper office. He was a big man in a dark coat and fedora: mid-thirties with heavy eyebrows, stained teeth, and massive hands. He gave Oriana a creepy feeling. It wasn't so much his looks; what put her on edge was the way the man looked at her — not a lascivious leer, but more of a silent, predatory, hooded stare. It was how she imagined a cobra stared at its victim before it struck.

"Miss Soroka, I think you may be the last person to see Vitaly Privalov last night. Did you meet with him as planned?"

"Yes, we met at the Normandie Soda Bar. He wanted to talk to me about my articles."

"What time was this?"

Oriana was struck by the quality of Nikolaev's English. He had a theatrically deep voice and spoke English fluently with a strong Russian accent. With this man, she thought, you immediately had the sense that he had no small talk, that there was something distant and contemptuous in his manner. He spoke in a low-volume monotone, and it left Oriana with a chilling sense of menace. "We met at seven. Why do you ask? Has something happened to him?"

"I need to find him. It's very important — he is wanted at the embassy. Where did he go after your meeting?"

"Home, I guess. He didn't tell me, and I didn't ask him. Is there a problem, Mr. Nikolaev?"

"Where did you go after the meeting?"

Oriana stiffened. "That is none of your business, Mr. Nikolaev, and I don't like your tone."

Nikolaev said nothing. For several seconds he glared at her. Oriana thought he looked affected, the way some boxers tried to intimidate their opponent before a fight. "If you hear from him, you will phone me at the embassy." He turned and pushed his way back through the revolving doors.

* * *

Privalov walked back to where he'd parked the car. Snow swirling off the nearby buildings had left the car windows with a thin dusting. The temperature was dropping again, and there was a sharp bite in the wind. At the driver's door he fished in his trouser pocket for the key, but then stopped and stepped back. No, it would be better to leave the car here. The only sign restricting parking on this street indicated that you had to have a permit to park here between the hours of 9 PM and 7 AM. The car could probably stay here for a day before anyone identified it as the missing plainclothes RCMP vehicle. He smiled at the thought. He put the key back in his pocket, walked around the vehicle, and climbed over the snowbank, and walked the half-mile to the Colonial Coach bus terminal on Albert Street.

The Ottawa bus station was a cavernous, dingy shed fronted by a two-story terminal building. The terminal had two ticket wickets, a baggage room, a small diner, washrooms, and offices upstairs. Privalov noticed that there were thirty or forty people milling about inside the terminal waiting for buses. At least half of the travellers here were men, and, with the exception of two or three, all were dressed much as he was, in long, dark, heavy wool coats and wearing scarves and dark fedoras. Privalov looked around him. There were no police in sight. That was certainly unlike Russia. It would be unthinkable at a train or bus station not to have pairs of Soviet militia officers strolling around, observing the travellers and keeping a careful eye on things.

He approached the ticket wicket on the far wall. The clerk looked intensely bored. When Privalov asked for a ticket to Montreal, the man rolled his eyes as if world-weary and put upon. "Next bus for Montreal leaves in forty minutes, bay number nine. Be on time, sir. It's the connecting run from Toronto, and it's only stopping long enough to take on passengers. That'll be a dollar thirty-five, please."

Privalov collected his ticket and went to the men's room. He found an empty stall and sat there with his thoughts for half an hour. When he emerged, there was a short line-up at bay 9. The bus was four minutes early, overheated, smoky, and half full. He found an empty seat by a window near the back and heaved a sigh of relief when he heard the hissing of the airbrake release as the driver pulled out of the terminal onto the street. So far, so good. It was a huge relief getting out of Ottawa so easily, but now he needed a drink.

✳ ✳ ✳

Oriana had a sinking sensation in her stomach. She was lonely and anxious. Declan hadn't called her. Her boss left her feeling humiliated and inadequate.. And now her meeting with Nikolaev not only eliminated whatever thrill came from playing at the edges of espionage, but she felt vulnerable, and angry at herself for being a bundle of insecurities.

She'd always tried to think of herself as being strong, and self-reliant. At least on most days, that's what she told herself. Now she was tense, and shaky. She had promised herself she wouldn't do this, but as soon as she found herself alone in the newsroom, she dialled Declan's office number. He picked up on the second ring.

"Declan, I can only talk for a few moments," she blurted without preamble. "I'm in the office, and people may return any second now."

"Oriana, look — I'm sorry I haven't called. You've got to believe me; I honestly haven't had five minutes. Things have been frantic here. How are you?"

"I'm fine. I understand," she lied. She lowered her voice and spoke quickly. "A Russian guy by the name of Nikolaev has been around to see me."

Reg Jones walked into the office holding a coffee and a cigarette. He sat down heavily at his desk and gave Oriana a friendly smile.

Oriana's voice went up a cheery octave. "Okay, I've got to run now. Can we follow up on this later?"

"Yeah. I haven't had lunch yet. Can you meet me at Katz's at one?"

The fresh air and exercise from Oriana's walk to the delicatessen boosted her confidence. She made a point of arriving at Katz's at five minutes past the hour. Connelly was already sitting facing the door in the booth at the back. Mrs. Katz gave her a motherly smile when she entered.

She slid onto the bench with her coat still on. Connelly smiled and took her hand.

"Are you okay?"

"Oh, never better. I just thought I should tell you about this Nikolaev guy. He came around to the paper this morning. He gave me the creeps. He was asking about Privalov. Do you know him?"

"Yeah. What did you tell him?"

Connelly looked up as Mrs. Katz appeared beside their table with a tray of smoked meat sandwiches and coffee. He thanked her and turned to Oriana. "Hope you don't mind. I'm really pressed for time, so I ordered for both of us as soon as I got here." As soon as Mrs. Katz left, he leaned forward. "So, what did you tell him?"

"That we met as planned, we discussed my articles, and then he left. I told him I haven't seen Privalov since. He really didn't say much else. How did it go at your end?"

Connelly exhaled heavily and looked sideways. "Not for publication, please. Don't be offended by my saying that, but yeah, Privalov came along with us. Things looked good, but as of early this morning he's gone on the loose. Bashed one of our guys with something heavy, and he's still in a coma."

Oriana winced. "I hope he's going to be all right. Any idea where Privalov is?"

"No. From what you say, sounds like the embassy doesn't know either. We're pretty certain now that he was the one who killed Shemyakin."

"Really? How do you know?"

"Can't say just now, but I definitely want to catch him."

She raised her eyebrows. "You've been busy."

"No question of that — it's been frantic. That's why I haven't called. I'm sorry." Connelly felt himself redden slightly and changed the subject. "How have things been with you?"

Oriana's jaw dropped a fraction. "The truth? It's been a disastrous day."

"How so?"

"I got up at five this morning, went to work, and wrote one of the best articles of my career. My boss, who completely lacks any kind of judgment, is out to get me. Oh, and he's also an obnoxious bozo. He randomly covered my article in red ink, and he's sticking what's left of my best work ever on one of the back pages. At the end he actually said, 'Look, Oriana, I've given you a chance at something bigger, and frankly, I think you're letting us all down. I expect better than this.'"

Connelly frowned. "What did you say?"

"I got angry. I told him I've done what he asked, that this is serious journalism, but I'm not very good at hiding my feelings. I blew it."

"How?"

"I didn't tell him that he was a talentless shit and a sorry imitation of a real editor. Well, I did, but not in those words. I said that he'd wrecked my article and told him that he had to let me get on with my job and to quit behaving like a domineering and insecure twit."

"Did you actually say that?"

"Pretty much." Oriana put her clenched fist in front of her mouth and then pulled it aside. "I think I'm going to lose my job. Just before I came here, he sent me a memo via his secretary. He said that tonight he wanted me to interview the editor of the new *Good Housekeeping Cookbook*. She's in town tonight. That's his way of telling me this is what he thinks of my abilities as a journalist, and that I'm off any kind of major assignment and my days are numbered. He doesn't have the courage to fire me for being insubordinate because it would make him look weak, so he's going to make sure I get every menial job on the paper. He's a sneaky, tyrannical little prick."

Connelly bit back a smile. "That sounds pretty grim. What will you do?"

"Not certain at this stage. If worst comes to worst, I can always be a waitress. I've done that before." She paused. "Yeah." She rolled her eyes. "I did that before when I was at school. But the truth is I'm not certain what I'm going to do. It's a matter of keeping my sanity and my pride and surviving. I've got to think this through." She shifted in her seat and looked uncomfortable. Now it was her turn to change the direction of the conversation. "So, if Privalov's gone, and he's obviously keeping away from the embassy, where do you suppose he's going?"

"That's a good question." Connelly's tone was noncommittal.

"Let me think aloud for a second." Oriana was whispering, utterly absorbed. "We know that he hasn't checked in with the embassy. And if he thinks you know he's Shemyakin's murderer, he has to stay underground. He'll have gone into hiding from everyone. Does he know that you think he's the killer?"

Connelly looked hesitant. "Well, I have to make the assumption that sooner or later he'll figure that one out himself." As soon as he said this, he pulled back from the table. He'd already gone too far telling her about Privalov's escape... A moment later, he relaxed: he trusted her and respected her intellect and judgment. She was a bright woman, and he wanted a second opinion on what Privalov's next move might be.

Oriana, reading his mind, said, "Don't worry, Declan. You don't need to explain the Official Secrets Act to me. This'll go no further than us. Besides, Jacobsen's not getting another word from me on this subject."

"No, that's not what I was thinking. I trust you. Go on."

"I was just thinking, if I were Privalov, where would I go? I'd want to get out of the country. But I don't think I'd go to the United States. Not to stay, anyway. That's too obvious, and he's smarter than that. I'd try to get to some other country: South America or Australia. Or..." Her eyes flashed. "What if, and this is a big if, what if Shemyakin's death was a deliberate execution by the Russians and Privalov is planning on making his way back to the Soviet Union? What if they're helping him?"

* * *

Cormier put the phone down, stood up from his desk, and walked upstairs to the superintendent's office. He tapped on the side of the open door. Ferrall was behind his desk, frowning at a file, an unlit pipe in his hand.

"Sir?" Cormier said. "I just talked to the hospital. Voigt's come out of his coma, but the bad news is that in the last hour he's had what they call an early post-traumatic seizure. He's going to be in hospital for a while. I've sent one of Russell's guys around with a car to bring his wife to the hospital. The doctors are concerned that there may be serious brain damage. They don't know at this stage."

Ferrall shook his head and grimaced. "I hope not. He's a good guy. He just got married this summer. Thanks for the update. I'm going to go see

184

him later this afternoon." He put his pipe down. "Have you had time to prepare a Most Wanted bulletin for Privalov?"

"Just having it typed as we speak, sir. Anything special about it?"

"Yeah, let's keep this one out of the press for the next while. Send it to all the major police forces across the country, customs and border points, airlines, and shipping terminals, but keep it off the press release. Also, could you have the Department of External Affairs query the Soviet embassy on our behalf? The Russians won't reply if we do it. Call Chuck Fisher. Let's see if they respond to him."

Chapter 17

AS THE BUS ROLLED OUT OF OTTAWA and across the snow-covered farmland of Eastern Ontario, Privalov felt an overwhelming sense of weariness. His limbs were leaden and his head began to nod. He sat up and rubbed his face. This was no time to drift off; he needed to stay alert. He'd sleep tonight. The strain of the last several weeks, especially last night and this morning, had taken a toll on him. He understood that. The prolonged stress left him perpetually weary and on edge. He didn't pretend to understand stress and fatigue in any kind of anatomical sense, but he'd experienced enough of it in his lifetime to realize that whatever reserves of energy and courage one had, those reserves were depleted at a much faster rate when worry and anxiety upset one's emotional balance. He'd rest soon enough.

He stared out the window looking at the furrowed lines of harvested corn fields, irregular brown stalks protruding through twenty-five centimetres of granular, blown snow. In the distance was a small line of trees and a cluster of farm buildings. Memories flooded back of that iron-cold winter in the Ukraine nine years ago. He had been a junior artillery officer then. It was Europe's coldest winter in a century.

It was strange, he thought, how most days you managed to put those harrowing times behind you; but then, when you least expected it, something yanks up the half-decomposed remains of a memory that you assumed you'd buried. The icy fields, the distant plumes of smoke over the farm buildings — it all reminded him of the afternoon outside Halynka. That was his first winter offensive of the war. They were well past the west bank of the Dnieper River and his battery had suddenly been raked by German counter-artillery fire. The battery had just started setting up its howitzers in a frozen field much like the one outside his window: packed snow in sharp, deep furrows, six guns in a line, a hundred men offloading and stacking ammunition, digging, dragging equipment, and bedding in the guns. In a matter of seconds, or at least it seemed like seconds, more than half the battery was killed. There was no warning, no ranging rounds to indicate that the Germans were bracketing them. They must have been shooting from the map. Suddenly, hell exploded all along the gun line, and then just as suddenly it stopped. Over half the men in the battery were casualties. Torn, bleeding, screaming, mangled, burned, lifeless, writhing, and frightened. Soviet soldiers and patriots. Most of the wounded died from shock or exposure later that night when the temperature plunged even further.

That day, and so many like it, was why he believed in the Soviet Union. He would never forget those men, or the hundreds of others he saw die over the next three years. His country would never be subject to that kind of horror again. He was intensely proud to be doing his duty. Today, he still served the Soviet Union. He was honouring the sacrifice of those men. Their memory invigorated him.

The bus rolled on into Quebec. Privalov looked at his watch. It would be dark in an hour and a half.

Before last night, Privalov had never talked to any of the Mounted Police who were tasked with watching them and countering their efforts. This wasn't a friendly pickup game of football, where, after the match, workers from two different factories could all go down to the canteen and have a drink together. He rubbed his chin. Connelly and his men seemed like reasonable, intelligent people. They were nice enough, but naïve if they thought they could dangle a life in Canada in front of him and expect him to cheerfully throw away his country, his wife and son, his honour, and his beliefs.

The window was beginning to frost over. He rubbed the cold glass with the bottom of his fist. Most of the Germans he'd fought and killed were probably reasonable men at one time or another too, but these same men had slaughtered millions, smashed Soviet cities, and turned the Motherland into an abattoir. There were no chances or half-measures to be taken when it came to security. These Westerners, these reasonable men, could just as easily be led by butchers who were prepared to destroy Soviet cities with their atomic bombs. It was not going to happen again, not while there was breath in his body.

The sun was already turning orange in the west when the bus pulled into the station on the corner of De Maisonneuve Boulevard and Berri Street in Montreal. He got off and strode through the terminal, looking neither left or right, walking as if he knew where he was going. He didn't know the city well. He walked south for twenty minutes until he reached the old port area down by the river. He was sure nobody had been waiting for him at the bus station and that he hadn't been followed. Down here in the streets close to the St. Lawrence, the wind was damp, and Privalov's feet were wet and numb from walking through salt-laden slush. The cold pierced through his wool coat, and he pulled it around him. He needed to rest, to think, to review his plans. He looked around for a hotel, somewhere he could find something to eat, get some rest, and restore himself for the rest of his journey.

The street he found himself on, Rue St Louis, was a darkened residential strip with broad metal flights of stairs at the front of most houses. Even the French neighbourhoods in Ottawa didn't have such staircases. He'd seen some other houses like these farther north when the bus entered Montreal, and he wondered if the strange metal stairs had something to do with Montreal's winter conditions. He walked two blocks north to Dorchester Boulevard, a main thoroughfare with streams of traffic. He stood shivering on the corner under a streetlight, watching rush-hour vehicles roar past. It was only a few minutes before a taxi cruised toward him. He raised his arm in the universal signal and the cab pulled over for him. He climbed in the back and the driver said something unintelligible. He slammed the door, asking the driver, "Do you know where the Ritz-Carleton Hotel is?"

The driver turned around, laughing. "Yeah, yeah. I'm a Montreal cabbie. I know where the Ritz is." He shook his head and muttered something indistinct. Privalov guessed it was probably something disrespectful along the lines of "Do you think I'm stupid? Of course I know my way around here."

Privalov had never been to the Ritz, but he knew from Shemyakin's vivid descriptions of the high life here in Montreal that it was one of the city's most luxurious hotels. It was unlikely anyone would be looking for him there.

A few minutes later the cab pulled up in front of a square twelve-story building. Out front was a tall doorman in a top hat, white gloves, and a maroon overcoat. He looked like he was in charge of the place. The driver turned about.

"This is it, sir. A buck-fifty."

Privalov struggled to one side and fished in his pocket, dragging out a five-dollar bill. He handed it to the cabbie, who looked at him blankly.

"Is there a tip in this?" the cabbie said.

"Yes, yes. Tip, of course."

"How much?"

"How much is a tip?"

"Twenty cents'll do fine, sir." He handed the change over the front bench seat.

Privalov climbed out of the cab and hurried past the doorman, deliberately ignoring this ridiculous-looking man with his red coat, top hat, and false confidence, a capitalist lackey who looked like he'd escaped from a circus. The doorman gave Privalov a smile, throwing him off his stride. Was the man giving him a condescending grin? He didn't want to admit it, but the whole setup intimidated him. He strode past him without returning the doorman's glance.

Inside the Ritz, the light in the lobby had a warm, orange glow. The floor was carpeted with a massive, rich, carpet in what looked like an Oriental design. There were two separate sets of couches and easy chairs around coffee tables, and there was piano music playing softly in a room off to the right. Across from the front door was a long front desk, from behind which two young women in maroon blazers smiled at him. Privalov forced a smile and walked forward.

"I would like a room for tonight, please."

"Yes, certainly, monsieur," said one of them. "Will you be staying for just one night?" The woman had a dazzlingly perfect smile and a slight French accent.

"Yes, just one night."

"And do you have any luggage, monsieur?"

"No. No, I am from the Latvian trade delegation visiting Ottawa and was at a conference here in Montreal. Because I have a headache, I have decided to stay here tonight, and I will go back to join the delegation tomorrow morning."

"That's fine, monsieur. A single room will be twelve dollars. Just so you know, monsieur, we don't take Diners Club cards yet. Hopefully we'll have that later this year. So, will you be paying by cheque or cash?"

"Cash, thank you." Privalov handed the woman a twenty-dollar bill.

She smiled and handed him his change. "Could you please sign the register, monsieur?" She pushed a leather-bound book toward him, along with a room key.

Privalov studied the existing entries in the leather book and printed out 'Georgs Bartulis' — it was the only Latvian name he could think of. Under his address he simply scribbled, 'Riga, Latvia.'

The woman smiled again. "The grill is open until eleven tonight, the café closes at nine, and we have room service throughout the night. Checkout is at noon. Your room is 705. The elevator is just over there on the right. Bonne soirée, Monsieur."

"Is there a tip here?" he asked.

"No, monsieur, but you can leave one for the chambermaid in your room in the morning if you wish." She smiled radiantly.

Privalov crossed the lobby to the elevator, thinking that the doorman could take a lesson in manners from the women behind the front desk. His confidence was returning, but he had a gnawing uncertainty at the pit of his stomach. In normal circumstances he wouldn't have felt the least bit anxious or self-conscious. He would have enjoyed the opportunity of chatting with two pretty desk clerks, but there was so much he didn't know about the normal things in Canada: bank withdrawal limits, taxis, and tipping, and what the hell were Diners Club cards? He knew he spoke good English, but he had a strong accent. He stood out like a broken tooth, and it left him feeling vulnerable and a touch awkward. He hated that feeling. Nonetheless, he was grateful he could get a room in this country without showing identification. In Russia they wouldn't hand him the room key until the transaction had been cleared with the local militia, and if they were feeling surly, they could leave you waiting for an hour or more.

His room was smaller than he expected, but so beautifully appointed. Thick carpets and heavy curtains that went to the floor, a small desk with a modern radio, a winged chair, a beautiful wood dresser, a high, comfortable double bed with a satin bedspread, and more pillows than anyone could ever possibly sleep on. The bathroom floor, ceiling, and walls were all clad in miniature white tiles, and there were more thick towels than a man could use in a week. Soap, shampoo, and a razor laid out... It was bourgeois extravagance — but he loved it. No wonder Shemyakin had spent so much time in Montreal staying in such hotels.

He sat on the winged chair and picked up the leather-covered room service menu. He wouldn't risk going to one of the restaurants. He hadn't eaten since breakfast with Connelly this morning at the lake. It was hard to believe; that all seemed like days ago now. He picked up the bedside phone.

"Yes, this is Mr. Bartulis in room number 705. I would like to order a hot roast beef sandwich, please." He licked his lips. What he really wanted was to order a bottle of cold vodka, but that would be too Russian, too obvious. "Can you please also send me a bottle of whisky? Yes, Scotch whisky. Yes, Glenlivet is very good. Thank you."

Twenty minutes later there was a soft knock at his door. He knew who it was, but his heart leapt. The police might also knock gently. He opened the door slowly. Outside stood a short young man in a maroon uniform with a trolley and trays. Just like in the American films, he wore a silly round hat like a dancing monkey. The man picked up one of the trays and indicated he was coming inside. Privalov stepped away from the door. The man put the tray, an ice bucket, and a whisky bottle on the desk. He handed

Privalov a pen and a receipt.

"Please sign here, sir."

Privalov signed. The man stood back, smiling. Privalov studied him and then it dawned on him. "Is there a tip?"

"Yes, sir."

"How much is the tip?"

The man's smile turned to a smirk. "One dollar, sir."

Privalov fished in his pocket and peeled a dollar bill from a thick wad of bills. The man's eyes widened at the bulk of the money roll. Privalov instantly knew he'd been taken for a dupe. He clenched his jaw and his eyes narrowed. His right hand balled into a fist; he flicked his head and eyes toward the door, a silent command. "Get out."

* * *

Connelly was back at his desk. He had spent the day interrogating Karazin. He rubbed his eyes. He thought the word 'interrogating' sounded more brutal than the process really was, although their discussion had certainly been more than a friendly little interview. The big question loomed in front of him now: Was Karazin a plant? Was he simply a good actor who was playing them, feeding them false information, deliberately bewildering them, sending them on a wild goose chase? What could the Russians be up to? He longed for a cigarette. He had pushed Karazin hard today, and he didn't like doing that. Unlike Privalov, who he never warmed to, he couldn't help but like Karazin.

During the interview, Connelly had suggested to Karazin that he might have to send him back to the embassy. "You know," he'd said, "it might not be up to us. We might not have any say in things. If the politicians decide that they don't want to upset the Soviet Union, they might order you back. Not a lot we could do. You understand that?"

The man's eyes had darted back and forth at the suggestion, and he'd wriggled around in his chair. If he had been lying, he could certainly mimic all the physical reactions of fear and anxiety.

"Of course, if we can verify some of things that you're telling me," Connelly had continued, "then we can prove to the politicians that you're too valuable for us to send you back. We can help you, get you confirmed as a legitimate refugee. If we can do that, no one can touch you. You'll be safe, so work with me."

Karazin looked like he could hardly believe what Connelly was saying.

"You've got to help me, Alexander," Connelly said. "Who else did Shemyakin and Privalov meet? You read their reports. You encrypted them. You saw the answers sent back from Moscow."

At several points in the day the poor man had been on the verge of tears. "Yes, but I am never seeing the original names sent by them, only the code names. They were doing this on purpose so that only they and Moscow could be knowing the real names of who they were doing work with."

"What jobs did these men have? Where did they work?"

Karazin wracked his brain. "I am telling you about engineers and scientists and professors. Shemyakin was doing better success than Privalov. Privalov was being angry for this. There was one man — he was businessman. I do not have name from Shemyakin. He was working in Montreal." He shrugged. "I am never seeing his name, any names, but I think Shemyakin was doing sex with wife of business man."

"How do you know that?"

"Shemyakin was drinking one night and when I am making report, he is laughing, telling me he is getting out of embassy in Canada and being with women. He is pointing to report and making face, telling me if I want to fuck women in Canada, to have better job, like his job."

"What did you think of him telling you this?"

"I am thinking he is being low. He is not telling me as he is telling friend." Karazin swallowed hard and his voice rose. "He is showing himself about important job. He is being such pig. All clerks, we are hating Shemyakin, Privalov, and Nikolaev."

Connelly sat back. In his time, he'd done hundreds of police interviews, many of them with world-class liars, men who could convince you that the sky was bright green and that they were as pure and innocent as the driven snow. If Karazin was a liar, he was as convincing as anyone he'd ever seen. But after Privalov, he was beginning to have serious doubts about his own judgment. Had he been guilty of wishful thinking? Was he believing what he wanted to be true rather than what the evidence was pointing to?

That could be true in Privalov's case, but as far as Karazin was concerned, the things he was telling Connelly dovetailed pretty closely with what they knew about Shemyakin and his range of contacts. That range of detail was verifiable. On the other hand, they couldn't really verify any of Privalov's story because he hadn't given them much. That should have been a red flag by itself. Connelly stared, glassy-eyed, at the corner of his desk. Did the details from the two key informants in this problem sufficiently resemble one another, or were they too neat? What new information had Karazin given them? Was it possible that, somehow, the men Cormier had interviewed had advised the Russians of what they had already found out from them? Connelly toyed with the pen on his desk. It was possible, but was it probable?

As if on cue, Cormier walked into the office and sat down. "You look lost in thought, boss. How're you making out with Karazin? You think his story makes any sense?"

Chapter 18

PRIVALOV WOKE AT TEN TO NINE. He sat in his underwear on the edge of his bed looking at what was left of the Glenlivet bottle in front of the mirror. There was a little less than two centimetres of liquid left. The inescapable truth was that imperceptibly, over time, he'd become one of those men who could easily down a litre of alcohol by himself in a night. And the awful, irrefutable conclusion was that this habit had long since ceased having anything to do with pleasure. There was no joy, no fulfillment in this. He needed it. Yet when he drank, he became angry, and when he was angry his control evaporated. It was almost like a scientific observation. Drinking was what had got him into this mess in the first place. If he hadn't been drinking, he would have handled Shemyakin differently. If he hadn't been drinking, he wouldn't have put his family in jeopardy. If he hadn't been drinking, he wouldn't be on the run from his own people.

He scratched his face and grimaced. There was no point in worrying about what he couldn't change. What was done was done. For now, he had a plan and there was work to be done. He looked at his watch and turned on the radio to catch the morning news.

Privalov sat listening to the newscast and then, satisfied, switched off the radio. There wasn't so much as a word about him. He got up and shaved, showered, and dressed. As he approached the door to leave, he did a quick scan of the room. There was nothing to reveal who had been there. For a moment he considered leaving a tip for the hotel maid, but then thought the better of it. No one would see him anyway. At the front desk he paid his room service bill and did a quick but thorough examination of the lobby. Except for a cleaner and the front desk staff, the place was empty. There was no one suspicious lurking about who could have been posted to keep an eye out for him.

Outside, he strolled past the doorman and walked two blocks on

Sherbrooke Street. When he thought he was sufficiently far enough from the hotel not to be identified by anyone, he hailed a cab. He got in the back, telling the driver, "The corner of Rue St Hubert and Rue Villeray, please." Despite the cabbie's attempt to kindle a conversation, Privalov rode for fifteen minutes in silence to the offices of the Soviet Union's commercial consul. He was angry and his stomach was in a knot. The hotel doorman might not have known who he was, but the two clowns at the consulate knew he was a senior MGB officer and he intended that they were going to be suitably terrified of him.

Inside the main building, he walked up the dingy three-story staircase and pushed open the door. The indolent, bald little shit called Koslov was sitting in the outer office, flipping through the pages of a *Life* magazine. Koslov looked up blankly, jumping to his feet when he recognized Privalov. Privalov stormed past.

"Sit down and be quiet," he said curtly in Russian. He shoved the door of Alexeev's office, giving it a simultaneous kick for good measure. Alexeev looked up angrily from a tabloid newspaper.

"What? Oh, Comrade Privalov. I had no idea you were coming today." He struggled to his feet.

"No, of course not. I'm on important business. No one is to know that I'm in Montreal or that I have been here. Do you understand that?"

Alexeev nodded in bewilderment.

"Good. Now come with me and give me the keys to your car."

"You want my car, Comrade?"

"Don't make me repeat myself. Get up, get your coat, show me your car. Let's go."

On the way past Koslov, Privalov spat, "I'm here on highly sensitive business and there is a need for the utmost secrecy. If you so much as tell anyone, anyone at all, at any time, that I've been here, I swear I'll have your balls! Understand?"

Koslov nodded eagerly. "Of course, Comrade Privalov!"

Alexeev led him down Rue Villeray to a rusting nine-year-old black Chevrolet Fleetline parked in the street.

"Listen to me carefully, Comrade," Privalov said in terse Russian. "I'm on a critical task that involves the security of our country and the safety of our agents. I'll be back in Ottawa in a week. At that time, and only at that time, will you report your car to the Montreal police as stolen. It will eventually be found and returned to you. In the meantime, you will tell no one, not even the members of our embassy, that you have seen me." Privalov squeezed Alexeev firmly by the arm. "You must tell no one." He lowered his voice. "We have identified a traitor who is doing great harm to the

Soviet Union." He paused for a second. "I'm going to find him, and I will eliminate him. When it's done, I will call you and thank you for your work. In the meantime, you and Koslov must say nothing to anybody — not now, not ever. If you do, I will consider it the most serious and deliberate breach of security." Privalov dropped his head a fraction of an inch and squeezed Alexeev's arm again. "If somebody asks you about your car, tell them it's in for a repair to the transmission."

* * *

Superintendent Ferrall stood at the door to Connelly's office. "How are things going with Karazin?"

"He seems to be sticking close to his story, sir. He's given us a few new bits of information, but not a lot. He's confirmed that Shemyakin was running a businessman within Canada Radiotech International. I'm thinking that would be Howard Kendall. He's as good a person to start with as any, so when we get a moment, I'd like to look more closely at him." Connelly let out a long, slow breath. "The other thing I've determined is that the Soviets' current primary intelligence objective in Canada is cracking the technical issues around the Pinetree Line. Apparently, that was Shemyakin's main role. Karazin thinks that's the GRU's main intelligence collection effort. Privalov, on the other hand, was primarily involved in running long-term illegals and domestic recruits, mainly academics, scientists, key industrial executives, and government policy makers. Unfortunately, we don't have actual names, as the Soviet embassy uses code words as a form of double encryption in case their routine codes have been compromised. Karazin has no idea who they are exactly. I'll try to get some more bits of information on that one. The only other development is that the Russians sent Fedor Nikolaev around to talk to Oriana. Apparently, they're concerned that Privalov hasn't shown up at the embassy."

Ferrall nodded and said nothing for a moment, like a chess player contemplating his next series of moves. "You're certainly making progress," he said at length, then pursed his lips. "It's a lot more than we knew this time a week ago."

"Yeah, I suppose so, sir," Connelly said morosely, and dropped his pen onto the desk. "Look, sir, I've got to say, I think I let you down with Privalov. I should have seen through him. If I'd been a little more astute, maybe Voigt wouldn't be in hospital with a major concussion."

Ferrall smiled. "Don't spend much time worrying about that. It wasn't your fault. We didn't plan on holding him against his will anyway. Besides, you're not the first good cop who's been fooled by a con man. I'm pretty sure that you won't be the last, either." Ferrall fidgeted with his pipe. "Anyway, news from me. Apparently, Voigt's come out of his coma, but he's still in a pretty bad way. They're going to transfer him to the Civic Hospital's neurology department later tonight. On the case, Cormier's working all the ropes, but finding Privalov's turning out to be a dead end. The Russians haven't given any information to Chuck Fischer at External Affairs." Ferrall stepped sideways and closed the door to the small office. He sat down and spoke in a lowered voice. "Have you heard anything from the Brits or the Americans in the last twenty-four hours?"

Connelly gave a slight shrug. "No, sir. Were they supposed to call me?"

"Just wondered. I had a call an hour ago from the MI5 liaison office in the British embassy in New York. He says they've heard through their sources that we're having some movement on the Shemyakin case. They're after me to let them send someone up to serve as a liaison. Says it might have some bearing on their work at home. He was a bit vague on that aspect. Oh, yeah — you'll be happy to know he's promised not to send Guy Burgess. He apologized again about Burgess being sent up to Canada. He says they're kicking him out of the embassy and sending him back to Britain. Apparently, he's been something of an ongoing national embarrassment in front of the Americans as well."

Connelly shook his head. "No. That's all news to me. I haven't talked to anyone."

"I didn't think so. Just for your information, I've stalled them again. I told them not to do anything just yet, that I had to discuss it with my superiors. But you know, I'm concerned as to how they knew so quickly that we've had some movement up here. There has to be a leak somewhere." Ferrall shifted in his chair and lit his pipe. He tilted his head back. "Look, Declan, there are, to my knowledge, only nine people who are even aware of the operation we've been running here in the last few days. One of them is in hospital, and seven others are all meticulously vetted members of the Mounted Police." He leaned back, weighing his words carefully. "Declan, I've suspected for the last couple of days that there's a certain chemistry between you and Oriana Soroka. That's really none of my business." He looked Connelly in the eye and spoke slowly. "Unless, of course, she might have been the one who's somehow tipped off the Brits that something was brewing here."

* * *

Chez Victor was a tiny but chic bar and grill on the south end of Monkland Avenue in Côte-des-Neiges. Privalov sat brooding over his next moves in the corner booth furthest from the window. Before finding Chez Victor, he had been driving around town for two hours, searching for exactly the right kind of place. The problem was, he had never actually done anything like what he had planned, and that meant that he didn't know exactly what the right kind of place looked like. Everything about this search was entirely new for him. When he saw Chez Victor, he pulled over, parked the Chevrolet, climbed over a slushy snowbank, and found that he was the only diner at this time of the day. He smiled at the waiter.

"A whisky, please."

The waiter was a forbidding-looking man in his seventies. He had white hair and jowls, wore an apron, and had large black circles under his eyes. He simply nodded and returned with a tumbler, a cruet of water, and a small dish of mixed nuts.

"Will you be ordering lunch, monsieur?"

"No, thank you. This will be fine." Privalov fished out a two-dollar bill and placed it on the table. He hoped that he looked sufficiently sophisticated. "Can you tell me, please, where I can find girls here in Montreal? I am from out of town. You know? Some company." He forced a smile.

The waiter glowered at him. "This isn't the kind of place you're looking for."

Privalov smiled again and pushed the two-dollar bill across the table. "I know, but can you tell me where I should go?"

The waiter made a sour face and said, "At night, the corner of Rue Ste-Catherine and Saint-Laurent Boulevard. Now, finish your drink and get out."

Privalov nodded coolly. That wasn't a reaction he had expected. He took five minutes to finish his drink. There was no point in becoming indignant or angry with the waiter; it would only draw attention to himself. Back in the car, he sat thinking. This encounter with the waiter only proved that his plan made more sense than ever. There were so many things about this country, its people, and their behaviour, that he still didn't understand. If he was going to travel and not be identified or recognized as a foreigner, he needed someone to help him.

✳ ✳ ✳

At seven that night Privalov found himself eyeing the front door of the Café Raspoutine on Rue Sainte Catherine. From the outside, Café Raspoutine looked like it suited his purposes perfectly. It occupied seventy-five feet of seedy street frontage and had a blinking red neon sign advertising it as Raspoutine — Café Bar — Dance. Inside the front door a burly man in a suit, a broad red tie, suspenders, and baggy trousers demanded Privalov pay a two-dollar cover charge just to get in. Before tonight, Privalov had never paid a cover charge for anything. This evening, he willingly forked over the money.

Inside, the lamps had been dimmed with red shades. Privalov's eyes took a moment to adjust to the shadows. For an instant, the red tinge awakened a memory of the map lights the Red Army had used in the divisional command post bunker during the war. Red light didn't travel far, making it harder for the Germans to identify a headquarters. Privalov looked around the room. There was a bar and a half-dozen tables. The bartender, a powerful-looking bald-headed man, stopped whatever he was doing over the sink and stared at him suspiciously. Perry Como was crooning 'Some Enchanted Evening' out of a speaker perched on a shelf by the collection of liquor bottles. At the back, by a small dance floor, two very bored girls sat smoking at a black Formica table. Privalov noticed that neither one of them bothered to look at him. At the bar, two other men with their backs to him were deep in conversation.

Privalov, keeping his back to the wall, took a seat at one of the tables. The bartender folded his arms and, without saying anything, jerked his head upwards, the universally abrupt signal for 'What do you want?'

"Whisky. A large whisky," Privalov called out in a voice loud enough to make the two men at the bar spin around.

The bartender brought him his drink and demanded $2.50 for it. Privalov shrugged. The price was outrageous. He put the money on the table and lifted the glass as if toasting the barman. The whisky tasted like lighter fluid. He quaffed most of it in one shot. As he put the glass down, one of the girls sauntered over to his table and sat down. She had a hard face, heavy with makeup, but Privalov thought there was an adolescent look about her.

"Are you interested in some company?" she said.

Privalov thought the girl had an American accent. "Yes, but I want to meet a girl who is my age."

Privalov was uncertain whether the bar girl's reaction was closer to a sneer or a smile. "And how old is that?" she said.

"You tell me."

The girl patted his hand. "Buy me a drink and I'll take you upstairs to meet Angelina. She'll set you up with what you need. I drink champagne."

Privalov nodded. "Champagne. Of course. And how much is that?"

"Three dollars."

Privalov dug in his pocket and dropped three one-dollar bills onto the table. "Take me to meet Angelina."

The girl looked over at the bartender and flicked her head toward the back of the room, then took Privalov gently by the hand. He got to his feet, throwing back the rest of his whisky with his free hand. She led him to a stairway leading up to a hallway panelled with imitation wood pressboard. At the end of the hallway, she opened a door and steered Privalov into a sitting room. A strawberry blonde woman, middle-aged, with a curly hairdo and bright red fingernails, was sitting on a worn easy chair. An old wooden radio was softly playing big band music. The girl motioned for Privalov to sit on the couch.

"Angelina, this gentleman would like to meet someone closer to his own age. Can you help him?" She went out again, closing the door softly behind her.

Angelina smiled. "You've come to the right place, darling." She looked him up and down and smiled. "That'll be twenty dollars, in advance." Privalov leaned over and fished the money out of his pocket. He handed it over with a forced smile.

"Just wait here a minute. I think I know just the girl for you." Angelina patted him on the knee and left the room. She was back in a minute. "Down the hall, darling. Millie's waiting for you in room three."

Privalov smiled again, more naturally this time. At the end of the hall a man with a thin moustache, in shirtsleeves and a brightly coloured green tie, leaned against the wall.

"Room three's on the left." He pointed to his watch. "You got thirty minutes, not a minute longer."

Privalov stepped through the open door into the room. Millie had her back to the door and was stubbing a cigarette in an ashtray. "My rules are don't kiss me and don't touch my hair," she said without turning around.

Privalov closed the door and sat on the edge of the bed. "That is fine. I simply want to talk."

Millie turned around slowly. She was in her early thirties with light brown hair, short bangs clipped high on her forehead, and a cluster of tight curls pinned at the back. She had bright red lipstick and heavy pancake foundation. But for a professional call-girl, Privalov thought she looked decidedly unpretentious in a plain mustard-coloured dress and a grey cardigan.

"You want to talk?" she said. "Okay, I've done that before." She shrugged. "It's your dime."

"Yes, I want to make a deal with you. I'm looking for a female companion for the next several days."

Millie laughed. "That could get very expensive in this game, mister. What kind of a deal do you want?"

"I know this may sound quite strange, but please, listen to what I have to say."

Millie shrugged again.

"I didn't come here for sex. Up until last week, I used to work in Toronto at an international financial services company. I was being cheated by my employer, and so I left the company with a large sum of money, what I thought they owed me. It was a great deal of money." Millie stared at him with one eyebrow cocked, but he chose to ignore her reservations. "I have wired most of the money to a bank in South America. As of yesterday, the company discovered the money is missing and the police are looking for me. I have to get out of the country, but the police have my description and they will be watching all the border points and the airports for an unaccompanied man with a Latvian accent. I intend to get onto a ship in Halifax, but I need someone to help me get there, someone to accompany me and do the talking for me so I won't be recognized.

"I think there is less chance of being caught if I travel as part of a married couple. You can do the talking at hotels, and if for any reason we are stopped by the police you will talk for me. In this weather it will take us two days to drive there. I will pay you four thousand dollars if you come with me. We will drive, and if we are stopped anywhere, you will pretend you are my wife. I will give you a thousand dollars tonight, and the remainder on the last day when we are in Halifax. After that, you can go where you want. We will never see each other again. This is a very good deal."

Millie lit another cigarette and sat on the bed. "You will pay me four thousand dollars to drive to Halifax? Halifax, as in Nova Scotia? You know I can't even get onto Sainte Catherine Street by myself. You do know that, eh?" She looked at the door, and then back at Privalov. "I think you saw Ronnie the creep with the Clark Gable moustache?" Privalov nodded. "Mr. Brass-knuckles is the timekeeper and the bouncer here. He also guards the back stairs. He keeps us in here. This is a hard racket, and they play rough. I wouldn't even get by him, let alone make it to Halifax." She blew out a cloud of smoke.

"I will deal with Ronnie." Privalov spoke quietly as he laid a thousand dollars in hundreds and fifties on the bed.

Millie's eyes widened. "That's more money than I've ever had at one time in my whole life. My God, this isn't real! Listen, you try to bribe Ronnie, it's not gonna work." She laughed. "I know the guy. With him, you'll just end up unconscious in the alley with an empty wallet."

" I have said, I will deal with Ronnie. Thank you for the advice. Ronnie won't be a problem. I know this is asking you to make a quick decision, but will you come with me?"

"Listen, mister, I hate this fucking place, but I don't even know your name. How do I know I won't end up dead in some hotel room?"

Privalov shrugged. "You have to trust me. My name is Georgs Bartulis." He motioned toward the money on the bed. "My money is a sign of my good intentions. If my plan was to hurt someone, I could do it for much less expense. Also, I am paying you so much money because if I don't get out of the country in the next few days, I will almost certainly spend the next fifteen years in a Canadian prison. I don't want that. So, will you come with me?"

She looked at the money and then back to Privalov. "If we don't make it past Ronnie, though, do I still get to keep the money?"

Privalov grinned. "Yes. I told you not to worry about Ronnie."

"Easy for you to say, George." Millie shook her head. "This is stupid, and I really don't believe it, but for that kinda money, I'm in. I wanna see this."

"Get your coat." Privalov stood up. "Follow me."

* * *

"I had to ask you this. I'm sorry," Connelly said. He and Oriana were walking down the sidewalk on Sparks Street. Shops were locking up, the afternoon sunlight was fading, the shadows were long. It had suddenly gotten much colder. Queued up on the street, overcrowded, bread-loaf-shaped buses and trolley cars were loading drably clad civil servants and shopkeepers to carry them home to the city's new suburbs.

Connelly was flustered by Oriana's silence. "Oriana, personally I don't think you told the British," he said. "But they know about Privalov, and it's obvious something's up when they've found out what we're doing on the day after we launched the operation. It's suspicious. It doesn't mean you're a suspect, or that I distrust you, but we have to determine who's the leak, and we have to look carefully at every possible source. I'm sorry, Oriana, but it's my job. I have to ask you."

Acknowledging the RCMP's concerns aloud left Connelly feeling guilty as well as unsettled. His affair with Oriana put them both in a potentially serious conflict of interest. It was the serpent that lay patiently in ambush, the corrosive subtext of their relationship. Without having discussed it, they both knew the relationship was an unprofessional wrinkle in a potentially volatile investigation. The development with the British only aggravated things. Connelly rubbed his hand across his face and exhaled heavily. "For one thing, I don't think you have any motive to be talking to the Brits. Do you?"

"There you go again, Declan. You're interrogating me."

"I suppose I am, Oriana, but let's not be naïve. There are two aspects to our relationship." He lowered his voice, trying to sound sympathetic. "One side of our relationship is business, and the other is personal; and I'm afraid neither of us has been wise enough to keep the two apart. I'm trying to balance both, and I need your help and your understanding on this one."

Oriana stopped and turned. "All right, Inspector. I have spoken to no one about Privalov other than what I have written in the paper. And like you, it's caused me some concern as to whether or not I've done the right thing by becoming involved with you. Like you, I have a professional code of ethics that I think I've probably been more than a little bit careless with. But while we're at it—"

Connelly grabbed Oriana lightly by the elbow. "Please, Oriana, come on. Please, not so loud. We're in the middle of a busy street, and I don't want all of Ottawa to know about my personal life," he winced, "or a highly classified operation."

"Right." Oriana frowned and lowered her voice to a whisper. "While we're at it, did it ever cross your mind, Inspector, that there are now four parties to your dirty little secret? The RCMP, Privalov, me, and the Russians. Let's just say it's not me, and you seem to think it's unlikely to be the RCMP. Okay, let's assume you guys are squeaky clean and watertight. We both agree, it's probably not Privalov, because wherever he is, he's in no position to tell them, so that would tell me that it just may be the Russians who have, one way or another, let the British know what you're up to. Maybe the leak is with the Russians, not me or any of the others."

"I know. I've thought of that," Connelly said placatingly, "but you want to know something?" Impulsively, he gathered her into his arms and hugged her. "You should be working for us. You think like an analyst."

"No, I don't, Declan," she snapped, pushing herself away from him. "Don't try to jolly me. I think like a journalist. That's my job, but I've promised to keep quiet about this operation, and sometimes I wish I hadn't made that promise." She turned and started walking again, shaking her head. "My job's turned into a form of Chinese water torture anyway," she said over her shoulder. "You don't trust me, my boss is deliberately trying to ruin me, and I've done nothing wrong. I'm angry and frustrated."

Connelly hurried to catch up to her, then put his arm around her and gave her a squeeze. "Look, I'm not trying to patronize you. I trust you. As for your editor, yeah, there's no question, he's a nasty piece of work. Unfortunately, we all run into one or two of those. It's still tough — I get that. So what do you think you'll do?"

"I don't know, but what I wanted to tell you before we got sidetracked was that Nikolaev has been calling me all afternoon. I haven't returned his call."

* * *

It wasn't much of a decision. Millie scooped the money into a red leatherette purse. For months now she'd been intensely unhappy, glum, and sullen, conscious every minute that she was trapped, thinking that things would never change. The money and the glamour once promised to her had turned out to be an impoverished three-year, slow-motion nightmare. Greed, misery, and the sudden opportunity that Privalov offered to change her life made the decision simple. She wanted out. Her pulse raced and her throat went dry.

"Wait," she whispered. "We can't get out of here using the front door. The back stairs are the safest way out. They lead to the alley, but Ronnie hangs out in the room by the back stairs."

Privalov nodded. "Don't worry about Ronnie," he told her again. "Follow me. Act like nothing is happening."

Privalov put on his hat, opened the door, and stepped into the hallway. He could hear someone moving inside one of the rooms at the end of the hall. He had taken only three steps down the hall when Ronnie popped his head out of his room. Privalov thought he looked ridiculous in his high-waisted trousers and oversized green tie. For a fleeting second, he had an image of an ugly, venomous spider lurking in the shadows above its web.

Privalov stopped and raised his hands in a friendly greeting. "Ronnie! Ronnie," he called out with a cheerful smile. "You are just the man I must talk to! I really have to ask you something."

Ronnie's face screwed up into a surprised sneer. As Privalov closed with Ronnie, he whipped off his hat and, in one motion, flicked it into Ronnie's face. Ronnie's hands came up instinctively, grabbing at the hat. At the same time, Privalov launched a powerful knee strike into Ronnie 'sgroin, then twisted his foot so that the heel of his shoe scraped down Ronnie's shin and collided violently with the small bones on the top of Ronnie's foot. At the same time, he grabbed Ronnie's right wrist with his left hand. Ronnie groaned, slumping forward. Privalov clutched Ronnie's hair in his right hand, wrenching him upwards and back. Loosening his grip on Ronnie's right wrist, he slammed a backfist strike to his temple. Letting go of Ronnie's hair, he used his right fist to punch into the hard tissue on Ronnie's throat. Ronnie went limp and crumpled to the ground. A black-handled switchblade rattled to the floor beside him. It was over in seconds.

When Privalov saw the knife, his face flushed, his eyebrows narrowed, and his jaw dropped. He side-kicked down again, viciously stomping at the side of Ronnie's head, shouting hoarsely, "You — you thought you were going to use a knife on me! You would stab me with your knife? You..." He stomped again, crunching his heel on Ronnie's limp hand.

Millie, eyes wide, exclaimed in a breathy voice, "Oh my God, that's awful... The bastard deserves it, but that's horrible." She put her hand over her mouth, choking back tears. "I've seen him beat people, but this is horrible."

Privalov bent over, picked up his hat, and grabbed Millie by the wrist. "Come with me." They scrambled down the stairs. Behind them, Privalov heard a door open and then Angelina's voice crying out, "My God, what's happened?"

Privalov kicked open the fire door, and the two fugitives burst into the freezing cold of the alley.

Chapter 19

NIKOLAEV'S VOICE HAD AN ANXIOUS EDGE TO IT. "Miss Soroka, you must understand that I cannot go back to Moscow. I want you to help me. I need your help."

The sun had been down for well over an hour, and Oriana and Nikolaev were walking along the path on the narrow strip of parkland that ran beside the Rideau Canal. Their footsteps crunched in the frozen layer of snow on the pavement.

"I'm listening to you, Mr. Nikolaev. You asked me to meet you here, but what do you think I can do to help you? I can't grant you asylum. I'm a journalist. You need to talk to someone in External Affairs, or maybe even the RCMP."

"I don't know anyone who I can trust. I need an answer tonight, because tomorrow or the next day, they are recalling the key embassy staff. We will have to go back to Moscow, and after the death of Mr. Shemyakin, we will all be in disgrace. One of our embassy team has been killed like this. You must understand, Miss Soroka. It's not like here. There will be no trial. There is a chance that I could be sent to a labour camp for several years. Yet I have done nothing wrong. The mission will be seen as a failure. I had nothing to do with that. I need your help."

"If you haven't done anything wrong, Mr. Nikolaev, what do you have to fear?"

"This is not the time to play games, Miss Soroka." The anxiety in his voice had turned to desperation. "You understand the nature of my government. I need your help."

"Why did you come to me, Mr. Nikolaev? Why not go to one of your contacts at External Affairs?"

Nikolaev stopped and stamped his feet and hugged himself. "You must understand." He was wearing a thin coat and breathing heavily. In the cold air, his breath hung about his head like a misty shroud. "What if these people tell me to come back tomorrow, or the next day? You know what will happen to me if the embassy hears that I have asked for asylum? It won't be a sentence of five years in a labour camp, I can tell you that much. I can't trust the bureaucrats. They might take days to make up their minds, and by then it will be too late, and others in the embassy may find out what I am trying to do. Don't you see? You could find a place for me to hide for a few days, write a story about me. When the public knows about my problem, the government will have to accept me."

Oriana said nothing for a few moments, stepping to the side of the path, letting a middle-aged couple stroll past with their collie. The three of them smiled politely. Nikolaev stayed put, forcing the couple to step around him and into the snow. It was a small incident, but it reinforced the impression that there was something sinister and obstinate about Nikolaev. She didn't like him.

When they were well past, Oriana whispered, "Even if I wrote a story about you, Mr. Nikolaev, my publisher would have to approve it. He would probably want to run it past the newspaper's lawyer. The lawyer would almost certainly want to talk to someone in the government. Then, if the paper chose not to run it, and they might well do that, you'd be no further ahead. You have to understand these things, Mr. Nikolaev: by going the newspaper route, the chances of the embassy finding out about you seeking asylum would be greater than if you went to External Affairs." Oriana paused and looked attentively at Nikolaev. "If what you say is true, you should go right now to the RCMP. External Affairs is probably closed for the night. That's my advice to you, Mr. Nikolaev. If they take you, then I could look at writing an article once I have the opportunity to do a long interview with you."

Nikolaev threw his hands in the air. "No, no, no! I can't go to the police, not yet. You don't understand." He dropped his hands and began to shout. "You don't care what happens to me! You don't care about people, do you, Miss Soroka?" He turned and stormed back down the canal toward the city centre.

✳ ✳ ✳

"I'm tired, George. I've been driving for over two hours. I haven't had anything to eat since noon. Can we stop, please?"

Privalov nodded. Against his instincts, he found that he actually liked Millie. She was a cheeky woman with a streak of boldness and a sense of humour. He hadn't expected that. Apart from his wife and mother, he hadn't

207

had a lot of experience with women — and he hadn't seen much of them in the last four years. It was hard not to like Millie. Besides being disrespectful of authority, she could be cheerful and trusting. He was surprised to find there was a kind of innocence about her, and in the last several hours he was certain that he detected a kind of untutored intelligence behind her brash exterior. It was a mystery to him how she'd ended up where she was.

"How much petrol do we have?" he said, ignoring her request.

"Just under half a tank. We can't go on driving all night, George. Besides, it's starting to snow. You don't want us to end up in the ditch, do you?"

Privalov pursed his lips. "Yes. I think you are right. Can we get some fuel and something to eat near here?"

"I think so. I've never really been this far out of Montreal before, but I think Trois Rivières is a pretty good-sized city, and they should have what we're looking for. Listen, George, we've gotta find someplace to stay. You know, I'm not keen on driving all night, especially if it's gonna snow."

Privalov knew she was right. Besides, he was getting a headache and wanted a drink. "Okay. Show me what's up ahead."

They continued down the two-lane highway that ran abreast of the St. Lawrence River. Traffic was light. As the miles rolled by, Millie chatted freely about what she thought the future might be like in Halifax. She was finished with Montreal. She was going to rebuild her life someplace where nobody knew her.

"With this money, George, I can go to secretarial school. I can learn to type and take shorthand. No more tricks, no more johns, no more Ronnies running my life. I really can't believe my luck. It's something I've dreamed of doing for a long time now, but I never thought it would happen, not really. You know?"

"Well, now you have the chance and I'm glad I can do something for you," Privalov said, and meant it. For years, he'd had no one close to him to share his life. Millie had inadvertently tapped into a seam of generosity that he'd repressed for years. He enjoyed being with her and he found himself wishing for her success as much as she did.

But this new relationship with Millie brought other tensions to the surface. For several months now Privalov had been brooding on the unpleasant reality of the circumstances he found himself in. His life in the MGB had been a depressing, solitary existence, and this state of affairs wasn't likely to change. It was taking its toll on him. He knew that. He could feel it every day. He was unravelling at the edges. He was unhappy, perpetually angry, and he drank far too much — but he was not now, nor would he ever be, a traitor to his country, his party — or his family. Unlike what he had told the self-satisfied and overconfident Inspector Connelly, he desperately missed his wife, Ulyana, and their young son. For years now the two of them had exchanged long letters every week via the diplomatic pouch, and he missed her terribly. He knew she loved him, but letters could never be the same thing as being together.

The tale he'd told Connelly was close enough to the truth to be plausible. It was a dialogue he had practised years ago in several variations in Moscow. In the event that the Canadians tried to loosen his tongue with liquor, he had always kept things close to the truth. That way he'd always remember the details. But Ulyana hadn't moved in with an engineer in Gorky. She'd moved back home in that city with her widowed father, who was an engineer at Gorky's GAZ automotive plant. She and their three-year-old son Nikolai waited patiently for him in a cramped apartment. She was an intelligent, quiet, steadfast woman, and she'd promised to wait for him while he was on yet another foreign posting.

But that was the source of another problem for him. Privalov worried that Ulyana might not recognize the man who returned. Was he the same person she once knew? He was a harder, more disdainful man than he once was. He knew that. Had he lost whatever spark of exuberance and fun he'd once had? Nobody who was genuinely sociable or good-natured ever went very far in the MGB. Those character traits were vulnerabilities, and they were suspect. The generous, affable men were weeded out in selection and training. It made for a culture of caution and mistrust. Not that life in the MGB was always gloomy, of course. There were times when there was laughter, but it was laughter that almost always involved something cynical. Millie wasn't like that. He liked her laughter. It had no filters. Nobody in the embassy laughed like that; but then, perhaps her high spirits were a form of nervousness, a means she had cultivated to conceal tension and fear. Privalov couldn't afford to trust her; but still, he liked her.

Much as he loved the Soviet Union, in the last year Privalov had sometimes thought he might have made a mistake in joining the MGB — not that he'd had any real choice at the time. Who knows? Perhaps things could have been better. The MGB was an unrelentingly pitiless organization. There was no room for weakness. Constant suspicion and vigilance took its toll. Unlike the army, the MGB didn't cultivate a sense of comradeship, and it was different from any of the old-boy networks that characterized the other branches of the Party. You could never really be friends with anyone in the MGB. Interpersonal trust was a character defect, and other than his wife, Privalov knew he had no friends. The Ministry for State Security may have been the Shield and Sword of the Communist Party, but despite its noble purpose, it had its own brutal culture with its own harsh traditions and expectations. It wasn't an easy place to carve out a career. It forced you to repress the natural tendencies of companionship, tolerance, and compassion. In their place, it rewarded you with the prestige and status that came from power and authority.

Privalov looked out at the wood lines, the long white fields and the distant lights of farmhouses rolling by in the night. Power and authority were characteristics he'd always wanted for himself. But the problem was, they came at a price. Over the years he had gradually and willingly allowed himself to assume the character the MGB tacitly demanded of its agents. This wasn't the first time he'd worried that, in the same way an actor takes on a new role, he might have assumed his current personality. It wasn't the sort of thing he could talk to any of his peers about, but he wondered whether, in the last few years, he had become increasingly aloof and callous because that's what his job demanded. There were times, when he was lonely and tense, that he saw himself as just some hapless dupe caught up in an elaborate masquerade. What he really wanted was stability, a life without the crushing drama.

He looked over at Millie singing to herself, peering over the steering wheel. He wasn't supposed to develop any kind of affection for an unwitting accomplice, the kind of person his MGB course instructors officiously classified as 'unconscious agents.' But Millie, with her heavy blue eye shadow, unsinkable spirits, and naïve candour, gave him hope. After all, wasn't Millie exactly the kind of person the Class Struggle was supposed to liberate — an unfortunate proletarian victim, a casualty of oppressive, bourgeois behaviours?

In thirty-six hours, Millie would be gone from his life, and sometime after that, he would be with Ulyana. There was no point filling his head with worry and doubt. Doubt and introspection were for weaklings. The respect and deference conferred on him by his position had in the past washed away any feelings of doubt. Soon enough he'd be back home, savouring his old status. He'd be safe, confident, knowing that he had done his duty correctly.

Millie slowed the car down. "Okay, George, I think this is what we're looking for. What d'ya think?" Off the road was a rectangular two-story red brick and stucco building with a large blazing red neon sign announcing 'Auberge Adelise, Restaurant, Bière et Vin, Chambres, Danse.' Half a dozen cars were parked outside.

"I think you are right, Millie. We should stop here for the night. Are you ready?"

Millie giggled and got out of the car. Slipping around to the passenger side, she opened Privalov's door. A frail, stooped man carefully eased himself out. He was wearing a hat and sunglasses, carefully tapping his way forward with a white cane. Millie took him by the arm.

"I'm ready now," he told her. "Take your blind husband inside. You will do all the talking. You must get us our room, and then have them send us up a bottle of whisky and something good to eat."

* * *

Cormier hung up the phone on his desk. It had been a long day. He looked up wearily at Ferrall and Connelly.

"Nothing, sirs. I wish I had better news, but I don't." He pulled a cigarette pack from his shirt pocket. "Nobody's reported seeing our car. I've checked with the Soviet embassy. They finally answered. They're up in arms. They claim they have no idea where Privalov is. I've had our officers visit the Soviet attachés in Toronto and Montreal, and as of three-thirty this afternoon, we've had people physically on every border point between Fort Erie and the Quebec–Maine border crossings. I've got people at the airport departure desks in Ottawa and Montreal. I've had the airlines and the train and bus stations canvassed. I've checked out all the local car rental agencies. I've circulated Privalov's picture to all the police forces in Ontario and Quebec."

He lit a cigarette. "You know, there's a pretty good chance he may have gotten out of the city before we could get our people out to all our border surveillance points. The long and short is that we've come up dry. I'm thinking we should talk to the FBI gentlemen, but I know that's a call that in this case is way above my level." He leaned forward on the desk with both elbows and said with a wry smile, "Oh, and for the record, I'm in the doghouse at home. I missed my daughter's team winning at the Ontario debating finals this afternoon. Other than that, I don't have anything to add."

"Right. Sorry about the debating finals, Marcel," Connelly said. "I'd like to say we'll make it up to you, but you know we can't." Connelly exhaled noisily and looked sheepish. "But please give Madeleine my congratulations."

"Not to worry, sir. It's not the first time, or the last time, I'm sure. We've all been there," Cormier said.

Connelly nodded. "Marcel, you've done great work, but I think we should expand the search to include all the Seaway ports as well as the docks in Montreal, Quebec City, Halifax, and Saint John, New Brunswick. If I was Privalov, I'd be angling to get out of the country, and I think after American border crossings, getting passage on a ship will be his most likely

211

escape route. He knows we'll be watching the airports closely."

Ferrall sucked on his unlit pipe. "I agree with that. Let's get someone on all those. We can handle the four ports. Provincial police in Ontario and Quebec can do the Seaway ports." He waved his pipe in emphasis. "You've done good work, Marcel. Don't be discouraged. Something's going to break on this one." He turned to Connelly. "On another matter, Declan, bring us up to date on what you've learned from Mr. Karazin."

"Actually, it's been a good day, sir. He's very cooperative, and, unlike Privalov, I genuinely feel sorry for this guy. Earlier today he seemed pretty choked up about his family — I think that was authentic." Connelly looked sheepish. "Time will tell."

He took a small notepad from his pocket. "In terms of hard, actionable information, he's provided us descriptions of Soviet intelligence targets and priorities in Canada as well as descriptions of some of the objectives and target industries for Soviet illegals in the United States as well as the ones they're developing deep covers for to be used later in the States. There are some other new developments. In addition to getting information on the new Mid-Canada Radar Line, the Soviets are planning on putting more resources into getting technical information on the design for the new CF-100 aircraft, the Orenda jet engine, and the new Civilian Flight Mapping System. All of these projects are currently in the design stages in Toronto."

Connelly flipped the pages of his notebook. "Karazin's provided no names, of course. He doesn't have clearance for any of the encoded names, but he's given us enough information to start beating the bushes for some of the leads. We also have a very good description of recent developments in Soviet training and preparation of overseas agents for the MGB, which will be useful for our allies." He put the notebook back in his pocket.

"I'm confident Karazin will provide us more information, sir. Like I said, he's pretty tired and strung out just now. He's a bit of a nervous wreck. I don't want to burn him out. I'd like to be able to tell him what sort of new life we can provide for him. Although he hasn't said it, I think he's worried about that. I'm getting a translator over from the Directorate of Defence Intelligence Language Services here tomorrow, so that should help. Like I said, he's tired and his English gets hard to follow. The adrenalin rush is wearing off, and he's a bit down. I can't say I blame him. Apart from that, I think he's a gold mine."

Ferrall nodded. "Anything else?"

"No, sir, that's about it in big-picture terms. As for detail, the transcripts of my interview will be ready late tomorrow. I'll prepare an initial report and summarize our findings. I imagine this will be going up the chain pretty quickly?"

"Yeah. That leads to my next points." Ferrall sat down and rubbed under his eyepatch. "Damn eye socket's bothering me. Okay, before that, first thing, I've had an update on Constable Voigt. His condition's improving slightly. He's alert. His speech is still slurred, but the doctors are more optimistic than they were this morning. So that bad news is showing some improvement. As for things with Mr. Karazin, the chain of command right up to the prime minister has been advised. Fortunately, nobody higher up has seen fit to try and manage the details of this thing for us.

"Marcel, your point's well taken. I've already been in contact with the FBI. Hal Mauro from the embassy came by to see me again this afternoon. He said it was just a routine visit," he paused for effect, "but I have my doubts. He didn't seem surprised when I told him about our developments here. I told him that the two defections had to remain completely out of the public eye until we choose to declassify the information. I promised we'd unhesitatingly share whatever information we get, but I refused to send Karazin down to the States. He understands that, but he advises me that the Congressional Intelligence Committees will exert pressure to interview him in Washington. I told him that issue will be determined by the prime minister. Our position is that he has to be interviewed here, under our terms. If we start parading our walk-ins around internationally, we'll never get another defection. Mauro has no problems with that. I expect that, given the precedent set at the end of the war by Igor Gouzenko's defection, the prime minister will be onside.

"Last of all, gentlemen, early this afternoon I had a phone call from a Colonel Sykes who works for the British military attaché in Washington. He said he was phoning at the behest of Mr. Kim Philby. Philby's the number two man at their embassy. He was Burgess' boss. Apparently Philby's having kittens about events in Ottawa. Sykes was guarded in his speech, but he certainly has the sense that something's going on here. He insisted we have a liaison officer visit us from Washington tomorrow to discuss what he calls 'matters of recent development.' I'm afraid I didn't improve the relationship with our British cousins. I told him that we weren't accepting any liaison visits and wouldn't be releasing interview summaries for at least a week, but to rest assured we'd keep them very much in the loop.

"As for just how the Americans and British seemed to know so quickly that something's going on here, I have a theory." Ferrall stopped and rubbed beneath his eye patch again for a moment. "Only a few of us knew about Karazin, and I don't believe the leak's here. So, the only other people who know both men are missing are the Russians."

* * *

The Auberge wasn't keen on doing room service, but Millie managed to convince the front desk clerk that her husband was recuperating from major surgery and needed the privacy. The food turned out to be surprisingly good. She ordered the house special for both of them: a chicken pot pie and homemade vegetable soup. For an additional four dollars she persuaded them to send up a bottle of blended Johnny Walker.

George seemed like a decent enough guy while they ate. He actually made polite conversation, asking where she came from and about her childhood and her future, never making mention of her recent employment, which she thought was very sweet of him, but a little stuffy. He even tried to make a few jokes, but they weren't very funny. She only laughed to be nice.

It was afterwards, when he began tucking into the whisky bottle, that things began to turn ugly. For the first several inches, George didn't say much. He grew quieter for about an hour, and to entertain herself Millie fiddled with the radio until she got an American station from upstate New York that was broadcasting the Jack Benny Show. It was fun, kind of goofy, with lots of laughs and wonderful song and comedy routines. Exactly the kind of thing she needed to take her mind off all the changes that had happened today.

It was just near the end of the program and two-thirds of the way down his bottle when George began to rant and rave about God knows what. Half of it was in Latvian, or whatever language it was they spoke there. He started going on about the Americans trying to run the world, and just as they were signing off with the theme song, he jumped up and turned the radio off. He smashed his fist down on the night table and shouted something she didn't understand about President Truman and nuclear testing. It was the look in his eyes that really set off her alarm bells. He looked like Ronnie before he did a number on someone.

That's when she grabbed her purse and headed for the door. "I'm going downstairs, George. I'm getting some fresh air and something to drink, by myself. I'll be back when you've settled down."

Chapter 20

SUPERINTENDENT FERRALL WAS SEATED in front of Assistant Commissioner Murray's desk. "So, sir, in summary, things are going better than I anticipated, but not how we'd planned. No sign of Privalov, and Karazin seems to be working out reasonably well." He picked up his briefcase and stood to leave, anxious to get back across town to his own organization.

Murray rose from behind his desk. "That's good work, Rory. Bad luck that Privalov has taken off on us, but now you have a prime suspect, and we certainly didn't have one forty-eight hours ago. So, I'm not too worried. If he's still in the country, I'm sure we'll eventually catch him. Karazin's been a stroke of good luck. He's going to give your organization a lot of credibility." Murray flicked his lighter and lit a cigarette. "Not your fault, but you needed to catch a break. For now, Karazin takes the pressure off us for an American or British intervention. I spoke personally to the minister and the commissioner this morning. They're delighted at the way things have turned out. The good news there is that they're happy and there's no sign of them wanting to meddle and screw things up. You've got a free hand, so congratulations."

"Thanks, sir. Now that we've got a better idea as to who killed Shemyakin, we've still got lots of work to do following up on Karazin's information. And to do that I need more trained people."

"Yeah, I hear you, but before you go, here's the bad news." Murray's voice dropped. "I'd planned on moving Wallace Graham out of the Privy Council Office and exiling him into the Financial Policy Planning Directorate."

Ferrall nodded but remained tight lipped.

"I think he beat me to it." Murray tapped his cigarette ash into a large glass ashtray and took a long drag. "I've just heard that he's being transferred this morning to a special, newly created position on the House of Commons Standing Committee on Justice and Legal Affairs. He was asked for by name by someone in the Prime Minister's Office. The guy's an institutional weasel."

"Well, from my perspective, that's good news, sir. It keeps him from poking his nose into Special Branch."

"I still have a problem with that, Rory. I don't trust Graham — and I'm telling you this because I think he's a security risk and he directly affects your organization. I'm going to speak to the commissioner. I'm not finished with him. He's not going to repeat his little stunt with Connelly or anyone else. Graham can still cause trouble for us in his new job. I especially don't trust him when he has unfettered access to political policy makers. Besides, I'm sure he's set his sights on something better. I think this is just temporary. He'll be smarming and worming his way into some other lucrative post-retirement position where he can be a menace for years."

Ferrall cleared his throat. "Well, for what it's worth, sir, like you, I don't trust Graham, but I don't believe he was the source of the leak concerning our two defectors." He set his briefcase down again. "You know, since I started this line of work, I've found that one of the problems with people like Graham is that after a while, every misfit and malcontent begins to look like a Soviet agent. It's easy to become delusional. You end up suspecting everybody, when most of the time it's just plain misconduct. Case in point. As of this morning, both the Brits and the Americans seemed to know about our two defectors. Graham knows nothing about Karazin, so it can't be him, and the only others who know that they're missing are the Russians. So, somehow, the information is going from within the Soviet embassy to the British embassy in Washington and the FBI."

"Interesting." Murray impatiently tapped his cigarette on the ashtray again as he thought about this. "I'm sure you're right. So, what will you do with that deduction?"

"I'm not certain, but can I hold on for a bit before I give you an answer to that one? I've got to do some leg work."

✳ ✳ ✳

The next day, Privalov was deliberately restrained, doing his best not to snap at Millie. When she had come back to their room the night before, he'd told her, "Listen, I'm sorry. I'm very sorry. I get angry sometimes when I drink too much. I've been under a lot of pressure." In the hour she was gone, he'd finished the bottle, but somehow managed to reason himself into a state approximating composure. He told her, "I would never do anything

216

to hurt you. We both have too much to lose. We need one another until we get to Halifax. After that, I'll give you the rest of what I've promised you, and we'll go our own ways."

Millie had made a show of considering the offer. She'd thought it through when she was downstairs. Millie had seen plenty of drunks in her life and figured she could handle this one. George was easier than most. After all, he'd shown no interest in wanting to have sex with her. There was just that explosive temper — she'd seen it twice now.

The remaining three thousand dollars, and the glitter of a new life, made the gamble irresistible. They agreed to sleep in the same bed. It would look too suspicious if she'd asked for a separate room at that late hour. Millie put a pillow between them and slept fitfully, wrapped in a separate blanket. By seven thirty the next morning, they were back on the road.

It wasn't until later in the day, as Privalov's head cleared, that he grew more conversational and pleasant. Ten hours of slow, torturous progress in intermittent flurries and drifting snow brought them to the outskirts of Moncton. Millie, again wary of driving in the dark on icy roads with bad visibility, insisted that they stop for the night.

"We'll be in Halifax tomorrow, by mid-morning at the latest," she claimed.

In Moncton they ceased being a couple; instead, they told the front desk that Millie was Privalov's attendant. They had separate but adjoining rooms, and the next day before eight they were back on the road. Just before noon, Millie parked the car in front of a seedy, three-story, grey stone building, the Empire Arms, on Halifax's Hollis Street.

She turned to Privalov. "I've filled my part of the bargain. Now, you owe me some money."

Privalov looked surprised. "When we get our rooms, I'll pay you inside. There is no need to rush things."

"No, George. This is where I get off. In public, in broad daylight. I wasn't born yesterday. I got you here safe and sound. Now, you pay up as promised, or I'm going straight to the police."

Privalov's eyes widened with surprise and outrage. "I had no intention of cheating you," he said indignantly. This wasn't entirely true. He'd considered stiffing Millie so that he could return the bulk of the money when he got to Moscow. The money would be further proof of his integrity and his loyalty.

He reached into his pocket and fished out a key. He dangled it in front of Millie. "I've got it. It's in the trunk. Stay here." He scrambled around to the back of the car. The damp wind off the harbour made him shiver. Halifax's damp ocean cold had a raw bite to it, different from the drier cold in the interior, he thought. As he fumbled with the trunk's lock for a moment, he wondered if feeling cold differently was even physically possible, or was it just some psychological perception. The trunk sprang open. There were more pressing issues to keep focused on. He walked back around to the passenger-side door and climbed in beside Millie with the briefcase.

Inside the car he counted out three thousand dollars. Millie carefully counted the money and wrapped the bills in a roll with a hair elastic. She snapped her purse closed.

"Good luck, George." She opened the driver's-side door.

"Where are you going now?" Privalov said.

"It doesn't matter. I'm not telling you. I'm not telling anyone where I'm going. I helped you get here, George. I kept my part of the bargain. You just gave me a new life, and now you'll never hear from me again. Best you don't know. Bye." Millie stepped out into the street. When she was around the corner, she flagged a taxi. "The train station, please." Thirty minutes later, she had a ticket with an overnight berth to Toronto.

Privalov left the white cane in the car and checked into the Empire Arms. Today he wore dark glasses, but now he moved much more slowly, had a pronounced limp and curvature of the spine, and spoke slowly with an exhausted and painful wheeze. He signed the register as Wojciech Kowalski of Hamilton, Ontario.

"My luggage hasn't arrived," he told the front desk clerk, "but when it does, call me in my room and I'll have it sent up."

Once in the room, he ordered a bottle of Ballantine's and began scouring the telephone book. His first call was to the Shipping Registry Office for the Port of Halifax. "Can you please tell me the name of the Soviet ship that is here in Halifax?" he asked the woman who answered.

After a moment of rustling papers, the woman was back on the line. "Which ship are you looking for, sir? There are two: the *Dimitry Laptev* and the *Novouralsk*."

Privalov had to think quickly. "They didn't tell me. The bigger one, I think."

"That would be the SS *Dimitry Laptev*, sir. She's at Pier 4, sir, taking on grain. She should be alongside until tomorrow at three or four in the afternoon, and then she has to be out of there. Is there anything else I can help you with?"

"Yes please. What is the other ship?"

"That's the SS *Novouralsk*, sir. She's a large fishing seiner, presently up at the north end undergoing repairs. She'll be there for at least another week or two. Will that be all, sir?"

"Yes. Thank you." Privalov hung up. How foolish these people are, he thought. In the Soviet Union, the list of ships in any harbour is a carefully guarded secret. Here, they advertise such information so that hobbyists can gawk at the ships as if they were rare birds. Even more foolish, they sell us grain and service our fishing trawlers. Westerners are so greedy that we weren't considered an enemy until we started shooting at them.

There was a knock at the door. Privalov put on his dark glasses and hobbled across the room. His whisky had arrived.

Chapter 21

COLONEL INVESTIGATOR TARABIN INHALED rigorously on his cigarette as he read the sheet of onionskin paper Nikolaev handed him. He exhaled slowly as his eyes crept from word to word.

1 - Classification Level - Top Secret / Most Important / Of Particular Importance - North American Operations Full Stop

2 - To - First Chief Directorate - Foreign Operations, First Department: Deputy Director Counter-Intelligence Full Stop

3 - From- Colonel Investigator Yevgeny Tarabin Full Stop

4 - Title - Preliminary Report and Recommendations of the Enquiry into the Death of Anatoly N Shemyakin Full Stop

5 - Investigative team believes Anatoly M Shemyakin murdered by Americans Full Stop Subsequent to this murder, Vitaly A Privalov likely subsequently kidnapped by Americans working in conjunction with Canadian Police Full Stop

6 - Believe Alexander V Karazin has defected. Full Stop Also believe Karazin has been working for Canadian Counter-Intelligence Special Branch for indeterminate period of time Full Stop Damage Assessment: Severe Full Stop Compromised operations include all technical intelligence-gathering in Canada and likely disclosure of illegal and resident program in Canada Full Stop

7 - Recommendations: Treason unlikely but ambassador and first secretary must be replaced immediately for reasons of incompetence and negligence Full Stop Replacements must be prepared for complete

Colonel Tarabin returned the paper to Nikolaev and took off his reading glasses. "I want you personally to encode this, triple-check it for accuracy, and then send it out." He took another energetic drag on his cigarette. "No one else is to see it. After you have completed that, burn this original copy as well as the encoded ticker tape and then report to me. Don't put this in the log book. Do you understand?"

"Yes, sir."

"Good. Don't let it go to your head, but you are the only person I trust in this shithouse that's supposed to pass for an embassy. Don't let me down."

✳ ✳ ✳

Privalov limped painfully as he eased himself down the Empire Arms' front step. It wasn't an act. On his advanced training course at the Academy for the Ministry of State Security, they had taught him that putting a sharp stone in your shoe was a reliable technique for giving you a genuine limp — it also prevented you from ever forgetting about it should you have to move around under stress.

Privalov hobbled to the curbside and climbed into the taxi's backseat. The cab driver was a chatty sort. He was upset with the National Hockey League's recent decision to increase the goalie's crease from 3 × 7 feet to 4 × 8 feet.

"They're makin' the game way too easy, don't ya think? Why even bother havin' a goalie?"

Privalov answered his attempts at conversation with monosyllabic grunts. He gave him a dollar tip when the cab reached the fenced perimeter at Pier 4 on Upper Water St. Bent over, he shuffled toward the small security building beside the entrance gate, stopping outside to catch his breath.

"Can I help you, sir?" A white-moustached commissionaire with Great War medals was screwing the top onto a steaming thermos at his desk.

"Yes. I have come to talk to my cousin on board the *Dimitry Laptev*. Can I go and see him?" Privalov put his cane down and leaned heavily on the counter, his breath coming in great, harrowing gasps.

"You can't just go up to the ship, sir. I'm sorry." The commissionaire sounded genuinely sympathetic.

Privalov looked crestfallen. "I hear this ship is leaving today. I came all the way from Fredericton to see him. I have not seen him since before the war. We were separated after the German invasion."

"I'm sorry, sir, but you can't go up there without an escort from the ship signing you in." He shrugged. "Port Authority rules. Nothing I can do."

"Sir," Privalov said, pointing to the commissionaire's service ribbons, "I see you are a veteran. In my war, I too was a veteran. The Free Polish Army. I fought with Canada." He lifted his arm up ruefully and pointed at his leg. "I was wounded with Canada. Can I phone up to the ship?"

"Suppose that can't hurt." The commissionaire smiled. "They only speak Russian up there, though, you know. Can you do that?"

"Yes, where we come from in Poland, we speak Polish and Russian."

"Come on back here, then, sir. Let's give it a try." The commissionaire shoved the phone across his desk and Privalov struggled around the counter.

The phone whirred in Privalov's ear and a Russian voice answered. Privalov broke into curt Russian. The commissionaire looked up, startled at the change in tone. Privalov continued speaking, then grimaced at the commissionaire, holding the receiver to his chest. "You are surprised at my tone of voice? You don't know Russians and their insistence on regulations, my friend. Poles are not like that. Russians only listen to orders."

A few seconds later there was another voice at the end of the line. Privalov placed the phone's receiver beside his ear once more and then barked a stream of something unintelligible to the Russian at the other end.

When he was finished, Privalov handed the phone back to the commissionaire. "They are sending someone down to sign me in." He shook his head. "You don't know Russians like I know them. Half my village was Russian. If I was polite, they would have just told me to fuck off."

A minute later, two scruffy-looking Russian seamen in coveralls ambled down the gangplank. The older one was blond and tall; the other, just out of his teens, was olive-skinned with jet-black hair. They looked scornfully at Privalov. Privalov pulled out his diplomatic passport and an identification card and spoke gruffly for a minute in Russian. The two sailors looked astonished. The blond seaman nodded his head earnestly. Privalov pointed to the register, snarling an order. The man scribbled something and passed the book to Privalov, who signed his name.

As the three men walked up the gangway, the commissionaire thought Privalov had suddenly developed a confident exuberance that wasn't there five minutes ago. Something strange here. He scratched the back of his head; the Polish guy's back wasn't nearly as bent, either. He picked up the phone.

Privalov sat at the small desk inside the captain's cabin and put his head back. His face had lost its colour; his head ached. He exhaled noisily and licked his lips. He leaned forward and, looking at the anxious expression on the captain's face, he said, "Comrade Captain. This is a very long story. I can tell you just a little bit of it on our sea voyage. For now, just send a secure cable to your fleet security office and tell them I'm here. I'm not leaving until we get to Russia. I want you to get us out to sea and into international waters as soon as you possibly can. Now, get me a bottle of very cold vodka." He leaned down, took off his right shoe, and shook out a small, sharp piece of gravel. He'd made it.

✳ ✳ ✳

It was dark. Oriana and Connelly walked unhurriedly arm in arm down the sidewalk on Argyle Street. It had been warmer earlier in the day, and now that the sun was gone the thin film of thawed snow had turned to an invisible sheet of black ice. The footing was treacherous, but they chose to walk to the movies rather than take a cab.

"I never figured it'd turn out this way," Oriana said. "I always expected to be in journalism for the rest of my life. What I didn't know was where it would take me. I don't know why I expected more. I suppose that was a bit presumptuous on my part. Life moves in unexpected directions." She laughed.

"So, what did Jacobsen say when you told him?"

"I just put my letter on his desk and said, 'Read it. I quit.' He looked like I'd just shot him. It took him a moment to work up the nerve to ask me why. I said 'You've demoted me for no reason, not once but twice, and you've undermined me at every turn. Why would I stay? You're a dishonest, pompous incompetent.' At that point, I turned and walked out."

"How do you feel about it?"

"Wonderful."

"That's great. So, what exactly is it you're going to be doing?"

"Well, just before I quit, I got a call from a contact I knew when I worked in the parliamentary press gallery. He's started a new firm doing market research and opinion polling."

"Do you know anything about that?"

"Not a lot. He knows that. I told him I had no experience in that field, but he wants me to organize the setup of phone centres and hiring here in Ottawa. He said I knew Ottawa and that's what he wants."

"Well, good for you. I suppose one of the benefits of not being a reporter is that there's no longer a conflict of interest between the two of us."

"I'd thought of that too. I'm glad you feel the same way." She snuggled into him. "I suppose you can't tell me how that whole business you've been working on has turned out?"

"No. I can't say much." Connelly smiled. "Let's just say, I think we'll have Privalov in one of our cells in the next hour or so."

Chapter 22

CONNELLY TOOK A DEEP BREATH. This had to be some kind of misunderstanding. He stood in the hallway outside Ferrall's office door. Cormier stood behind him.

"Sir, Marcel tells me that you gave an order to let Privalov sail. That we didn't arrest him."

Ferrall sat back. "That's correct. Both of you come in here and shut the door. You deserve to know something."

The inspector and staff sergeant trooped behind Ferrall and stood in front of his desk. Ferrall was thin lipped.

"Sit down," he told them tersely. "That's right. Privalov's going back to Russia. We could have picked him up, but we're not doing that. When I got word that the Halifax detachment had requested permission to board the Soviet freighter, I denied it. I didn't want Privalov tipped off to what we are up to. An opportunity presented itself and I wanted him thinking that he got away clean on his own steam. Here's why.

"Yesterday, Hal Mauro of the FBI was back in my office. He made me an offer. As we know, the FBI does the domestic counter-intelligence in the States, but they're dependent on the CIA for all externally sourced intelligence that affects them. According to Mauro, the CIA tells the FBI only what they want the FBI to know and only when they want the FBI to know it. The FBI's very unhappy with that. Mauro wants a more direct and dependable source of information with us, a straightforward sharing of intelligence, just like we do with criminal intelligence."

Cormier sat quietly, tight-lipped and angry.

Connelly nodded. "Okay, sir. What's this got to do with Privalov?"

"Bear with me. This is the part that never leaves this room. You two need to know because you've been in on this from the beginning. Mauro's offer is based on the FBI providing us details of all CIA operations here in Canada, for this case and in the future. Mauro's not being a nice guy. Thanks in large part to your work, he figures that Special Branch is about to get a lot bigger and more effective. He wants first dibs on any of our findings that impact the U.S. In return, we find out what's going on in our own backyard."

Ferrall paused for effect, looking both officers in the eye. "Now, Mauro's been digging and found out that this guy calling himself Jay O'Neil is a CIA operative. We'd already figured that one out. What we suspected and Mauro confirmed was that O'Neil was feeding false information to the Soviets through Shemyakin. What we didn't know was that O'Neil was also feeding Privalov false information about Shemyakin. He got Privalov to believe Shemyakin was a traitor and was working for the CIA. Nobody expected Privalov to get drunk, go berserk, and murder Shemyakin, but that suited O'Neil's purposes even better."

Cormier sat forward, the beginnings of a smile on his face.

Ferrall continued, "The plan was to roll up Shemyakin's operation and have him sent back to Moscow, and in doing so reinforce a whole trove of O'Neil's falsely planted information. But then the situation changed. Unbeknownst to the CIA, we nabbed Privalov, the Soviets also brought in their own investigation team, and then Privalov walked off on us."

"Okay, sir, so why let Privalov get away scot-free? We had him," Cormier said.

"Two reasons. First, remember that I keep telling you we aren't in the police business of bringing criminals to justice. As small as we are right now, we're a counter-intelligence agency. So, I don't intend to go through the motions of charging Privalov with murder. The Soviets will just claim the case is rigged. They'll continue to refuse to cooperate, they'll invoke diplomatic immunity, and they'll send Privalov home where we can't touch him. We won't be any further ahead, and we'll look ineffectual."

"Yeah, but hasn't most of that happened already, sir?" Cormier said.

"It has, but I've added a wrinkle. After talking to Hal Mauro, I made a secure call to the British embassy in Washington. I spoke to their number two man there, a Mr. Kim Philby. Philby's in MI6 and he runs their intelligence liaison. I gave him the update that he's been clamouring for, but with a few additions."

Ferrall picked up his pipe and began twisting its stem. "Now, Mauro and the head of the FBI, J. Edgar Hoover, are convinced that the Brits in Washington are leaking like a sieve. They just haven't figured out yet who specifically is doing the leaking, but they're convinced that everything the Americans tell them is going directly to Moscow via the British embassy. The CIA refuse to believe it. The FBI want to use this case to prove the

CIA wrong.”

He waved his pipe. “You see, Philby and the head of the CIA, James Angleton, are the best of pals from the war. The CIA aren’t listening to the FBI and believe the leak is coming from somewhere back in the UK. What I did was tell Philby, in the strictest confidence, mind you, that we were trying to rescue Privalov, that Privalov, not Shemyakin, was working for us all along, and that Privalov killed Shemyakin when Shemyakin began to suspect him of working for us. That’s why we brought Privalov in, to rescue him when the Soviets brought in their own MGB counter-intelligence team. I told him Privalov is thoroughly disillusioned with Stalin and the way the Communists are running Russia. But he’s a brave man, and he insisted that he has to go back to the Soviet Union and continue to work for us from the inside. That way, Privalov also protects his wife. I told Philby that as reluctant as I was to do it, we had to let Privalov go and make it look like he escaped.”

Connelly sat back and nodded. Cormier inhaled deeply. His eyes widened and he turned his head slightly.

“Jesus, sir. The Soviets won’t believe anything coming out of Ottawa for a while after this. And, you know, this means that you’ve just signed the man’s death warrant.”

“Yeah.” Ferrall raised his eyebrows. “I’d thought of that.”

CONFIDENTIAL

NOT RELEASABLE TO THE PUBLIC

RECEIVED

11 / 3 / 11

A novel

by A E MERRICK

THE TRUTH WILL SET YOU FREE

11 / 3 / 11

9/11 was an inside job.

The moon landings were faked.

JFK is alive and well and spends his days with Elvis.

Everyone knows what happened on 11/3/11. But do they really know the truth?

John Doe – JD to his friends – knows for a fact that things are not as they seem. The world is wearing blinders, but he has his eyes wide open. And the more you truly know, the crazier you seem.

Dive into a rabbit hole of conspiracy theories and see the world through JD's eyes. AE Merrick's debut novel is a wild ride through mind control, paranoia and isolation in search of the ever-elusive truth.

About the Author

A.E. Merrick is a Toronto-based dilettante who has experimented with a number of different identities, occupations, and pastimes. They are uncomfortable with publicly searchable databases of personal information. They write truth rather than fiction. 11/3/11 is their first novel.

A MILITARY THRILLER
INTERDICTION
MATT HARDMAN

INTERDICTION

The world of private security is a lucrative one, a collection of corporate armies built to compete in what has become a thirty billion dollar a year industry. Staffed largely by regular military and special forces veterans, these companies provide services to governments and the corporate world.

What would happen if one of the world's most powerful private security firms went rogue?

Daniel Evans has just been sworn in as the 46thPresident of the United States and his first major initiative is to fulfill his biggest campaign promise—the complete withdrawal of all American military personnel from the Middle East.

Nicholas DeGuerra is the CEO of TitanX Security, the world's largest private security company. He's a self-made man, a former Delta operator turned businessman who knows that the new president's policy is a threat to his financial security. He's just launched a desperate operation to save his company and his fortune.

Brian Thompson is a United States Navy Chief nearing retirement and looking forward to life after the military. A staffing shortage puts him onboard USS James E. Williams, an aging destroyer deployed to the Horn of Africa.

When a Pakistani nuke is stolen, the President of the United States sends Thompson and the USS Williams on a last-ditch interdiction mission to intercept the weapon and derail DeGuerra's plan.

ABOUT THE AUTHOR

Matt Hardman is a retired U.S. Navy Chief Petty Officer. While on active duty, he served onboard a submarine, two aircraft carriers, two amphibious transports, one submarine tender, and one destroyer. During his final tour of duty, he served as the Engineering Department Chief, or "Top Snipe," for the USS James E. Williams (DDG 95). He holds a bachelor's in Intelligence Studies and Counterintelligence from American Military University and a Master's in Writing from Johns Hopkins University. Matt Hardman is also a husband and father of six children and currently resides in Calvert County, Maryland.

DOUBLE † DAGGER

Double Dagger Books is Canada's newest military-focused publisher. Conflict and warfare have shaped human history since before we began to record it. The earliest stories that we know of, passed on as oral tradition, speak of war, and more importantly, the essential elements of the human condition that are revealed under its pressure. We are dedicated to publishing material that, while rooted in conflict, transcends the idea of "war" as merely a genre. Fiction, non- fiction, and stuff that defies categorization, we want to read it all.

Because if you want peace, study war.

www.doubledagger.ca

234

ABOUT THE AUTHOR

Michael Goodspeed has had a lengthy career as an Army officer as well as having been a video producer and worked in the telecommunications industry. He has degrees in English Literature and History, Business Administration, and Strategic Studies. He has lived and worked across the Americas, Europe, the Middle East, and Africa. He is the author of numerous articles for scholarly journals and newspapers and has had four books published: two social histories and two historical novels. His most recent novel, Dead Spy Cold Grave is an historical espionage thriller set in the early days of the Cold War. He divides his time between Toronto and a lake in Northern Ontario.